"It's not you...okay? It's...th..."

He was silent behind her. But his fingers moved lightly against her stomach. Almost as if he were caressing her.

"We're safe."

Her gaze slid to the right. His gun was there. Within easy reach. "Sometimes, I don't ever feel safe." As soon as she said the words, Noelle wished that she could call them back. She'd never made that confession to anyone.

"Why not?" His hold tightened.

Noelle shook her head. She was feeling warmer, so much warmer now. The shivers and shudders were easing. "Because I'm never sure what waits in the darkness."

WAY OF
THE SHADOWS

BY
CYNTHIA EDEN

Published in Great Britain 2014
by Mills & Boon, an imprint of Harlequin (UK) Limited,
Eton House, 18-24 Paradise Road, Richmond, Surrey, TW9 1SR

© 2014 Cindy Roussos

ISBN: 978-0-263-91369-9

46-0914

Harlequin (UK) Limited's policy is to use papers that are natural, renewable and recyclable products and made from wood grown in sustainable forests. The logging and manufacturing processes conform to the legal environmental regulations of the country of origin.

Printed and bound in Spain
by Blackprint CPI, Barcelona

New York Times and *USA TODAY* bestselling author **Cynthia Eden** writes tales of romantic suspense and paranormal romance. Her books have received starred reviews from *Publishers Weekly*, and she has received a RITA® Award nomination for best romantic suspense novel. Cynthia lives in the Deep South, loves horror movies and has an addiction to chocolate. More information about Cynthia may be found on her website, www.cynthiaeden.com, or you can follow her on Twitter, www.twitter.com/cynthiaeden.

A big thanks to Denise and Shannon at Harlequin
Intrigue—thank you so much for giving
me the opportunity to write about the Shadow Agents.

For my wonderful readers…thank you for all
the support that you've given to the men and women
of the EOD. I hope that you've enjoyed their tales!

Prologue

The darkness was all she knew. It surrounded her, seemed to suffocate her. It bound her as deeply, as securely as the ropes around her wrists.

Fear coiled around Noelle Evers as she waited in the dark. She was waiting for her own death, and she knew it. That certainty was there, filling her mind—that and nothing else. So when the door opened and she heard the squeak of wood, Noelle tensed.

The light spilled forward. The wood squeaked again. Someone was coming toward her....

The beam of a flashlight slit through her eyes, blinding her because it was such a sharp contrast to the darkness.

"Found her!" A man's voice called. It was deep and rough, heavy with relief. "She's alive!"

Noelle squinted as she tried to see past that bright light.

More footsteps thudded toward her. Then hands were on her. Rough, strong hands. They pulled at her ropes then yanked her out of the chair and to her feet.

"It's all right," that deep, rumbling voice told her. "You're safe now."

She didn't believe him.

There were more lights then, sweeping into the room. It looked like…a cabin? She was in a cabin? In the darkness, she hadn't been able to tell anything about her surroundings, but she could now see glimpses of an old, log-lined cabin.

She licked her lips. Her mouth felt so dry. She had to swallow three times before she managed, "H-how did…I g-get here?"

His face was in shadows, but he was tall, with broad shoulders and a gun strapped to his hip.

Noelle backed up when she saw the weapon. Her feet slipped on something. She glanced down and saw a twisting mass of rope near her feet.

"Easy," he told her, and his grip tightened around her arms. "I'm a deputy. We're all with the Coleman County Sheriff's Department, and we're here to take you home."

She'd…she'd been at home…sleeping in her bed…. Noelle remembered that. She'd gone to sleep—and awoken to darkness.

"Sheriff!" Another voice cried out then, breaking with what sounded like fear.

The deputy pulled Noelle close as he hurried toward that cry.

The flashlights all hit the far left corner of the room. They fell on the man sprawled there. A man who was dead—his throat had been cut. The man stared sightlessly back at them while his blood formed a dark pool beneath him.

The deputy's hold on Noelle tightened. "Who is that?" he demanded.

Noelle started to shake.

"Ms. Evers…" His voice gentled a bit. "Is he one of the men who took you?"

Tears leaked down her cheeks. "I don't know!"

Voices rose. Shouted. More men and women came inside the cabin. More lights.

Too bright.

Noelle's shoulders hunched. She looked down at her wrists. They were bloody and raw. And her hands—her hands were stained with blood. So was her gown. The gown she'd worn to sleep when she climbed into her own bed.

This isn't my home. But she couldn't remember how she'd gotten there. Noelle only knew darkness.

The deputy pulled off his coat. Carefully, he put it around her shoulders. "Tell me what happened." He was leading her from the cabin keeping his fingers around her arm. "Get me a medic!" He called out to another one of the men swarming the area.

Then she was outside. The night air was crisp, but she could still smell blood.

Because it's on me.

"I want to go home," Noelle whispered. "I want to see my parents." Noelle was seventeen. She was a sophomore at Coleman High School. She was cheering at the football game on Friday. She was—

Noelle's knees gave way and she would've hit the ground if the deputy hadn't grabbed her. He lifted her up against his chest, holding her tightly. *"Medic!"* the deputy yelled.

She wasn't just shaking any longer. Noelle's eyes rolled back in her head as giant shudders jolted through her.

The deputy carried her to a gurney. He and the medic strapped her down. "What the hell is happening?"

"Noelle!" She heard the scream distantly, but she knew that voice. It was her mother's voice. Noelle tried to respond, but she couldn't speak.

"She's seizing," the medic snapped. "We need to get her stable!"

The darkness seemed to close in again. She didn't want to go back into the dark.

Something bad waited in the dark.

Death waited.

But Noelle couldn't fight, and the darkness took her once more.

THE NEXT TIME Noelle's eyes opened, she was surrounded by a sea of white. The scent of antiseptic told her she was in the hospital even before the room came into focus.

She blinked a few times then saw her mother's tear-filled gaze. "You're okay, baby," her mom whispered.

Noelle didn't feel okay.

"We need to ask her some questions."

Noelle's gaze darted to the left at those words. Her father stood close by. He looked pale, and...older than she'd ever seen him.

Right next to her father, Sheriff Morris Bartley stood, his stare on her. He leaned toward Noelle.

"She just woke up," her father gritted out.

"I know." The sheriff sighed. "But she's the only one who can tell us what happened. I got a dead body, and I got her and I need to know—"

The darkness waited.

Noelle gave a hard, negative shake of her head.

"Noelle, how did you wind up in that cabin?" the sheriff asked her.

"This needs to wait," her father barked.

The machines around Noelle began to beep, faster, louder.

"Who was the dead man? Is he the one who took you? Is he—"

"I don't remember," Noelle whispered. Her throat hurt. *She* hurt.

The sheriff exhaled on a rough sigh. His hands gripped his hat. "Start with what you know. Tell me who took you from your house. Tell me how you got to that cabin and how—"

"I don't remember." Her voice was even softer now.

The sheriff's brows shot up. "Did you leave your house willingly? Is that what happened? Did you—?"

He didn't understand. "I don't…remember anything."

Her mother gave a little gasp.

"I was in my room, in my bed." Noelle's heart galloped in her chest. The machines raced. "Then I was in the dark." She blinked away the tears that filled her eyes.

Something happened in the dark. Something bad.

"I don't remember," she said again, and it was almost as if…as if the words were a vow.

The machines beeped louder around her. Noelle's mother pulled Noelle into a tight hug.

And, over her mother's shoulder, Noelle glanced up and met the eyes of the sheriff. There was concern in his gaze and suspicion.

I don't remember.

There was only darkness in her mind, and Noelle didn't know if that was good…or bad.

Chapter One

Fifteen years later...

The plane dipped, hitting another hard patch of turbulence, and Noelle Evers locked her fingers around the armrest on either side of her body. The private plane was currently flying over an area of pure-white land in Alaska, and Noelle was afraid they might be diving right *into* that snowy landscape at any moment.

"Relax," a low, gravel-rough voice told her. "We'll be landing in just a few more minutes."

The voice—and the guy who went with that voice—pulled Noelle's attention from the narrow window. She looked at the man seated directly across from her.

Thomas Anthony.

Tall, dark, deadly...and, currently, her partner on this assignment. Thomas "Dragon" Anthony was a man who seemed to always put her on edge.

"If you're going to be working with the EOD," Thomas murmured as he lifted one dark eyebrow, "rough flights will be the least of your worries."

Noelle forced herself to take a long, deep breath. She didn't want to show any weakness in front of Thomas. The man made her far too...nervous. Too *aware*.

Noelle was new to the EOD—the Elite Operations Division. She'd been recruited by EOD Director Bruce Mercer a few months back. Normally, the agents in that secretive group were all ex-military. They belonged to some of the most elite military units operating in the world. The agents were recruited to join the EOD because of their skills and because they were deadly when it came to their missions.

Noelle wasn't ex-military. She didn't specialize in killing or hunting prey. Instead, her specialty was getting *inside* a killer's mind. Before Bruce Mercer had used his pull to get Noelle into the EOD, she'd been working as a profiler at the FBI.

But then one of the EOD agents had gone rogue...and Mercer had brought her in to profile the agents there.

To hunt a killer within the division.

"You don't fit, you know," Thomas added in that deep, dark voice of his. A voice that made her tense and think of things she really shouldn't.

The plane bounced again. Noelle swallowed. "You mean because I lack the military training?"

"I mean because when we get into a life-or-death situation—and we will—you won't be prepared to take the necessary action."

Her eyes narrowed at those words. *Way to insult your partner on the first case.* "Look, I might not be an ex–Army Ranger—" as *he* was "—but I worked at the FBI for five years. I've been in plenty of dangerous situations, and I've handled myself just fine."

Thomas's lips quirked a bit. They were sensual lips, with a faintly cruel edge. Thomas was a handsome man, if you went for the deadly, dangerous type. As a general rule, Noelle definitely did *not* go for that type. She preferred safe guys, with a capital *S*.

And everything about Thomas spelled *DANGER*. From the top of his midnight-black hair down to his well-worn hiking boots, the guy just oozed a threat. Maybe it was because she'd read his file. She knew just what he was capable of doing—what he *had* done. Thomas didn't need any weapon when he went after his targets. He could kill—and had—quite easily, with his hands. He'd earned the nickname of Dragon while at the EOD because he was a martial-arts expert—he attacked with brutal control, and his opponents never had a chance against him.

Cold. Hard. Dangerous.

Thomas had a firm, square jaw, a blade-sharp nose and sculpted cheekbones that gave him a strong, fierce appearance. His deep, golden eyes reminded her of a lion's gaze. Maybe because every time she looked into those eyes, Noelle felt as if he were a predator and she was his prey.

We're partners. Partners. Mercer had sent them on this trip to Alaska because they were supposed to be hunting a killer. Together.

"You've never killed anyone," Thomas said as he tilted his head to study her. "Death is a way of life for EOD agents."

"Yes, well, I'm sure this will shock you, but FBI agents see plenty of death, too." Death was rather her specialty. "I know killers, and you can trust me to do my job."

Her job… Her job was to question the suspect they were pursuing. To break through the very public façade the man presented and to determine if Alaskan Senator

Lawrence Duncan was the man who'd recently plotted the destruction of the EOD.

Thomas's eyes narrowed just a bit as he gazed at her.

And there it is again. He was looking at her with a touch of familiarity. As if he knew her.

Too well.

But Noelle hadn't met Thomas Anthony until she started work at the EOD just a few months before. They were most certainly not intimately acquainted.

No matter how Thomas might glance at her.

"You're doing it again," Noelle blurted. Then she could have bitten her tongue when his face tensed. She was normally so much better at controlling her emotions and her responses to people, but Thomas just put her on edge.

"Doing what?" Thomas asked voice totally emotionless.

"Staring at me…as if—as if we're—" She floundered because what Noelle really wanted to say was… *As if we're lovers.* But they weren't. No way would she have forgotten him.

It was just…the intensity in his eyes…the heat…

"I make you nervous," he said.

Why lie? "Yes."

"Because you know what I've done." His gaze slid to the files on the seat beside her. "You read all of our files, right? When you were trying to decide which EOD agent was actually a psychotic killer in disguise."

That had been her *first* assignment at the EOD. This outing to Alaska was her second.

"So, what's the verdict, doc?" The *doc* was mocking, but Noelle was a doctor, a psychiatrist. She'd been trying for years to understand the demons that chased people.

Ever since she'd woken up in a small, southern hospital with her life shattered around her.

"Tell me…" Thomas continued with his gaze assessing. "Am I dangerous? Am I psychotic? Is that why you tense up every time I get near you?" He leaned forward. "Are you afraid I'll hurt you?" Then, before she could respond, his jaw hardened even more. "Because that's not the way things work at the EOD. You trust your partner, or you don't trust anyone."

She couldn't seem to take a deep enough breath. Thomas filled the space around her so completely.

The pilot's voice floated over the intercom then, announcing their impending landing.

Thomas leaned back.

But Noelle's hand flew out. She touched his wrist.

Thomas stilled.

"I know you're not psychotic. You're a soldier. A damn fine one, at that," she added because it was true. "And if I seem nervous…" *Tell him.* "It's not you, really. I have a…very hard time getting close to people." Mostly because Noelle had made a habit of putting a wall between herself and others.

Once, that wall had been necessary for Noelle's survival. But now, she didn't know how to live without that protection.

His gaze dropped to her hand.

Noelle slowly pulled her fingers back.

After a moment, Thomas's stare lifted once more to her face. "You'll be closer to me than you will be to anyone else."

Goose bumps rose on Noelle's arms. Was that a promise? Or a warning?

Then the plane began its descent, and she held back the other questions she wanted to ask him.

THOMAS ANTHONY WAS used to danger. He was used to pain. He was used to surviving any and every hellhole on earth. As an Army Ranger, his job had been to get the mission accomplished, no matter what.

But his job had never involved working intimately with Noelle Evers, not until now.

She doesn't remember me.

He'd known that, of course, from the beginning. From the first day he'd glanced up at the EOD and found himself staring into her warm, hazel eyes. Just looking at her had been like a punch to his gut. He'd wondered if she'd seen the flare of recognition in his eyes, but...

No, she hadn't shown any awareness of the past they shared.

That was a good thing. Her not remembering helped him. Because if she ever did remember what he'd done...

She'd be terrified of me.

Even more afraid than she already was.

And, despite her words, Noelle was afraid of him. Thomas knew a whole lot about fear, and he was certain of the emotion he saw in her eyes.

"The senator will see you now," Paula Quill said as she pointed toward the closed door on the right. The woman's blond hair was pulled back in a perfect twist, and her face was schooled to show not even a hint of curiosity about their visit. As the senator's assistant,

Thomas figured the woman was used to keeping that mask of hers in place.

They were in the senator's mansion, a too-big, mausoleum-type place Thomas didn't like. But they'd needed to track the man back to his lair, even if that lair was in one of the most isolated spots in Alaska.

"He's waiting in his study," Paula added. Paula was pretty, a woman in her early twenties, and based on what Thomas knew about the senator, Paula was *exactly* the guy's type. The senator was single, and from all accounts, quite a ladies' man.

The EOD also suspected the man was a killer.

Noelle breezed past the other woman and headed into the senator's study.

Noelle and Paula…they were night and day. Paula was icy reserve, cold perfection.

But Noelle…with her dark, red hair and her striking face…she was heat. Fire.

Passion.

The senator turned at Noelle's approach, a fake smile on his face. Senator Lawrence Duncan was forty-two, rich and currently the chief suspect in the recent bombing of the EOD office in Washington D.C.

Someone with a whole lot of power had hired an assassin—a man known as the Jack of Hearts—to take out EOD Director Bruce Mercer *and* to destroy the EOD in the process.

Right now, all of their intel was pointing to Senator Duncan as being that person in question.

"Senator Duncan." Noelle's voice was smooth, giving no hint at all to her southern roots. "Thank you for seeing us today." She offered the senator her hand.

And he held it far too long. "How could I refuse?"

Duncan murmured. "Though I'll confess, I don't quite know why the FBI wants to see me."

That was their cover. They were acting as FBI agents because even U.S. senators didn't have clearance to know about EOD missions.

But if this guy is the one we're after, he already knows far too much about the EOD.

"We have some questions to ask you," Noelle murmured. "About a killer who was recently hunting in D.C."

Paula pulled the door shut, sealing them inside the room with the senator as she left.

The senator's gaze swept over Noelle. He was still holding her hand and looking far too appreciative as his gaze dipped over her.

Noelle was a fine-looking woman, no doubt about it. Tall and curved, Thomas had seen plenty of men pass admiring stares her way. And every time those guys gazed at her with desire flaring in their eyes, Thomas wanted to drive his fist into their faces.

He cleared his throat. "I'm Agent Thomas Anthony," Thomas said. A full, fake dossier had been created with his FBI credentials, just in case the senator wanted to dig. "And we certainly appreciate your cooperation." Bull. Thomas didn't appreciate anything about the jerk, and if the guy didn't let Noelle's hand go in the next five seconds—

Noelle pulled away from the senator. "Are you familiar with the killer known as the Jack of Hearts?"

Duncan blinked. "Ah…I read about him in the paper. Wasn't he the serial killer who left playing cards at the scenes of his kills?"

Not exactly. Jack had been a murderer all right, but

he'd been an assassin, not a serial killer. His kills hadn't been for pleasure. They'd been for pure profit.

"That's him," Noelle inclined her head toward the senator. Thomas noticed her gaze swept around the study.

Thomas followed her stare. Duncan was a hunter. The trophies from his kills filled the walls of the room. And so did pictures. Pictures of cabins. Of boats. Of smiling women who stood at his side.

"Ah, well, I've certainly never met the man." Duncan took a seat behind his desk. He motioned toward the couch on the right. "So I don't see how I can—"

"When the authorities caught up with him," Noelle interrupted smoothly. "He was planning to escape on your boat, the *Dreamer*. It was docked in D.C., and Jack had intended to slip away on that vessel."

The senator's eyes flared with surprise. "I hadn't realized that. I heard he was at the dock, but not that he was planning to use *my* boat."

Thomas thought the senator's response seemed a little too perfect. Almost rehearsed.

"Do you have any idea why he might have selected *your* boat?" Noelle didn't sit on the couch. Neither did Thomas. They both kept standing. Noelle pulled a photograph from the manila file she carried, and she pushed it across the desk toward the senator. "Take a look at Jack, and tell me…have you seen him before?"

The senator's gaze darted down to the photo, then right back to Noelle. "I see so many people on the campaign trail. Our paths could've crossed, and I wouldn't know it."

"Why did he choose *your* boat?" Thomas demanded because the senator had conveniently not answered that particular question.

Duncan's gaze—a dark brown—darted toward him. "Agent…Anthony, was it? I have no idea why he chose my boat. Perhaps it was just convenient for him. The right escape boat, at the right place."

Thomas wasn't buying that. "Before he died, the killer implied he knew you. That you'd *hired* him to do work for you in the past."

The senator's jaw hardened. "I have dozens of people working for me at any given time. You can check with Paula to see if this—this man was part of our extended staff, but I've certainly had no personal experience with him."

"I'm not talking about hiring him to work as part of your campaign team." Thomas knew his voice had roughened. He also knew Noelle was carefully studying the senator's reaction to their questions. "I'm asking if you hired him to kill for you."

The senator shot to his feet. "This is outrageous!" He pointed toward the door. "Leave. Now. I will not stand for this sort of harassment!"

"It's not harassment," Noelle said quietly. "It's just questioning. And we thought it would be better for you if we did that questioning here, away from prying eyes, instead of back in the limelight of D.C."

Anger burned in Duncan's stare. "Now I see why I warranted a *personal* visit from the FBI. It's certainly not every day that I'm tracked to my home like this…." His breath heaved out in what was probably supposed to look like an affronted rush. "I don't like the accusations flying from you two."

"We've made no accusations," Noelle replied. Thomas had to admire her. She was good at keeping her emotions in check. "We're simply asking you questions."

"You're *done* with your questions." The senator stomped toward the door. "You want to see me again, you talk to my lawyer." He yanked open the door and gave them a hard glare. "Hope you enjoy your trip back to D.C. By the time you get there, I'll have already talked to your supervisor. You'll both be lucky to have jobs waiting on you."

Oh, Thomas was sure the jobs would be waiting. He was also sure they wouldn't be leaving Alaska anytime soon.

The mission isn't over. It's just started.

"Thanks for your time, Senator," Noelle said. "It's certainly been enlightening."

Duncan frowned at that, but Noelle just headed right past the guy.

Thomas took his time following her. He'd been around men like the senator before. Men born with silver spoons shoved deep in their mouths. He often wished those guys would choke on them.

"You and your partner should be careful," the senator muttered. "This is a dangerous part of the country."

Thomas froze. Had that jerk just *threatened* them? He turned his head and met the senator's dark stare.

"No one comes into my home and tries to destroy me," the senator spat at him. "No one. You've just made a very powerful enemy."

Thomas fought the urge to roll his eyes. "Right. In case you can't tell, I'm terrified right now."

The senator frowned.

It was Thomas's turn to smile. "Something you should know, too. I'm a bit of a hunter, like you." He motioned to the trophies on the wall. "Only I don't hunt animals. I take out the humans who are too dangerous to be walking the streets."

"I—" The senator's face reddened.

Thomas leaned in closer to him. "We know what you did. We know what you are. Soon, the whole world will know, too."

The senator's shoulders hunched.

Thomas nodded. "We'll be seeing you again, soon." Because they hadn't come all the way to Alaska for some quick turnaround trip. They'd come to Alaska to get the proof they needed. Proof of the senator's guilt. They weren't leaving until they'd accomplished their mission.

Satisfied he'd made his point, Thomas exited behind Noelle. Paula watched them with wide, wary eyes. Thomas knew she'd overheard plenty of their conversation. *If you're smart, lady, you'll get away from the senator, as fast as you can.*

But Paula appeared to have frozen in place.

Thomas and Noelle didn't speak again until they'd left the senator's mansion. Once they were back inside their rented SUV, Thomas glanced at Noelle.

She was staring up at the senator's home.

"Don't keep me in suspense," he drawled as he cranked the vehicle. A light dusting of snow had started to fall. "What did you think?"

She didn't glance his way. "It's too early to tell."

He didn't buy it. Noelle made her living by reading people. By looking past the bright, shiny surface they presented to the rest of the world. He pulled out of the winding drive and headed back toward the cabin in town that the EOD had rented for them.

They hadn't bothered with getting a room in the local lodge—they'd needed more permanency.

They were planning to stay in Alaska for the long haul.

Until we can bury the senator.

"But I do know he was lying to us," Noelle added.

Thomas wasn't a profiler, and he knew that. The guy had barely been able to hold eye contact with him, and the senator had reacted far too strongly to their questions.

"So he's our guy." Thomas kept his hold steady on the steering wheel. He'd driven on snow-covered roads plenty of times. But those roads were sure different from the dirt roads of his youth.

"I think he could be. The man is controlling, dominating, and he's—" Noelle hesitated. "I think there may be quite a few layers to the senator."

"Yeah, well, your job is to peel away those layers, isn't it? To find out what hides underneath." That knowledge made him nervous. He didn't want Noelle to ever see beneath the surface he presented. Thomas had told her before she shouldn't profile him, but he'd caught her staring at him a few times, her eyes curious.

What does Noelle see when she looks at me? He knew what he saw when he looked into her eyes.

The thing I want most.

But when she stared at him, Thomas wondered if she just saw a killer.

Unfortunately, that was exactly what he was.

"THEY NEED TO VANISH," Lawrence Duncan said as his fingers tightened around the phone he had pressed to his ear. "Hell, yes, I know the risks, and that's why I'm telling you…*they can't make it out of this area.*"

His heart was racing in his chest. It had been pounding too fast from the moment his study door had opened and FBI agent Noelle Evers had walked inside. He'd recognized her instantly, even after all those long years. "She's a threat," he said flatly. "One that should have been eliminated by now."

Silence stretched on the phone line.

"Do it," Lawrence snarled. "Or I will." Even though he hated to get his hands dirty. But too much was at stake in this situation. They were already too exposed. And when Noelle put the pieces together—

I'll lose everything.

He heard the rough rasp of breathing on the other end of the line. Lawrence waited, hoping to hear—

"They'll die tonight."

He smiled. "The snowfall is just going to get heavier. They're on their way to their cabin now. That means they are heading *your* way." He'd taken the liberty of acquiring all of his information earlier. His assistant, Paula, had a knack for discovering information. Even before the agents had entered his home, Lawrence had known where they'd be staying in town. "With weather like this, it will be easy enough for them to have an accident."

A fatal one.

The senator hesitated. "Just…don't leave obvious wounds on their bodies."

"Don't worry, there won't be any bodies to find."

The words should have chilled Lawrence, but he'd

lost his conscience long ago. The first time he'd seen a kill, his life had changed.

And the blood had stained his hands ever since.

THEY'D BEEN DRIVING for about twenty minutes when the bright flash of headlights illuminated their rental vehicle. Thomas narrowed his eyes as he glanced in the rearview mirror. He could hear the growl of a fast-approaching vehicle behind him.

Even as the snow continued to fall in heavier waves.

"Where'd he come from?" Noelle asked as she turned in her seat to glance back.

Thomas's hands tightened around the wheel. Adrenaline spiked in his blood as the other vehicle's engine growled again and seemed to come even closer.

"What is he doing?" Alarm sharpened Noelle's voice. "Maybe we should slow down, in case he wants to pass."

The road was narrow and surrounded by trees. Up ahead, an old bridge crossed over what looked like an ice-filled lake.

"We're not slowing down," Thomas said because his instincts were screaming at him. A dark road. A driver who was—

The other vehicle slammed into the back of Thomas's SUV. The impact was jarring, and he had to fight to keep the SUV from swerving off the road. "Hold on," he growled to Noelle. "Just hold—"

The other driver came at them again, hitting even harder this time. The SUV's wheels slipped on the icy road as the bridge loomed before them.

"It's a truck," Noelle gasped out. "I can see its outline. It's big and—"

It hit them again. Noelle's words ended in a scream

because the SUV flew across the slick road. They were heading for the bridge. The SUV started to spin as the tires slid right over the ice.

"Thomas!"

The SUV slammed into the side of the bridge. The impact was on Noelle's side, and Thomas's gaze immediately jerked toward her as fear clawed through him.

Her hair had fallen over her face, and the echo of her scream seemed to shudder through his whole body. "Noelle?"

Thomas could hear the other vehicle's motor growling again. The SOB was going to come at him again. And if the truck hit them, they could easily plunge into the frigid water.

They had to get out of there, fast. "Come on, baby," he said, the endearment sliding from his mouth without thought because it was *her*. "We have to move."

The bright headlights were on them again. Coming fast, too fast.

Noelle's head lifted. She blinked at him. "Thomas?"

He yanked her free from the seat belt. He was already out of his, too. He shoved open his door.

The vehicle slammed right into Thomas's open door. Metal crunched, groaned—and the door ripped away as the truck drove their SUV harder into the side of the bridge and its old railing.

"Climb out the back!" Thomas yelled. "Hurry!" He pushed her into the rear seat. He had his weapon in his hands, and he turned back, aiming toward the other driver.

Who are you? What in the hell is happening?

His bullets blasted through the other vehicle's windshield. The truck stopped its advance. Noelle had made it into the backseat. She forced open the rear door, and Thomas followed her, barely fitting in the small escape space because the vehicle was wedged so closely to the railing.

He'd just cleared the vehicle when—

The truck hit them again. Only this time, the railing broke. Glass shattered. Metal crunched. And the wooden barrier splintered.

Thomas grabbed tightly to Noelle, and he lunged forward with her, hurtling them toward the woods near the edge of the bridge. They hit the snow and rolled down the ravine, tumbling again and again as they flew toward the bottom.

The SUV crashed into the frozen lake, sending chunks of ice into the air.

Thomas and Noelle finally stopped. They were about two feet away from that lake. Noelle was on top of him, and he quickly reversed their positions, holding her tightly. He could hear the growl of the other vehicle's engine, and then...

"He's leaving," Noelle whispered.

Yes, he was. Because he thought he'd gotten his prey?

The engine's snarl grew softer as the truck drove away.

The snow kept falling.

Noelle pushed against his shoulders. Thomas rose slowly, and he pulled Noelle to her feet. Their SUV was partially submerged and sinking fast. Damn it.

"Are you all right?" Thomas asked her as his eyes swept over her. He didn't see any injuries, but he wanted to be sure she was all right.

"He just tried to kill us!" She sounded incredulous.

She was also shaking.

Because it was cold out there. He shouldered out of his coat and pushed it toward her. When she tried to refuse, Thomas just wrapped it around her shoulders. "Senior agent," he snapped at her, still remembering the flash of fear he'd felt in the SUV. "That means you do what I say. Right now, I'm saying…*take my coat.*"

She pulled the coat closer. Thomas yanked out his phone. They'd rolled a good twenty feet from the road. A heavy darkness was already sweeping over the area. He lifted the phone—and realized it had been smashed to hell and back during the tumble.

"Tell me your phone's working," he said.

"I…I think it's in the SUV."

Hell.

The temperature was too low. It was getting too dark. No one was going to see them down there, and if anyone did happen to come along that lonely stretch of road again, it could very well be the same jerk who'd just tried to kill them.

Noelle started to climb back up toward the road. He caught her arm, stopping her. "Was your gun in the vehicle, too?" Thomas demanded.

She gave a grim nod. "Yours?" Noelle asked softly.

"You know I don't need a gun to kill." She was still shivering. They had to get to safety, fast. "But I've got the weapon."

"Stay to the shadows as much as possible," Thomas told her, keeping his voice quiet, too. In this area, any noise would carry easily. "He could come back, but we have to travel close to the road because running through the wilderness sure isn't an option for us." Not unless they wanted a slow death.

"I thought I saw a turnoff, a mile or so before the bridge," Noelle told him. When she spoke, a small cloud appeared before her mouth. *It's too cold out here.* "Maybe there's a cabin there. Someone who can help us."

Maybe. Right then, that turnoff sounded like their best chance. He kept his hold on her arm, and they started walking through the darkness.

Chapter Two

"You need to strip."

The cabin door slammed closed behind Noelle. At Thomas's growled words, Noelle stiffened. "Excuse me?"

They'd been walking for what felt like an hour. They'd taken the turnoff from the main road and slogged ahead until they'd found this place—a rundown, one-room cabin, which looked as if it hadn't been used in years.

It was as cold inside as it was outside. Noelle couldn't stop the shivers that rocked her body.

"Your core temperature is too low," Thomas told her flatly. "We have to get warm. The snow wet our clothing, so we have to ditch it." He was leaning over what looked like one very ancient fireplace. "Lucky damn night," he rasped. "There's some old wood here."

Uh, yeah, but how were they going to *light* that fire and—

He pulled out a small kit from his pocket and went to work. A flame flared seconds later.

Her breath expelled in a relieved rush.

Still kneeling in front of the fire, Thomas glanced

back at her. "There was no way I'd come into the Alaskan wilderness without a fire kit."

She shivered. Again.

"Strip," he ordered once more.

The cabin was deserted, so they sure weren't going to get any rescue crew out there that night. But if they didn't warm up, soon, Noelle realized the odds of them making it until morning weren't going to be high.

Thomas headed toward her.

Noelle tensed.

"There you go again," he said, and he sounded angry. "When will you learn, I'm not going to bite?"

"I—"

He brushed by her and yanked open a small closet. No, he yanked *down* that closet's door; the old thing just literally fell off its hinges. "This will have to do for kindling 'cause we aren't finding any dry wood outside." He broke the door into heavy chunks. He had the fire flaring even higher when he added it. His back was turned to her as she inched toward that inviting warmth.

"My clothes are hitting the floor," Thomas told her bluntly. "Yours need to do the same."

Because they were soaked. But…

He stripped out of his sweater. Dropped the shirt he'd worn under it for layering. When he bent to remove his boots and socks, the firelight flickered over the tight muscles in his chest and arms. He had to work out—a lot. She'd never seen anyone with such sculpted muscles. As she stared at him—probably too long and too hard—Noelle could just make out the…scars on his body. Twisting, sharp, they snaked around his abs and lined his back.

She remembered the wound notations in his files.

He'd been captured on a mission a while back. Held. Tortured. But, by the time rescue had come, all of his captors had been dead.

Thomas turned then. He still wore his jeans. His eyes met hers. "It's not personal," he told her in his deep, dark voice. "It's survival."

She felt her cheeks burn. Well, at least burning was better than freezing. Noelle fumbled and her clothes started to hit the floor. His jacket. Hers. Her sweater. Her undershirt. Her boots. Her socks.

Her fingers were fumbling, uncoordinated, as she tried to unhook the snap of her jeans.

"Let me." His voice was rougher than before, and his fingers were suddenly working at her waistband. He was so close, seeming to surround her with his strength. Noelle tried to pull in a deep breath, and his scent—masculine and crisp—wrapped around her.

Her zipper eased down with a hiss of sound.

She jerked back from him. Nearly fell. Would have, if Thomas hadn't snagged her arm so quickly. "Easy," he murmured.

Easy was the last thing she felt right then.

His fingers slowly uncurled their grip. "I'll spread out our clothes to dry. We should try to get some rest near the fire."

Noelle didn't hold out a lot of hope regarding rest. She bent and pushed her jeans down her legs. Then she looked up. Thomas had turned his back to her, but he'd stuck his hand out behind him, obviously waiting for her jeans. She pushed them into his hand.

"The rest," Thomas pressed.

"No way," Noelle said, aware that her voice held a sharp snap. "I'm keeping on my underwear, and I want you to do the same." Her panties and her bra were dry enough, and she was absolutely not planning to flash him any more than necessary.

Noelle thought she heard Thomas sigh, but he bent and finished spreading out her clothes. And his. And—

"Sorry," he said, voice a bit wry as she jerked her gaze off him and back toward the fire. "But I'm not wearing underwear."

No, no, he *hadn't* been.

Noelle dropped toward the fire. She sat on the floor and pulled her knees up toward her. She was still shivering, and the tips of her fingers and toes were starting to ache.

A few moments later, Thomas eased down next to her. He reached for her.

The flinch was instinctive. She'd been withdrawing from people ever since—well, ever since she'd been seventeen years old and she'd woken, terrified, in a cabin that had actually looked a whole lot like the one they were currently in.

Her shoulders hunched.

"We need to share body warmth," he said again. "Don't worry I think I can control myself here."

Okay, now he was just mocking her.

But his hands gently curled around her, and he eased her fully down on the wooden floor next to him. Then he curled his body around hers. His left arm slid under her head, almost like a pillow, while his right curled around her stomach and pulled her back against the warm, hard cradle of his body.

"I *think* that I can," he added roughly, his breath blowing over the shell of her ear.

The fire crackled in front of her.

Noelle swallowed and tried to figure out what she was supposed to do in this situation. Being naked and trapped in a one-room cabin with Agent Thomas Anthony certainly hadn't been on her to-do list.

"I think we have confirmation of the senator's guilt." His rumbling voice seemed to roll right through her.

"We visit the senator," Thomas continued grimly, "then less than half an hour later, some maniac tries to kill us. Connecting those dots sure isn't hard."

No, it wasn't, and Noelle had never been the type to believe in coincidences. She tried to put a little more space between their bodies.

Thomas just pulled her right back against him. "He left the scene because he thinks we're dead."

"If we hadn't cleared the SUV right then, we would be dead." Her own words were quiet and they gave no hint to the terror that had rocked through her as she fought to get out of the vehicle. As cold as it was outside…if they'd plunged beneath the ice in that lake, survival would have been only a dim hope. "But I don't know if the senator did this himself. He strikes me as more of a guy who hires out his dirty work." After all, that was exactly what they thought he'd done in D.C.— hired Jack to take out the EOD.

And as far as getting rid of her and Thomas, well, she was sure that counted as dirty work.

"He just tried to kill two federal agents," Thomas's lips brushed against her neck. Had he meant to do that? Surely not. "Whether he did it himself or he hired someone, we're getting the guy. At first light, we're finding a way out of this place, and we're going after him."

First light. That certainly seemed very far away.

"He panicked." That was the only explanation she

had. "Something set him off during our meeting." Something they'd said or done.

"He got set off because the FBI was at his door. The guy's probably trying to run as fast and as far as he can right now."

Noelle wasn't so sure. If he thought they were dead, why would he bother to run?

"But I'll find him," Thomas vowed. "I won't stop until I do."

The fire surged a bit higher then, sending sparks into the air.

"We should get some sleep." His voice softened a bit. "Who the hell knows what we'll face tomorrow."

Since they'd just survived one attempt on their lives, Noelle knew he was right.

Her gaze drifted away from the fire. She glanced at the flickering shadows lining the walls. This place... It was just like the cabin that haunted her nightmares. Those nightmares chased her wherever she went, no matter what she did.

"You're too tense," he said. "Look, I get that you don't like me, but—"

"I like you just fine." How awkward was this conversation? But he had a right to know... "It's not you that I'm afraid of, okay? It's...this place."

He was silent behind her. But his fingers moved lightly against her stomach. Almost as if he were caressing her.

"We're safe."

Her gaze slid to the right. His gun was there. Within easy reach. "Sometimes, I don't ever feel safe." As soon as she said the words, Noelle wished she could call them back. She'd never made that confession to anyone.

"Why not?" His hold definitely tightened then.

Noelle shook her head. She was feeling warmer, so much warmer now. The shivers and shudders were easing. "Because I'm never sure what waits in the darkness." But she wasn't talking about the darkness outside the cabin. She was talking about the darkness in her own mind.

He was silent behind her.

And Noelle found she couldn't stop talking, not to him. Not then. "When I was seventeen, I was…taken." Just saying the words hurt, but it also seemed a relief to put them out there. "I was missing from my home for over forty-eight hours before the police found me." She was glad she wasn't looking into his face when she told this story. Noelle wasn't sure she wanted to see his reaction. "Forty-eight hours," she said again, whispering the words. "And to this day, I still can't remember a single thing that happened during that time." When she tried to remember, she only saw the darkness.

"Maybe you're better off not remembering."

That was what her mother had told her, over and over. Her mother had thought it would be better to just move forward. To put those two days into the back of her mind and pretend they hadn't happened.

But they *had* happened. They'd changed her.

"When the police found me, a dead man was in the cabin with me."

Silence. Then, "You think you killed him?"

"I was tied, bound to a chair. Someone else was there." The man's accomplice? Another shudder had her body quaking. But she didn't know if that shudder came from the cold or from the fear in her belly. "A killer was there, and I can't remember a thing about him."

That scared her more than anything else. Because that man—that killer—he could be anyone. He could be anywhere. She could have met him a hundred times and never known.

She'd become a profiler because of what happened. Because she wanted to be able to see the murderers out there. To look behind the masks they wore.

What she'd discovered during the course of her career was that monsters were real. They just wore the guise of men.

Her eyes squeezed closed. She didn't know why she'd revealed so much to Thomas. In the harsh light of dawn, she knew she'd regret sharing so much with him. But, right then, she still just felt that strange relief.

And the fear slid away as the fire warmed her and he held her close. It was odd to feel so secure…in the arms of a dragon.

THE DOOR TO Lawrence Duncan's study opened with a rasp of sound. Lawrence glanced up, expecting to see Paula, but she wasn't in the doorway. Still, he smiled when he saw just who *had* come to pay him a late-night visit. "I take it that you accomplished our task?"

His visitor took a step inside his study. "Their vehicle won't be found."

"Good." His eyes narrowed as he studied the man before him. "This shouldn't have happened, you know. I'm supposed to be clear. Instead, I'm cleaning up your messes." His breath heaved out. "Noelle Evers. She should've died years ago, and we both know it."

The floor creaked as the man edged closer to Lawrence. "I didn't want Noelle to die this way. I wanted—"

"To cut her throat yourself? Yes, well, I know how

you enjoy getting up close, but that wasn't going to happen." Lawrence shot to his feet and paced toward the window on the right. When he looked out, he just saw darkness. "She's not some scared kid any longer. She's FBI. And if we hadn't taken her out then—"

His words ended, cut off with a gurgle of sound because—because a knife had just sliced across his throat.

"I was saving her for later." The words were snarled into Lawrence's ear. "She would have been special. Now she's *gone*."

Lawrence's hand flew to his neck, but he couldn't stop the flow. His knees gave way. He tried to grab for the window curtain, but his bloody hands just slipped over the fabric. He hit the floor.

His eyes were open and staring up at the killer above him.

"You were a threat, too," the killer told him. "Because you knew what I'd done." He smiled down at Lawrence. "But you won't tell anyone now, will you? You *can't* tell anyone." His smile faded away. "And I won't be on your leash any longer. From here on out, no one controls me."

SHE WAS ASLEEP in his arms. Noelle's breathing was easy and soft, and all of the tension had drained from her body. She was a silken weight against Thomas, and her scent—light and sweet—wrapped deeply around him.

He'd told her that it wasn't personal. That it was just about survival.

He was such a liar. With her, everything was personal. It had been, for far longer than she realized.

His left arm was still under her head. His fingers were starting to go numb, but Thomas didn't care. She was comfortable, and he had no intention of moving. He'd dreamed of holding her before, but he hadn't ever thought he'd actually get this close to her.

Some dreams were so much better in reality.

His lips brushed lightly over her hair. If she'd been awake, he wouldn't have dared such a move. But asleep…

I'll make my control hold. It was a good thing she wasn't aware right then. There'd be no hiding the arousal he felt when she was near.

He figured an hour had passed. The flames were still crackling. They were secure for the night, but he had no intention of closing his eyes anytime soon. With his perfect temptation nestled so closely to him, sleep wasn't exactly high on his priority list. Besides, he wanted to keep her safe, and keeping Noelle safe meant someone had to stay awake for guard duty.

"Let me go…"

The words were so soft that, at first, he thought he'd just imagined them, but then Noelle began to struggle lightly against his hold. "Please," she whispered, and the plea cut right through him. "Don't hurt me."

Never.

She twisted in his hold, her struggles growing stronger. "Let me go!"

"Noelle." He knew she was having a nightmare. She'd revealed so much to him in the darkness. "Noelle, you're safe." With him, she'd always be safe. He wished she would realize that.

She rolled then, and he eased his hold as she turned toward him. Her body came flush against his, and he was stunned to see her eyes were wide open. "Noelle?"

"I won't tell," she said, and her voice was wrong.

Too soft. Too lost. "Just let me go." Her hands pushed against him.

He shifted his body, caught her hands and pinned them lightly to the floor. "Look at me." Thomas said the words deliberately because he knew Noelle wasn't seeing him. She was just staring at images from her past.

How often did this happen? How often did she get trapped in the same nightmare?

"Don't hurt me..."

She was breaking him. Thomas had to make Noelle see what was right in front of her. Damn it, he'd worried when he saw this place it might stir up her past, but he hadn't exactly been given a choice. It had been this dump of a cabin or nothing, and he hadn't planned to just stand by while she suffered.

"Noelle..." Her name was a growl of frustration. Then he did the only thing he could—Thomas kissed her.

He'd often thought about kissing Noelle, tasting her. But he'd sure never imagined their first taste would be like this.

Her lips were soft beneath his. He kissed her slowly, carefully. He wanted to pull her back from the past and get her to see the present. To see him.

She stiffened against him as he kissed her. He knew awareness was flooding back for her. He knew he should pull away.

He also knew that he wanted her more than he'd ever wanted any other woman.

So when her lips parted in surprise, he didn't do the right thing. He didn't pull back and ask her if she was okay.

He kissed her harder. He thrust his tongue into her

mouth, and he savored her. With every movement of his lips against hers, Thomas just wanted more.

He wanted everything.

One day, he'd get it.

Her breasts were pressed to his chest. Her smooth legs were trapped between his thighs. And—

She was kissing him back. Slowly at first then with more passion, with a need he hadn't expected.

Desire surged within him. *Noelle wants me, too.* He'd never expected to find the passion hiding behind her fear.

His heart thudded in his ears. He was so close to having her. Only the thin scrap of lace she wore shielded her from him. When he'd first seen the black bra and that tiny bit that passed for her panties, lust had surged through him.

He wanted to touch every inch of her then.

He freed her wrists so he could explore her body. He'd make it good for her. He'd give her so much pleasure. Enough to chase away any nightmares that ever dared to whisper through her mind again.

When he let her wrists go, her hands immediately curled around his shoulders. He kissed his way down her throat. Her pulse raced beneath his mouth, and Thomas had to lick that spot right there. She moaned lightly, and his teeth grazed over the flesh. He wanted her so much his whole body seemed to flash molten hot.

"Thomas?" Desire was in her voice, and he loved the sound of his name on her lips.

His hand was on her rib cage. He wanted that bra gone. He wanted—

Her.

"Thomas…no, we're partners." Confusion fought with the desire in Noelle's husky voice. "I— *We can't.*"

Oh, they could. They could do it so well and so long, but Thomas stilled at her words. His head lifted. He met her stare, and he knew she'd read fierce hunger in his eyes.

Her hands seemed to burn against his skin. He was so close to the thing he wanted most. So very close.

Thomas pulled away from her and rose to his feet. His jeans were still a little damp, but he pulled them on. Staying naked with her sure wasn't an option then. He turned his back to her as he yanked up the zipper.

"I…I didn't mean to let things get so far." Her soft voice came from behind him.

He sucked in a deep breath, then glanced over his shoulder at her. She'd sat up and her hands were now curled around her folded knees. Damn. Noelle was the sexiest thing he'd ever seen. "You were having a bad dream."

Her brows rose at that.

"I kissed you to try and wake you up." Only she hadn't been sleeping, not really. He thought maybe she'd had more of a flashback than a nightmare. Thomas cleared his throat. "I'm the one who didn't mean to let things get this far." Not yet. He had plans for Noelle, and those plans hadn't included this pit stop at a run-down shack in the middle of nowhere.

"I don't remember the nightmare." Her gaze dropped from his. "But then, I never do."

He turned to fully face her. The fire crackled behind him. "Maybe it's good to get a few things out in the open now."

Her chin lifted as her eyes found his once more.

"I want you."

"We're partners—"

"It's a temporary assignment, and we both know it. Mercer doesn't plan to keep you in the field. He wants you in the EOD main office, working up your profiles. This is a one-shot mission for us." So the normal rules weren't applying. When it came to Noelle, Thomas had no rules. "I want you," he said again, "and unless I'm mistaken, you want me, too."

She didn't speak.

His jaw locked. He'd felt her desire, tasted it. He knew—

"I do," Noelle said, the words so quiet he had to strain in order to hear them.

His heart seemed to stop at that admission.

"But I know better than to take everything I want. Especially when what I want can be dangerous to me."

"You can trust me," he growled. He wasn't a threat to her. Damn it, yes, he knew the stories that circulated about him at the EOD. That the Dragon was a cold-blooded killer with ice in his veins and that he killed without remorse. *That isn't me.* He needed Noelle to see him for the man he truly was.

Her body tensed. "I can't trust myself."

He didn't even know what that meant.

But before he could question her more, he heard the faint roar of—an engine?

He saw Noelle's head whip toward the door, and he knew she'd heard the sound, too. He grabbed for the rest of his clothes and dressed as quickly as he could. Noelle was scrambling to her feet and pulling on her still-wet clothing.

His fingers curled around his gun. Was that a rescuer

coming to find them, someone who'd been alerted by the smoke rising from the old chimney? Or was it the maniac in the truck, coming back to finish them off? Thomas had known the fire would pose risks for him and Noelle. The smoke would give away their location, but staying warm had been a priority.

The roar of the approaching engine grew louder.

Noelle hurried to Thomas's side. "Stay behind me," he told her with a firm glare. "Until we find out just who is coming this way."

"You're the one with the gun," she said with a shrug as she lifted her hands. "Letting you take the lead is more than fine by me."

He cracked open the front door. He could see the bright glint of headlights coming toward the cabin. That roar—it was from what looked like a snowplow. Thomas could just make out its bulk.

He inched onto the sagging porch, keeping his gun at his side. A quick count showed him three vehicles were coming his way, and none of those vehicles looked like the truck that had run them off the road. Actually one of those vehicles—

A siren screamed on. Blue lights flashed.

Right. One of those vehicles looked like a deputy's car.

More bright lights flooded the scene, illuminating Thomas and Noelle on the porch. Thomas wisely kept his weapon hidden.

Noelle's arm brushed against Thomas's side. "We're FBI!" Noelle called out as she moved forward. They were both supposed to keep using that cover, no matter what.

Doors slammed. Two men ran toward them. "We

were hoping it was you," one of the man huffed out. "I'm Sheriff Glen Hodges. Your FBI boss has been calling our office for hours because you missed some sort of check-in."

Ah, that boss would be Mercer, and yes, they had missed their check-in. Thomas was actually surprised Mercer hadn't sent the National Guard after them. When it came to protecting his agents, Mercer was as fierce as any lion.

"We saw the smoke," the man beside Sheriff Hodges said, as he rocked forward onto the balls of his feet. "No one has been using Brian Lakely's place in years, so we thought it might be you."

Thomas advanced toward the men.

"Did you have car trouble?" Hodges asked, shaking his head. "How the heck did you wind up out here?"

"We had car trouble," Thomas agreed softly. "And the trouble started when some bozo ran us off the road and left us for dead."

"What?" The shocked exclamation came as the sheriff shot back a good two feet. "But we don't have trouble like that out here in Camden—"

"Well," Thomas drawled, "it looks like you do now. Because someone out there just tried to kill two federal agents." Thomas planned to get his hands on that *someone* very soon.

Senator Duncan, I'm coming for you.

Chapter Three

"Uh, are you real sure you want to do this?" Sheriff Hodges asked as he slammed his car door and turned toward Noelle and Thomas. The snow was still falling.

They were outside the senator's home. She and Thomas had insisted they be brought straight over. Noelle wanted to look into the senator's eyes and *see* his reaction to their survival. If he was the guy who'd just tried to send them to an icy grave, his reaction would tell her everything she needed to know.

"Senator Duncan…" The sheriff's voice was cautious. "He has a lot of power around here."

"We're not worried about his power." Noelle brushed past the sheriff and headed for the gate that led to the senator's property. It was ajar, so she just kept marching right up to the front door. She was wearing a thick coat about two sizes too big, a spare that Hodges kept in his trunk. Gloves covered her fingers, and a big woolen cap swallowed her hair. Thomas followed right on her heels. After what they'd been through, there was no way they'd allow the senator to slip through their fingers that night.

"Maybe you two should go to the local doc's place," the sheriff said as he rushed after them. "Make sure you're not suffering from some kind of trauma."

Noelle wasn't concerned about trauma. Before she could slam her fist against the door, Thomas beat her to it. He pounded hard enough to shake the façade.

Lights flooded on from the interior of the house.

"I'm gonna be in so much trouble," Hodges muttered.

The man needed to grow a backbone.

Eyes narrowed, Noelle focused on the door. When it swung open a few minutes later, a disheveled Paula Quill stood in the doorway.

"Agents?" Paula shoved back her hair. "What are you doing here?"

Noelle advanced and Paula fell back. Noelle figured that counted as an invitation to enter the place. "We're here to see the senator, *now.*"

"But it's the middle of the night!" Paula's hands tightly gripped the front of her robe. "You can't just barge in here—"

That was exactly what they'd just done. Noelle glanced to the left and saw a light was on in the senator's study, and its door was slightly open. Just like the gate. The senator should really watch that tendency to keep inviting folks in.

"The senator is *sleeping,*" Paula snapped as she moved to stand directly in front of Noelle. "You'll have to come back in the morning if you want another appointment with him."

Noelle simply walked around the other woman and headed for the study.

"Sorry, ma'am," Thomas murmured to Paula, "but this appointment can't wait."

Noelle's steps quickened as she approached that study door. Thomas was close. She could hear him following her. "Senator Duncan," Noelle called, raising her voice, "I hope you—" She fully pushed open the door, and her words broke off.

Noelle didn't see the senator in the office. He wasn't at his desk.

"I *told* you," Paula said, voice tight. "He's asleep. He's upstairs! Now, leave."

But…Noelle could smell something in that room. A familiar, gut-tightening scent. Instead of leaving, she advanced. Every muscle in her body tightened.

She glanced over her shoulder and saw Thomas's eyes were narrowed and currently sweeping over the room.

She looked behind the desk. Looked behind the leather couch…

And saw the body.

"That's not sleeping," Thomas said flatly as he peered down at the senator. "That's dead."

Paula ran toward the sofa. When she saw Duncan, Paula screamed.

"OUR CHIEF SUSPECT is dead."

Noelle glanced over when Thomas made this grim announcement. They were at the sheriff's station in Camden, in fresh clothes, and the two of them were currently heading the investigation into the senator's death. When they'd found the body, Sheriff Hodges had pretty much gone into shock.

"Things like this just don't happen in Camden…" Those had been the sheriff's hushed words once Paula Quill finally stopped screaming. It had taken at least fifteen minutes to calm down that woman.

To Noelle, it appeared as if the quiet town of Camden was having one hell of a night.

"Yeah, Mercer, I'm sure the guy in the truck wanted us dead. It was no mere hit-and-run. We were targeted." Thomas turned toward Noelle as he kept the phone to his ear. "My money was on the senator being behind that attack, but with him dead..." Thomas exhaled. "I'm not sure what's going on now."

Neither was Noelle.

"Right," Thomas said into the phone as his shoulders straightened. "We'll keep the FBI cover, and we'll report back on everything we find." He ended the call and tossed his phone onto the nearby desk.

They'd taken over one of the empty offices at the sheriff's station so they could have some privacy—and a base for their operations.

"Mercer wants us to stay here until we find the killer." Thomas ran a hand through his hair. "Our FBI cover positions us to lead the case, so he thinks we can control the investigation."

They could. If Sheriff Hodges called to verify their credentials, Noelle knew Mercer would just pull strings to make sure that verification went through without a hitch.

"Tell me what's happening," Thomas said as he crossed his arms over his chest and studied her. "You're the one who knows killers so well."

Yes, she did. Noelle cleared her throat. "The senator knew his killer. There was no sign of a struggle, and since none of the alarms were triggered in the house, I'm thinking Duncan even let the guy inside." A bad mistake. He'd trusted the wrong person. "There were no hesitation wounds on the senator's body. The knife sliced straight across his carotid artery. The senator... he would've been dead in moments." With his throat cut, the man hadn't been able to cry out for help. He'd just been able to die.

Noelle forced herself to take a long, deep breath. "I think we're looking for a man who has killed before." If it had been the killer's first time, the attack would've been more disorganized. Senator Duncan might have even been able to fight back. "And knife attacks... they're more personal. Using a knife is a type of intimate kill for many perpetrators."

His golden eyes gleamed. "So you think the man we're looking for was a friend of Duncan's."

"Friend, relative, maybe even an employee. He was someone who had access to the senator. Someone who could come to his house late at night and expect a meeting." She wasn't going to ignore the obvious. "I can think of one main reason for a meeting that late."

Thomas nodded. "A meeting that probably occurred right after our *accident* on the bridge." His hands dropped back to his sides.

Yes, they had both heard the M.E. reveal the estimated time of death.

"We already suspected that the senator didn't like to get up close with his dirty work. He sent someone in D.C. to attack Mercer, so maybe he sent someone to take care of us, too." She licked her lips. "Only that *someone* turned on the senator." *Why?* It was her job to find out why. Her job to understand the killers. Their motivations. Their darkness.

"You think we're looking at a professional."

"Of a sort, yes."

"So..." Thomas cocked his head to the right as he studied her. "What will this professional do when he realizes that he didn't succeed in taking us out? *If,* of course, he was the one who came after us."

Well, that was easy enough to answer. "There are two choices. He'll just cut his losses and get out of town or he'll try to finish the job."

Thomas's lips curved into a chilling smile. "I'd like to see him try."

HIS HANDS WERE SHAKING.

The killer glanced down at them. They were trembling again. And even though he'd thrown away his bloodstained gloves, he could swear he saw red on his fingertips.

Duncan's gone.

It felt so good to be free of the jerk. Duncan had always been controlling him…warning him.

No more.

The sun had risen. The snow had finally stopped falling. It was *his* day. No more taking orders. No more hiding.

He'd do what he wanted.

The FBI agents were gone. *She* was gone.

And the senator's body would be found at any time. He was free.

The sound of laughter drifted on the wind. The light, musical sound caught his attention. He glanced over at the diner on the right. It had just opened for breakfast. He watched as a young girl—looked as though she was barely sixteen—tried to push back the drift in front of the entrance. She was laughing because the snow kept falling back on her. Her red hair glinted in the light.

He stared at her, remembering the past.

She was so busy at her job she didn't even see him.

The road was empty. The diner always opened first thing. It would be a while before any locals wandered into the place.

He started walking toward her. She didn't even look up as he approached. He could see her name tag.

Jenny.

Jenny must be new at the diner. He'd never seen her there before.

Then he was just a few feet from Jenny.

Her hair was a deep, dark red. She'd braided it and the braid hung over her shoulder. He was so close to her. Close enough to touch.

Jenny looked up then, and she gasped when she saw him. A hand rose to her chest, and the shovel slipped from her fingers.

He smiled at her. "Morning, ma'am."

She blinked, and some of the alarm faded from her gaze. That was good. That was real good. He didn't want her scared. Not yet.

He drew even closer to her. Close enough to catch her scent. She smelled sweet. He liked that. His gaze slid toward the diner. The shades were still pulled. He couldn't see in. That meant no one could see out.

"We'll be open in about ten more minutes," Jenny told him. "The cook's getting things going now."

The cook. That would be the big, ex-lumberjack named Henry. But if Henry was getting things going in the kitchen...

Then he can't see us out here.

And Jenny was so perfect. She reminded him of what he'd lost.

His hand lifted and brushed over her cheek.

Her eyes widened as she sucked in a sharp breath. "Mister—"

"It will hurt, Jenny," he warned her.

Too late, Jenny opened her mouth to scream.

She never had the chance to make a sound.

NOELLE WAS ABOUT to fall flat on her face. It took all of the energy she had to climb the steps leading up to their cabin.

This place wasn't like the one-room shack they'd slept in before. This cabin was more like a luxury resort and as far from the place in her nightmares as possible.

The EOD was footing the bill for these digs, so Noelle was more than happy to escape to the fine lodgings.

She'd been up for over thirty-six hours, minus that one rough hour of sleep she'd gotten while she'd been in Thomas's arms.

Her gaze slanted toward him. *I want you, and unless I'm mistaken, you want me, too.* His words kept echoing through her mind.

The problem was Noelle wasn't used to taking what she wanted. She was used to closing herself off from others. Used to waking from dark dreams she could never fully remember—alone.

"We need to head back to the sheriff's station at eighteen hundred hours," Thomas said as he secured the front door behind them. He glanced around the cabin. A spiral staircase led upstairs. "That gives us a few hours to sleep."

And sleep was certainly her priority because of the whole almost-falling-on-her-face bit, but…

She kept thinking about what it had been like to be held in his arms. To kiss him. To touch him.

His head cocked as his eye raked over her. "Something wrong?"

"I'm just…trying to figure out who could've killed the senator." Well, she should be doing that, anyway.

He grunted as he headed toward her. "Mercer is arranging for new clothes to be delivered to us."

Since their bags were at the bottom of an icy lake, she appreciated the arrangement.

"Get some sleep, get some food, and then you'll be able to work up a profile."

He sure sounded confident. But it wasn't as if she just waved a wand and magically figured out a killer. "I'll need to head back to Lawrence's place. I want to search every inch of that house."

He flashed her a hard smile. "Already on the to-do list. Mercer wants us to find evidence proving Lawrence is our guy—and if the senator was working with anyone else in the attack against the EOD, we need to find out just who that person is."

Right. Because the case wasn't closed, not even with the death of their chief suspect.

"There are supposed to be two bedrooms upstairs," Thomas added as he glanced up at the winding staircase. "Pick which one you want, and I'll take the other."

I'll take the one with you.

Wait, no. She had *not* nearly said that. She must be more exhausted than she'd realized. Noelle turned on her heel and hurried toward the stairs.

"Do you need to talk?"

Her hand curled around the bannister. His voice had been so rough. "About what?"

"About the nightmares you have."

How could she talk about what she didn't remember?

"You begged someone not to hurt you. Pleaded for them to let you go." The hardwood floor creaked beneath his footsteps. "And you promised not to tell…"

She glanced over her shoulder at him. "I don't remember any of that." Her heart raced in her chest.

"You do when you let down your guard. When you sleep, that veil in your mind falls away."

She shook her head. "I… No, you're wrong."

He was just a few feet away. "Have you ever thought that maybe you just don't want to remember?"

The dead man on the floor…the blood on her hands…

"I want to remember." Those forty-eight hours had shattered her life. Her mother had wanted to push them away while Noelle had desperately wanted to grab that time back.

His gaze held hers. "There are plenty of moments from my life that I wish I could forget."

She thought of the scars on his body. His captivity. "What if you had the scars, but no memory of how you'd gotten them?" She didn't have scars on her body. Not on the outside, anyway. But those two nights had left deep marks inside of her. "Every time you looked at them, wouldn't you wonder?"

He took another gliding step toward her. She tilted back her head to keep meeting his gaze.

"When I look at the scars I have now," Thomas said, "I remember how much my captors enjoyed cutting into me. They wanted me to break." His eyes narrowed. "I didn't. No matter what they did to me, I didn't break."

No, the Dragon hadn't. But had she? In those lost hours, what had Noelle done?

"Then I remember what it was like to kill them."

His hands fisted. "You know what I am and what I've done. But when I close my eyes, I don't like seeing the bodies in my mind."

You know what I am. She reached out to him and pressed her hand to his clenched fist. "You're a soldier. You survived. You fought. *That's what you did.*"

His gaze fell to her hand. Her skin was so pale while his was a dark tan.

"You need to be careful," Thomas warned her. His stare was still focused on her hand.

"Careful?"

"You already know I want you, and right now...my control isn't real strong."

She pulled back. "I didn't mean—"

A muscle jerked in his jaw. "I know what you meant, but I'm running on no sleep and the memory of you being nearly naked in my arms. So you should go to your room, I'll go to mine, and when we wake up in a few hours, we can just pretend we never crossed the line between us."

The line between partners...and lovers?

"I'll stay hands-off, and we'll keep things just business." The gold in his eyes heated. "And we'll get the job done here so we can head back to D.C."

That was the right thing to do. They had to work together. But... *I want him.*

Noelle turned away. She climbed up the stairs. She was right at the top when she just had to look back once more.

He was still standing at the base. That hot, golden gaze was focused on her.

"When did we meet before?" Noelle asked quietly.

A mask seemed to slip over his face.

"Don't lie to me." So, maybe she was also running on no sleep and the memory of him being so warm and naked beside her. Because she sure felt as if she'd been pushed to the edge. "You're familiar to me. And sometimes, sometimes…like right *now,* I'll catch you looking at me as if—as if you know me."

"I do know you," he growled. "We're working together and—"

"You knew me before the EOD. You even slipped up once." Another day, another case, but the words had nagged at her. "You told me that you'd seen me, but I hadn't seen you."

He glanced away from her, giving Noelle his profile. "You don't have clearance to know about all the cases I've worked. So all I can say is that our paths have crossed."

There was more. "Do you always keep secrets from women you want to have sex with?"

His shoulders stiffened. "I keep secrets from everyone." He turned on his heel, giving her his broad back. "Get some sleep. Eighteen hundred hours will be here before you know it."

Frustration had her muscles knotting, but she spun around and pretty much stomped her way into the room at the top of the stairs. The room was filled with heavy oak furniture, and a big, wide picture window overlooked the snow-covered land around the cabin.

The bed was a massive four-poster, which waited in the middle of the room. Noelle stared down at the covers, then she just let herself fall, face-first, into them.

She wanted sleep to take her away because the look in Thomas's gaze… It had unnerved her far too much.

THERE WERE NO creaks from upstairs. No soft rustles of clothing. Noelle had been up there for fifteen minutes, and Thomas was pretty sure the woman had crashed.

He pulled out his phone and called Mercer. The situation was about to slide out of his control, and he needed to know what to do when—

"Don't tell me you've found another body," Mercer said, his words rumbling as the EOD Director answered the call on the second ring.

Thomas's gaze stayed locked on the staircase. "Pairing me with Noelle was a mistake."

Silence.

"She wants me to tell her how I know her." He hated looking right into her eyes and lying. The lies were cutting him up inside.

"You're in Alaska to track down the man who hired the Jack of Hearts to kill me...and to destroy the EOD."

"Yeah, well..." His hand raked through his hair. "All signs indicate that guy is on a slab in the county morgue right now. We'll do recon work after we've had a little time to rest, but Noelle is pushing, and I want to know just how much—"

"You can reveal?" Mercer's tone was measured.

"It's been fifteen years. She still has nightmares."

"I thought she might." It almost sounded as if sympathy was in Mercer's voice. Obviously, they had a bad connection. Mercer felt sympathy for no one. "And that's why she's paired up with you."

"I'm not following you."

"If anyone can help her to remember, it's you. After all, you were there, right?"

He swallowed. "You put us together—because you thought she'd remember me?"

"Well, I'd hoped Noelle would remember you the first time she saw you at the EOD. Maybe get a flashback. Something. That didn't happen, so I figured we needed to step up the game."

Only Mercer thought playing with someone's life constituted a game.

"She's not a victim anymore, she's an agent." Mercer's voice hardened. "Fifteen years ago, we had to protect your cover. You had to vanish from the scene."

But he'd left her behind, and she'd been…shattered.

"Come now, Agent Anthony, I know you've seen her since then. You've watched over her all these years."

Damn it. Mercer and his all-knowing intel. "What I do on my *own* time is none of your—"

"You should be thanking me. I mean, at least you don't have to sneak off to check up on your profiler on your rare off days. Now you get to be up close with her, 24/7."

This was insane. "She doesn't *remember* me."

"She will." Flat. "I think it's possible that Noelle will discover a whole lot while she's in Alaska." A pause. "I want her to rip apart Senator Lawrence Duncan's life. She's just the woman for this job."

Thomas's brows pulled together. "Have you told me everything about this mission?"

"Oh, son, I never tell anyone…everything."

Hell.

"I know you'll guard Dr. Evers. That's your job right now. To make sure that nothing happens to her while she's in Alaska. If I'm going to get to the bottom of this mystery, I need her."

So, Noelle was the brains while Thomas was the kill-ing power. He'd always been a weapon, of one kind or another. From the time he'd turned eighteen...

I have my memories, and sometimes, I hate them.

"I'll keep Noelle safe."

"Of course, you will." Now Mercer sounded certain. Almost smug. "It's what you've been doing for the past fifteen years, isn't it?"

Mercer *had* been watching. Far too much.

"Even when she became an FBI agent, you couldn't let go. You thought she still needed you."

No, Mercer had that part all wrong. It wasn't about what Noelle needed.

I need her.

There was so much death in his life. Everywhere he turned. But Noelle, she was the one bright light in the darkness that always seemed to surrounded him.

"This time, she does need you," Mercer's voice held an edge. "So stay close, no matter what happens."

Thomas ended the call. He took his time climbing those stairs. When he got to the top, he saw the door to Noelle's room had been left ajar.

His fingers pressed against it, opening it just a few more inches. Noelle was on the bed. Her thick hair was a curtain, spilling down her back.

Would nightmares come to her again?

If they did, Thomas hoped she would come to *him*.

Chapter Four

Senator Lawrence Duncan had believed in surrounding himself with the finer things in life.

Noelle put her hands on her hips as she studied the senator's closet. The massive closet was easily the size of her D.C. bedroom *and* living room and filled with designer clothing.

"He was ex-navy," Thomas said. "This place sure is a long way from his life on the ship."

She knew all about Lawrence Duncan's background. He'd grown up poor in Camden, Alaska. He joined the navy when he was eighteen. He'd been an enlisted man for eight years, and when he'd gotten out of the service, the guy had seemed to skyrocket to power overnight. He'd come out of the military with some incredible connections, or else he'd obtained some very deadly secrets during his time in the service.

"He was married twice," Noelle murmured as she studied the closet. Each item was perfectly in place. "Both women left him citing irreconcilable differences." But she'd interviewed those ladies before coming to Camden. Fear had flashed in their eyes when they spoke of their husband.

Dominating. Controlling. Their voices had become whispers when they talked about the senator.

"He was sleeping with his assistant." Thomas propped his shoulder against the bedroom wall.

"Her and plenty of other aides." She turned away from the closet. She'd searched in there, twice, and found nothing of any real value. But...something *had* to be in the house. This place was Lawrence's sanctuary. After he'd left the navy, he could have started over any place. But he'd returned to Camden. He'd torn down his old house and had this mansion built right in the same spot.

She and Thomas had already confiscated all of the senator's computer equipment. An initial search of the material hadn't shed any additional light on the attack in D.C.—*or* on the senator's death—but they had specialists back at the EOD who'd tear that equipment apart. If there was intel to find there, they would.

She went toward the window on the left. Looking down, she saw the slumping roof of what looked like an old shed behind the main house. About fifty yards back, right at the tree line.

The shed made her curious. "He replaced everything else." No, not just replaced. He'd *destroyed* everything else on that property. "Why not that shed? Why is it still out there?"

Before Thomas could answer her, Noelle turned and hurried from the room. Sheriff Hodges glanced up when she rushed down the stairs. His hand was on Paula's shoulder, as if he'd been comforting the woman. Paula's eyes were watering, and her nose was red.

"I should have heard him. I should have helped him!" Noelle didn't slow to help console the other woman.

She figured Hodges had things covered. She made her way to the back of the house and threw open the rear door. The icy air hit her, seeming to chill straight to her bones.

Thomas was behind her. Not speaking but following closely. When they got to the old shed, she saw a big wooden board had been positioned to block the entrance. She grabbed for the board, but Thomas was there, and he heaved it aside.

She pushed open the shed's door. But it really wasn't so much a shed. It reminded her more of an old barn.

The roof was high, there was no floor, just what looked like dirt and straw and—

A trunk sat, half-hidden beneath some old blankets, positioned against the far back wall. Her steps quickened as she approached it.

"Why are we out here, Noelle?" Thomas asked her.

"Because I need to understand Lawrence. He came back here to this exact spot to start his new life, for a reason." She dropped to her knees and pushed aside the blankets that covered the trunk. Then she saw the padlock. The trunk was old and weathered from time, but the padlock was shiny. New.

"If the senator had something valuable, he wouldn't leave it out here." Thomas's words were clipped. "That's probably just some kind of equipment in there he used on his land. He didn't want it stolen so—"

She'd spotted a hammer hanging on a nearby shelf. Noelle grabbed it and started pounding at the lock.

"*Noelle!* Hell, wait, we can get the sheriff to—"

The lock broke. Noelle shoved it aside. She wasn't even sure what she'd expected to find but—

Photographs.

There were dozens of photographs inside the trunk. The old, Polaroid type. The white edges surrounded the images.

Her fingers were shaking when she reached for the first one. The light from her flashlight bobbed as she tried to focus in on that photo.

A photo of a young girl, a teen, blindfolded, tied to a chair.

A girl with red hair.

The print fell from her fingers, but then Noelle dove forward. Her light shined on all of those snapshots.

Red-haired girls. Teens. Bound. Blindfolded.

"Noelle!" Thomas's fingers curled around her, and he yanked her to her feet.

But it was too late. Because she'd just found another photograph, only this photograph was familiar.

"That's me," she whispered as she stared down at her picture.

Like the other girls, she was blindfolded and tied to a chair.

That image... Dear God, had been taken fifteen years ago, during the two lost days of her life.

"THERE ARE TEN different girls in these pictures." No emotion entered Noelle's voice, and it was that complete lack of emotion that worried Thomas the most.

They were back at the sheriff's station. It was long past midnight, and Noelle—she'd pinned all of the photos to the wall in their makeshift office. Those images had already been faxed to the EOD. But...

"Are you okay?"

She flinched at the question, and instead of answering, she said, "They're all about the same age. Sixteen or seventeen, females, with red hair—"

His fingers curled around her shoulders and he turned her, forcing her to face him. "Are. You. Okay?"

Her pupils were too big. Her face too pale.

"We have to operate under the assumption the photos are—are trophies that Senator Lawrence kept close because he wanted to relive the abductions—"

"Noelle, you're in the damn photo!"

Her gaze fell to his throat. He saw her swallow. "We always knew that a second man had to be involved in my abduction." Her voice still had no emotion. "I was tied up, so I couldn't have been the one to kill him. Someone else was there the whole time." Slowly, her lashes lifted. "It's possible Senator Lawrence was that someone."

No, it wasn't.

"This is the first lead I've ever had." Her lower lip trembled, but she caught it between her teeth. After a moment, Noelle said, "This is *my* life, and the man who could've told me the truth is dead."

Thomas wasn't exactly mourning the guy.

She pulled in a deep breath. "The EOD is searching Missing Persons databases now, using image-recognition software, but this—this isn't the usual type of case for Mercer's team."

No, it wasn't.

"The FBI should be investigating, and Sheriff Hodges, he *thinks* he's got the FBI." She shook her head. "We have to call them in. The real FBI. If any of those girls are still alive—"

"Do you think they are?"

Because he was watching her so closely, Thomas saw her eyelids flicker.

No, she doesn't.

"Tell me why killers keep trophies," Thomas demanded. Because, yes, he knew exactly what those images were.

"To remind them of the crimes."

"Cadaver dogs are on the way." He'd been pulling some strings of his own while she worked to identify the victims. "There might be more than just photographs buried in that old shed." There had been no floor there. Just earth…

A graveyard? Maybe. He'd be finding out soon.

"I got away." Her voice was a thin whisper. "Maybe some of them did, too. If there's another survivor, if we can find her, then we can figure out how the senator fits into all of this."

Provided Mercer didn't yank them off the case. Because Noelle had been right about the EOD not handling missing-persons cases, and with a potential serial killer involved— Hell, no, this wasn't business as usual for them.

Thomas was used to facing terrorists, arms dealers, but this… This was beyond his realm.

But it was exactly where Noelle thrived.

She'd turned back to study the photographs. "He used a Polaroid so that he wouldn't have to develop his film." Her fingers hovered over the image of herself. "Technology wasn't so advanced back then, he couldn't just snap a picture with his phone, and he wouldn't have wanted anyone to know what he was doing."

"It's possible that all of those images are from at least fifteen years ago."

She nodded. "But a killer like that, he wouldn't just... stop." Softer, she added, "He couldn't. The compulsion to kill would be too strong."

This whole situation wasn't making sense to Thomas. "The guy was a senator. You don't get much more of a high profile. He had guards, reporters, hell, nearly *everyone* dogging his steps. Wouldn't someone have noticed if the guy was abducting girls?"

The image of Lawrence Duncan as a serial killer just wasn't fitting for him.

"He was a hunter." Noelle was still looking at the snapshots. "Maybe he just found something that he really enjoyed hunting. Something...or someone."

Thomas stiffened at her words as memories flooded through his mind. A forest. Darkness. A girl's scream.

Damn it, he *had* to tell her. Mercer could fire him; Thomas didn't care. The photographs changed everything. *We always thought it was just her.*

But it was now obvious Noelle hadn't been the only victim.

"There's something you need to know," Thomas told her, aware his voice had come out a bit rough.

She didn't glance his way.

"Noelle, *look* at me."

Her body turned. Her gaze found his.

"You were right," he said. He didn't know how she was going to react, and in that moment, fear crouched beneath his skin. "We met before you came to work at the EOD."

She stepped toward him as her brows rose. "When?"

"Years ago." He exhaled once more. "It wasn't for long, just an hour, maybe two." Two hours that changed his life and hers.

"Thomas?"

"The first time I saw you...you were running, in the woods..."

Surprise flashed over face. "What are you talking about?"

"You screamed for me to help you."

Her body trembled. The little bit of color in her face drained away. He lunged toward her, worried she might be about to pass out. He grabbed her, holding her tightly. *"Noelle?"*

Her hands twisted so that she was holding him, too. "Why are you saying this? Why are you—?"

The door behind Thomas flew open and crashed into the wall. "I need you two!" Sheriff Hodges yelled. "In the bull pen, *now!*"

That man had the worst timing in the world. Thomas threw a glare over his shoulder, and he didn't care if the sheriff saw him basically embracing Noelle right then. "We're busy. It's just gonna have to wait—"

"The hell it is." Red stained the sheriff's cheeks as he pointed to the pictures on the wall. "I just got a report of a missing girl. A girl who looks just like those others pinned up there."

Then Thomas heard it. The soft sound of...sobbing? Coming from outside the room.

"Jenny Tucker has been missing since around six this morning," Hodges told them. "We don't... *Things like this don't happen in Camden.*"

Noelle shoved past the sheriff as she made her way to the door. "Yes, they do."

She yanked open the door and hurried out of the office. Thomas spared a hard glance for the sheriff. Hodges appeared to have aged about ten years. The lines near his eyes and mouth were deeper, and the sheriff's shoulders slumped. "I don't… I don't know what to do. I arrest a few drunks every now and then." He swallowed, and his Adam's apple bobbed. "You've got to help us, Agent Anthony. This isn't what I do."

It wasn't what Thomas did, either. He was used to going right after a target and taking out his prey. Not playing a cat-and-mouse game with a serial killer.

He turned on his heel and followed after Noelle. She'd stopped beside a woman with short, red hair. The woman was huddled in a chair, and tears streamed down her cheeks.

"I—I thought she was working late.… I kept waiting for my Jenny to come h-home.…" Her body shuddered. "It was… It was her first day. She was gonna work weekends at the diner."

Noelle patted the woman's shoulder.

"Sh-she never came home."

The floor creaked behind Thomas.

"Jenny's like the girls in all those pictures," the sheriff said, his voice low and carrying only to Thomas's ears. "Is she…is she already dead?"

"I don't know." His hands had fisted at his sides. "It's too early to know anything. The girl could've run off with a boyfriend. She could be at a friend's house. We can't make any conclusions yet." But his gut was tight, and he couldn't help remembering another long-ago night. One that had been filled with the sound of screams…and the red of blood.

THE SMALL CABIN was perfect. Isolated. Secure.

He'd lit a lantern so he could see the girl. She was bound, blindfolded and shivering from the cold.

She hadn't talked much. But then, with a gag in her mouth, talking wouldn't be easy. When she'd woken up, she'd cried for her mother, but he'd stopped those cries easily enough with the gag.

He stared down at her. She was slumped in the chair. Just watching her brought back so many memories for him.

He'd been a different man back then.

Unfocused. So eager for the cries...

Everything had changed for him, though. In one night. With one kill.

Everything.

He couldn't go back to being the same man. The spike of adrenaline in his blood—it just wasn't the same with the girls any longer. He didn't feel the rush. The thrill.

His hand tightened around the knife in his hand. There wasn't any challenge with little Jenny. Once, there had been. No more.

He was used to bigger game now.

He turned from the girl. He needed to head into town for a while. Had Duncan's body been found? He needed to make sure his bases were covered, and he needed to line up a new job. After he killed Jenny, he'd have to leave the area for good.

It was time to move on.

Camden was a wasteland. Ice and snow. Next time, he'd try someplace warmer.

Maybe he'd head back to Alabama. Or Florida. The memories there were so much damn better.

"WE HAVE TO call in the FBI." Noelle turned toward Thomas as soon as he cut off the engine of their rental car. It was another SUV, which the sheriff had gotten for them. They were parked just a few feet away from the entrance of the only diner in Camden—the presumed spot of Jenny Tucker's abduction. Noelle had known she had to get out here to investigate for herself, but that investigation just wasn't going to be good enough.

Thomas frowned at her. "As far as the locals are concerned, we *are* the FBI."

She shook her head. "The EOD doesn't investigate abductions like this. You *know* that."

Hostage retrieval. Unconventional warfare. Target destruction. She knew the key words for missions the EOD agents took. But this case…

My past.

It was different.

"Mercer will pull us off the investigation as soon as he finds out what's happening. And we can't just leave the girl out there. We *have* to call in the FBI." She had friends at the FBI who should be working this case. If she put in just a fast call to them, those special agents would be on the first flight out there.

But does Jenny have that long?

"I figure that I'm staring at Jenny Tucker's best hope of survival," Thomas said flatly as his gaze held hers. "Mercer told me that you were the best profiler he'd ever seen. If anyone can catch the guy out there, I think it would be you."

But Thomas didn't get it. She shoved back the hair that had fallen over her forehead. "My mind… It's all messed up." Her voice thickened and she tried to swallow the lump in her throat as Thomas watched her with that deep, golden gaze. "Every time I try to think about

Jenny or the man who took her, I just see my own picture, pinned to the wall at the station."

Her past. The secrets she'd sought for so long—they were all tangled up in what was happening in Camden.

Her breath seemed to burn her lungs. "I don't have the distance needed for this case. It's too personal." She couldn't separate her own feelings from what was happening. Jenny... *Jenny could be me.* Only Noelle had gotten lucky. She'd been rescued.

Jenny hadn't.

"I don't think distance is what this case needs." His words were a deep rumble as his finger slid over the steering wheel. "I think you're what that girl out there needs. If she really was taken, then you know exactly what that is like."

No, she didn't. Because she couldn't remember anything about her abduction.

He hesitated a moment as he studied her, then he slowly inclined his head. "But I'll talk to the boss, if that's what you want. We'll get other FBI agents down here."

"Thank you," she whispered.

"But *you* need to stay on point. We both do. We can't blow our cover, because I think this is about a whole lot more than one girl's abduction. The senator was murdered, and we still need to figure out how he fits into this mess."

Yes, they did.

Noelle turned from him and pushed against the handle of her door. His hand flew out, stopping her before she could leave the vehicle. "You're not alone in this, understand? Whatever happens, whatever we discover, I'm going to be right by your side."

She nodded. "Because you're my partner." She'd learned that about the EOD. A partner always had your back. A partner would protect you to the bitter end, a partner would—

"No, that's not why." His fingers lifted and curled around her chin. That golden gaze of his heated even more. She saw the need in his eyes. Her heart raced faster. "You can count on me."

She had to look away from that deep stare because Noelle was afraid Thomas would see too much in her own eyes. She'd been alone for so long. But he was offering her something else. Something she was afraid to take.

She pushed open her car door and the cold air rushed against her skin. The lights from the diner were on, glowing brightly even though it was close to ten o'clock.

Noelle stared at the area around the diner. A few old buildings, which were boarded up. A lone road, which stretched away and disappeared into the darkness.

Camden wasn't a thriving town, she had read during her pretrip research. It had lost most of its residents as the younger generation moved off to bigger cities. Because the businesses were vanishing and the people were leaving, there just hadn't been anyone out there to see Jenny.

Before they'd left the station, the sheriff had checked in with all of Jenny's friends. No one had seen the girl, and the friends had all claimed Jenny had no boyfriend. They'd been adamant she *couldn't* have run off with someone.

The snow crunched beneath Noelle's feet. She saw the open sign on the diner's door. A man, tall, with dark hair, was inside and heading toward the front.

Thomas was at Noelle's side. He grabbed for the handle and pulled open the door. The bell overhead gave a light jingle of sound.

"Sorry," the man inside rasped. "We're closing."

Noelle pulled out her ID. "Henry Price?" The sheriff had given her the guy's name.

The man nodded as his gaze jerked down to her ID.

"I'm Agent Noelle Evers, and this is my partner, Agent Thomas Anthony. We need to ask you some questions about Jenny."

Henry rubbed a hand over his bleary eyes. "Already talked to the sheriff on the phone."

"And now you're going to talk with us," Thomas said simply. The bell jingled again as the door closed behind them.

Henry shook his head. "I don't know anything. The girl was here this morning. I told her to go and clear the snow from the front, but instead of doing her job…" He turned away and headed for the kitchen. "She just left. You try to help some people, and they just turn on you—"

"Mr. Price." Anger snapped in Noelle's words.

Henry stopped and glanced back at her. A frown pulled down his brows.

"I don't know what you *think* is happening here," Noelle told him, her voice tight with barely held fury, "but Jenny Tucker's mother is down at the sheriff's station right now, her heart breaking because she believes that her daughter was abducted."

He waved his hand. "She's a teenager. They're always trying to cut out of this town and find some adventure."

"None of her friends believe that she cut out of town.

And…other evidence…we have suggests that Jenny could be the potential target of a kidnapper in the area." She wouldn't tell him about Jenny matching the physical description of the other victims. They still didn't know what had become of those victims.

Henry blinked as what could have been worry flashed in his eyes. "I didn't hear anything. I mean, if someone took her, she would've screamed right?"

"Not if she didn't have the chance." Thomas's voice was cold.

Henry's gaze flew to the door. "The shovel was outside. When I went looking for her, it was propped right on the side of the building. Like she'd just gotten bored, left it there and walked away."

Thomas took a step forward. "We're going to need that shovel."

They'd dust it for prints. Maybe they'd get lucky. If the girl's abductor had touched it with his bare fingers and the guy was in the system, they could get a hit on his identity.

Henry nodded. "Yeah, yeah…" He turned away once more.

Noelle grabbed his arm. "I need you to think very hard for me. When you went outside and you saw that shovel, did you notice anything else?" Snow had fallen since this morning. By now, it would've covered any signs left behind by Jenny and her abductor.

Henry frowned down at her hand. "I don't… I don't think so."

"Were there footprints in the snow?" she pressed. "Any vehicles that didn't belong?"

His eyes narrowed as he glanced back up at her face. "I think I saw one set of footprints leading toward the parking lot. That's why I thought it was just Jenny leaving."

One set. Which would imply Jenny *had* left on her own. Or else her abductor had carried her off.

"You have any customers here who seem particularly interested in girls around Jenny's age?" This question came from Thomas.

Henry blanched. "No, man, just...*no*."

Noelle dropped her hold on him. She wanted to get outside and take a look around that parking lot. "If you think of anything else, let us know."

"I'll get the shovel."

"*I'll* get it," Thomas said. "We don't want to destroy any evidence that might be left on it."

"I used it all day," Henry said as he hurried down the narrow aisle that led to the kitchen. "I didn't think... I used it *all damn day*."

Noelle turned away from the men. Her gaze fixed on the diner's windows. If Henry had been working in the kitchen when Jenny was taken, no, he wouldn't have been able to see anything at all out there.

She headed for the front door. The bell jingled again. Noelle shoved her hands into the jacket pockets and glanced around the diner.

Noelle tried to picture Jenny in her mind. Jenny's mother had brought a photograph of the girl to the station, and Jenny had certainly looked a lot like the images of the other girls they'd found.

A lot like me.

Jenny would've been working on that little sidewalk area. Excited and nervous because it was her first day. If someone had approached her, she would've just thought it was a customer, coming in early.

So you would've talked with him. Let him get close.
Close enough for him to attack her.
One set of footprints…

Her gaze slid to the right, toward the parking lot. The perp would've needed to be strong enough to carry Jenny away. And skilled enough to make sure Jenny never had the chance to cry out for help.

Noelle headed toward that parking lot. It was empty now, and the trees that surrounded the area swooped forward, arching in close.

It was a bitterly cold night, and the wilderness stretched as far as Noelle's eyes could see. If Jenny was out there, she could freeze to death during the night.

Provided the man who took her didn't *kill* her first.

Before she'd left the station, Noelle had heard the weather report come in—a bad winter storm was expected. Heavy snowfall. No one should be out on a night like this one, not with the storm coming. It was supposed to hit strongly just after midnight.

I don't want to find Jenny's frozen body tomorrow. I don't want to be the one who has to look into her mother's tear-filled eyes and tell her that her daughter isn't coming home again.

A twig snapped, the sound coming from the darkness about twenty feet in front of Noelle. She tensed as adrenaline flooded through her body. That sound could've been caused by an animal. It could've been caused by *anything*.

Even a perp who'd come back to the scene of his crime.

Noelle raced forward. Animal or man, she was about to find out exactly who she was dealing with out there. Her hands flew up, and she shoved aside the bushes in her path. She yanked out the flashlight she'd pushed into her coat earlier, and she whipped it up, shining the light.

No one was there.

At least, no one she saw.

But Noelle heard the rush of thudding footsteps, fleeing to the right.

She lunged that direction, but her feet got caught in something, and she twisted, falling down hard. Her left hand shoved into the snow and touched rough, frozen fabric. She yanked it up.

A scarf?

"Noelle!" Thomas's shout seemed to shake the trees.

She could still hear footfalls. She shined her light down. The snow was falling once more, but...

I see them.

She could see the outline left by a pair of boots. It wasn't an animal who'd been watching her in the darkness.

Was the scarf Jenny's? Maybe the perp hadn't taken Jenny away in a car. Maybe he'd just carried her off. Maybe Jenny was closer than they realized.

"Thomas, follow me!" Noelle called, and she didn't pause any longer. She raced right after that trail of footprints. The snow would just keep falling as the storm swept in and, soon, would obliterate the tracks. She couldn't let that watcher get away—not until she found out who the individual was and why that person was in the woods.

The innocent don't run.

But this guy was sure fleeing fast.

So she just had to be faster.

Chapter Five

Noelle had vanished into the woods. Thomas swore as he gave chase, shining his flashlight on the ground so he could follow her footprints.

He didn't know why she was running off, but he sure wasn't about to let her head out alone. Whatever she'd seen, Noelle was desperate to follow that lead.

And he was desperate to follow *her*.

His feet pounded into the snow. His boots were sinking into the soft fall, and the suction made every step that much harder.

He threw a fast glance over his shoulder. He couldn't see the lights from the diner, not anymore. There was darkness all around him and—

He glanced forward and his light hit Noelle. She stood in the middle of a clearing, with one of her hands locked around a flashlight and the other hand around her gun. Since she'd lost her own weapon in the icy water, she'd gotten that gun from the sheriff.

"There are two sets of tracks here," she said, voice tense.

His light flashed to the ground. "Who are we following? Did you get an ID on—"

"I didn't see him. I *heard* him, and I followed his footprints, but there are *two* sets now."

Two sets, which appeared to be the same size and shape.

"We have to split up," Noelle said, her words tumbling out. "I think the perp took Jenny into the woods. He didn't drive away with her. He carried her off. He's out here now, watching us."

Leaving a trail for them to follow?

Thomas's light fell over those prints again. The snowfall was getting harder.

"They'll be covered soon." She surged to the right. "You go left. I'll—"

He grabbed her arm, stopping her. "This is a trap." He knew it with certainty because he'd laid similar traps before.

Two sets of footprints to throw off those who pursued. To divide them up.

To make the attack easier.

"No, no, he's here. I heard him." She twisted her hand, trying to break loose from his hold and the light from her flashlight bobbed. But he didn't let her go. He *couldn't.* "Jenny won't survive if she's out in the open! We have to follow him, now!" She tugged again. "You go left. I'll go right."

He didn't let her go *anywhere.* "There's more snow to the left." The tracks were covered just a bit more. Because those tracks had been placed earlier? "We both go right."

And he led the way, with his flashlight positioned just over his gun. When it came to hunting deadly prey, Thomas was the one with more experience.

But I've been with her in the wilderness before. Noelle didn't remember that terrible night, but he did. There hadn't been any snow on the ground then. Just a hot, long southern night. A night of fear and death.

It was easy enough for a good hunter to cover his tracks, even out in the snow. Grab a branch, drag it behind you, and your trail was gone.

Whoever they were after… That person *wanted* them to follow.

Their prey was leading them somewhere. To Jenny? To death?

Thomas was about to show the fool he'd made a serious mistake.

Thomas was never the hunted. He'd been born to be the predator.

NOELLE EVERS WASN'T DEAD. She wasn't trapped beneath the frozen waters of the lake. She'd survived.

And she's hunting me.

He wanted to laugh, but sound carried too easily in the wilderness. He'd snapped that twig for her before because he'd just had to be sure, had to determine with one hundred percent certainty he was looking at Noelle.

The snow had fallen around her. Her red hair had been hidden under her cap. But when she'd called out—

I know her voice.

Noelle had changed so much over the years. Not easy prey any longer. Not like Jenny.

Noelle was following his trail. Hunting *him.*

She had a weapon. She had training. She was…

Perfect.

But Noelle wasn't alone. The other agent was with her. Moving like a shadow in the darkness. The man was a killer; he easily recognized the type. Instead of alarming him, the knowledge had his grin stretching even more.

And Lawrence had just wanted me to end them so quickly. Lawrence had never understood. It wasn't just about the kills. It was about the hunt.

He was about to enjoy the best hunt of his life.

Come to me, Noelle. Come in close, and let's see if I can make you scream the way I did before.

THE TRACKS ENDED—vanished into the rough edge of stone that lined the rising wall of a mountain.

"Where did he go?" Noelle spun around, shining her light. Her voice was high, nervous.

Thomas glanced up at the mountain. He suspected the man they were after had climbed up, which meant...

You know this area, well, don't you? How long have you been hiding in the Alaskan wilderness?

His light hit the edge of the mountain.

"Up there." Noelle's voice was fainter now as the wind began to howl more around them. The approaching storm was moving in fast. "We have to follow him!"

She tried to put her hands in the faint ridges between the icy rocks. Thomas pulled her back before she could climb. "We need to head back to town, Noelle."

Shaking her head, Noelle jerked away from him. "Jenny could be up there! We have to find her!"

"You can't scale the rocks." She thought she was going to free hand her way up that frozen surface? Hell, no. She'd fall and break her neck. "We'll go back to town and get help." Maybe a chopper could fly them up the mountain. They'd do a search. Look for any cabins that would be a good base site for the man they were after.

"We don't have time for that. Jenny needs us!"

There was no sign of the man on the face of the mountain. "He might not even be up there." His gaze turned to the wilderness. "He could be watching us, from out there."

Noelle shuddered. From cold? From fear?

"We're not equipped for this search. We need supplies. Dogs."

"And Jenny needs us!" Noelle shook her head. "I'm not just going to leave her."

"Are you going to die with her?" His words were brutal, but Thomas had to make her see reason.

Noelle gasped and lurched back a step.

"Because if we stay out in the open, if we keep blindly following this man's path tonight and that storm hits, you could die. You're already shaking apart in front of me, and hypothermia will set in before you know it."

"She needs us," Noelle said again as her chin notched up.

"And she could be anywhere. We're going back for the dogs." He yanked out his phone, but of course, there was no cell service out here. Nothing.

Noelle's light hit to the left. To the right.

"I can't just leave her," Noelle told him.

She was going to *have* to leave her.

"You stay, you die with her." There was no way Thomas was going to let that happen on his watch. Even if he had to carry her out of there, Noelle was leaving the woods.

"I DON'T NEED you anymore." He let the knife trail over Jenny's skin. She was crying. Shaking. So useless to him. "You weren't what I was hoping for."

It had been because of Noelle. He'd gone a little...

mad there for a moment. Forgotten all of his training. That wonderful training and control Lawrence had worked hard to give him over the years.

Lawrence had wanted to use him. He had. For so long.

But Lawrence had made a mistake.

They're my kills. My choice.

The knife cut through the gag that covered her mouth.

"P-please…" Jenny begged him. "Let…me go."

"It doesn't work like that."

"I won't tell anyone about you! *Please!*"

Ah, there she went. Making promises. But Jenny knew what he looked like. If she got to Noelle and the other agent, they'd want her to describe her abductor. They'd even sit her down with a sketch artist. Get her to come up with a composite of him.

Then his picture would be everywhere. The EOD would make sure of that.

I know all about the EOD, but they don't know about me. They have no clue just who—what—I am.

Their mistake. They thought the Jack of Hearts was the greatest threat they had to face. They were wrong. It was time to show them the error of their ways. Time for him to get all of the respect he had coming.

They'd thought Jack was a serial killer?

Jack was nothing.

He stroked the back of his hand over her cheek. "I have plans for you."

Jenny whimpered.

"I'M NOT LEAVING HER." Noelle shook her head, sending snowflakes falling around her. "You go back to town. You find the sheriff and get the dogs out here—"

Thomas shoved his gun into his holster and let his flashlight's attached cord loop around his wrist as he grabbed both of her shoulders. "You think I'll just leave you out here to die alone? *We're partners!*"

She knew that. "She could be me," Noelle whispered as she stared up at his face. Her own light was hitting the ground, so she couldn't see his expression. "I was alone. I was trapped. The only person with me was a dead man."

His hold tightened on her.

"I was bound to a chair. If the cops hadn't found me…" A tip. They'd gotten a tip, which no one had ever been able to trace. "I could've died in that cabin." Starved to death, slowly. But Jenny wouldn't have to worry about death by starvation. Not when it was so bitterly cold outside.

She'll freeze to death by morning.

"You're not her." His voice was grim. "And I'll be damned if I let you die for her. You are coming with me. One way or—"

A scream ripped through the silence of the night.

Thomas stilled. Then, in the next instant, he'd torn away from Noelle. His gun was in his hand again as he rushed toward that dying sound.

A sound that hadn't come from high up on the mountain, but one that had come from the right. Farther into the woods.

They fought their way through those trees, ran ahead even as another scream echoed in the night.

Then Noelle saw it. The hard, stark outline of a little cabin.

The cabin waited. The doors shut. "Please…please don't make me go back in there…."

Those words whispered through her mind. Noelle's *own* words, her broken voice, and she shook her head, hard, as she drew closer.

The cabin was pitch black. Thomas's flashlight hit the shut front door.

He ran toward it and kicked it in.

Another scream came then.

Noelle rushed in behind Thomas, providing cover for him. But there was no attacker in the room.

A young girl sat in the middle of the room, a rickety, wooden chair beneath her. Her arms were pulled behind her back. A blindfold covered her eyes.

The cabin was so familiar, for an instant, Noelle remembered… *"Please, I don't want to be alone! Don't leave me alone!"*

And a man's voice had replied to her.

He'd said, *"I'll always be with you."*

Hard shudders shook Noelle's body as the past and present seemed to merge around her.

Thomas crouched in front of the girl. "Jenny Tucker?"

She jerked. "Yes! Yes, help me!"

Noelle surged forward. She ran behind the girl and yanked until the binds around Jenny's wrists were gone. The girl's skin was icy. Her fingers… Her fingers were blue.

"H-he's c-coming back."

Thomas pulled the blindfold from Jenny's eyes. Jenny blinked up at him.

Noelle tugged Jenny to her feet. "He's not going to hurt you anymore. We're going to get you out of here."

Jenny shook her head. Tears slid down her cheeks. "I'm sorry…"

Noelle's nose burned. What was that acrid scent?

Her flashlight hit the walls. They looked...wet.

"We need to get out of here," Noelle yelled as she re-alized that, yes, Thomas had been right. They'd walked straight into a trap.

That smell—it was the heavy scent of gasoline.

Thomas picked Jenny up in his arms and sprinted for the door.

"H-he told me to scream...to scream until help came."

They were almost at the door but—

A blast seemed to shake the cabin. Fire blazed in-side, rushing toward them, following the trail of fuel spread throughout the cabin.

Jenny screamed.

And the fire raged.

There was only one window in that cabin. One to the left, and fire already covered it. The front door was gone. A wall of flames stood in its place.

Thomas sat Jenny down on her feet. The girl im-mediately fell, and Noelle ran toward her, pulling her up before the flames could lick across the girl's skin.

Thomas shrugged out of his coat and wrapped it around Jenny's body. His gaze lifted and met Noelle's. "You get out first."

Uh, how?

"Cover up with your coat. Make sure none of your flesh is vulnerable." He coughed a bit because the smoke was rising fast. "The coat is going to ignite, so you'll have to strip and roll in the snow as soon as you get outside."

He wanted her to run *through* the fire. Right. But...

"You don't have a coat." He'd just given his only protection to Jenny.

His jaw locked. The blaze let her see him clearly. "I'll be right behind you."

He'll burn. "Thomas…"

The flames flared higher. "Go!"

Tears stung Noelle's eyes.

"He could be waiting out there," Thomas warned her. "Get your gun, and cover me when I come out. I *need* you to get out there and cover me."

She was supposed to let him get hurt?

"Go, *Noelle, go*… I'll be right behind you."

And, over the roar of the fire, the voice from the darkness of her past spoke again. *I'll always be with you.*

A long tremor shook her body. Noelle ran toward the flaming doorway, and she jumped through the fire. There was a loud *whoosh* of sound, which seemed to fill her ears. Heat surrounded her, so hot, so—

Her body flew through the air, and she hit the snow. She rolled because Thomas had been right. Her clothes were on fire. She pushed out of her coat and kept rolling, then hurried back up to her feet, even as she pulled out her weapon.

I'm not burned. I'm not—

Thomas flew through the fire. The flames came with him when he left the cabin. He hit the snow, too, hard, and Jenny tumbled out of his hands. The coat Jenny wore was blazing. Noelle shoved it away, even as Jenny yelled for help.

Jenny wasn't burned, though; she was safe.

"Thomas?" Noelle whispered.

He yanked off the smoking ski mask he'd used to

cover his face. He was twisting, trying to put out the fire consuming his clothes and pants.

Noelle helped him, securing her weapon and slapping at the blaze. Her gloves burned away.

The fire died.

Thomas glanced up at her.

"Are you hurt?" Noelle whispered. She didn't see any burns, but maybe it was just too dark to notice them.

He caught her hands. Her gloves were gone, only bits of fabric remained. "Are you?" Thomas demanded his voice an angry growl.

Noelle shook her head.

Somehow, they'd both made it out of that hell.

Jenny was sobbing.

Thomas rose to his feet. He picked Jenny up in his arms. "Watch my back," he told Noelle.

She had her weapon ready again. The killer had to be close. He'd set the fire just moments before, but…

It wasn't the time to chase after him. They had to get Jenny to safety. Jenny was the key. She could help them identify her attacker.

Noelle hurried her steps and followed closely behind Thomas. His hold was gentle on Jenny. He had to be freezing, but he didn't slow at all. He was fast and strong, and his grip on the young woman was unbreakable.

For an instant, the snow-covered landscape vanished, and Noelle saw—

Not flames. Not snow. A forest. Woods. Noelle remembered the moonlight that had trickled through the tops of the trees. She'd stared up at it as he'd held her. His grip had been so strong. So solid. She'd been…safe.

Noelle's grip tightened on her gun as the image

faded. She glanced back over her shoulder. The cabin was burning; the hungry flames consumed the place, destroying any evidence that might have been left behind.

But…

Jenny is safe. She survived.

Noelle was used to finding the bodies of the victims in her job as a profiler. She usually arrived too late to help anyone. But this… This was different.

We saved her.

She kept her gun up as she hastened after Thomas and Jenny.

I'll always be with you.

The voice whispered through her mind, and the voice—it belonged to Thomas.

JENNY WAS LOADED into the back of an ambulance. Thomas watched its lights flash on as the siren's cry filled the night. Jenny had been sobbing when she was loaded up. She'd told him again and again how sorry she was. *He made her lure us into that cabin—he wanted us all to burn.*

"I can't thank you two enough." Sheriff Hodges came toward him. He stared at Thomas, then Noelle with wide eyes. "That girl… You saved her."

They'd nearly died with her. Thomas looked back at the wilderness. "When are the dogs getting here?" Because every moment that passed was another moment the perp could use to flee.

"We can't send them out, not with the storm."

He'd been afraid of that. The snow was already falling so much harder, and the howl of the wind was constant now.

The sheriff ran a gloved hand over his face. "Word came through on the radio a little while ago. The storm's due to hit any minute. It won't be safe to send anyone out. The snow's gonna be too thick. The snowstorm will last all night."

And it would give the killer out there the perfect cover for his escape.

"Jenny wouldn't have lasted until dawn." Noelle's voice was soft. "If he hadn't killed her, then the storm would've."

Thomas could feel the push of the impending gales. As he'd carried Jenny, he'd fought to stay upright as the wind and the snow blasted against him.

"You two need to get secure for the night." Hodges gave a firm nod. "I'll get my men to check the area once more, but then I have to send them in. I won't lose any of my people for that guy."

No, they couldn't put lives on the line.

And so the perp gets away, for now.

The sheriff nodded once more, then turned away. The wind battered against Thomas. He was wearing a borrowed coat a sheriff's deputy had given him. Noelle was wearing a similar one, only its bulk seemed to swallow her.

She stared up at Thomas with unreadable eyes. Strange, he'd believed he'd gotten pretty good at reading Noelle's feelings. But right then, he couldn't tell a single thing about her thoughts.

Thomas cleared his throat. "We should get back to our place." Driving would be a nightmare if they waited much longer. It was a good thing their rented cabin was near town.

Noelle nodded, but she didn't move. "Do you jump through fire often?"

He hadn't expected the question. He felt his lips curl in a grim smile. "Only when I have to."

She inclined her head and spun, heading back toward the diner and their vehicle. Thomas saw Henry was out, watching them with wide eyes. The sheriff had taken the shovel in as evidence. Maybe they'd get lucky on the fingerprint check.

Maybe not.

But at least they'd found the girl.

When he'd rushed into that cabin and seen her there, the blindfold covering half her face, her red hair streaming behind him, it had been as if Thomas had run straight into a nightmare from his past.

Only I wasn't the white knight then.

He'd been the man ignoring the cries for help.

They reached their SUV. Snow coated the windows, and Thomas shoved it away. When the vehicle was clear—well, *clearer*—he glanced at Noelle. Her eyes were on him.

What is she thinking?

"I was wrong about you," Noelle said, and the howl of the wind nearly swallowed her words. "The profile that I had in my head… It was all wrong."

He stiffened at her words. "I warned you before that you shouldn't profile me." Because he'd been afraid she wouldn't like the man who truly lived inside him.

"I just didn't realize how good you were at keeping secrets and telling lies."

She knows. "Noelle?"

She climbed into the vehicle. Thomas jumped inside with her. It was as cold in the SUV as it was outside.

And the snow was falling in ever harder waves. He turned on the ignition. It took three tries for the motor to finally kick to life. The windshield wipers slashed across the glass, but they didn't help him see any better.

The sheriff had been right. Thomas figured he and Noelle would be lucky to make it back to their cabin before the storm hit with its full fury.

He spared another fast glance for Noelle. She was staring straight ahead, her attention seemingly on the snow that blasted down on them, but he could feel the tension emanating from her body.

Oh, yeah, the storm was about to hit, and he had a feeling it just might wreck his world.

HE'D LEARNED TO cover his tracks when he was ten years old. But he didn't slow down to erase his footprints. There was no need then. Mother Nature was erasing the tracks for him.

The fire was out. He didn't even see the smoke drifting up into the sky any longer.

He'd watched the blaze, just for a moment, and he'd seen them escape.

Worthy prey.

Noelle had come out first. She'd been burning. He'd smiled at the sight. But the flames had been extinguished all too quickly. The male had followed her—and he'd brought out Jenny.

Jenny shouldn't have made it out of the house.

Now two have survived.

That wasn't acceptable. He'd have to correct that situation.

Jenny would be easy enough. She didn't have any fight in her. But Noelle... Now, there was his challenge.

He'd take her out first. Her and the agent who seemed to always be at her side. The fellow thought he was some sort of protector. No, he was just a dead man walking, and he didn't know it.

He'd kill Noelle and her shadow.

It was just that the *shadow* had seemed familiar to him. Something about the man's profile. His voice. *I feel like I know him.*

His breath heaved from his lungs. The snow fell harder.

A storm...it would be the perfect cover. When the snow fell so heavily, no one would be looking for an attack.

No one would see him. Not until it was too late.

Chapter Six

The snow pelted down on their cabin. Noelle pulled the oversize coat closer to her body as she glanced back over her shoulder. Thomas shoved the door closed, pushing his shoulder into the wood, then securing the lock.

It was cold inside, but cold wasn't the reason why Noelle was shivering.

Her past was coming back to her, and the images that kept flashing through her mind didn't make any sense. They couldn't be real. Not unless—

"I'll get the fire going," Thomas said as he stalked toward the large fireplace. "You should head upstairs. Get in a warm shower. Wash away the ash and get some feeling back in your limbs."

There was no emotion in his words, and he wasn't looking directly at her. She found, right then, she couldn't take her gaze off him.

He bent near the fireplace. A few moments later, flames flashed up.

A shudder shook her as she remembered the fire that had nearly taken their lives.

Still crouching, Thomas glanced back at her. The

gold of his gaze reminded her of the fire. "Go on up-stairs," he said again. "You're shaking."

"It's not from the cold." Well, okay, perhaps part of it was. She crept closer to him and to the warmth of the fireplace. Her hands were fisted in the pockets of her borrowed coat. "I need to ask you some questions."

He looked toward the stairs. "The power might not stay on long, not if the storm is as strong as I'm thinking it will be. You should shower first, then we can talk."

She braced her legs and straightened her shoulders. She'd waited long enough for this conversation. "Tell me about the first time that we met."

His eyelids flickered as he slowly rose to his full height. He wasn't looking at the stairs any longer. He was focused on her, and his stare was guarded. "Why does that matter?"

"Because I... I remember your voice."

His jaw hardened.

"I can hear your voice in my head. You're saying that...you'll always be with me."

He didn't speak.

"But you've never said those words to me."

He turned back toward the fire.

"At least, you haven't said them since I started with the EOD. So that means you had to tell them to me *before* Mercer brought me on." She was trying to keep her voice even and calm, but her heart was galloping like mad in her chest. "And the only *before* for me, the only time I don't remember, is the forty-eight hours of my abduction."

He looked back at her. His expression was unread-able. "You've had one hell of a night. We both have. After you've slept, I bet things will be clearer for you."

"Doctors told me that same line for weeks." Anger snapped in her words, and she tried to pull back the old fury. "'Things will be clear…' and 'Give it some time…' and 'You just need rest.'" Her laughter held a bitter edge. "I've heard all of that a dozen times before. And guess what? Rest doesn't help. Time doesn't help." Her lips pressed together, and after a tense moment, Noelle demanded, "But you know what *did* help? Seeing that poor girl tied to the chair." She took a step toward him. *"Just like me."* Because it had been as if she'd stared into a mirror of her past.

A muscle flexed along Thomas's jaw. "She's not you, though, Noelle. You're just getting things confused."

She sucked in a sharp breath. "Stop lying to me."

He shook his head.

"You are. You're lying. From the moment I saw you at the EOD, I felt like we'd met before."

"Other missions," he growled out. "Our paths have crossed. I can't tell you what I was doing then; you don't have the clearance."

"Forget clearance!" The words came out as a yell as she shot forward and grabbed his arms. "This is my life! Tell me!"

He stared into her eyes. "I've seen you. You haven't always seen me. The FBI works plenty of cases that merge with the EOD. Sometimes, you guys thought you were hunting serials, but you were after assassins. It was our job to contain those killers. My team did its job."

"No, there's more to this." Earlier, she was sure that he'd started to tell her more. Back at the station, before they'd learned about Jenny.

"I've told you the truth."

Her temples were throbbing, her heart breaking. "Not

all of it." She blinked because her eyes were filling with tears, and she would *not* let them fall. "I thought we were partners. I thought we could count on each other." She dropped her hold and stepped back. "I guess I thought wrong." She whirled away from him.

But his hand locked around her shoulder, and he spun her right back to face him.

"Thomas—"

His mouth crashed down on hers. She was so shocked by the move she just stood there a moment. Then...

"Damn it, I'm sorry." He tore his mouth from hers, but he didn't let her go. Thomas stared down at her with glittering eyes. "Let's try that again...."

And this time, the kiss was softer. Tempting her, not taking or demanding, but seducing her instead.

Her emotions were about to rip her apart. She shouldn't just be standing in his arms.

I'll always be with you. The memory of those words didn't scare her. The words made her feel safe. The way being with Thomas always did.

Her hands rose to curl around his shoulders. She shouldn't be in his arms, no, but nothing had ever felt more right to her before.

His mouth pressed to hers, and her lips parted. He kissed her, deeply, sensually, and she rose onto her toes in front of him. The anger that had been blasting through her changed. Desire rose, igniting like a fire-storm because, suddenly, it was all too much. The past. The present. The fire. The fear.

She didn't want to think anymore. She only wanted to feel. And Thomas, he was very, very good at making her feel.

Her hands shoved against his coat. He let her go, just

for a moment, and that coat hit the floor. He stared at her, and she could read his gaze then, no problem. Lust and heavy desire shined in his eyes. "Noelle…"

She shook her head. She'd asked him to talk. He'd refused. Now… Now she just wanted to keep feeling.

Noelle tossed aside her coat. Kicked off her boots and ditched her socks. She was stripping in front of him, when she'd never had the courage to do this before, not in front of the only two lovers she'd had. She'd been so nervous with them. So afraid.

But there wasn't any room for fear. Not with him.

Thomas pulled her against him and kissed her again, even as his hands slid over her flesh. His fingertips were rough, callused, but he was so careful as he caressed her. She arched into his touch. Wanting more. Needing more. She needed everything he had to give.

Lies. Truth. She didn't know the line between them anymore.

She didn't know what was memory. What was hope. She only knew desire.

He pulled her down onto the rug in front of the fireplace. She could hear the wind howling outside. She could feel the mad drumbeat of her heart, shaking her from the inside.

He ditched his clothes, and then he—he just gazed down at her.

"You're the most perfect thing that I've ever seen."

No, she wasn't. Her breasts were too small. Her legs too long and—

He bent his head and took her nipple into his mouth. A surge of heat had her gasping his name. He kept kissing her breast, licking her nipple, even as his hand slid down her body. Her legs spread for him, and his fingers explored her flesh.

"Warm," his voice rumbled against her, "so...*hot and perfect.*"

She felt as if she were burning then. The cold was long gone. Her breath heaved out in pants as he took his time learning her body. Stroking. Licking. Touching.

Kissing.

Everywhere.

Her nails bit into his shoulders. It had never been like this for her before. The passion so intense, her body responding so quickly. Maybe it was the adrenaline. The fear. The fury.

Or maybe it was just the man.

He positioned himself between her legs. His eyes blazed and—

"I need to protect you..."

Understanding dawned for her. She shook her head. "I'm safe." She was on contraception, and she was clean. All of the agents underwent regular physicals and—

"I'm clean," he gritted out, "and I want you...more than I've ever wanted anyone or anything."

"Then take me," she heard herself whisper.

His fingers caught hers and he pinned her hands to the rug. He stared into her eyes, his face a mask of stark need as he thrust inside her.

He drove deep and filled her completely. She gasped at the sensation because it had been so long for her, and sex with her other lovers had never been like this.

Heat. Need. Passion.

He withdrew. Plunged deep. Again and again. Her legs wrapped around his hips as she surged up to meet his thrusts. Every hard glide of his body pushed him right over her sensitive core, and her body tightened. Release was close, so very close and—

Noelle screamed when the pleasure hit her. No gentle wave. No crest of release. But an avalanche, which rolled right over her, stealing her breath and making her heart slam into her ribs. She cried out Thomas's name, so lost in him she could barely see. Her body trembled, spasmed and she held on to him as fiercely as she could.

Then he drove into her once more. He stiffened, and the growl that broke from him was her name.

She tried to focus on him because she wanted to see him in that moment. The hard angles of his face. The pleasure in his eyes.

He bent toward her. He kissed her.

And he kept thrusting.

Her breath caught and she arched toward him. Because she realized the pleasure wasn't over.

It was just beginning.

WHEN NOELLE OPENED her eyes, she was still by the fire. The rest of the house was dark, but the fire blazed. Thomas was in front of the hearth, wearing a pair of jeans. He bent forward as she watched and he stirred up the flames.

"The power's out," he said, without looking back at her.

A soft cover surrounded her body. She didn't even know where that cover had come from, but she pulled it closer.

"We should stay down here," Thomas said, his attention seemingly on the blaze. "It's warmer here, as long as we keep the fire going."

Keeping the blanket with her, Noelle sat up. She brought her knees in front of her and watched Thomas.

"I didn't…mean for that to happen." His voice was low, rasping, and his shoulders were tense. "I know I pounced on you and—"

"If this is the part where you apologize," she said, a bit surprised by the bite in her own voice, "don't. I knew exactly what I was doing and exactly what I wanted."

He looked back at her.

"You," Noelle told him simply. "I wanted to be with you."

He swallowed. She saw the faint movement of his Adam's apple. "There are things you don't know about me."

She lifted her brows at that. "I'd say I know you pretty well by now." Biblically well.

He glanced toward the fire once more. "You know what you read in the files Mercer gave you, but with me… He wouldn't have shown you everything."

Noelle forced herself to take slow, deep breaths. "And why not?"

The flames crackled.

"My father was a solider." Thomas spoke slowly. "He was a damn good fighter and a good man." His hand lifted and he stared at it for a second. Then he struck out with a powerful force that seemed to whip through the air around him. His hand was perfectly straight as it moved in a series of fast, hard glides—attacks that were both beautiful…and brutal. "He taught me how to fight when most kids were learning how to read and write. He wanted me to be prepared, always prepared for what life might throw at me."

She waited.

"My mother didn't like being a soldier's wife. She left, and she took me with her." His jaw hardened. "And he died on his next mission."

"I'm sorry." The words felt so hollow to her.

"My dad was good at what he did. His walls were full of medals and commendations. But when he lost us, I think he just stopped caring." He rubbed a hand over his face. "I realized then just how dangerous love could be to a man. Love makes you weak. Vulnerable."

She shook her head, even though he couldn't see the move. "It doesn't have to be like that."

"It does…when love becomes an obsession. When it's all you think about. When you can't do your mission because you're seeing a woman in your head. You're worried about her, thinking about her, and you can't protect your team, much less yourself."

She didn't know what to say then.

"I intended to live my life without any commitments. The missions *were* my life, and women… Sex was a necessity I took care of when I needed it."

Noelle stiffened. Her hold on the cover tightened. Okay, he'd better not have just said she was some kind of itch he'd *taken care of.* The man needed to think again. He wasn't—

He faced her. "You're different, and I can't afford the weakness that you make me feel."

That was both good *and* insulting. "I'm not a weakness to you."

"Yes," he said softly. "You are. More than you know." He rolled back his shoulders. "I should've known once wouldn't be enough with you."

She distinctly remembered at least two times. During the third, she'd—

"I should have kept my hands off you, but I couldn't."

Noelle cleared her throat. "I didn't want them off. I wanted you."

He shook his head. "No, you just wanted to stop being afraid, and I was close and convenient."

Oh, the hell *no,* he hadn't just said that. Noelle jumped to her feet. The cover almost fell, so she scrambled to keep it over her. Then she stalked toward Thomas, and she jabbed him in the chest with her index finger. "Listen up, soldier," Noelle snapped at him.

His brows lifted.

"You are many things, but trust me, convenient isn't one of them." Not by a long shot. "You're infuriating, you're secretive and you're deadly. *Convenient* doesn't even make your top-ten list."

"Then why were you with me? Why did you give yourself to me?" The words held a hard demand.

She licked her lips and swore she could still taste him. "Because I needed you right then…" She thought of his words. "More than I needed anyone or anything." Even the secrets of her past. Secrets her gut told her he knew.

He didn't speak. Maybe he was back to being Strong and Silent. That was okay. Noelle found she had plenty to say. "What happened between us tonight wasn't about the past. It was only about the present. About me needing you. About you needing me. I'm not looking for forever." Was that why he was giving her the spiel about sex being a necessity? She straightened her shoulders and vowed not to crumble. "I just needed you, because when you look at me—" and she'd seen this in his gaze "—you see *me.* Flaws. Strengths. You seem to see all of me, and you want what you see."

He didn't realize how important that was to her. She felt broken on the inside, but he looked at her with such hunger, such desire.

Maybe it was time for them to be completely honest. They were alone in the cabin. Separated from the rest of the world by the storm. "I know you were there," she whispered.

Because Noelle was watching him so closely, she saw the slight hardening of his mouth.

"It's not me being confused. I hear your voice, and I know you were there when I was taken." There had been so many law enforcement personnel swarming the little cabin when she was rescued. Had he been a deputy back then? A face that she couldn't remember, but a voice that had stayed with me? "What I don't understand is…why…after everything, you just won't admit the truth to me. It's my life. I should have the highest possible clearance when it comes to *me*."

His hand rose. The back of his fingers brushed over her cheek. He swallowed and whispered, "I was there."

It took an instant for those words to sink in. "When the rescuers came for me?"

His eyes closed. "I saw you in my mind for years after that night. I hated to leave you, but I didn't have a choice. The mission I was on meant that I couldn't be compromised. Other lives were at stake."

Her heart should have been racing. Instead, its beat was slow. Everything felt slow for her right then. "You didn't answer my question."

His eyes opened.

"Were you there when the rescuers came?" She remembered a deputy, a guy with a wide-brimmed hat who'd pulled her from the chair and guided her from the cabin. After she'd gotten outside, the deputy had vanished. But he'd been…good to her. He'd pulled her from the darkness and—

Thomas shook his head.

Her heart stopped then. "Thomas?"

"I was told never to talk about that night."

She couldn't have this conversation covered only in a blanket. And she couldn't leave the room right then, not if her life depended on it. "Who told you?"

"Mercer."

The puppet master. The man always pulling the strings. The man who'd been in and out of Noelle's life for years. *"Why?"*

"Because EOD agents can't be compromised, you know that."

She had to figure this out before she shattered. "You're thirty-seven."

His head inclined toward her.

"Fifteen years ago…you would have only been twenty-two." The background file Mercer had given to her had indicated Thomas hadn't joined the EOD until he was twenty-seven, after he'd spent years working operations as an Army Ranger.

"I was twenty-two, and I'd been killing for the government for years by then."

"You weren't EOD." He *couldn't* have been.

Thomas simply stared back at her.

"Tell me!"

"I've been with the EOD since I was twenty-one years old." His lips twisted. "I told you, I was very, very good at my job."

A wave of dizziness had her stepping back from him.

"Mercer knows what happened to me, too, doesn't he?" He's known, and for years, he's said nothing.

Thomas nodded.

"Why? It's my life!" Anger was cracking through her.

"But other lives were on the line. We thought… We thought your abduction was an isolated incident." He tried to reach out for her, but she flinched back. "I didn't know there were other girls involved, not until we found those pictures."

Had Mercer known? Was that why he'd been so adamant she investigate the senator? "Tell me everything."

"Clearance—"

"Don't!" How dare he throw that up to her? "You just made love to me. There were no barriers between us. It was you and it was me." She heaved out a breath. Her heart wasn't beating slowly anymore. It was thundering in her chest. "I've had a void in my mind for years. A void that you could fill. All you had to do was speak. Just…tell me." She was about to rip that cover in two with her grip. "Do it now, Thomas. Tell me. I'm not crazy. I remember your voice, I remember—"

"You were in the woods." His voice was flat. Ice cold. "I heard your screams, so I ran to investigate."

Her knees almost gave way. She grabbed for the mantel and kept one hand around the cover that shielded her.

His hands were fists at his sides. "You were fleeing in the woods. You were hysterical, crying, saying that a man was chasing you." The faint lines around his mouth deepened in the firelight. *"Hunting you."*

Goose bumps rose on her skin.

"I didn't see anyone, and you… You were too pale. Your pupils were dilated, and I thought—I thought you were on drugs. At first."

She could only shake her head. But…the doctors *had* thought she'd been drugged. *Rohypnol.* Since it could cause memory loss, that had been the drug they suspected the most. *And* since it could be untraceable in the blood after the passage of time, they'd figured her abductor must have given it to her.

"Then I saw your hands. You had bruises around your wrists. As if you'd been tied up. Restrained."

Her lungs were starving for air, even though she was breathing as deeply as she could.

"I never expected to find you in those woods. Saving you… It wasn't my mission, but… *I wasn't going to let anyone hurt you.*"

"They found me in the cabin." His story wasn't making sense to her. She'd been in the cabin, not out in the open, in the woods.

"Because I took you back there."

She stumbled away from the mantel. "I was tied up! *You* did that to me?"

He tried to grab her, but even though she'd craved his touch before, she couldn't stand it right then.

And she needed clothes.

Clothes!

She spun away from him. Grabbed a flashlight and then she was running up the stairs.

"Noelle!"

Her world was shaking, and she wasn't going to stand there, naked. She shoved open the door to her bedroom. Her flashlight hit on the bed. It was so cold in there. Icy.

She grabbed for her suitcase, even as she heard him thundering up the stairs behind her. She yanked on her jeans. Pulled on a T-shirt. Didn't slow down for underwear. Her teeth were chattering. So cold. So cold because—

The window was open.

Noelle froze.

"We've started, and we aren't stopping," Thomas said as he stormed into her room. "Mercer is going to fire my ass, but I don't care. I won't hold back with you any longer. After what happened tonight, I can't."

Her flashlight was on the window. "Why is it open?" It shouldn't be open. It had been locked when they'd left before.

Her light hit the floor. Snow was inside, some melted, some still a hard white.

"Where's your weapon?" Thomas asked her, voice whisper soft.

The window was open, and it looked… It almost looked as if there were wet boot prints on the hard-wood floor.

"Downstairs." There was no way someone could've gotten into the cabin, not while they were there and… making love.

Would I even have noticed an intruder then? No.

Thomas's hand closed around her arm. "You stay next to me, got it?" He didn't have his weapon, either. Both guns… They were downstairs. They'd put them aside in their frantic need for each other.

She turned toward Thomas. "Are we alone?" The storm was still raging. The wind was so strong. Maybe—maybe the window had just blown open. She pulled away from Thomas and went toward that window. Shut it. Locked it.

And Thomas was right by her, moving to keep his body beside hers. "We're about to find out," he told her, voice still low and soft. "You stay with me, and we're going to do a full-house sweep."

"*After* we get our weapons." His words about her past were swirling through her mind, but this…new fear was within her. Jenny's abductor had gotten away. Had he come after them? They went back down the stairs on silent feet. The shadows seemed to stretch all around them.

Noelle's skin crawled at the thought of someone being in that cabin with them, watching them while they made love.

Thomas's gun was just where he'd left it. So was hers. When the gun was in Noelle's hands, she finally felt better. They checked the cabin, moving room by room.

But no one was there.

No other windows were open.

It must've just been the storm. The wind…

Thomas headed toward the cabin's back door.

"What are you doing?" Noelle asked him.

He spared her a brief glance as he shouldered into his coat. He'd already donned his shirt and boots. "I'm checking the exterior perimeter."

Noelle shook her head. "In this storm? You need to stay inside." *And you need to finish telling me what really happened that long-ago night.*

But his jaw was locked and his body radiated determination. "The window was open. I'm making damn sure someone didn't open it. I want to check outside and see if there are any signs of an intruder."

"There won't be any signs. The snow would've covered any signs."

He motioned toward her gun. "Keep your weapon close until I get back."

No. He wasn't walking out into that storm without her. "If you're going, then so am I."

Thomas shook his head. "I need you to stay inside. The weather is going to be rough enough as it is. One of us has to make sure the interior of this place remains secure."

"But—"

But he wasn't listening to her.

Thomas was already gone.

Chapter Seven

Thomas mentally cursed himself as he trudged through the snow. He should never have lowered his guard. For someone to get close enough to the house…to get *inside* while he was there… Thomas knew he was seriously slipping. That didn't happen. He was always aware of his surroundings and of any threats that were close.

But when Noelle had kissed him back, when she'd responded so wildly, he'd lost control. He'd taken what he'd wanted for so long.

And he'd been blind to everything else.

Then…hell, he'd revealed too much. Mercer would nail his hide to the wall, but Thomas didn't care. Noelle deserved to know what was happening. *Especially* if the past was coming back—and it sure looked as if it was.

He headed around the cabin and shined his light up near Noelle's window.

Snow covered the area once more, and there was no sign up there anyone had been climbing on the cabin. No sign but…

His light lowered. It hit the ground. The snow was blowing wildly around him, flying hard. He turned to the left because over the howl of the wind, he'd thought he'd heard—

His light fell on the shadowy form of man. A man who stood less than fifteen feet away from him. The man was bundled up, with a thick ski mask covering his face.

He stared at Thomas for an instant, then he spun away.

"Stop!" Thomas snarled.

But the man didn't stop. He ran into the thick snow, heading for the line of trees.

And Thomas hurried after him as he fought the grasping hold of the snow.

THE THUNDER OF a gunshot rose over the howling of the wind.

Noelle lunged for the door when she heard that sound. Forget securing the interior of the cabin. Thomas needed her!

She already had on her borrowed coat, and she rushed for the door with her flashlight in one hand and her gun in the other. She didn't have on gloves, and the wind whipped against her skin.

"Thomas!" The gale seemed to yank the cry away from her.

Another gunshot rang out. It sounded as though it had come from the line of trees near the east. She fought the snow and struggled in that direction.

Her light flew around. She didn't see Thomas and couldn't see anything but the line of trees and a haze of white as the snow spun in the air.

Thomas wasn't answering her call. Had he been the one firing? Or had someone been shooting at him?

She pushed into the shadows of the trees. The cold

was already making her body shake. Her fingers had a death grip on the flashlight and the gun.

A shadow rushed to the side, moving in the corner of her light. She spun to the left. *"Thomas?"*

Then something hit her. No, *someone.* The tackle sent Noelle flying into the snow. She shoved up with her elbow, ready to break her assailant's nose.

"It's me!"

Thomas's voice.

"He's got a gun, baby, so be careful." He rose then. He didn't have a light, and hers had slipped from her grip. She floundered, trying to find it, but he caught her hand. "The light just makes us a bigger target."

Noelle thought she heard laughter then, tangled with the howl of the wind.

Thomas pulled away from her. He seemed to be swallowed by the thick snow. She scrambled to her feet. Her eyes were narrowed as she struggled to keep him in her line of sight, but he was moving quickly, even in that thick curtain. Heading deeper into the woods as he followed his prey.

Someone was in the house with us. Someone saw...

"I remember you..."

Did she hear those words? Imagine them? The storm was so loud.

"Noelle..." Something brushed over her arm, and she jumped as she spun around.

But... No one was there.

Her attention jerked back toward Thomas. He'd just rushed into a thick copse of trees. She hurried after him.

And tripped, slamming right into the ground.

Swearing, she fought to rise again, but her fingers

caught the—the rope that had been hidden near her feet. Rope that had been used to trip her.

A trap. For prey.

For them.

"Thomas!" Noelle screamed. "Stop! It's a setup!" The window, the shots… They were designed to lure them out into this wilderness.

She pushed onto her knees, then staggered after Thomas. He hadn't heard her cry. He hadn't stopped. She had to get to him.

Noelle shoved through the line of trees, and a hand grabbed her arm. She saw the thick outline of a man before her, a man covered in winter clothing, but—

Not Thomas.

She fired her weapon. The bullet hit him, she knew it did. This close, there was no way she could miss, but he didn't let her go. He tightened his hold on her and yanked her forward.

And he—he *threw* her.

Noelle screamed once more, but the wind was wailing around her. She expected to hit the snow when she fell, but she hit something hard instead.

Ice.

And she felt that ice begin to splinter beneath her hand.

The sound of laughter seemed to float on the wind once more.

"Noelle!"

Thomas. That wasn't laughter; that was *his* frantic voice.

She looked up. He was fighting to get close to her. *"Don't!"* She tried to yell as loudly as she could. She raised her arm toward him.

And felt more of the ice crack beneath her.

"Stay back!" Could he hear her? "It's giving way! We'll both—"

The ice broke, and Noelle fell into the frigid water. It was so cold it stole her breath. Her feet and legs seemed to go numb right away. She couldn't move them, couldn't kick. Her arms had flown out in front of her when the ice broke, and they were still above the surface. She slapped them down on the frozen plane, hoping to find a way to secure herself because she was going down. Her heart was racing. The water was freezing her.

"I've got you!" Fingers wrapped around hers.

Her gaze flew up. She could barely make out Thomas's form. He was lying on the ice, his body spread out. His fingers were around hers, but she couldn't feel his touch.

She couldn't feel anything but that Arctic water, and it was pulling her down.

"I'm getting you out!" He was yelling, but his words sounded like a whisper. "We have to keep our weight distributed. Don't stand up when you're clear...."

He was pulling her up. Inch by slow, desperate inch.

He thought she was planning to stand? Her legs weren't working, her teeth were chattering, and she was afraid she'd pass out at any moment.

But he kept pulling her. Slowly. Carefully. Her hips hit something solid. She could feel new splinters in that surface beneath her. *"H-hurry..."* Noelle managed to rasp because she was terrified more of the ice was about to give way. If she and Thomas both went in, they wouldn't come out.

He didn't hurry. He kept up that inching pace. Her whole body shuddered with cold. Her hands were numb in his grasp. Her face was against the ice. The cracks scratched her skin.

"We're almost there, baby. Hold on for me."

She wasn't holding on to him at all. She couldn't.

"Got you!" Thomas yanked her forward and into his arms. He fiercely held her. She should feel the warmth from his body. She didn't. Tremors shook her. Her gaze fell on the shadows behind them as Thomas tried to rub her arms and her legs. He was yanking at her wet clothes.

"B-behind…" Speaking was so hard. She tried to push at him. To warn him.

Thomas was too fixated on her.

"G-gun…" Where was his weapon? They needed it. Thomas's head flew up.

"B-behind…"

He pushed her down into the snow. His hand hit the ground near her and when it rose again, she saw he had his weapon. He fired. Once. Twice.

She'd seen the shadow out there watching them. Waiting for another moment to attack.

"He's running," Thomas snarled.

"F-follow…" The man had already gotten away once. They couldn't afford to let him vanish again.

"If I do, you're dead." He pulled her into his arms and kept his gun ready. "No, baby, that's not happening. You're priority."

She needed to help him. The attacker could circle back around. Everything that was happening… It was all one big trap. She had to help Thomas.

But she could only shudder.

He pulled her closer. "I've got you, and I won't let you go…"

THE SNOW WAS a blur around him. The agent had Noelle. He was trying to make his way back to the cabin with her.

His chest burned where Noelle's bullet had hit him. The blood was leaving a trail in the snow. But the storm would make that trail vanish. The storm would...

He leaned against a tree as he fought to catch his breath. The man's bullet had grazed his arm, cutting through the coat, but Noelle's had been the one to do the most damage. He'd just been caught off-guard by her. To see her, standing right in front of him, after all of those years...

She was a ghost from his past.

A ghost who had *shot* him. He'd reacted instinctively when the bullet hit. He'd grabbed her and thrown her toward the ice.

The ice had been meant for the man—the one called Thomas. The fellow was proving himself to be a worthy hunter.

But he'd still die.

And I remember you, Thomas... Because he'd crossed paths with that man before. Only Thomas hadn't been such a *good* guy then. Noelle had no clue about the man she thought was her partner.

No. Clue.

Thomas would die soon. So would Noelle.

It was just a matter of time....

The wound throbbed. He shoved more snow against it. Damn it, he was going to have to stop that bleeding. He could feel weakness pushing through his blood. But where the hell was he supposed to find help in this storm?

Gritting his teeth, he trudged forward. He'd stayed

alive through plenty of attacks. He'd survive this, too, and then…then he'd make Noelle Evers and her partner *pay*.

"NOELLE? BABY, LOOK AT ME." Thomas yanked the wet clothing off Noelle and tossed the items away. He'd made it back to the cabin with her. He'd locked the doors, secured the place in seconds, and now he was trying to get her warm again.

Her lips were totally devoid of color. Her face far too pale. Her skin was icy beneath his touch, and shudders racked her.

"It's okay," he told her, aware his voice was ragged. "I've got you." Fear still raced through his veins. When she'd gone through the ice, he'd been terrified he wouldn't be able to get her out in time.

"T-Thomas?"

"Yes, baby, I've got you." He knew he was just repeating himself, but he didn't care. He settled her on the rug in front of the fireplace and wrapped the blanket around her. Her fingers fumbled as she tried to hold up the fabric.

Get her warm. Keep her safe. Those were his two priorities. He stoked the fire, building up the flames, then he stripped as quickly as he could. But Thomas made sure to keep his gun close by. He was pretty certain the perp they wanted was still out in that storm, but he wasn't going to take any chances.

He wanted to search the whole cabin again, but he couldn't, not until he took care of Noelle.

He turned back to her. The blanket had slipped down to her hips.

"Baby…" He dropped beside her and pulled her

close. He stretched out with her, and he wrapped his body around hers as best he could. Flesh to flesh. His body could warm hers. He positioned the blanket around her and he just… He just held her. Held her and tried to fight the gnawing fear in his stomach.

He'd stared down terrorists, looked into the barrel of a loaded gun during a particularly brutal game of Russian roulette.

He'd battled through hellfire.

But he'd never been as afraid as he'd been when she screamed his name and fell through the ice.

Never again. He had to find that SOB out there. He had to stop him before the man came after Noelle once more.

His hands slid over her back. She was shivering, and her lips were pressed against his neck. He wanted to take all of her pain away. He wanted to do anything, everything to protect her.

Yet the only thing he could do was hold her. Hold her and try to give her his warmth.

The fire crackled, and gradually, the shivers eased from her body. His hands curled around her hips. She felt warmer. At least, he hoped she did.

"Thank you…" Her soft whisper blew against his neck. "I was…a-afraid I wasn't getting out of the water."

His hold tightened on her. "I never would've left you." If necessary, he would've gone in that water and found a way to pull her out.

He'd left her once before. Followed orders, even though every instinct he possessed had screamed against it. He wouldn't make that mistake ever again.

Her lips pressed against his throat. The lightest of caresses.

Thomas swallowed. "You should...probably not do that."

When she'd been shivering with cold, they'd had to be close *and* naked for survival.

But she was warmer, and he—he *always* wanted her.

She kissed his neck again. *"Thank you."* He felt the light lick of her tongue against his skin.

His eyes squeezed shut. The woman didn't seem to realize just how fragile his control was. When it came to her, hell, he couldn't *keep* control in place. Not a possibility.

Her legs shifted against him, parted so her thighs were on either side of his.

Bad, bad mistake. "Noelle..."

She kissed him again. He'd never realized how sensitive his neck was. When Noelle kissed him there, when she licked him with that delicate little tongue of hers, a wave of arousal shot right through his body. He was already hard for her, with her naked body rubbing against his, how could he not be? But now...

My control is shredding.

"I want in you," he told her, and he didn't see how he could be more blunt. "So you need to pull away. You're weak, you need to rest and—"

Her head lifted. The fire had dried her damp hair. He could see the shine of her eyes. "I want you in me," she said softly.

And he was lost.

His hands slid around her body, found the center of her need. He caressed her. Felt that last thread of his control give way—

Thomas thrust into her—drove into her until he was

hilt deep. She might have been cold before, but right then, she was blazing hot. Her sex clamped tightly around him, and Thomas was pretty sure he was about to lose his mind.

Noelle pushed up, bracing her hands against the floor. Her breasts were so close, he had to lean up and take one into his mouth.

Then she started moving. Rising. Falling. The rhythm was maddening. He needed more. He needed deeper, but Noelle was going slow. Slow and sensual. Every glide of her body had his muscles aching with the effort to hold back.

He wanted to take, and he would, but first...

Noelle.

He kept stroking the center of her need. He knew now just how she liked to be touched. Knew the caresses she needed. Knew just how to make her eyes go blind and to make her gasp.

When she moaned his name, he smiled.

When she came, crying out, her body tensing, he took over.

His hands locked tightly around her hips. He lifted her body, up and down, again and again, driving in the rhythm he needed. When it wasn't enough, when he needed more, deeper, he twisted with her, putting her beneath him on that rug.

And he took her. Claimed her. Pleasure flooded through him.

He kissed her when the release erupted. Kissed her and tasted life and hope. Tasted everything he'd ever wanted.

Thomas knew that, in an instant, he would kill to keep her by his side.

THE STORM HAD PASSED. Noelle stared out at the sea of white around the cabin. In the distance, she could hear the rumble of snowplows.

The road in front of their cabin was covered, but she knew they'd be getting out of there soon enough.

Her gaze slid toward the trees that lined the property. Had the perp survived the night? She bet he had. But…

"My bullet hit him," she said quietly. Thomas was behind her. Not talking. They hadn't talked much during the remainder of the night.

They'd made love, and exhausted, she'd fallen asleep in his arms. When she'd woken up, he'd been dressed. Armed.

And the day had dawned.

"I grazed him," Thomas said, as he drew closer to her. "Or at least, I think I did."

Her shot had been at near point-blank range, so Noelle figured the wound she'd inflicted had to be bad. "He'll need medical help." She glanced toward Thomas. "I hit him in the chest. Not his heart, but enough of a wound that the guy can't just keep walking around without treatment." Not even close. "*If* he survived the storm, he'll be looking for someone to patch him up." So they'd check first with local doctors and veterinary personnel. Someone with medical training.

"He'll look, unless he's the kind of man used to taking care of his own wounds."

Noelle thought of the scars on Thomas's body. "You've done that."

"When it comes down to either being able to stitch up yourself or dying, yeah, you learn to stitch that skin pretty fast." His voice was grim. "I've dug bullets out.

Hell, I've even cauterized knife wounds. In the field, you do what you have to do, and you keep going."

The words of a soldier. But they weren't looking for a soldier. They were looking for a killer.

Or are we looking for both?

The whir of the snowplow was louder.

"The sheriff will be coming for us," Thomas said. "We'll talk to Jenny and get her to describe the man who took her." He glanced up at the now-clear sky. "And we'll talk to Mercer. Find out what the EOD has learned about those victims."

Before they did… "We need to talk first," she said as she gave a determined nod.

His gaze instantly became shuttered.

"No more secrets, no more lies."

He flinched at that. "I haven't lied to you."

It almost seemed surreal to have this conversation with him. After everything that had happened the night before, they should have been close. Heck, it didn't get much closer than being someone's lover. But there was a wall between them.

Secrets.

And, yes, despite what he'd just said…lies.

"I want to know everything." They were alone. Now was the time to put it all out on the table. "From the moment that you saw me—running in those woods— until the moment you left me tied in that cabin." Because, yes, that part was obvious. She'd been left there with a dead man.

The sound of the plow grew louder. They'd tried to call the sheriff earlier, but they still had no service in the area. While they had a few more precious moments of privacy, she needed to hear the rest of Thomas's tale.

Even though part of her was almost afraid to hear what he had to say.

Hiding from the truth won't do any good.

"You heard me screaming in the woods, and you found me." She looked down at her wrists. "I'd been tied up, bound—"

"And he was hunting you."

Her head whipped up. Thomas wasn't looking at her. He was staring out at the snow.

"I knew what he was doing pretty quickly. Another hunter always knows...."

She shook her head, but he didn't see the movement.

"You were leaving a clear trail for him to follow. Broken branches, blood on the rocks. He expected to find you out there, but he didn't expect me." His voice was low and rough. "He jumped out of the bushes with a knife, and he went for your throat."

Her hand lifted to her throat. "The man...the man found with me that day... *His* throat had been cut."

Now he did look at her. His eyes blazed with emotion. "I wasn't going to let him kill you. And, like I said, he expected you—" his right hand flexed near his side "—not me. I got that knife away from him, and he was the one who died."

Her breath rushed out. "All of that was in the woods? But—but his body was found in the cabin. *I* was found in the cabin."

He looked away from her. "I was working a case. Undercover. Domestic terrorists were in the area. I...I couldn't be found with you. I couldn't be caught up in an investigation about a missing teen girl and her dead abductor."

"You left me." Saying the words…hurt. Her hand lowered to her chest and rubbed over the ache there.

"Yes," his voice was soft. "I left you. You kept trying to follow me, so I had to tie you up. I couldn't have you walking from one danger straight into another."

The pain in her chest seemed to get worse. "You were following orders." Mercer's orders. She'd thought Mercer was her friend. They'd met years before when she first joined the FBI. He'd taken an interest in her. Her supervisor had been in awe of the guy, and even though she hadn't realized quite how powerful Mercer was, Noelle had known he was a man who could help her.

Only he'd actually been the man hiding her past from her.

The pain of betrayal was there, and she wondered if it always would be.

"That's what a soldier does." Anger roughened Thomas's words. "And, yes, damn it, that was what I did." He swung to face her. "I took you to that cabin. I…called in backup."

"Mercer…"

"EOD agents put the body inside."

She'd gone over the reports. There hadn't been enough of the dead man's blood in the cabin, so the police had thought his body had been dumped there, but they'd never been able to find the kill site.

The EOD were too good at covering their tracks.

"I didn't want to tie you up. Your wrists were already raw and bloody."

She blinked away tears.

"You wouldn't stay behind. You kept trying to follow," he said quietly. "I didn't…I didn't have a choice."

"Actually, you did. You've known this for years, you could've said—"

"Before I left you at that cabin, I told you that you couldn't speak to the police about me. I told you I was working a case and lives were on the line." He yanked a hand through his hair. "At first, I thought you *were* covering for me. Doing what I'd asked because you promised me that you'd keep quiet."

She frowned at him.

"Later…later I realized you just didn't remember, and by then, I was in so deep at the EOD that telling you the real truth wasn't an option." His hand dropped. "I even thought it might be better for you. Not knowing. You seemed to be making a good life for yourself. You graduated at the top of your college class. You went to Quantico. You had a wide circle of friends. Hell, you were even involved with that jerk psychology professor for a time."

She took a step back as realization slammed into her. "You were watching me." That was her gut response. He wasn't just quoting facts he'd discovered in some background report on her. The anger that hummed in his voice when he talked about her ex, Jim…it was too strong. Too personal.

He'd even told her before that he'd seen her, but she hadn't seen him.

Because he was watching me?

"I needed to make sure you were all right."

The growl of an engine grew louder. A snowplow? The sheriff? She didn't look away from Thomas to find out. "How long have you been watching me?"

"It's not… I check on you, okay? When I'm back in the U.S. Between assignments." He seemed to be weighing his words and responding so carefully. "I just like to make sure that you're safe."

I'll always be with you.

"The EOD gathered a lot of intel on your attacker, and we thought it was just one guy, working alone. You seemed to be the first victim he'd taken. Mercer believed that, with his death, it was over, but I…just needed to be sure." He sighed. "I needed to be sure because at night, when I closed my eyes, I would still hear you screaming for me to help you."

There it was. All of the secrets from her past. The truth she'd sought for so long, and now, hearing all of those details just made her feel numb. Like she'd just taken a dive into another ice pond.

But it made sense. His story explained the strange connection she'd felt with Thomas. The awareness. He *was* her past. The man who'd saved her in the dark.

He saved me, then left me.

No wonder her emotions had been all over the place with him.

She'd even…even wondered if she might be falling for him.

"Say something," he gritted out, his eyes glinting.

"What do you want me to say?" That emotionless voice didn't sound right. It didn't sound like her voice at all.

"Yell at me. Curse me. Tell me I'm a jerk for keeping the truth from you." He took another step toward her. "Tell me that I should've chosen you and turned my back on the EOD."

Her eyes widened. "Is that what you want me to say?" As she stared into Thomas's eyes, Noelle saw his guilt. Heavy. Thick.

"You were seventeen." Another step brought him even closer. "You were terrified. You…you asked me to stay with you. You begged me to stay."

She shook her head. The memory was right there. "And you said you'd always be with me."

"I'm sorry," he rasped.

So was she.

The growling of that engine was so close. She rushed away from the window and yanked open the front door. Noelle saw not one but two vehicles driving up behind the snowplow. One was the sheriff's car and the other, a dark SUV. As she watched, they braked and the passenger door of the SUV opened. A man jumped out. Her eyes narrowed as she stared at him.

He wore a thick coat, but she could tell his shoulders were broad. His back was straight. He yanked off his woolen cap as he headed toward her. The closer he came, the more she noticed the gray at his temples, his stony visage….

"No way," Noelle whispered. Sunglasses shielded the man's eyes, but she knew they would be green—and sharp.

Another man flanked the guy, a man who walked with a tense alertness, which broadcasted his military background.

She knew the second guy was a bodyguard, even before he turned and blocked the sheriff from heading up to the cabin.

And the man striding so confidently toward them was none other than—

"Mercer?" Thomas said, shock in his voice.

He should be shocked. As a rule, the EOD boss didn't do field work. He stayed in his office, and he pulled the strings. But, thanks to the recent attack at the EOD, there *was* no D.C. office.

"Inside," Bruce Mercer snapped. "You never know who's watching."

He was the man who'd kept her past from her. The man who knew where all the bodies were buried in D.C.

And because he was there, right in front of her, Noelle knew the situation in Camden, Alaska, had to be very, very bad.

If Bruce Mercer was there, then death wasn't far behind.

Chapter Eight

"Judging by the way Noelle is looking at me, I guess you told her everything, Agent Anthony?"

They were inside the cabin. Mercer was pacing near the fireplace while the man he'd brought with him—Thomas easily recognized Aaron Black—stood guard near the door.

For Aaron to be there, *with* Mercer, Thomas knew the situation had to be serious. He'd worked with the ex-SEAL before on cases that didn't involve hostage rescue. They'd involved cleanup.

Target disposal.

Death.

"*You* should've told me the truth," Noelle said, voice sharp. "As soon as I came on with the EOD. You should've—"

"I thought the past was dead and buried. Part of it was dead." Mercer waved toward Thomas. "Thanks to Agent Anthony."

His back teeth locked. Mercer wasn't exactly helping the situation.

"We thought the man who'd taken you—"

"Justin Hardin," Noelle bit out. "His name was Justin Hardin."

Mercer would know that. The man knew everything.

"We thought he was working alone. Our intel was wrong. We didn't realize just how mistaken we'd been until you uncovered those photographs at the senator's place."

Now he understood why Mercer was in Camden. "You identified those girls."

"Yes." Mercer turned sharply on his heel and faced Noelle. "They were taken from different states. Two even from different countries, *before* you went missing. The geographical area was so wide that we never connected the dots together." He exhaled. "That was a mistake that we have remedied now."

Noelle's arms were crossed over her chest. "Those girls were all taken that long ago? Then they—"

"I don't believe any of those girls are still alive."

Noelle's shoulders sagged.

Thomas narrowed his gaze on Mercer. "Since when does the EOD get involved on a serial's crime?" They didn't, not unless…

"The girls were taken from different states and different countries." It was Aaron who spoke. His voice was low and devoid of accent. "The techs at the EOD matched all of those abductions with ports of call that Senator Lawrence Duncan visited while he was enlisted in the navy."

Noelle shook her head. "He didn't do this! He's dead, and Jenny Tucker was abducted *after* Duncan's body had already been found. Her mother saw her leave the house that morning, and we know Duncan was killed during the night."

"Our mistake before," Mercer said, cutting through her words but sending a sympathetic glance her way, or at least, as sympathetic as Mercer got, "was think-ing there was only one killer involved. Obviously, there were two."

Red flashed on Noelle's high cheekbones. "Justin Hardin is *dead*."

"Hardin was hunting you," Aaron said. His gaze slid to Thomas. "We, um, learned that from Agent Anthony. He was the man after you in those Alabama woods."

He wanted to cross to Noelle's side. This situation was so messed up.

"But Hardin had a partner." Aaron's head inclined toward Noelle. "One we missed."

"You're *still* missing the truth!" The red grew darker on her cheeks. "If there was a second killer, there would be more victims." She pointed at Mercer. "You said the girls were all taken before me. The killer wouldn't just stop after my abduction. He wouldn't simply *quit* kill-ing. It doesn't work like that. Killing would be a com-pulsion for him. He'd keep taking victims because he *had* to. If we're dealing with a serial, he'd have a ritual that he followed and—" Noelle broke off as her eyes widened. "Hunting."

"Yes," Mercer said softly.

Thomas was lost. His stare drifted between Mercer and Noelle. What was he missing?

"He kept killing, but he changed his prey." Noelle's gaze seemed unfocused, and Thomas knew she was try-ing to profile the man they were after. "He was hunt-ing girls before, teenagers, but… Something changed."

"Maybe the fact that his partner died?" Aaron tossed out. "Maybe that sent the guy into a tailspin."

Noelle rubbed her temples. "He's hunting. Last night,

when he lured Thomas and me outside of this place, he was *hunting* us."

Mercer frowned. "He was here? What the hell? Why didn't you say something sooner?"

Because they hadn't exactly had the chance. Thomas locked gazes with the director. "We pursued him in the storm last night. Noelle shot him, but he got away."

"He got away because of me." Noelle's chin came up. "The attacker threw me onto weak ice and I fell through. Thomas had to pull me to safety."

Aaron lifted a brow. "Uh, you went through the ice?"

"I survived." Her voice was cold. Noelle started to pace. "He's a hunter, and he knows this area." Noelle's gaze snapped toward Thomas. "He started by hunting girls—they both did—but... After the partner died, maybe our guy realized he needed more of a challenge. He had to go for tougher game."

"And that's precisely what he did." Mercer nodded grimly. "I got Sydney to pull up every piece of intel we had on the late Senator Duncan."

Thomas knew Mercer was referring to Sydney Ortez. The woman was a genius with computers and information retrieval.

Mercer continued, "It seems that the senator's enemies—a few in the U.S. but particularly abroad—had a tendency to vanish."

"They were hunted," Thomas surmised. "By the senator?"

Mercer hesitated.

"He didn't get his hands dirty," Noelle said, and her words sounded so certain. "Not in the attack in D.C. and not when we were pushed off the road that first night. Duncan was a background guy. A puppeteer..."

Just like Mercer?

"He had others do the bloody work for him," Aaron said. His hands were loose at his sides.

"Yes." Noelle licked her lips. "If the earlier abductions all matched up with the senator's ports, then Duncan probably knew the killer. He knew what he was doing."

Of course, the senator wouldn't have stopped the killer.

"I was looking at it all wrong." Noelle kept pacing. "I thought the pictures we discovered at the senator's place were trophies. Mementos to remind Duncan of the victims, but they weren't."

"So what the hell were they?" Aaron asked. His blue eyes were narrowed and his jaw was locked.

Noelle stopped pacing. "They were blackmail material. He knew the killer's identity, and Duncan used those images to get the killer to do *his* dirty work."

"Like an attack dog on a leash." Thomas saw the situation perfectly now. "But if that's true, then something in those photos should tell us our killer's identity."

Mercer nodded. "And that's where Noelle comes in." He advanced toward her. "You're the one who can figure this one out. You're the one who can put the pieces of this puzzle together and help us determine just who this sick bozo is before he has the chance to hurt anyone else."

HE WAS STILL bleeding and he was getting weaker by the moment. The bullet was lodged in him. He had to get it out, but every time he tried to get a hold on the thing, he just made the wound bigger. Deeper.

The snowplows were out, clearing the little town of

Camden. He was in the shadows because that was his custom. He'd spent most of his life hiding, one way or another.

When you had a monster inside, you had to be careful. If the world saw you for what you really were, they'd destroy you.

His father had told him that. His father had seen him for exactly what he was. His old man had hoped the military would change him. Focus him. And, in a way, it had.

Because in the navy, he'd met Lawrence Duncan.

He watched as a bundled woman made her way to the small pharmacy in town. Figured that place would open first.

He would've preferred to find a veterinarian or some kind of doc, but the pharmacy tech would have to do. There wasn't anyone else who could help him, not now.

He made his way across the street. Saw the blood that dripped from him and splattered down in the snow. He should clean up his trail. But...

Too weak.

He pushed open the pharmacy door. The lights weren't on. Power wasn't back on in the town. He'd tried to use a phone before, but he hadn't been able to connect. The storm had knocked all communication down.

"We're not quite open yet!" A cheery voice called out. "Give me just a few minutes, and I'll help you."

He pulled his knife from its sheath. He walked down the narrow aisle. Saw the woman as she shrugged out of her coat. She was built like Noelle, long, slender, almost delicate lines. But her hair was a dark black, not a red.

"Be with you soon!" She said, not glancing back.

Her mistake.

He grabbed her and put the knife to her throat as he jerked her back against his chest. "You'll be with me right now." He had a ski mask over his face, so he twisted her around toward him, all the while keeping that knife right at her throat.

"Please…" she whispered.

He shook his head. "I'm not planning to kill you." Not yet, anyway. "Because you're going to help me, aren't you?"

The knife cut into her neck.

And she nodded.

"JENNY…" NOELLE KEPT her voice low and gentle. She didn't want to upset Jenny. The girl had already been through enough.

She was at Jenny's house. Jenny's mother was behind the girl, pacing nervously, and the sheriff watched from a position near the door.

"We need to take her over to Harrison County Medical," the sheriff said, voice tight. "Get her thoroughly checked out and—"

"No!" Jenny's desperate cry seemed to echo in Noelle's ears. Jenny glanced over her shoulder. "Mom, you promised I wouldn't have to go anywhere! I don't want— I need to stay here!"

Jenny's mother caught her daughter's hand and held tight. "You're not going anywhere."

The sheriff growled.

Noelle squared her shoulders. "I know the officers collected your clothing last night."

"Evidence," Jenny whispered as her gaze dropped down to her lap. "They said it was evidence. They—they sent me back home in borrowed clothes this morning."

Noelle glanced toward Jenny's mother.

"The storm trapped us at the sheriff's station. That's as far as the ambulance could get in that weather." Her gaze cut to Hodges. "But my girl is fine now. She doesn't need a hospital." Her breath heaved out as she pointed at the sheriff. "And he asked us questions all night, so I don't see why we have to answer any more now!"

"I promise, this won't take long." Noelle saw Jenny flinch. She wanted to reach out and touch the girl, offer comfort, but Jenny seemed frozen before her. "I need you to describe the man who took you."

"I *did* already!" Jenny's voice broke a bit. "I told the sheriff…he was tall, wide shoulders. He had dark hair and stubble on his face."

"Caucasian, African-American—"

"Caucasian," Jenny whispered.

"Were there any marks on his face? Any scars or tattoos that you noticed?"

Jenny shook her head.

"What about his eyes? What color were they?"

"Brown. I think they were brown."

"Good, Jenny. You're doing really, really well." Noelle knew interrogations with victims had to be handled carefully. If you pushed too hard, victims could break. If you didn't push hard enough, they might not be able to tell important details. "When he spoke to you, did the man have any accent?"

Another shake of Jenny's head was her answer.

Okay. Time to try a different tactic because, unfortunately, the man Jenny had just described could be *anyone*. "When we found you in the cabin, you were screaming."

A tear leaked down Jenny's cheek. "He told me that I had to scream."

"Because he wanted—"

"He wanted you to die." Jenny glanced up at her. "You're Noelle, and he said you had to die."

Chill bumps rose on Noelle's skin. "He mentioned me by name?"

"Yes."

"What did he say?"

"I wasn't…good enough. But you—you would be more fun. So I had to scream so he could see you. He said…he said he just wanted to see you."

No, he'd wanted to kill her. He'd wanted to kill them all.

"He told me that he liked to see his girls."

The photos. "Did he take any pictures of you while you were in that cabin?"

"Yes." Shame burned in that word. "I was crying and begging him, and he was taking my picture. He was… filming me with his phone."

Because the sicko didn't use a Polaroid any longer, but he still needed the memories of his victims.

"This is very important." Noelle leaned toward Jenny. "Did you ever hear him talking with anyone else? Did you *see* anyone else with him?"

Jenny bit her lower lip. "I don't…I don't think so."

"Are you sure, Jenny?" Because the man had worked with a partner years before. Maybe he was up to his old tricks. Two hunters.

A game? A competition?

"I only heard him. No one else."

Noelle smiled at her. "Thank you, Jenny. You've been

very helpful." She rose from the couch and turned for the door.

Jenny grabbed her hand. "When am I going to stop seeing him?"

Noelle stilled. Then, slowly, her gaze slid to find Jenny's.

"Every time I close my eyes, he's there." Jenny swallowed and the little click of sound was almost painful to hear. "When will that stop? When will he get out of my mind?"

"When I catch him and lock him in a cell. Then you won't ever have to worry about seeing him again."

Jenny nodded and she let go of Noelle.

"Thank you for your time." Noelle inclined her head to Jenny and Jenny's mother. Then she left because looking at Jenny was far too much like looking at herself.

The sheriff followed her out. Noelle had been given a new coat from the sheriff's department, one that fit better, and it helped to block the chill in the air.

The door shut behind them. "I need to head back to the station," Noelle said. Thomas and Aaron were out running down leads and searching the area. They thought if the perp was looking for medical aid, he might be staying close to the town—and they were determined to find him.

When the sheriff didn't speak, Noelle glanced his way. He was watching her with a hooded gaze. "Sheriff?"

"Locking him up won't stop that girl's nightmares." His hand rasped over his stubble-covered jaw. "You and I both know that, don't we?"

Her head tilted as she studied him.

"Camden was a quiet town before all this mess started." His lips pressed together and formed a grim line. "But Los Angeles, well, it had more than its share of crime."

So there was more to the sheriff than met the eye. Wasn't that the story with everyone? "You came up here to get away."

"I got tired of arriving too late."

She knew exactly what that was like.

"You're not FBI."

Noelle didn't so much as blink. "My ID says otherwise."

He laughed, but the sound was grim. "This ain't my first rodeo, and I know FBI agents when I see them. They're stiff, by the book, and they sure as hell don't race through fire without so much as twitching." He pointed at her. "It was the other agent who gave things away. Military. Covert, I'm betting."

"The past few days have been very stressful," she said carefully. "I think—"

"That bigwig who flew in on his *own* chopper, he isn't FBI. I don't know what organization you all work for, but I do need to know this." He exhaled on a rough breath. "Is my town safe? Or will more people be hurt soon?"

Watch what you say. "We are going to catch the man who's behind Jenny's abduction."

"Yeah, but are you and that team of yours going to do it before or *after* I have to clean up more bodies?"

THE SNOW WAS RED.

Thomas stopped instantly when he caught sight of

the red drops. He lifted his hand, an old habit, as he signaled to Aaron.

Aaron bent low and gazed at the blood and at the faint trail that led across the street. The trail ended right at the door of an old pharmacy.

The lights were out in that pharmacy. Odd, since power had come back to the city an hour ago.

"Cover me," Thomas said flatly. He advanced toward the building, aware of Aaron following him. Thomas had his gun out, and he was more than ready to use it on the man who'd nearly killed Noelle the night before.

There were more droplets at the door, as if the guy had paused for a moment before he'd gone inside. Thomas reached for the knob. It twisted easily in his grasp. He shoved open that door and rushed inside.

Aaron was right on his heels.

Drops of crimson dotted the aisle. He followed them, then saw the heavy, blood-soaked cloths on the counter.

A quick search showed no one was in the pharmacy. The back door was unlocked. Just like the front.

"Looks like the guy got away again." Aaron shook his head. "But we had to be close."

Thomas studied the discarded bandages—and the bullet that had been left behind.

"He dug it out, huh?" Aaron whistled. "I had to do that once. Thought I'd pass out before the bullet came out of my stomach."

Thomas's gaze swept the scene once more. "He didn't dig it out himself." That just made things so much worse.

"What? How do you know?"

Thomas grabbed the purse that had fallen on the ground near the red-stained counter.

"Hell," Aaron muttered.

Thomas pulled out the ID inside. Sarah Finway. A Sarah Finway who was most definitely *not* there any longer.

"He's got another victim," Thomas said.

NOELLE STARED AT the photos on the wall. All of those girls. Scared. Blindfolded. So alone.

But you weren't really alone, were you? Because their abductor had been the one to take the photos.

"I've got more men coming in," Mercer said.

She nearly jumped at his voice. She'd been so intent on those girls Noelle hadn't even heard him enter the little office.

"They'll be here in two hours."

Right. When Mercer said jump, people flew.

"They'll search every inch of the senator's house, and if there's more evidence to find," he nodded and said, "we'll have it."

Her phone rang. Noelle glanced down, saw it was Thomas, and she answered immediately. "Did you find him?"

"He's got another victim."

Her fingers tightened around the instrument.

"A woman who worked at the pharmacy, Sarah Finway. The guy's blood is here, but he's not and neither is she."

Her heart thundered in her chest. "We can use his blood for DNA. If he's in the system, we'll have an ID."

"But we won't have *her*." Frustration boiled in Thomas's voice. "The guy knows this area. He'll stash her, and then he'll kill her, all while we're running down DNA."

Thomas wasn't used to this part of the business. EOD agents were men and women of action. They didn't run DNA checks. They didn't stalk after criminals. They went in. They attacked. They completed their missions.

And Thomas was right. By the time they got a DNA hit on the perp, Sarah Finway could be dead.

"I'm going to keep searching with Aaron. If we find anything, I'll call you."

"He knows this area. Be careful because you don't want to walk into another of his traps."

"I want to find the guy," Thomas fired back. "If he wants to hunt someone, if that's the way he likes to play, then he needs to come hunt me, not some innocent civilian."

When the call ended, Noelle kept holding the phone and staring at those pictures. "I need to talk with the sheriff," she said, not looking over her shoulder at Mercer. "And then I want to head back to the senator's place and talk with Paula Quill." Because Paula had been the senator's confidant. If there had been someone in and out of the senator's life for the past fifteen years, then Paula should know.

Mercer's footsteps padded out of the office. She knew he'd pull the sheriff in, one way or another. No one said no to Mercer. At least, not for long.

She put the phone down on the desk and let her gaze trek from image to image. They'd gotten names for the girls. Dates of their disappearances. She'd put the images in order based on those dates, and her focus shifted to the first girl who'd vanished.

Emma Jane Rogers. Age sixteen. She'd lived in Charleston.

"The first kill is the one that matters most," Noelle

whispered as she leaned toward the image. There had to be something in the picture that could help her. Why had the killer begun with Emma Jane? Why her?

Had all of the others girls been taken because they *looked* like Emma?

Her finger pressed against the photograph. Emma Jane was wearing a necklace. They'd blown up the photo, and Noelle could see it appeared to be half of a heart. The kind of necklace young couples often wore. The girl would have one part, and the boy would have the other.

There were two images of Emma Jane. In one of the images, that necklace around her neck was clear.

In the other image, it was gone. Blood dripped over her neck, as if she'd been sliced with a knife.

As if someone had sliced the necklace off her?

Noelle quickly checked the other snapshots. None of the others were wearing any sort of jewelry. Their necks also didn't show any signs of having been cut. There were no injuries on those girls in the other photos at all.

These are the before shots.

Were there after shots someplace? Images that showed what had happened to the girls after the hunt was complete?

Noelle knew that there must be.

"Here's the sheriff."

Noelle turned at Mercer's flat words. He had a tight grip on the sheriff's arm. Hodges was glaring at him.

"I was in the middle of a briefing with my men!" Hodges sputtered. "You don't just drag a sheriff away—"

Mercer laughed. "I drag anyone away." He pointed

toward Noelle. "Now, answer her questions because if anyone can figure out this guy, it's her."

She already had puzzle pieces flying through her mind. "He's a local, Sheriff. Someone who knows this area extremely well. He'd keep to himself. He's a male… probably in his late thirties, close to Senator Duncan's age. He's ex-navy, so he might be sporting some tattoos that he got during the service."

Hodges shook his head. "This is a town of barely a thousand people. I know everyone."

"And that's why you know *him*. He might come in and out, drifting in when Senator Duncan is in the area. He won't stay all year, but he *knows this place*. He'd be the best hunter in the area. He'd have to be. So think of someone who's gone after big game. Someone who—"

The sheriff stiffened.

"You know who it is," Mercer growled.

"There *is* a guy like that. His name's Patrick, Patrick Porter." Hodges shook his head. "He's the best hunter in the area. He comes through the area because he likes to go after bears." His gaze darted to the photos on the wall. "Lot of hunters come through here because they want to go after the big game, but Porter… He comes back each year. And he always gets his prey."

Her heart raced in her chest. "Is he here now?"

"I don't know." Hodges ran a hand over his face. "But he usually stays at the old Burrows cabin. It's about four miles north of the senator's place."

A perfect fit.

"Get your men out there," Mercer snapped. "Now."

Noelle yanked out her phone as the sheriff rushed away. She had Thomas back on the line seconds later. "We have a target. His name's Patrick Porter, and the sheriff said he's at a cabin about four miles north of the senator's home." That would sure put the guy in close enough proximity to kill. "The sheriff is heading there now."

"You know he probably has a few cabins out there, Noelle," Thomas said. "Places to hide his victims."

Yes, she knew that. "But he might have left us something we could use at the Burrows place." Or maybe the guy wasn't thinking clearly because of his injuries. She'd seen plenty of perps slip up over the years. "Get back to the station, and we'll go after him with the sheriff." Because she planned to be on the scene.

She pushed the phone into her pocket and spun back around. She marched for the door, but Mercer put up his hand, blocking her. "You need to be careful."

His words had her pausing. Since when did the EOD director worry his agents couldn't do their jobs?

Her eyes narrowed on him. "I might not have military experience, but I survived just fine as an FBI agent. If you don't think I can do this, then you never should've brought me on the team."

"I know you can do any job." He shut the door, sealing them inside.

Noelle gave a frantic shake of her head. "Thomas is on his way. I need to get directions for that cabin. I should—"

"Thomas briefed me on what happened last night."

For an instant, her cheeks burned. No *way* was he talking about what she suspected. There were sure some things the boss didn't need to know.

"You nearly died. If you'd been alone, do you think you would have made it out of that water?"

"You might be surprised," Noelle said as she lifted

her chin. "I'm a lot stronger than you give me credit for being."

He laughed at that, the sound low and rough. "Oh, I know you're plenty strong. All of my agents are. I didn't keep the truth from you because I thought you were weak." His head tilted. "Is that what you think?"

She didn't know what to think.

"You changed Thomas on that mission. He was still young, a new agent, but he was focused totally on the job. Until you. He tried to go back for you—twice— even though we told him that you'd been taken in by the local cops."

Her lashes lowered to shield her eyes.

"He was undercover. He saved your life, but by staying on his mission, he saved the lives of hundreds of other people, too."

Noelle swallowed.

"Don't blame him. If you're furious, and you've got a right to be, blame me."

Her lashes lifted. "I do."

He nodded. "Fair enough."

She didn't see where a whole lot was fair right then. "I don't have time for this now. Sarah Finway is out there, and she needs help." She pushed past him and grabbed for the doorknob.

"That's why you're an EOD agent. Because you put others first. It's what our job is about. We have to give up the things that we want most, in order to get the mission accomplished."

There was a note of pain in his voice, which pulled at her. She glanced back.

"You didn't have the clearance to know about Thomas's actions. Not until you joined the EOD."

"That's why you pushed for me to join the division."

He inclined his head.

"And this particular mission? Did you know about the link to my past?" The guy seemed to know *everything,* while Noelle felt as if she were floundering around in the dark.

"I knew that Senator Duncan was connected to the destruction of the EOD office. I'd been recently looking into his past, and I was noticing connections that alarmed me. Enemies who were vanishing... I was putting all of those dots together and getting a picture of a man who was a national-security threat." His eyes narrowed. "I sent you on this mission because I knew you could figure him out. I paired you with Thomas...because I knew it was time for you to understand the past."

"You should have *told* me."

His eyes glinted. "Every day I make decisions that impact thousands of lives. The jobs my agents do... They're dangerous. They're deadly. They are jobs most people will never even know about." He heaved out a hard breath. "I have to make judgments. I do the best that I can." He backed away from her. "You're alive, Agent Evers, because one of my operatives saved your life. Now it's your job to save the lives of others."

Mercer had never seemed quite so human to her as he did in that moment. There was pain in his voice, and she'd caught the faint tremble of his hands.

"This case is personal to you," Noelle noted quietly.

"Senator Duncan almost took out dozens of agents who were in the EOD building. Damn straight it's personal." He pinned her with his stare. "So we're closing this case. We're bringing down this Patrick Porter. We're going to learn everything about him and his

connection to Duncan. No one messes with my agents."
His eyes sharpened on her. "Not any of them."

"LET ME GO," Sarah whispered as she sat in the old,
wooden chair, her hands bound behind her back.
"Please…I won't tell anyone about you."

They always said the same thing. Always made
promises they couldn't keep.

It was the lies that got to him.

She'd lied to him. She'd started this whole chain of
events.

"I helped you," Sarah said, the tears making her
voice husky. Tears were so useless. He wished she'd stop
shedding them. "I dug out the bullet. I sewed you up."

A twisted, tangled mess of stitches.

"Please," she said again. "Just let me go…I am *begging* you…"

Well, if she was going to beg…

"You aren't my usual type." These days, he went
for a much bigger challenge. He used his knife to cut
through her ropes. She rose to her feet, stumbling a bit.
He motioned to the door. "Go."

She didn't move.

He rolled his eyes, then roared, *"Go!"*

She rushed for the door.

His hold tightened on the knife. "I'll give you a five-
minute head start. Since you did help me…it's the least
you deserve."

Her head jerked back toward him. Her eyes widened in horror.

He smiled. "You're wasting precious time."

Because after the hell he'd been through, he needed

a hunt. Sarah wasn't his first choice, but she'd do. And she'd send a message to Noelle Evers.

I can kill whenever I want. He was the perfect killing machine. No one could stop him. No one would stop him.

Sarah screamed as she ran into the wilderness. She wouldn't be screaming for long. He'd make sure of that.

He looked down at the blade. And he remembered another girl. A knife had sliced against her throat. She'd begged, too. Asked him to believe her. To trust her.

He'd also given her a chance to survive. But she hadn't run fast enough. They never did.

He waited, counting, then... "Time's up."

The thrill of the hunt heated his veins.

Chapter Nine

The sheriff's men had fanned out to search the area around the Burrows cabin. Thomas watched as those men made heavy paths in the snow. Aaron was behind him, and Noelle was at his side.

"It's too easy."

Noelle glanced over at his words. "You know he's not here," Thomas told her flatly. "He took her someplace else."

She started heading toward the cabin just as the sheriff appeared in the doorway. "Place is clear!" Hodges called out. "It looks like no one's been here all season!"

"Appearances can be deceiving," Thomas heard Noelle murmur as she kept walking toward the cabin.

"I'm betting the guy has half a dozen places he uses for hiding up here," Aaron said. His gun was holstered at his hip. "If the sheriff is right about him coming up for big game, then he'd have to know the area."

That was their problem. The man knew the area better than they did, and that was why he kept getting away. "He's not going to stay up here forever," Thomas said. "If we don't find him soon, he could slip away."

And take the answers they needed with him.

Noelle disappeared into the cabin.

The sheriff joined his men on the search.

Thomas had just taken a step forward when he heard the cry. Sharp and high. At first, he thought it was an animal. One that was hurt.

But then the cry came again, echoing up to him.

A scream.

Thomas whirled around. Aaron had already taken off, running toward the scream. Other deputies were scrambling to follow. "Be careful!" Thomas bellowed. "He likes his traps!" Thomas didn't doubt for an instant the man would use human bait to pull them into another one of his hunts.

He glanced back toward the cabin. Noelle had just run outside. Her eyes were wide and desperate as she hurried after him.

They both knew that scream belonged to Sarah Finway, and the fact they didn't hear any other cries...

We're coming, Sarah. Just hold on.

HE LIKED THE way the snow turned red. That was always a bonus he got when he hunted in the colder climates. Sarah had gotten farther than he'd expected. Probably because she knew the area nearly as well as he did. She'd used some shortcuts that he just had to admire.

A gurgle came from her lips.

He wiped the knife on his coat. The blood smeared. "It's okay. You just stay here and try to breathe, nice and slow. That will help you survive longer." He needed her to live for a few more minutes. He put the knife in its sheath. Then he drew out his gun.

Her eyes widened. Another frantic gurgle broke from her lips.

"Shh..." He aimed the gun at her head.

Tears leaked from her eyes.

"This isn't for you. Don't worry." He'd heard the sound of those engines. They'd been coming closer as he hunted. If he hadn't taken Sarah down when he had, she just might have made it to safety.

Yes, she'd been much better prey than he'd expected. "This gun is for the ones coming to save you." Because he wasn't going out of this battle quietly. It was time everyone knew about him.

No more shadows. No more secrets.

He already knew Jenny had spent the night at the sheriff's station. The storm had kept her there, so she would've had the whole night to talk about him—to tell the authorities what he looked like.

So he figured he had two choices—keep running... or go out fighting. Go out by showing them all *exactly* who they were dealing with in this battle.

For years, no one had known of his existence.

Soon, no one would ever forget him.

He just wished he had his rifle with him, but the handgun would have to do. He slipped back into the shadows cast by the snow-covered trees, and he waited.

"SARAH FINWAY!" SHERIFF HODGES called as he raced to keep up with the pack searching for Sarah. *"Sarah!"*

Thomas saw the sheriff had his gun out, and Hodges was sweeping to the left and right. They'd tracked that dying scream out here, but there was no sound now.

Other than the frantic cries from the sheriff and his deputies.

Aaron's shoulder brushed against Thomas's. "I don't like this." His voice was low.

Thomas didn't like this situation, either. They were

surrounded by trees, so there were dozens of places for a perp to hide. The sheriff and his men were making enough noise to wake the dead.

"Footprints!" One of the deputies called out. "Here! I've got her!"

He had her *only* if those were Sarah's footprints.

Thomas's instincts screamed at him. Noelle started to follow the others. He grabbed her arm and barked out, "Stop!"

But it was too late. He heard the sharp thunder of gunfire. One blast. Two. Three.

Yells and screams filled the air.

"Damn it," Aaron growled. "It's like sheep to the slaughter!"

Thomas took cover, with Noelle right at his side. The deputies were firing back, but they seemed to be shooting wildly in all directions. They needed to calm down and focus.

"Where is he?" Thomas heard one deputy demand, voice breaking.

They didn't see their attacker, but they were still shooting?

"Stop firing!" Thomas shouted. He couldn't figure out anything with the chaos around him.

After a few moments, they did stop.

"The sheriff," Noelle whispered, horror in her voice.

Thomas peered around his cover. He cursed when he saw the sight before him. The sheriff was on the ground, a bloom of red on his body. And the woman—had to be Sarah Finway—she was just a few feet away from him.

It looked like the sheriff's chest was still rising and falling. Thomas wasn't so sure about Sarah.

Noelle lunged forward.

Thomas yanked her right back.

"Let me go!" she fiercely fought his grip, but her voice was whisper soft. "I have to help them!"

"Don't you see what he's doing? The sick freak is using them as bait. He'll shoot whoever goes out there next."

"They need *help*." She shook her head. "I can't stay here and watch them die! I won't!"

Thomas tightened his hold on her. He studied the sheriff's body, trying to figure out the angle of entry. The trajectory of the bullet. The wind.

His gaze darted to the right. To the trees located there. Higher land. Best elevation. Perfect hunting zone.

He motioned toward Aaron, indicating the target zone. Aaron slipped back and, keeping to cover, began to advance to the right.

"Thomas...he's *dying*."

Yes, the sheriff was, but Thomas couldn't let her die, too. None of the deputies were going to help because they were too worried about getting shot.

"Give me cover," Thomas growled to her. "To the northwest."

"What? Thomas, no, I meant for me—"

He was already gone. He rushed out, kept his body low and dove toward the sheriff.

Gunfire blasted right near his face, missing him by about two inches.

"No!" He heard Noelle scream. Then she was firing back, giving Thomas the cover he so desperately needed. He grabbed the sheriff's arm and pulled the guy toward the trees. The bullet had sunk into the sheriff's stomach, and he was bleeding heavily.

"Get him…" the sheriff wheezed. "Shoot the… S…O…B."

The woman was still lying out there. Sarah Finway. Thomas knew more bullets would fly his way, but he braced himself, lifted his gun and went back toward her.

Gunfire erupted. There was a rough, choked cry.

Thomas used his body to try and cover the woman, but Sarah—

She's gone.

He couldn't find her pulse.

"I've got him!"

Thomas's head whipped up at Aaron's yell. And, sure enough, Aaron was standing with a bloody man in front of him. Aaron's gun was at the guy's temple.

Thomas's gaze trekked over the man's face as stunned recognition flooded through him. *I know him.*

Noelle raced from her cover then. She didn't go toward the killer. She ran for the sheriff. She fell to her knees and tried to apply pressure to the wound.

The man Aaron held began to laugh. "You think this is the end?" Blood dripped down the side of his face. "You have no clue!"

Aaron's mouth twisted into a snarl, and he slammed his gun into the side of the man's head.

The killer fell, and that sick laughter stopped.

Thomas's attention jumped to Aaron.

The ex-SEAL shrugged. "What? I thought he was about to attack. Sounded like a threat to me." His shoulders straightened. "Besides, Mercer wants this man brought in…by any means necessary."

Mercer's favorite order. *Any means necessary.*

"We're losing him!" Noelle yelled.

Thomas glanced back. Two of the deputies were

around Sarah. The others were standing nervously beside Noelle and peering worriedly at the sheriff.

"We have to carry him out of here!" She whirled toward Thomas. "Help me!"

Always. He rushed back to her side, but when he saw the sickly pallor in the sheriff's face, Thomas knew the odds weren't good for the man.

The memory of the perp's laughter drifted through Thomas's mind.

You think this is the end? You have no clue.

Hell. What would happen next?

SHE HAD BLOOD on her hands. Noelle stared down at her palms. Mercer had used his chopper to airlift the sheriff to the nearest hospital. She could still hear the *whoop-whoop* of the chopper's blades.

Sheriff Hodges had been alive when they lifted off. Gut wounds could be so tricky. Would he be able to hang on and live long enough to reach the hospital?

Noelle wasn't so sure.

"We did it," Aaron said as he watched the aircraft rise. "Chalk up another capture for the EOD."

She didn't share his enthusiasm. "We lost Sarah Finway." She turned toward him. "And Sheriff Hodges will be very, very lucky if he survives."

"But Patrick Porter won't *ever* hurt anyone else again." Aaron nodded grimly. "We can be sure of that."

She needed to wash her hands. She needed to change clothes. She also needed to interrogate Patrick Porter. *I'm sure that's not his real name.* Patrick would be full of secrets.

Mercer and Thomas had secured the man in the sheriff's station. She knew Mercer would be transporting the guy out of the area at the first opportunity.

She wanted her answers before that transfer. She wanted to know everything.

Noelle marched toward the station. Aaron followed closely, but he didn't speak. There were deputies inside the station, just two men. The others had gone with the sheriff. Mercer's orders. She knew he just didn't want a big audience around for what would come.

Once inside the station, she headed toward the small bathroom first. Noelle washed the blood away and tried not to remember the desperate look in the sheriff's eyes.

Failed.

Noelle knew that desperation would haunt her for the rest of her days.

A knock sounded on the bathroom door. "Noelle?" Thomas's voice called. "I've got fresh clothes for you."

She opened the door.

"Courtesy of Mercer," he said as he lifted a bag toward her.

Right. Mercer the Magic Man. He could do anything. She took the clothes from him and started to shut the door. Thomas's hand flew out, stopping her.

"He's going to try messing with your head." The words were a grim warning.

"I already know that." She was used to killers and their mind games. Finally, an area that was her specialty.

"Don't believe him. Don't believe the lies he's going to tell. Don't trust him."

Her head tilted. There was an odd note in his voice that made her nervous. "I know killers, Thomas. So that means I'm used to their lies." Some killers could lie so perfectly. They'd fool lie detectors. Fool law enforcement. Deceive everyone.

But she was ready for what was coming. Noelle didn't need Thomas to warn her.

"Mercer says...he wants to start the interrogation in five minutes. He's hoping to transfer the guy out by dawn."

That didn't give them a lot of time. "Mercer wants containment."

Thomas inclined his head. "He's already working on the cover-up."

Right. Because the world couldn't find out that a trusted senator had been bent on destruction—or that he'd been working side by side with a suspected serial killer.

Part of the EOD's job was to sweep away the dirty, dangerous secrets like this one.

Thomas's hand dropped. "I've always wanted to protect you."

She blinked at him.

"Remember that."

Then he was gone.

Her hands tightened around the bag. She couldn't shake the feeling there was more going on with this case. More... Something that had rattled even the normally controlled Thomas "Dragon" Anthony.

She changed quickly and made sure all of the blood was gone from her hands. Her fingers were trembling slightly, and she clenched them into fists as she drew in a steadying breath. The case wasn't over. Not yet. It wouldn't be over until they uncovered all of the secrets Patrick Porter possessed.

After another bracing breath, Noelle opened the

door. She expected the narrow hallway to be empty. It wasn't. Thomas waited for her, with his back propped against the nearby wall.

"Thomas?"

He stared down at his hands. "I've done things in my life that I regret."

"We all do things that we regret."

His head lifted, and he gave her a sad smile. "I was trained to kill. Designed to be a perfect weapon. Trust me. There are things in my past better left forgotten."

Noelle cleared her throat. "Forgetting isn't all it's cracked up to be."

He straightened from the wall and reached for her. "Are you sure about that?"

His hold was strong, hard, and a bright intensity burned in his gaze.

"More of your past is going to come out, baby, and I need you to trust me."

Oh, but that did not sound good. "I do trust you."

"Enough to forgive what I've done?"

"Thomas..." He was scaring her.

His hand rose and curled under her chin. "I've watched you for so long that you seem like you're just a natural part of my life." His gaze searched hers. "But there are still secrets out there, and I don't want them to hurt you. I don't want *anything* to hurt you."

She felt as if she were missing something.

"I'll do what I must, in order to protect you."

She wasn't asking for protection.

His head bent, and Thomas pressed a kiss to her lips. He seemed to savor her. Almost helplessly, Noelle leaned toward him. After the madness of the past few days, Thomas was the only certain thing in her life.

When they touched, she needed.

When they kissed, she wanted.

He'd gotten past her guard when no other man had. Because of their shared past? Perhaps. But maybe it was just because he was…Thomas.

He let the kiss linger. She never wanted it to end. She wished they didn't have a killer waiting. She wanted to be with Thomas. To push away the fear and worry and simply *live*.

But he stepped back. "My first loyalty is to you. Remember that."

She could still taste him.

"From here on out, it always will be." He turned away from her and marched down the hall.

Noelle realized her fingers were trembling again, and a chill had slid down her spine. It was strange. Thomas's words had sounded like a warning.

But what else did he need to protect her from?

THE LITTLE SHERIFF'S station in Camden didn't have any interrogation rooms, but the place did sport two cells. And Patrick Porter was currently pacing the floor in one of those narrow cells.

When Noelle started walking toward him, he immediately stopped that pacing. His head snapped up, and he smiled at her.

She heard Thomas growl behind her.

She and Thomas were the only two conducting this interrogation. Mercer had gotten Aaron to install a video camera, and the feed was going back to him. Mercer wouldn't be making a personal appearance for this questioning period, though, not unless he absolutely needed to do so. Noelle knew when it came to EOD prisoners, Mercer had a policy of standing back.

Because he'd been burned too many times before.

"Did the sheriff die?" Patrick didn't sound particularly concerned about that possibility. Actually, he was more gleeful.

Noelle shook her head. "He's stable." At least, that was what she'd been told moments before. "He's on his way to the hospital. Your bullet missed its mark."

The glee faded as the faint lines near his eyes tightened. "I don't miss my mark."

"You did this time." She nodded toward him. Blood had broken through on his shirt. "Maybe the wound I gave you made you weak."

He laughed. "Nothing makes me weak." His gaze slid to Thomas. "Bet you can't say the same."

Thomas didn't say anything.

"We want to know where the bodies are," Noelle said softly. "That's the only reason we're talking to you right now. We know about all of the victims, starting with Emma Jane in Charleston."

"You have no clue about my victims." Disgust laced the words.

"We found your photographs. We saw the girls—"

Patrick laughed. She truly hated the sound of his grating laughter. His eyes were still on Thomas, but they were starting to fill with what looked like…recognition? "I'll be damned," the killer said as he advanced toward the bars. "It really is you…and she has no clue, does she? *Dragon*."

Thomas still wasn't speaking.

Patrick's fingers curled around the bars. "Your hair's shorter. Your face is harder. Looks like you broke your nose a few times over the years." He laughed. "They've got *you* in here? Don't they know what you've done?" His gaze came back to Noelle. "What he did to *you*."

When they'd been in that hallway, Thomas sure hadn't mentioned he knew the suspect. But then, he'd been busy kissing her. Noelle's heart was galloping in her chest, but she didn't let her expression alter. *Dragon.* The guy could've learned of Thomas's moniker in a dozen ways. He could just be playing with them now.

"I want to know where those girls are," Noelle said again.

Patrick's hold tightened around the bars. "Get the Dragon here to tell you."

A knot of tension formed at the nape of her neck. *Push him. Don't let him get to you.* "I know you were involved with Emma Jane. She was your girl, right? And she tried to leave you."

Now, *that* got his gaze flying toward her. "You don't know a damn thing about Emma!"

"I know that you two had matching necklaces. Hearts. You gave one half of the heart to her, and you wore its mate. When she betrayed you, well, that was when you snapped. You kidnapped her. You tortured her. Then you killed her."

Silence.

Patrick rested his forehead against the bars. "Every killer starts somewhere, right, Dragon?"

She didn't like the way the guy kept baiting Thomas. Worse, she didn't like the ice that kept growing in her gut. Ice that told Noelle she was missing something. Something very, very important.

"Are all the girls dead?" She stepped a bit closer to the cell. Not too close, though, because she didn't want him to be able to grab her. "Senator Duncan had pictures of them in his shed, but they were *your* pictures, weren't they? Pictures you'd taken to remind you of the kills."

"Duncan is dead," Patrick murmured. "And he never even saw the attack coming."

Beside her, Thomas shifted his stance, a ripple of movement that seemed menacing.

"Duncan thought he could control me, but I got tired of playing by his rules." Patrick's stare, a bright, glinting blue, raked over her. Dark stubble lined his jaw and his skin was a deep gold. "Especially when he sent me after you."

She stared back into those blue eyes and knew she was staring straight at evil.

"I remember you. I never forgot you." His head lifted from the bars as he laughed. "Dragon, there, he killed the wrong man. Did you know that? Justin Hardin wasn't the one hunting you. He was just the one to keep you in that cabin. You fought him, though, and you got away. You ran. Justin wasn't good at hunting, not like me. He called me, said he was going after you. Promised he'd have you waiting for me…"

"I wasn't waiting," Noelle snapped out as more pieces from her past slid into place.

"Because the Dragon killed Justin." He shook his head and focused on Thomas once more. "Did you do it to protect the girl…or because you didn't want Justin telling what he knew about you?"

Noelle rocked forward onto the balls of her feet. "How about you tell me how those pictures wound up with Senator Duncan, or maybe…maybe you want me to guess on that? Because I've got some ideas…"

Patrick shrugged. "Then let's hear them."

"You were stationed together with Duncan in the navy." They had EOD agents pulling up the senator's enlistment records. "I bet you kept those photos close, because you'd need them close." Looking at them would've been a compulsion. "But if you were bunking with Duncan, he would've had access to your area. I think he found them, only, instead of turning you in, he kept the photos so that he could blackmail you."

Patrick gave a low whistle. "You're only half right."

She didn't like the coldness in his stare. The man was in total control. She needed to rattle his cage and make that control shatter. "You were going after girls then…" Time to press for more. Time to *shatter*. "But after your enlistment, after you started fighting and killing in battle, did you think they were too easy? You're the big game hunter. And they weren't big enough game."

His gaze drifted dismissively over her. "No, you weren't."

Thomas stepped forward.

"The girls—you—were expendable. Weak. They all cried and begged too quickly. Some didn't even have the sense to run. I mean, hell, everyone is supposed to have a survival instinct, right? Isn't that what the experts say?"

She didn't respond.

"But they didn't. They died easily."

She studied him carefully. There was no emotion in his voice. No remorse. No glee. He was simply stating a fact. She'd wondered before if he were a psychopath. She wasn't wondering any longer. "Why didn't Duncan turn you in?"

But she knew…

Noelle didn't like the sardonic little smile curling Patrick's thin lips. "Most people would've turned me in. I mean, that would be the *right* thing to do, huh? That's what you think, don't you, *Noelle?*"

From the corner of her eye, Noelle saw Thomas clench his hands into fists.

"But Duncan wasn't like most folks. He was like me."

One psychopath, finding another.

"He kept the photos and told me he'd turn me in unless I did a job for him. Someone had made him very, very angry, you see, and he wanted that person eliminated."

"Then he should've done the job himself." This tight snarl came from Thomas.

Patrick shrugged. "Not his way. He gave me the prey, and he told me to hunt. I did."

Mercer's suspicions had been right. This guy had become Lawrence's attack dog.

"I found out I liked my new prey. They fought harder. They made me have to work for the rush."

The rush he'd first got when he killed Emma Jane. "Emma Jane was a crime of passion." Strange, when he was so passionless now. "Emma Jane was probably the only person you ever really connected with, and she betrayed you."

He lunged forward and grabbed the bars. "I was eighteen! I'd just enlisted. She couldn't even wait two months for me to come home. *Two. Months.*"

The pieces were all in place for Noelle now. "You killed the other girls because they looked like her." *I looked like her.* "You thought we'd give you the same rush, but we weren't Emma Jane, so you needed to try something else." Duncan had entered the man's life at the perfect time.

Or the worst.

"I was good at killing." Patrick's words were hard, biting and eerily reminiscent of what Thomas had once told her. Almost helplessly, Noelle's gaze slid to Thomas. He was glaring at the man behind bars. "Duncan made it worth my while. Duncan paid me for my work, and I had one hell of a time." His voice was calmer now. "After all, I'd lost my pickup man." His blue stare locked on Thomas. "Courtesy of the Dragon. And, damn, but Justin was good at picking the girls. The kid always knew exactly what I liked back then."

"We're going to need a list of all your victims." Families deserved to get closure. This man before her, he could've killed so many people.

But Patrick just smirked. "Like I'm the only killer in the room." He nodded toward Thomas. "Why don't we do some sharing? Get him to tell you all about his kills, and then I'll tell you mine."

She kept her shoulders locked. "I don't need to know about what Thomas did in battle—"

Patrick's laughter cut her off. "I'm not talking about battle. I'm talking about what he did…for fun. Like when he was down in Alabama. How many did you kill then? Not counting my pickup man, of course. Because he was probably just a bonus for you."

Thomas was as still as stone.

"Not gonna tell her? How about I start… It was a whole gang that went down, after you turned on them…."

His mission. Patrick couldn't learn about the EOD or about what covers Thomas had used over the years.

"In a few hours, you're going to be transferred to a maximum-security holding facility. You won't get out again, and you'll be very, very lucky to see the light of day ever again."

But Patrick was still focused on Thomas. "When I first saw you with her, I didn't get a good look at you. You're good at changing your appearance, though, aren't you? Blending in. Showing people what you want 'em to see."

"If you cooperate, we can help you." Noelle doubted that there was actually much help Mercer would allow. Maybe a slightly bigger cell? No, probably not. This guy would be locked away forever. But what he didn't know...

"You're missing what's right in front of you!" Patrick exploded.

Noelle didn't flinch.

"He's a killer! Worse than me! You think he's some kind of hero? Don't you know what he did to you when he had you in that cabin?"

Goose bumps rose on Noelle's flesh.

This was the monster who'd tried to destroy her life.

"He's just like me," Patrick told her, and he was so smug. "Only...I bet he's killed *more* men than I have. Think about that the next time you decide to have sex with him in front of a fire."

He *had* been there.

Revulsion twisted her stomach.

Patrick was laughing again and— Thomas moved in a flash. His hand flew through the gap between the bars. He grabbed Patrick around the neck and yanked the man forward. Patrick's head slammed into the bars. Bones crunched, and Noelle was pretty sure the perp's nose broke. Judging by that spray of blood… Oh, yes, it was definitely a break.

Patrick started howling and swearing.

Thomas withdrew his hand, stepped back. His eyes were on Noelle. "He won't tell us anything. Leave him here. The boss can work him over later."

She was sure the interrogations the EOD conducted were probably very different from standard FBI techniques.

Her gaze slid to the cell. Patrick Porter could answer all of the questions that she had about her past. He could tell Noelle why he'd picked her. Why he'd picked them all.

But…

It won't happen.

The man enjoyed his power too much, and if they were going to break through to him, they had to take the power away. The best way to do that was to act as if he didn't matter.

"We're done." Noelle turned away from the killer. Talking to him made her skin crawl. She was sick of maintaining an icy image when, in truth, just being close to Patrick made her feel as if she were splintering apart on the inside.

"Done?" Patrick snarled. "We're done when I say! Now get me a doctor! He broke my damn nose!"

"Your nose is the least of your worries." Thomas sounded totally unconcerned. "Just wait until you get in your new home. That's when the real fun will begin."

Noelle grabbed for the door.

"Wait!" Patrick yelled after her. "You can't just leave me in here! I thought you wanted to deal! You wanted—"

Noelle glanced back at him. *Play the part. Play the part.* "Right now, I just want you to rot. You see, I think I was wrong. You don't have any information that I need to hear."

His face went slack with shock. Ah, nice. A new emotion.

She turned away from him and marched out of the holding area and didn't start shaking, not until the door closed behind Thomas. Not until they were away from the monster who'd changed her life.

Then her body trembled so hard she thought she'd collapse.

"Are you okay, Agent Evers?"

Her head jerked up at Aaron's question. He was a few feet away, frowning at her.

She didn't want him to see her break. All of the other EOD agents seemed to be so contained and strong. She couldn't crumble in front of him.

Thomas stepped in front of her, blocking Aaron's view. "She's fine. We're both exhausted, and we're getting some sleep before the plane takes off in a few hours." He jerked his thumb toward the closed door. "Keep a close eye on him. I don't trust the guy not to make some kind of last-ditch escape effort. Guys like him would rather go out with a bang than be chained up."

Then Thomas looked back at her. "She's fine," he said again, as he stared into Noelle's eyes.

Then he was pulling her down the narrow hallway. He shoved open the door to the office they'd commandeered before, and he hurried her inside.

When the door shut behind them, when they were finally alone, Noelle let the tears come.

Chapter Ten

It was a good thing bars had separated him from Patrick Porter because Thomas had sure wanted to do more than just break the man's nose.

That SOB had planned Noelle's murder. He'd been the one who intended to hunt her like an animal, then leave her remains in the woods of Alabama.

He'd been laughing, so smug and confidant.

And Noelle was crying.

Thomas stared at her a moment, and he felt absolutely lost. Her tears… They *hurt* him and seemed to strike out right at his heart. And she was hunching her shoulders and trying to cover her face so he wouldn't see. As if she needed to hide from him.

There was no part of Noelle that ever needed to be hidden from his sight. To him, every single inch of her was perfect.

He caught her hands, pulled them down and held them tightly in his. Then Thomas bent toward her and pressed a kiss to her cheek. He could taste the salt of her tears. He *hated* her pain.

I want that man in the ground.

"What can I do?" Thomas knew the words sounded

like little more than a growl, but his rage was too strong for anything else. "Tell me how to help you."

She shook her head and tried to pull away.

He just held her tighter, and he kissed her other cheek. Crying had always made him uncomfortable. Truth be told, emotion made him uncomfortable, but with Noelle, everything was different. Her hurt seemed to be his. He felt it slicing through him like a knife.

"I've seen men like him before." Her voice was soft. Husky with pain. "I've brought them in for the FBI. I've seen the broken victims left in their wake." She swallowed and whispered, "Now I'm one of them."

"No." A sharp comeback. "There is nothing broken about you. You're the strongest woman I've ever met."

She blinked up at him. Her eyes were so gorgeous, even glistening with tears. Hell, maybe they were more gorgeous that way. Did she have any clue she was bringing him to his knees? "You got away," he told her, fighting to keep his hold light on her. "You got away, and *you* were the one who finally brought down this jerk."

"The EOD—"

"We couldn't have done this without you, and you know it. It's not about being a victim. It's about being a survivor. Survivors are the brave ones. The powerful ones. That's you, baby. Through and through." He had to kiss her, so he did. Thomas lowered his head, and his lips brushed against hers. He'd meant for the kiss to be easy. Light.

At first, it was.

Her hands rose and curled around his shoulders. She pulled him closer and kissed him harder.

And the desire he felt for her raged hotter.

In an instant, the kiss wasn't about comforting her.

It wasn't about taking away her pain. It was just about them. The consuming need they felt for each other.

He locked her against his body, holding her flush against him. She had to feel his desire, because there was certainly no hiding it.

Then she—

Pulled away.

Thomas sucked in a hard breath and clenched his hands into fists. Noelle didn't look at him as she backed off, putting a careful distance between them.

"Noelle…"

She jerked at his voice.

He frowned at her, then he remembered all of the things Patrick had said. Things he'd feared the man would say. Because he and Patrick Porter… Their paths had crossed before. Only back then, the man had been using an alias.

So had Thomas.

"It's not true," he told her. He needed her to look at him. Hell, he needed her back in his arms.

"I don't want to be here," Noelle said, her voice still whisper soft. She stalked for the door. Before she could leave, his hand flew out, and he shoved the wooden door closed.

"It's not true," he said once more.

Her head turned. Her eyes met his. She wasn't crying anymore, but there were secrets in her gaze. Thomas was pretty sure he'd sell his soul if it meant he could learn what they were.

"I didn't do anything to hurt you all those years ago, I swear." He had to make her believe that. It was so important she trust him.

Noelle blinked. Then she smiled. A slow smile that

made him ache. Her hand rose and touched his cheek. "Oh, Thomas, I know that. You saved me then. I didn't doubt that truth for an instant."

For a moment, *he* was the one who couldn't speak. Her faith in him seemed so strong. Staggering. No one had ever believed in him the way she did. "I—" He broke off, cleared his throat and tried again. "I need you to know that I have met that man before."

He felt the tension that hardened her body. "When?"

Aw, damn, this was going to hurt the most. "When I was working undercover in Alabama." So long ago. "I got the intel I needed on that group, and the EOD stormed in, but before I did…I had to pass the group's initiation."

"What did you do?"

Her voice was so hoarse.

"I fought four men."

She pulled away from him.

"I didn't kill them, I swear, but…if I hadn't fought, they would've pegged me for an agent. I had to prove myself." He had. "There were three of us there for the initiation. A group circled us, threw back in the men who tried to run. Porter— I turned once and he was in front of me. He knew I wasn't one of the ones running. He was laughing." He swallowed bile. "Cheering me on as I attacked." *Dragon, Dragon!* He'd just gone by that tag back then, to better fit in with the group.

The guy had even come up and congratulated him on a good fight afterward.

She paled before him. "I have to get out of here. I just— I need to leave."

He was afraid she was leaving him. "I was undercover. My job was to infiltrate and bring down that organization."

"No matter the cost."

She'd been the cost.

Thomas shook his head. "If I'd known for a minute that he was the man who'd arranged your abduction—"

"Why didn't the EOD apprehend him then? If the rest of the group got *contained,* then why not him?" Emotion ripped through her words. Pain. Fury. "Why was he left free to hurt and kill?"

"Because he wasn't there when the EOD team came in. Something had spooked him and he ran."

Her laugh was cold. Mocking. "*I* spooked him."

Thomas frowned at her.

"He must've gone back to hunt me. I wasn't there, the cops were, so he knew he had to clear out." A bitter smile twisted her lips. "No one else had seen him there, so he just slipped away. Or, sailed away, I guess, since he just boarded the naval vessel and headed to the next port."

Then he'd kept killing. Only his prey had changed, and he'd started working with a new partner.

"I'm sorry," Thomas told her. The words weren't enough. They never would be. For so many years, he'd hated the choices he'd made. A young girl, left alone. He hadn't realized that someone else was out there, possibly still after her.

"So am I," Noelle said. Then she jerked open the door and straightened her shoulders. When she left this time, he didn't follow her. He knew she wanted to get away.

From me.

So he let her go.

"THIS ISN'T OVER!" Patrick Porter yelled as he grabbed the bars. The woman had left and the agent—*Dragon, you liar*—had followed on her heels.

They thought they were done? That they just got to walk away while he was tossed into a cell to rot?

No. That wasn't the way his story would be ending.

"The blood's gonna be on you!" His bellow seemed to echo back to him. "Another body…*on you, Noelle!* You thought it was bad when you were the victim? How's it gonna feel when you realize you let her die? *You. Let. Her. Die!*"

AARON BLACK FROWNED as he glanced toward the holding-room door. The jerk in there had been yelling his head off for the past ten minutes. Making threats. Demanding his freedom.

Talking about a victim.

It could be pure bull, of course. A last-ditch effort to save himself. Aaron had seen it before. When facing nothing but a dark cell for endless days, men would lie. They'd promise anything. Everything. Tell any falsehood imaginable.

But…

Sometimes, they would also tell the truth.

He stepped closer to the holding room.

NOELLE STOOD IN the snow. Her eyes were closed. Her hands outstretched. She was just a few feet away from the sheriff's station. A monster was inside that station. A man with a soul darker than hell.

She had to face him again. It was her job. But every time she looked into his eyes, Noelle felt as if she were a helpless teen again. Lost and so scared.

Waiting to die.

Snow crunched to the left, and in an instant, Noelle spun around with her gun up.

Her firearm locked right on Bruce Mercer. He lifted his hands toward her. "Easy. I'm not the enemy."

Sometimes, it was hard to tell which side Mercer was really on. "You kept my past from me." She holstered her weapon.

"I thought the danger was gone." He exhaled and advanced toward her. "I was very wrong."

Her eyebrows shot up. Had the great and oh, so powerful Mercer just admitted to being wrong? Human?

"You weren't alone."

She had no idea what he was talking about.

"Has Agent Anthony told you that part yet?"

"He told me that he'd seen Porter. While he was undercover in Alabama, Thomas *saw* him with that terrorist group."

"Ah, yes, well, is it surprising that Porter would have ties to others who wanted to maim and kill? Like to like, you know."

Yes, she knew plenty about the darkness that hid within men.

"We didn't have an ID on Porter then. Just a basic physical description. He slipped away." Mercer heaved out a breath as he stared at the mountains in the distance. "We try our hardest, but there are always some that get away. For every killer we stop, another one is out there, waiting in the wings." His voice lowered. "Some days I wonder if it will ever end."

She rubbed her arms. The snow had felt good before, seeming to cool the fire that burned within her as it fell again, but now...

"Thomas was at the hospital because he needed to see you. He even went in your room, but you didn't recognize him. You didn't know him at all."

Those words had her breath catching.

"Maybe Thomas told you he'd watched you over the years, but I don't think you realize...quite how much. When your mother died, he was at the funeral. When your father passed, he was at the nursing home. When you graduated from college, he was in the audience. When you went on your first case with the FBI, he was shadowing you."

She could only shake her head. That made no sense to her. *"Why?"*

"Because fifteen years ago, Thomas Anthony met a girl in the woods. A girl he said was the bravest, strongest person he'd ever met. He told me the girl was hurt and scared, but she kept fighting to survive, no matter what."

She looked away from Mercer. She didn't want him reading the expression in her eyes.

"Because fifteen years ago..." Mercer said again. "I think a twenty-two-year-old agent fell in love with that girl. With her strength and her courage, and he couldn't bear to imagine her alone in the world. He wanted to keep her safe. To watch over her. So he did, in his way, and with every year that passed, every day that he watched her prove again and again just how strong she was, I think he fell for her even more."

No, no, that couldn't be true. "He would've said something to me."

Mercer laughed at that.

Her head whipped back around toward him. She could *never* remember hearing Mercer laugh.

"Thomas Anthony is a good agent. One of the best I've ever seen, but that man doesn't connect easily with others. He keeps his emotions to himself."

"Then how do you know—"

"Because you're not the only one who is good at reading people. And if you weren't so blinded by your own feelings, you'd see that Thomas Anthony would die in an instant, if it meant keeping you safe. He'd lie, he'd kill, he'd cheat. He'd do anything for you."

Her heart was thundering in her chest. "Why are you telling me this?" *Now?*

"Because the mission ends in just a few hours. When we board the plane, that's the end for your partnership with Thomas Anthony."

Noelle shook her head. "But the EOD—"

"Oh, don't worry about us. We'll always be around." He gave a little nod. "But your period as an EOD liaison from the FBI, that's over."

It was the last thing she'd expected. "You're *firing* me?"

His lips twitched. "No. I brought you on because I thought being around Anthony would stir some memories, and if that didn't work, I thought, well…" His words trailed away. But surely, Bruce Mercer wasn't suggesting he'd tried to play matchmaker for her and Thomas? Mercer was a power player. Not some closet romantic who—

"You deserve some happiness. So does he." Mercer rubbed his chin. "I'm not saying I won't be using you again. You're the best profiler I've ever come across, but in the future, you won't be partnered with Anthony. So whatever you two decide, there's nothing at the EOD that will stand between you." His hand dropped as he gazed at her. "The only thing between the two of you is what you put there. Ghosts from your past. Fears about your future. It's all what *you* see...or what you don't."

He pointed down the road. "Thomas went back to the cabin you two rented. He said he was tired. Maybe you should go there and try to get a little shut-eye, too." Then he turned and made his way back inside the sheriff's station.

Noelle sucked in a deep gulp of air. One. Two.

Then she found herself hurrying forward. She got the keys to the extra rental truck, and she was on her way back to the cabin before she gave herself a second to think.

She parked the truck and hurried inside the cabin. She opened her mouth to call out to Thomas, but stopped when she caught sight of him near the fireplace.

He wore only a pair of loose jogging pants. His back was to her. Strong, broad. He was moving fluidly, as his hands struck out above him and his feet lifted in a series of blurring kicks.

Martial arts. She didn't recognize any of his moves but she'd read in his file he'd studied tae kwon do, jujitsu, krav maga and aikido.

She shut the door behind her then leaned back against the wall and just watched him.

Admired him.

His muscles stretched. Flexed. His skin gleamed golden in the firelight. He turned to the left. Then the right. His strikes were fast and powerful.

And she kept watching.

Noelle wasn't sure how much time passed, but after a while, Thomas turned to slowly face her. His eyes seemed to reflect the fire.

"What was…?" She stopped, cleared her throat and tried again. "What was that?"

"Choong-Jang, a black belt form for tae kwon do." He rolled back his shoulders and regarded her with a locked jaw.

"Does that…help you relax?"

"Sometimes." He shook his head and took a step toward her. "Not this time."

She tensed. Mercer's words seemed to echo through her mind. She wanted to ask Thomas if the EOD director's story was true. Had Thomas really been there, in the background for so much of her life?

She stopped less than a foot away from him. Helplessly, her gaze slid over his body. The man had a truly magnificent chest. So muscled. Strong.

"The scars will always be there."

Her gaze jerked up to his face. "I wasn't looking at your scars." She'd been more focused on the muscles.

His laughter was rough. "They slide all across me. It's hard to miss them."

"I think I was distracted by other things," she murmured, aware her cheeks were stinging.

One dark brow rose.

She tried to pull in a steadying breath. It didn't work so much. Noelle didn't feel steady at all. She was nervous. Tense. And…

"We go back to D.C. soon," she blurted.

He nodded.

"Mercer told me that my job as an FBI liaison with the EOD is done. For now, anyway."

That news had him frowning. "You're leaving?"

I don't want to leave him.

"How often have you watched me?" The question slipped from her.

His hand rose to stroke her cheek. "I don't want to scare you. I *never* want to do that."

She turned her head and kissed his palm. She felt the tension thicken around them. "You don't." The darkness that clung to him had never frightened her. The power he possessed just made her feel safe because Noelle knew he'd protect her.

It was what he'd always done.

"I used to dream about you," he whispered, the words rough. "At first, the dreams were the girl I left in that cabin. You were scared and you were crying out for me."

Pain echoed in his voice.

"I'm not scared any longer." She'd worked hard to become stronger.

"Then the dreams changed because *you* changed." His hand slid away from her as his shoulders straightened. "I started to dream about the woman you'd become."

Maybe…maybe Mercer was right. "What do you want from me?" Noelle asked him and she held her breath as she waited for his response.

At his sides, Thomas's hands balled into fists. "I'm a desperate man. I've been that way…too long." His gaze held hers. "I want whatever you'll give me."

I'll give you everything. Maybe she already had. She moved toward him and eliminated that little bit of space. Her hands curled around his shoulders. Then Noelle put her lips on his.

She was making a choice. Choosing *him*. Noelle needed Thomas to understand that. Just as she needed him to choose her. Her mouth moved lightly on his, caressing.

His hands rose and locked around her hips. She could feel the strength of his arousal pressing against her.

"I don't want just one more night." His words were growled against her lips. "With you, I want forever. I can't have another taste just to lose you when we leave this place."

His words broke her heart. Noelle shook her head. "You won't lose me." He was what she wanted. The past was done. The ghosts—*dead*. She wanted to focus on the future, and she wasn't going to let any fears hold her back.

Mercer had been right on that score.

Thomas kissed her again, and the kiss was harder. Deeper. He took control, and she felt the passion pour through her. She couldn't get close enough to him. Couldn't feel him enough.

They stumbled together up the stairs. When she slipped, his grasp on her tightened. He lifted her up, holding her easily.

She kept kissing him.

Then they were in the bedroom. He tugged off her clothes, stripping her quickly, and her hands swept over his shoulders. His chest.

He eased her toward the bed, but Noelle didn't fall back on the mattress. Instead, she lowered to her knees before him, and her lips skimmed over the scars on his chest and stomach. Scars that mattered to him but not to her. The scars told her how strong he was. How he'd survived.

But that was all.

To her, Thomas was perfect.

He caught her hands, though, when her lips skimmed low on his stomach, and he pushed her back. "I can't—" His words ended in a growl as he lifted her up and settled her on the bed.

This wasn't about seduction or finesse. This was about need and desire in its most primal, pure form.

He ditched the rest of his clothes. His fingers caught hers, pinned them to the bed. With his eyes on her, he thrust inside. Her breath caught as he surged deep, then her legs lifted and wrapped around him. She held him tight, and when he began to thrust, she met him, arching her body eagerly.

They rolled over the bed, twisting and turning as the passion surged hotter and harder. Her nails scraped over his back. The pleasure was just out of her reach. *So close.*

His fingers freed hers. He touched her between her legs, finding just the spot that had her gasping, then shuddering in release.

He was with her. Thrusting deep and hard. Shaking the bed. Shaking her. Making the pleasure ripple through her once more.

"Too…good…" He groaned the words. "Can't…get enough…with you…."

Noelle felt the same way with him. She wondered if it would ever be enough, or if the need would grow and—

He drove into her once more.

Pleasure lashed through her.

His release swept over him, stiffening Thomas's body, and he held her in a grip of steel.

Noelle couldn't catch her breath. Her heart raced frantically, the sound a drumbeat in her ears. She was panting hard, her whole body quaking, and she tried to grab back control because there was something very important she needed to tell him.

I love you.

The truth had hit her when she was at the sheriff's station. When Porter had tried to shatter her trust in Thomas, and she'd realized *nothing* could break her trust in him.

Not because he was her partner.

But because he was the man who'd worked his way into her heart.

Her lips parted.

Thomas kissed her again.

"YOU'RE KILLING HER!" Patrick yelled, his voice echoing back to him. "This one won't be on me! It's on you! *All of you!*"

The holding room door flew open and banged against the wall.

Patrick lowered his head so the man who'd rushed in wouldn't see his smile.

"You had your chance to talk," the guy snarled. "You didn't. If you can't stop the screams, then I'll just shove a gag in your mouth."

Patrick's head snapped up. "That's not the way cops work."

"Who said I was a cop?" The man demanded.

Thomas stared into the fellow's cold eyes. He took in the guy's battle-ready posture. The hands, which were loose at his sides and the grim face, which could've been staring into hell.

I'll show him hell.

"You'll be leaving this place in about three hours,"

the man told him flatly. "Settle down until then, or I will settle you down."

Patrick stared back at him. Didn't speak.

The guy gave a grim nod and turned away. Patrick waited until the fellow reached for the door.

"She'll still be alive in three hours," Patrick mused. "At least, I think she will. Guess it depends on how long she can stand the cold out there, all alone."

The man glanced back at him. Patrick knew the guy was trying to judge him. To see if he was telling the truth or if he was just spinning a new lie.

"I got tired of Lawrence Duncan sending me out to do *his* work. I was tired of killing for him," he waited a beat, then added slyly, "and for her."

"Her?" The guy's brows climbed.

Patrick gave a slow nod. "They were working together. Always were. She would slip in and get the intel he needed. People talk so much easier to a pretty face, and Paula sure has a pretty face." He whistled, remembering the other features he enjoyed about her. "But I figured, if I'm done with Duncan, then I'm done with her, too."

"You're trying to say you've abducted—"

"The senator's aide, Paula Quill." His fingers curled around the bars. "And if you want her to keep living, *you'll get me out of here!*"

Chapter Eleven

He wasn't going to let her go. Thomas lifted his head
and stared down into Noelle's unforgettable eyes as he
tried to find the right words to tell her. No one had ever
meant as much to him as she did, and the last thing he
wanted to do was mess up anything with her.

He'd already botched things enough already. He had
to use care.

And not bulldoze his way ahead.

He withdrew from her body, hating the separation
because the woman felt like heaven. If he had his way,
he'd stay curled with her for hours. Days.

But…

Duty waited.

So did the plane.

Before they boarded and left Alaska, he needed to
clear the air between them.

But his phone was ringing. Thomas frowned as the
buzzing reached him. The sound was coming from
downstairs because he'd left it down there earlier. When
Noelle had kissed him, answering it had been the last
thing on his mind.

Noelle blinked, obviously hearing the sound, too.
"Ah, are you expecting someone?"

No, Mercer had said they were clear until takeoff. He brushed his hand over the silken length of her arm. "I'll be right back. Don't...don't move, okay? We need to talk." As soon as he could figure out how to say the right words.

She gave a slow nod.

Thomas yanked on his jogging pants and hurried downstairs. The caller wasn't giving up; that was for sure. Thomas grabbed the phone, then tensed when he saw the number on the screen. He lifted the phone to his ear. "Anthony."

"Do you know where Paula Quill is right now?" Aaron demanded.

Thomas glanced toward the stairs. "The senator's aide? She's been staying at his house in Camden, so check for her there."

"We did. We've called and sent a deputy over to that place, but the staff there say that they haven't seen her since before the big storm swept in."

"So she went out to visit friends before the bad weather hit." His eyes were still on the stairs. He didn't hear any sound from overhead. "Get the woman's cell number and—"

"We've called her cell." Tension deepened Aaron's voice. "There's no answer."

Thomas hesitated. "Why are her whereabouts so important to you?"

"Because that joker in lockup is screaming that he has her hidden in the wilderness, and he says the only way she makes it out alive is if he goes back in for her."

"*What?*"

"So we need you and Noelle back at the station, right now. Because if he's not lying..."

Thomas's gaze was now on the darkness beyond the window. *If Patrick is telling the truth, then Paula Quill could be out there right now, dying.*

Thomas ended the call and raced back up the stairs. As soon as Noelle saw his expression, she leapt to her feet. "What's happening?"

"Patrick Porter may have taken another victim." They wouldn't know for sure, not yet, but… "We have to get back to the station."

She yanked on her clothes. "Who's the victim?"

He dressed quickly, his movement jerky. "Paula Quill."

"The senator's aide?" She shook her head. "What do you think…? Is he—is he lying?"

Thomas hoped so, but a knot had formed in his gut. They finished dressing. When she started to rush past him, Thomas caught her arm. "Before we go, there's something I need you to know." Because he never wanted secrets between them again.

Noelle glanced back at him.

I don't want to mess this up. She means too much to me. The woman deserved wining and dining, not some rushed confession on their way to interrogate a prisoner.

"Thomas? What is it?"

"I will not leave you again." The words rumbled, too deep. "You can count on me, no matter what."

Her smile came then, spreading slowly over her face and lighting her eyes. "I already knew that."

Okay. *Do it.* "Did you know I love you?"

Wait. Hell, he'd meant that to come out better. But charm had never been his strong suit.

She blinked up at him.

He cleared his throat. "I wanted you to know that."

He knew she didn't love him, but maybe they could have *something* when they went back to D.C. "I don't want us to end when the plane touches back down in D.C."

"Thomas—"

"Let's finish this case. Find out if Porter is telling the truth or just jerking us around and then…" He pushed back his shoulders. "Give me the chance to prove that you and I can work out. We can have something together." *Something worth fighting for.*

Her gaze searched his. Thomas wasn't sure what she was looking for. If he knew, he'd give her everything she needed. "Noelle—"

His phone started ringing again.

Damn it!

"Give me the chance," Thomas said again. Then there was nothing more to say. They had a killer to face.

"WE FOUND THESE images on Patrick Porter's phone." Mercer's voice was grim.

Noelle stared down at the images. They showed a familiar woman—Paula Quill—tied to a chair. A blindfold covered her eyes.

"The jerk *told* us where to find the images on his phone. He's taunting us, and he likes the power he has," Mercer added.

Noelle looked up at the EOD boss.

"No one has seen Paula Quill in over twenty-four hours," Mercer said.

"No one but Patrick," Thomas said. "The time stamp on that image is six hours ago."

Six hours. Time to live. Time to die.

Her gaze slid toward the holding-room door.

"He told Aaron that he'd lead us to Paula." Mercer paused. "No, he said he'd lead *you* to her, Agent Evers."

"That's not happening!" Thomas snapped. "No way is Noelle going out in the wilderness with that guy!"

"Yes, well, I figured you'd say that, Anthony." Mercer started to pace. "If the woman is out there, we need the search dogs. We need to patrol the area and find—"

"The area is too big. He left her out there to die." Noelle's voice was certain. She turned back to face Mercer. "He knew we were closing in. He wanted leverage." No wonder he'd been so willing to sacrifice the other women. He'd had a backup plan all along. His ace in case he was captured. "Paula Quill is that leverage. If we don't agree to go after her, then Paula is dead."

Mercer shook his head. "The EOD—"

Noelle's hand lifted. "Doesn't negotiate. Right. I've heard the spiel before." She pulled in a deep breath. "But I'm not EOD, not any longer. I got fired, remember? Now I'm back to being plain old FBI."

Mercer studied her, his eyes narrowed.

"I'm not letting a woman die on my watch."

Thomas surged toward her. "He sets traps. You know his game. And you're just going to walk out with him—"

She laughed. "No, *we* are." Because if Patrick had said he'd only take her to find Paula, then she knew exactly what he intended to do. "Patrick Porter wants me dead. I was the first victim who got away. He wants me out there, where he's in control. He wants to kill me because I'm the one who came back and destroyed everything for him."

A muscle flexed in Thomas's jaw. "I'm *not* letting that happen."

Right. She nodded. "I knew I could count on you."

His brows shot up.

"You come with us. You watch my back. I'll watch yours. We'll get Paula out—"

"How do you know the guy will even lead you to her?" Mercer demanded as his words cut through hers.

Noelle had to shrug. "He wants me to see what he can do. It's all a game to him."

But he wasn't going to win the game. She was. No matter what she had to do, she'd beat him.

She headed toward the holding room. Mercer caught her arm. "He said that Paula Quill was working with the senator. That she helped gather intel and plan hits on the senator's targets."

Her eyes widened. *Paula isn't just an innocent victim.* "And you think she was tied to the attack on the EOD."

"She's a person of interest." His lips tightened into a thin line. "I need her brought in alive."

Because Mercer still wanted to know why the EOD had been set up for the attack in the first place.

"You've both got current tracking devices?" Mercer asked, frowning at them.

At the EOD, all agents had small devices implanted just beneath the skin. If his agents were taken by the enemy, Mercer wanted to be able to make certain they were rescued, no matter where they went.

Thomas nodded. So did Noelle. She'd gotten her chip right after she'd started in her liaison role.

Mercer's attention shifted to Thomas. "Never let her out of your sight."

"Don't worry—it won't happen." Thomas was adamant.

Mercer held his stare a little longer, then he stepped back. He waved toward the holding-room door. "Do what you need to do."

Noelle straightened her shoulders and marched forward. She schooled her expression so no emotion showed on her face when she entered the holding room—and saw Patrick in his cell. He smirked at her. He was so confident of his control and power. She needed to destroy that confidence. She *would*.

Aaron stood just a few feet away, and he was glaring at their prisoner.

"Saw my pictures, did you?" Patrick asked her, voice nearly purring with satisfaction. "I was wondering how long it would take you to see them."

"Why didn't you tell us—immediately—that you'd taken her?" Noelle asked.

"I *would've* told you, but you're the one who stopped talking to me." His eyes sparked with fury. "So if she dies, you're the one to blame for that."

Thomas stalked to Noelle's side. "You really think you're just going to walk out of here with Agent Evers?"

"I think if I don't go, you'll never find Paula."

His voice had softened a bit when he said the other woman's name. Because she was his victim and he enjoyed his victims so much?

Enjoyed their suffering, their pain.

Noelle's head inclined a bit as she studied him.

"Paula will vanish and her death will be on you two."

He shook his head. "And here I thought you were supposed to save people."

"We did save Jenny," Noelle pointed out to him because she wanted to see his response.

The fury flashed in his eyes again. *"Jenny,"* he bit out the name, "wasn't worth my time. She wasn't a challenge. She wasn't anything to me. Just bait, to lure you out."

"Isn't that what Paula is, too?" Thomas wanted to know. "Bait. You stick her in the middle of nowhere, and you expect us to just follow your lead…right into whatever hell you've got waiting for us?"

Patrick laughed. "You have to do it! Because if you don't, you both know she's dead." He pointed toward Noelle. *"She* can't live with a death on her. You…" He waved dismissively toward Thomas. "You don't care. People don't matter to you."

Yes, they did. He didn't know Thomas at all.

Patrick's eyes were on Noelle. "But she won't let an innocent die. She can't. Seeing Paula tied up like that, it was like seeing yourself, wasn't it?"

She didn't let any emotion break through. "You're a control freak, a man who thinks that he's the strongest and the toughest in any room that he enters. But you weren't always that way. In fact, you first killed Emma Jane because you felt weak." She was about to show him just how much she knew. "You got a rush from her death, one unlike anything you'd ever felt before."

He was still smirking at her. *That smirk is going to vanish.*

"I don't think you meant to *hunt* her. I think Emma Jane got away from you. She ran. You had to chase her. That's when you began to like the hunt so much."

His smirk slipped.

"You tried to recreate that rush by taking girls who reminded you of Emma Jane, but that just didn't work." She shook her head. "Then, of course, you found out your partner had been killed. That made you feel lost, isolated—and powerless. You hate to feel like you lack power—"

"Because I don't! I never lack power!"

"Lucky for you, though, Duncan entered the picture then. He used you, but he also refocused you. The rush came back because your prey was more challenging, and you continued this way…for a while."

His breath heaved out. "You think you're so smart—"

"It was only a matter of time until you killed him. You couldn't keep following his orders forever, even if you enjoyed the work. Following *his* orders meant he held power, not you. So when he pushed too far, when he told you to kill me and Agent Anthony *his* way, you snapped."

Patrick glared at her. *And the smirk is gone.*

"You'll always snap in the end." Noelle sighed as if she pitied him. She didn't. She hated him. "Control is your weakness."

His hands flew out from behind the bars, lunging toward her, but he was too far away to do any damage. His fingers stretched uselessly into the air.

"You think you'll get power by taking me into the wilderness, leading me on a hunt for Paula, then killing me." She glanced from his hands to his face. "That won't happen."

"Your death is overdue," he snarled at her.

"So is yours," Thomas fired right back.

Patrick's hands jerked backed through the bars.

"I go with you," Thomas said, voice hard. "You're cuffed, and you're within sight at all times. You take us to Paula and—"

"And what do I get?"

Noelle knew it wasn't really about what he'd get. Obviously, the man planned to try and kill them out there. But she played along, for now. "You get to walk outside once a day when you get to your future prison home. You can see the sun, and not live every single minute pinned behind bars."

She waited.

Patrick's jaw was clenched.

"Deal?" Noelle pressed because she didn't know how much time Paula had left.

"Deal," Patrick snarled. But his eyes… His eyes were glinting with triumph.

THOMAS STAYED RIGHT beside Noelle as they approached the cabin. A helicopter had brought them in as they'd followed Patrick Porter's gritted instructions.

Those instructions had taken them back to the general area where they'd found Sarah Finway's body. Where Patrick had been waiting to attack them all before.

Had Sarah seen Paula? Had the two women been kept together? And when Patrick decided he needed to make one of them scream, had Sarah been his unlucky choice?

Noelle had seen Thomas's face tense as they drew closer to the area, and she knew the same questions were plaguing him. Had they been so close to another victim and hadn't even realized it?

The chopper had landed and it waited a good two

hundred yards away. They'd trudged through the snow and the woods. Patrick was cuffed and far too confident.

That confidence was about to end.

It wasn't the first time a prisoner had offered an exchange to Noelle. It also wasn't the first time Noelle knew that prisoner was planning a double cross.

A death.

Aaron was shadowing them. He'd been the one flying the chopper, and Noelle knew the guy hadn't stayed behind. He was just remaining out of Patrick's sight as he trailed them, waiting for the moment to strike.

They cleared a deep thatch of trees, and Noelle saw the cabin. It was nestled under the broader trees, its exterior nearly covered by thick snow. No wonder they hadn't spotted it from the sky. It was too well camouflaged.

"Built it myself," Patrick said as he expelled a rush of air, which appeared as a white cloud before his face. "That way, I knew no one would ever be able to find the place." He waved his hand. "Go on in… She's waiting for you."

Right. As if they were idiots.

Thomas lifted his weapon and pointed at Patrick. "You could have the place rigged to blow. As soon as we walk in, boom."

Patrick just shrugged. "I could…"

Noelle's gaze returned to the cabin. Something about this scene nagged at her.

Snow crunched beneath Thomas's boots. "And that's why you're going in first."

Patrick opened his mouth to reply.

"There's no smoke," Noelle said. She glanced around. "'Course, there's no smoke," Patrick muttered. "She's tied up. She can't start a fire, and I sure as hell wasn't starting one. Why give away the place's position?"

No fire…but also no pile of snow in front of the door. It had been snowing off and on during the past seven hours. It was particularly heavy right after they brought Patrick into the sheriff's station. If no one had been at that cabin in hours, the snow should've piled up in front of the door. Instead, it looked as if the path to the door had been freshly cleared.

Something glinted in the window of the little cabin.

Her eyes widened as Noelle realized she was staring at the barrel of a gun. She started to scream a warning to Thomas, but he was already moving. He grabbed her, wrapping his arms around her, and she slammed back into the ground just as the thunder of gunfire exploded.

Gunfire…and laughter. Patrick's laughter.

She spat snow out of her mouth and tried to shove up, but Thomas wasn't letting her go.

"Shooter in the cabin," he growled into her ear.

Because Patrick *had* found another partner.

"Can't see him," Thomas whispered. "But he has eyes on us."

Patrick was running toward the cabin.

"Stop!" Thomas yelled at the guy.

Patrick only ran faster. Another shot blasted from the cabin.

And a shot also blasted from Thomas's gun. The bullet caught Patrick in the shoulder. The man spun around, snarling.

Thunder echoed once more. No, not thunder. The roar was more gunfire, coming from the cabin. The bullet ripped right past Noelle's head, so close she felt its heat against her.

"We need cover," Thomas said, "*Now.* You run for the thicker trees, and I'll watch your back."

Translation—she ran and he fired, making himself a target. Not a plan she loved. Not even one she liked. Noelle yanked out her own weapon.

Patrick was stumbling toward that cabin door. He was close, just about five feet away from the entrance.

Gunfire erupted once more. Patrick's body jerked when he was hit, his body moving like a marionette on a string. Blood sprayed into the snow, turning it red.

Patrick's partner had just shot him. Noelle sure hadn't seen that coming. Noelle had thought she and Thomas were the targets.

"*Go!*" Thomas yelled to Noelle.

Patrick slipped. Fell.

Thomas fired into the cabin. Noelle rushed to the cover of the woods, and Thomas was right behind her.

And—and Aaron was there. She saw the darkness of his hair, and he started shooting, providing cover fire for her and Thomas as they got to safety.

When Noelle turned back again, Patrick was lying in the snow, and the red beneath him was spreading.

"What in the hell is happening?" Aaron demanded. "I thought this was a rescue mission!'

Thomas shook his head and never took his gaze from the cabin. "It was a trap, all along."

"For us? Or for that jerk out there, bleeding out?"

Patrick was moaning and begging for help.

Fury and fear churned within Noelle. *Did your victims beg, too?*

"Is the woman in there?" Aaron wanted to know.

They hadn't gotten a glimpse of the shooter, not yet.

But Noelle didn't need a glimpse. "She is."

Aaron grunted. "So, we're looking at two people in—"

"Only one," Noelle interrupted. "Just one."

As comprehension sank in, Aaron whistled. "Paula Quill got free and found a gun in the place, huh? Payback is a—"

The cabin's door opened then. A small, hunched figure appeared.

Paula.

She had a gun in her hand. She lifted the gun and aimed it at the begging Patrick.

Paula walked forward. Her grip on the gun was steady and her steps were slow.

She's going to kill him.

"Stop!" Thomas shouted.

Paula's head jerked up. So did her gun. She pointed it at Thomas.

"No, Thomas," Noelle said as Thomas stepped forward, "that woman isn't a victim." Noelle was seeing her for exactly what she was.

Patrick's partner.

Paula fired. So did Thomas. His bullet hit its target, and Paula fell back, slamming into the side of the cabin.

But her bullet had hit, too. Thomas's blood sprayed in the air, and Noelle gave a frantic cry as she grabbed for him.

No, not Thomas. Not—

Aaron sprang forward, running toward Paula.

Thomas grabbed Noelle's hand. Blood streamed from a wound near his upper arm. "Just a flesh wound, baby. I swear, I'm fine."

And she realized she'd been pleading, so desperate for him to be all right.

His hold tightened on her. "It would take a lot more than this to slow me down."

Yes, yes, it would. Relief had her feeling light-headed, but they didn't have time to waste. She and Thomas rushed after Aaron.

The other agent had already kicked the gun away from Paula. Paula's wound was almost an exact mirror image of Thomas's.

But Paula was screaming, and Thomas was eerily silent.

Aaron locked his hand around Paula's uninjured shoulder. "Wrong move, ma'am, *wrong*."

"Help...me..." Patrick pleaded when Noelle drew closer to him.

She stared down at his bloody chest. His breath was wheezing in and out. If he didn't get medical attention, he'd be dead in moments.

Noelle dropped to her knees beside him.

"What are you doing?" Paula shrieked. "Let him die! After what he did to you, *let him bleed out!*"

Noelle shook her head. "That's not who I am." She ripped his shirt away. Saw the gaping wounds. She tried to apply pressure.

"He has to die!" Paula screamed. "He killed Lawrence! He abducted me! *Let. Him. Die!*" She started sobbing then, deep, wrenching sobs, which shook her whole body.

Aaron swore. "Look, it's going to be all right..."

Noelle frantically shook her head. "He didn't abduct her—"

But it was too late. Aaron had lowered his guard, and Paula—Paula grabbed his gun.

She lifted the weapon, aimed for her target. But her target was right behind Noelle, and when Paula fired, standing less than five feet away while Noelle crouched on the cold snow, Noelle knew that bullet was going to hit her. It would hit her, then go *through* her as it rushed toward Patrick Porter.

She tried to brace herself. *Thomas, I—*

The bullet didn't hit her.

Thomas jumped in front of Noelle.

The bullet hit him, and Noelle screamed.

He had his gun up, but Thomas didn't get the chance to fire. The weapon slipped from his hands as he staggered back and fell into her. Noelle wrapped her arms around him. Held him tight. "Thomas, *Thomas!*"

Aaron wrestled the gun from Paula. The woman crumpled then, crying pitifully, but Noelle knew it was all an act. A show.

Thomas slumped against Noelle.

She felt the stickiness of his blood. Not from the wound near his shoulder, but from the wound at his heart.

He hit the snow beside her. She grabbed for him, shaking him. "Thomas!" His eyes were closed.

The wound... Desperately, quickly, Noelle looked for the entrance wound. An inch from his heart. But there was no exit wound. If there'd been an exit wound, she would've been hit, too. Instead, the bullet was lodged inside him.

Her head whipped toward Aaron. "We have to get him to the chopper, *now!*" Thomas's blood wasn't just on her fingers now. He was bleeding so much that the blood coated her hands.

No, no, no.

Aaron swore and rushed toward her, pulling Paula in his wake. The woman was still sobbing, still—

"I...love you..."

Thomas's rasped words had pain welling within Noelle. She held him tight, tried to stop that precious blood from pumping out of him. "I love you, too!"

His eyes were still closed and with every second that passed, he seemed to be growing paler.

"Thomas, I love you, too! Do you hear me?"

She didn't think he did.

Terror clawed through her.

"You said you wouldn't leave me alone. Not ever again."

He barely seemed to be breathing.

"Don't leave me. *Don't.*" She pressed a kiss to his lips. "I. Love. You."

But Thomas didn't answer her. When Mercer and two deputies rushed through the woods moments later, Thomas was unconscious. Unresponsive.

They loaded him into the helicopter. Patrick was pushed in beside him.

Patrick was still wheezing. His color had turned ashen. Thomas... She couldn't hear his breaths at all.

She held him tight. *I won't let you go.* "Keep your promise," she whispered as the tears burned her eyes. Then she looked toward the open door of the chopper.

Aaron stood there. A deputy had cuffed a sobbing Paula.

"Don't let her go!" Noelle cried out. "She's the key to this mess."

Paula's head lifted. Her gaze darted from Patrick to Thomas.

Paula smiled.

The chopper lifted in the air.

THOMAS KNEW HE was in a hospital even before he opened his eyes. It was the smell that told him, that antiseptic scent and the steady beeping of a nearby machine.

He remembered getting shot. Remembered the desperate fear he wouldn't get to Noelle in time to save her. So when he forced his eyes open and struggled to speak, her name was the first word he uttered. "No…elle…"

"I'm right here." Her hand squeezed his. "Do you hear me? I'm right here."

He turned his head. The glow of the sun was behind her, and damn if the woman didn't look like an angel to him.

His perfect dream. Right there.

"You're smiling." Noelle sounded worried. "Is that because of the drugs? Because when a person takes a bullet to the chest, a smile after surgery isn't the typical response."

Thomas shook his head.

"I'm calling the nurse." She lunged toward the call button.

"I…remember."

Noelle paused at his gruff words. "You remember the shooting? That's good. I was—I was worried you'd—"

He shook his head again, turning slightly against the pillow. Surprisingly, he felt no pain. Must've been the drugs. Like pain would've mattered to him right then. No, not when he *knew*. "You…love me."

He wondered if she would deny it.

"Of course, I love you," Noelle said as she bent close to him. Her beautiful eyes gleamed with tears. "I'm just surprised you didn't realize it sooner. I mean, I could barely get within ten feet of you without stumbling over my words every time we talked."

He'd thought that was fear. That he made her too nervous.

Noelle pressed a light kiss to his lips. "You're the most dangerous man I've ever met, and you're the only man who has ever made me feel completely safe when I'm with him."

His heart ached, and that wasn't due to the wound. "I'd die to keep you safe."

A tear spilled from her eye and slid down her cheek. "You almost did. How about you don't ever, *ever* do that again?"

He wouldn't make any promises. When it came to Noelle, he'd do anything if it meant she was alive and happy. Her hand still held his. He lifted their joined hands, ignoring the slight burn of the IV, and he pressed a kiss to the back of her hand.

"I love you." Saying the words to her seemed as natural as breathing. He'd never given those words to another woman, and Thomas knew Noelle would be the only one he ever did say them to. She'd held his heart for so long. Her courage had drawn him in. Her intelligence. Her goodness, which seemed to shine from within her. After spending so much time in the shadows and in the darkness, he'd been drawn to the light that was Noelle.

To him, she was… Hell, she was everything.

"Marry me."

Not the most suave of proposals.

But—

"Yes."

The machines around him raced, and Noelle pushed closer to him. "I don't want to spend my life without you, Thomas. I don't want to be alone anymore. I want *you*."

She was all he'd ever need.

His dreams. His hopes.

His.

Noelle pressed a kiss to his lips once more, and Thomas knew he was the luckiest damn man on earth.

Yeah, she was an angel, all right, and she was *his*.

Chapter Twelve

Noelle entered the interrogation room with slow, determined steps. Her heels clicked softly on the floor as she made her way toward the prisoner.

The woman sat at the table, a guard stationed behind her. The woman's blond hair had lost some of its polished shine, and the long locks were pulled back into a limp ponytail.

As Noelle drew closer to the table, Paula Quinn glanced up, a smile on her face. "So, I finally merited an audience, huh?"

Noelle didn't speak.

"Too bad about your partner…" Paula leaned forward. "I was out of my mind when I fired that shot, of course. Patrick had kidnapped me, and I—I just snapped."

Cry me a river. Noelle didn't believe the woman's lies for a moment.

"I was aiming for Patrick. Not the agent." Paula's voice lowered with what sounded like sorrow. "I'm so sorry that Agent Anthony died…"

The door opened behind Noelle. She didn't glance back. She didn't need to. Shock swept over Paula's face when she saw the identity of her second visitor.

"Agent Anthony isn't dead," Noelle said. She also didn't think Thomas should be back to work, but since he wasn't *technically* in the field, Mercer had given the clear for him to come in on the interrogation.

Noelle was back to working as a liaison, at least until the situation with Paula Quill was resolved. Mercer wanted the woman to break, and Noelle was about to make that happen.

Then, when the case was officially closed, she had a wedding to plan. After all, a woman had her priorities. And getting hitched to Thomas—definite priority. But, sending this killer in front of her to jail for the rest of Paula's life? *Current goal.*

This was the woman who'd nearly taken Thomas away from Noelle. Damn straight she was going to do everything possible to break Paula.

Noelle sat in front of Paula. Thomas pulled out the chair right beside her. He didn't even wince when he sat down. The guy was far too good at camouflaging his pain.

"He's alive!" A wide smile broke over Paula's face. She lifted her hands, showing the cuffs that circled her wrists. "I'm so glad! I never meant to shoot you. I meant to shoot—"

"Me?" Noelle finished softly.

The smile slipped from Paula's face. "Of course not! I was aiming for Patrick."

"But in order to get to him—" Thomas's voice cut like a knife "—you were ready to shoot through Noelle."

Noelle slanted a quick glance his way. Did he even realize his voice had softened when he said her name? That had been…sweet. As sweet as she knew Thomas would ever get while they were at the EOD. After all, the man had an image to maintain.

"I—I was so scared..." Paula's shoulders shook.

Paula really was a terrific actress.

Noelle reached for the files that were waiting on the table. She flipped them open. "You started working for Senator Duncan over ten years ago."

"Ah...yes. Yes, I did..."

"And when you mention Patrick Porter, you always use his first name... That's an intimate association, so I assume you met him over the years while you were working with the senator?"

Paula's gaze darted to Thomas, then back to Noelle. "Patrick would come to see the senator every few months. They were friends." Her breath huffed out. "I can't believe that he killed him! And then abducted me!"

"Oh, I think you can believe it," Thomas muttered.

Paula's stare hardened for an instant.

Noelle asked, "You weren't aware that Patrick was killing for the senator?"

As Noelle stared at Paula, the other woman's mouth dropped open in a perfect O of surprise. "You can't be serious! There's no way—"

"Oh, I'm serious. You deleted the record of the kills from the senator's computer, but you weren't quite good enough at that deletion. We've got computer techs here... They can recover *anything* if you just give them time." Noelle smiled at Paula. "Serial killers like to keep souvenirs of their kills, did you know that? Patrick... His thing was pictures. Videos. When he had completed a kill, he'd send that image to Lawrence as proof the job was done. It was all of those images that you tried to delete. The video files."

Paula shook her head. "I have *no* idea what you're talking about!"

She could keep up the lies for a bit longer.

"The files were deleted *after* the senator's death."

"Then Patrick must've done it! He got into the system and—"

Noelle shook her head. "The only fingerprints on that keyboard were yours and the senator's."

Paula flushed. Her cuffed hands slammed against the table. "Then he used gloves. I don't know—"

"I think you know plenty," Thomas drawled as he leaned forward, "because you were featured in some of those videos." He reached for the laptop on the table. "Want to see them?"

Paula's face changed then. The pretty veneer faded. Evil flashed in her eyes.

"Patrick liked to work with a partner, and Lawrence, well, he was the more hands-off kind of guy, right?" Noelle asked, her voice emotionless. "So you were the one who went in with Patrick. The one who helped him lure those victims out. For the past ten years, Patrick had been killing men. The high-profile enemies of the senator. And to lure out prey like that…"

"You need the right bait," Thomas finished.

Bait that looked innocent but wasn't. Bait that would be too seductive to resist.

Thomas tapped a few buttons on the keyboard. A video began to play. Paula's soft laughter filled the room. Only this time, that laughter was coming from the recording. The woman was as still as a statue across from them as her eyes locked on the screen.

"Stop it," Paula whispered.

They didn't stop the video.

"I'm so glad we decided to get away for the week-end..." Now a man's deep, rumbling voice came from that video. *"Leaving D.C. was the best idea you've had..."*

"That's General Randall Adams. He worked for the Pentagon." Noelle shrugged. "You know that, though, right? Since the two of you were lovers. Randall's the one who first tipped you off about the EOD. You worried the EOD was closing in on you and Lawrence, that we'd realize—"

"I don't know anything about the EOD," Paula said, the words quiet but hard.

Thomas drummed his fingers on the table. "Once you came up on the EOD's radar, you knew we'd realize you'd been killing for years. We go after threats to security, and that's exactly what you are."

The video kept playing.

"Sometimes, Paula," Randall murmured, *"I wish you and I could give it all up. Just be together..."*

Paula's cuffed hands grabbed for the laptop. She shoved the top down. "I don't want to see anymore."

Noelle realized she'd been right. Of all the clips on that laptop, and there were plenty, the one of Randall had been the one Paula needed to see. "When Patrick kills him later—and Randall certainly wasn't easy to kill—your name is the last thing the general says."

The color was completely gone from Paula's face. Her lips twisted into a snarl. "Pointing at his accuser, is he?"

Thomas's fingers stilled on the table. "No, I think he was just calling out for the woman he loved."

Noelle turned her head to look at his hard profile.

"In those lasts minutes, you know what really matters," Thomas continued. His gaze flickered to Noelle. "You want to be clear, no words left unsaid, before you draw that last breath."

A sob broke from Paula.

Noelle had to swallow to clear the lump from her own throat. She could still hear Thomas's rough growl in her ears. *"I...love you..."*

"It was all Lawrence!" Paula said in a rush. "He's the one who made me work with Patrick! He found out that I'd killed my stepfather when I was sixteen." Tears trekked down her cheeks, but they weren't fake any longer. "He was hurting me, and I stopped him. No one would believe my stories about my stepfather, so I had to do something!" Shudders shook her. "Then Lawrence came along.... I—I thought he was going to help me, but he had other plans. Everyone always does...."

"Everyone but Randall," Noelle said softly.

Paula's shoulders bowed. "Lawrence flipped out when we got confirmation from Randall about the EOD. He was sure someone there—someone called Mercer—would be coming after him. That all the dots from his crimes would be connected. So, yes, he went after them. He didn't want the hit coming right back to him and Patrick, so he hired some guy for the job."

Jack.

"But since I'm here...and they're all dead..." Paula blinked away tears. "I guess the EOD didn't end, did it? Mercer... He's not dead."

Thomas pushed away from the table. The legs of his chair groaned. He headed for the door.

Noelle sat at the table for a moment longer. His job was finished. Hers wasn't. Now she needed to get the rest of the details. Names and dates. Closure would be given to families, and if Noelle's instincts were right, they would even get new leads to follow based on the information Paula would give them. Paula had been deeply connected in the senator's life. If there were others who'd tried to hide secrets in D.C., then Paula would know about them.

The woman would cooperate now. There was no reason for her not to do so.

The door closed softly behind Thomas.

Noelle stared at Paula.

"I loved him," Paula whispered.

Noelle reached for a pen and a pad.

"I loved him," Paula said again. "And after Randall was dead…I—I wanted to be, too.…"

THOMAS HEADED INTO the next room. He shut the door behind him. Mercer was standing at attention, just a few feet away from the observation window that let him watch Noelle and Paula.

"The EOD isn't dead," Mercer said voice curt. "And we won't ever be. No matter how many times they come after us." He turned, focusing on Thomas. "Because of men like you. Women like Noelle. Agents who will risk their lives to protect the division."

It wasn't the division Thomas had thought of when he'd leapt to take that bullet in Alaska. It was the only woman he'd ever loved. "I'm marrying her."

Mercer's left eyebrow shot up. "Does Noelle know? Or is this some—"

"Noelle knows I love her, and she's agreed to marry me." *And I know just how lucky I am.* "I won't have any more secrets between us. Not ever again." He was giving that warning to Mercer.

"Good. That's the way it should be."

"Sir—"

Mercer lifted a hand. "My agents sacrifice for the EOD. You think I don't know that?" And, for an instant, the mask Mercer usually wore fell away. "They give up their homes, their families... They focus on the missions. But life is more than just a mission." He came forward and slapped a hand on Thomas's shoulder. "A whole lot more, and I'm glad you finally realized that."

Thomas glanced toward the observation glass. Noelle was questioning Paula, and Paula was telling her everything.

But his gaze wasn't on the captured woman. It was on Noelle. He could see the side of her face. The soft profile. The delicate line of her jaw.

"I knew you loved her," Mercer told him gruffly. "I just wondered when you'd realize it yourself."

Those words had Thomas's stare jerking back toward his boss.

Mercer smiled. *Smiled.* "It's in how you look at her. Usually, you stare at the world as if daring someone to attack you. But you stare at her..." He exhaled and his hand dropped from Thomas's shoulder. "You stare at her as if it's Christmas morning, and you just found the presents beneath the tree."

Thomas swallowed. "She's what matters most to me."

"Then she needs to be the one person you hold tightest." Mercer gave a firm nod. "Don't let her go, and, son, you don't hesitate to tell that woman how you feel every single day of your life." For an instant, sadness flashed in his eyes. "Because the days pass too fast, and you never know when you could wake up and find—" Mercer broke off then. He turned away from Thomas.

"Wait for Noelle to finish up the interview. When she's done, you two take the next week off. I think you've earned that time."

Mercer headed for the door.

Thomas didn't move from his spot in front of the observation window. When the door shut behind Mercer, Thomas kept watching Noelle.

He knew what Mercer had been about to say. *You never know when you could wake up and find her gone.*

Yes, he knew about the director's past. Because he knew most of the secrets at the EOD. Once upon a time, Mercer had loved, too. But his wife had been taken from him.

You never know when you could wake up and find her gone.

Noelle turned her head then and looked toward the observation room. He stared into her eyes. The most gorgeous eyes he'd ever seen.

He wouldn't think of a life without Noelle. She'd been the one thing to get him through the darkest times of his life. No matter what hellhole he'd entered, she'd been there, the light in the darkness. The image of her had gotten him through so many times when he thought escape would be impossible.

No, he wouldn't think of a life without her. Because he didn't want to live that life.

He had his dream, he had Noelle, and Thomas knew he would fight heaven and hell to keep her by his side.

He stayed there, watching, until the interrogation was over, and when Noelle finally came into the room to find him, Thomas stalked toward her.

"Thomas?"

He pulled her into his arms. He still didn't think she

realized just how incredibly important she was to him. Maybe one day, she would.

"I love you." The words came from him so easily now. No stumbles. No hesitations.

She smiled.

For so long, darkness had been all he'd known. But not any longer. Now he had light.

He had love.

He had Noelle.

Thomas kissed her.

* * * * *

In seconds, he was up and at the window, gun in hand.

He saw a woman walking down the long lane, headed for the road.

It had to be Hope. Right height, right weight. Same sexy walk. But her hair was short and dark.

He slipped on his jacket and followed, gun in hand.

She stopped when she reached the road. He considered approaching. He should, really. But he knew that if he did, she'd simply lie about what had driven her to leave her warm bed at midnight.

And he'd be no closer to figuring out what made this woman tick.

So he stayed quiet, hidden by the trees. And in less than five minutes, an old car came along. Hope slid in and shut the door. The car drove away, leaving Mack McCann, who rarely got surprised by anything, standing at the side of the road with his mouth hanging open.

STALKED

BY
BEVERLY LONG

Published in Great Britain 2014
by Mills & Boon, an imprint of Harlequin (UK) Limited,
Eton House, 18-24 Paradise Road, Richmond, Surrey, TW9 1SR

© 2014 Beverly R. Long

ISBN: 978-0-263-91369-9

46-0914

Harlequin (UK) Limited's policy is to use papers that are natural, renewable and recyclable products and made from wood grown in sustainable forests. The logging and manufacturing processes conform to the legal environmental regulations of the country of origin.

Printed and bound in Spain
by Blackprint CPI, Barcelona

As a child, **Beverly Long** used to take a flashlight to bed so that she could hide under the covers and read. Once a teenager, more often than not, the books she chose were romance novels. Now she gets to keep the light on as long as she wants, and there's always a romance novel on her nightstand. With both a bachelor's and a master's degree in business and more than twenty years of experience as a human resources director, she now enjoys the opportunity to write her own stories. She considers her books to be a great success if they compel the reader to stay up way past their bedtime.

Beverly loves to hear from readers. Visit www.beverlylong.com, or like her at www.facebook.com/beverlylong.romance.

For my mother,
who told the very best stories
about Colorado.

Chapter One

Mack McCann wiped the sweat out of his eyes and reached for his cold beer. He'd been sanding boards in the unusually warm spring sun for what seemed like hours. But he was making progress. The McCann cabin, blown to smithereens seven months prior, would stand again.

It had to be ready for Chandler and Ethan's late June wedding. His sister had insisted that she wanted to be married at Crow Hollow. Ethan hadn't wanted to wait, but he'd agreed because he basically wanted to give the stars and the moon to Chandler.

It was pretty damn amazing that his sister had fallen in love with one of his best friends. He and Ethan Moore, along with Brody Donovan, had spent their formative years at the McCann and Donovan cabins. The three boys had spent summers traipsing around the forests and the lakes set high in the Colorado Rockies, not ever realizing that theirs was a friendship that would span the globe over the next twenty years.

Ethan had enlisted in the army and flew helicopters. Brody had gone to college, then to medical school, then surprised them all when he'd enlisted in the air force. And Mack, well, he'd done exactly what he'd hoped to do since he'd been about seven.

He'd become a spy.

Sort of.

Naval intelligence. He'd worked in more countries than he could remember, and in some of the best and worst conditions known to man. Silk sheets and lavish meals in Qatar, and dirt floors and beans in the Democratic Republic of the Congo.

He'd dined with presidents and princesses. He'd squatted alongside peasants washing their clothes in muddy rivers. His playground was anywhere there was information to be gained.

He'd been working 24/7 for the last sixteen years, and quite frankly, he was tired. And he hadn't been able to shake the feeling that there should be something more. So he'd made the decision to leave.

Of course, he'd cop to having a few moments of doubt over the past months while he waited for his discharge papers to be processed. But once he had fresh mountain air in his lungs, he'd known that coming home was the right decision.

He'd secured a new position as director of security for Matrice Biomedics. The job would keep him in Colorado, close to family. He'd delayed his start date until June 15th, almost six weeks away. Until then, he had few worries. His biggest one at the present time was what to have for lunch.

Fifteen minutes later, Mack was on his second sandwich when he heard the sound of an approaching vehicle. Had his father decided to come early? He wasn't expected until the end of the week. When the car rounded the final bend in the road, Mack shook his head in disbelief.

Bingham Trovell, the man who'd been his commanding officer for a good portion of his career, had his arm hanging out the window, waving like a fool. Mack waited until the car had stopped before approaching. "Has hell frozen over, sir? I can't imagine anything else that would get you on land."

Bing opened his car door and shifted two hundred and fifty pounds of black muscle out of the car. At fifty, he could probably still work circles around men half his age. He'd retired just three years earlier to a little boat and started calling the Mississippi home.

Bing looked at the package of hot dogs and buns that Mack had tossed aside earlier. "Good. I'm glad I made it in time."

Mack laughed and hugged the big man. "Come have a seat at my fire."

It was two hot dogs, two beers and forty minutes later that Bing dropped his bombshell. "I need a favor."

"Anything," Mack said, wiping his mouth with the back of his hand.

"I've got a friend who needs some security for his family. I told him that I knew somebody who could fit the bill perfectly. You."

Mack shook his head. "No."

"Were my sources incorrect? Are you not taking the job at Matrice Biomedics?"

Mack nodded. "I'm securing data and trade secrets and intellectual property. All the things I stole from the enemy. I'm not a bouncer at the front door."

"But you could be a bouncer. You have been a bouncer."

Mack couldn't deny that. His role in naval intelligence had morphed over the years, and there had been times when he'd been charged with ensuring the physical security of important places and important people. "I start working in mid-June. That means I have to have the cabin done by then so that it's ready for Chandler's wedding at the end of June. I promised her."

"We'll get the right people up here to finish the job. At our expense. You don't need to worry about that."

"Who the hell is this person?" Mack asked.

"He's my friend. My old college roommate, actually. Reverend Archibald Minnow."

Mack frowned at his friend. "The television preacher? That Archibald Minnow?"

"Yes. But it's not security for him. It's for his daughter, Hope."

Hope Minnow. Mack had always had the ability to recall information quickly and his three weeks in mountain air hadn't dulled his senses. "She was recently profiled in *People*. Short article. I read it and four others between dress changes."

Bing raised one eyebrow, making his already homely face look even less symmetrical. "Between dress changes?"

Mack waved a hand. "Wedding dresses. Most women want their bridesmaids with them. Not my sister. She wanted them and me." He'd been happy enough to go. There was nothing terribly taxing about being surrounded by four women who smelled wonderful and whose only expectation was a thumbs-up or -down on the dress. Plus, the upscale shopping area where the store was located had recently been targeted by street gangs looking for pockets to pick and purses to snatch.

Call him overprotective. He could take it. But it hadn't been that long ago that his sister had almost died at the hands of their crazy stepmother. Besides, Ethan couldn't go; no way was the groom getting an early peak at the dress. It had to be Mack.

"Well, I hope you found something lovely that fits you well in the hips," Bing said, his tone absolutely serious.

Mack set his gaze on the horizon. "You know," he said, "people get lost in these woods all the time. Their bodies don't get found until years later. By then, of course, all the meat has been eaten off."

Bing gave him a fast, crooked smile. Then he got somber. "Hope Minnow needs you."

"That wasn't my impression from the article. I think she needs her personal shopper, her masseuse and her flavored vodka. The paparazzi caught her at some event in New York City."

"She spends a lot of time there. The Minnows live in New Jersey in a more rural area. It's a forty-minute drive into the city with good traffic."

"Worth doing if you're looking for some action," Mack said.

"She's my godchild," Bing said.

"No offense meant."

"None taken. She was always the sweetest thing growing up. Got married a couple years ago but that didn't work out. After that, she seemed to change."

"Her image doesn't quite fit with the message Archibald Minnow preaches, does it?"

"Not hardly. And I won't defend the man's beliefs but he's been my friend for a long time and I'd like to help him. I definitely don't want anything to happen to Hope."

"What happened to the ex-husband?" Mack asked.

"William Baylor. He still works with Archie in the ministry. There are long ties between the two families. I guess his mother and Patsy Minnow were friends in college."

"Hope must have gone back to her maiden name?"

"Right away."

"It's got to be awkward with him still working with her father," Mack said. "She doesn't work for the ministry, too, does she?"

Bing shook his head. "No. I don't think Hope has any-

thing to do with the ministry or much to do with Archie.
He never talks about her."

"Does she work somewhere else or is she strictly a
party girl?" Mack thought back to the picture he'd seen
in the magazine. Long, sexy legs, short black skirt and
a top that showed just enough cleavage to make a grown
man beg for more. Pretty face with blond hair hanging
down to the middle of her back. Eye candy.

He didn't mind that, but he preferred a little more
substance. Although both eye candy and substance had
been sadly missing in his life the past few months as
he worked feverishly to finish up things before leaving
Uncle Sam's employ.

"She used to have a good job working at the Metropolitan Museum of Art in special events. She has a master's degree from New York University. But she left her
job when her mother got sick."

Maybe he'd misjudged. There could be plenty of substance there. "How is Mrs. Minnow now?"

"Better. Definitely good enough to travel, she says.
Patsy Minnow is a real sweetheart. I've always told Ar-
chie that he didn't deserve her. So, what do you think?"
Bing prompted.

It wouldn't be the worst assignment he'd ever had. And
he owed Bing. Would always owe Bing. "How long?"

"Just for a few weeks until Archie has the opportunity
to vet the qualifications of various security firms. He and
his wife are scheduled to leave the country the day after
tomorrow for ten days and he won't have a chance to address it before then. There's a small group going along,
including my wife and me. Otherwise, I'd do it myself.
He has to be very careful who he lets into his inner circle.
I've vouched for you and that's good enough. He knows

I would never disappoint him and I've told him that you would never knowingly disappoint me."

True. Twelve years ago, Bing had saved Mack from torture and a bad death when Mack had underestimated the enemy. Bing had done it at great risk to himself. That wasn't something a man took lightly. Mack looked around the yard. The cabin was coming along nicely. Somebody else could lay the floor and get the bathroom finished. If he babysat Hope for ten days, there'd still be plenty of time to paint and get the yard cleaned up. There was really no good reason to turn down Bing.

"Okay. I'm in," Mack said.

Chapter Two

Hope watched the seconds tick by on her bedroom clock.
Her curtains were open and she could see the sun high
in the blue sky. Clouds would likely roll in later, if the
weather forecaster on the news was to be believed. They
were calling for showers around dinnertime.

She waited another ten minutes, then rolled out of
bed, did twenty minutes of yoga, showered and pulled
her still-wet hair back into a low ponytail. She dressed
casually in black ankle pants and a gauzy royal-blue-and-
black shirt. She slipped her feet into her favorite one-inch
heels, perfect for walking around the city.

Which she did most afternoons.

Because strolling around New York was like nails on
a chalkboard to her father and that made all the effort
very worthwhile. Archibald Minnow was embarrassed
that his daughter was *without purpose*. That's how he'd
described her in a recent magazine article that had come
out shortly after the *People* article. She couldn't even remember which magazine because he did so many interviews. Blah, blah, blah. The church this, the church that.
He'd have tried to avoid questions about her. But in this
instance, they must have pressed and he had to offer up
something. *My daughter is a woman without purpose.
I pray for her daily and am confident that she will find*

her way. Now can we talk about the money we need to keep this machine running?

Although he'd never really say *machine*. Nothing quite so crass. He'd say all the right words. And the money would flow in.

And the cachet of the small-town preacher who had caught the attention of the right people at the right time and made it big on television would continue to grow. Archibald Minnow hadn't been an overnight success but pretty darn close. A meteoric rise, some said. From unknown to household name in just a few years.

And everybody who didn't roll *with him* got rolled over. Most got on board willingly, gleefully, praying for space inside Reverend Minnow's magic bubble.

Hope didn't believe in magic bubbles, and she'd stopped believing in her father a long time ago.

At a very disrespectful and slothful one-fifteen in the afternoon, Hope walked down the curving staircase. When she passed the kitchen, she stuck her head in. Mavis Jones stood at the kitchen sink, washing up a few dishes, likely from the lunch that she and Hope's mother had shared.

"How's Mom?" Hope asked.

"We played five holes of golf today before we took the cart back to the clubhouse. Not bad given that this was the first time we've been out this spring."

"Not bad at all," Hope said. Especially since her mother hadn't felt well enough to play at all last year. Radiation and chemotherapy had robbed her mother of many of the things she loved. It had been a very ugly time. Thank goodness that Mavis, who'd been her mother's friend for over forty years and widowed several years ago, had been there to help. Hope didn't know what they would have done without her.

"Hopefully you'll get a full nine in soon. And the day she walks eighteen holes, I'll dance naked in the street. Or something like that," Hope said, winking at Mavis.

"Me, too. Except who would want to see this old woman and all her sagging and jiggling parts?"

Mavis wasn't kidding anybody. She was still an attractive woman. "You sag and jiggle less than lots of thirty-year-olds," Hope said. "You know that."

The woman shrugged but looked pleased. "You want me to bring you some coffee on the veranda?" she asked.

"I'll get my own coffee," Hope said, walking into the kitchen. "You know you don't have to wait on me." She poured a cup and stuck two pieces of bread into the toaster. Once they popped, she spread the peanut butter on thickly, slapped the pieces together and wrapped her breakfast up in a napkin. "I'll see you later," she said.

When she opened the French doors to the veranda, the warm sun hit her face. Spring had come early this year to the east coast, and flowering shrubs had been in full bloom for weeks. The gardeners had planted annuals in the big urns that flanked the doorway and vines were already starting to trail down the sides.

She walked across the red brick and pulled out a chair. She put her toast and coffee down on the glass-topped table and sat in the sun, facing the heated lap pool that had been opened for the season just the week before. This was normally her favorite time of the day. She loved the solitude. Her father would be working and her mother resting.

But today, her quiet was infringed upon by voices. Men's voices. She stood up, shading her eyes against the glaring sun. Her father was in the yard, well beyond the formal garden area. He wore casual clothes, as if he hadn't yet gone into work. Next to him she recognized Bingham Trovell. Uncle Bing had brought her gifts from all over the world when she was a child. And he'd always had time for a story. To read one, to tell one, to laugh about one.

She didn't recognize the third man. He was dressed the most formally, in dark slacks and a light-colored sports jacket. He was too far away for her to make out his face.

Likely a potential donor. Poor Uncle Bing. Somehow he'd gotten sucked up into the appeal. Her father rarely gave tours of the grounds anymore, so this guy had to have enough bucks to make that happen.

They were walking toward the house. She got up and grabbed her toast and coffee, intending to leave before they saw her.

But her mother stood in the doorway. Still beautiful at 67, the former Miss Texas had put on at least five pounds in the last month. She was still way too thin but Hope was grateful for every ounce.

"Hi," Hope said. "I hear you played golf this morning."

"Yes, it was fabulous. Is that your lunch?"

Hope looked at her toast, still wrapped in the paper napkin. "Brunch. I'm going to eat inside today," she said. She waited for her mom to step aside. But the woman didn't.

Hope looked over her shoulder. The trio was closer. "Excuse me, Mom," she said.

"Do you have a minute?" her mother asked. "Your father and I would like you to meet someone."

"I was on my way out," Hope lied.

"Please."

Hope sighed. She couldn't say no to her mother. "I just have a minute," she hedged.

Her mother nodded and looked past Hope. "Hello, Bing," she said. "You're looking well."

"And you, Patsy." Uncle Bing took the last three steps, leaned in past Hope and kissed her mother's cheek. "You look radiant."

Then Uncle Bing turned to her and hugged her hard. "Good to see you, Hope."

Her father stepped close, in a Prada shirt, khaki shorts and deck shoes. At 67, he still had a full head of hair that he kept brown with some regular help from his hairdresser. He was trim, had all his own teeth and a good smile to show them off.

The camera loved him. And contributions from female fans almost doubled those from males.

As usual, he nodded in Hope's direction but didn't speak. Instead, he pulled out chairs at the table and motioned for them to take one. Her mother sat.

Hope checked out the stranger. Up close, she could tell that his clothes were expensive. He wore them with a casual elegance. His short hair was dark, with just a thread of silver at the temples. He was very tanned, very fit.

She wished he'd take his sunglasses off or that she'd thought to put hers on.

Uncle Bing waved a hand. "Hope, this is my good friend Mack McCann."

She extended her hand. "Mr. McCann," she murmured. When her hand connected to his, she expected his skin to be warm from the sun. But it was cool. There were calluses on his palms and his index finger looked bruised, as if he'd recently hit it with something. Both imperfections were strangely at odds with his otherwise sophisticated presence.

"Ms. Minnow," he replied. His voice was low, sexy.

"Let's get on with it," her father said.

Hope snuck one last look at her mother, who was looking at her expectantly. Expecting what, Hope wasn't sure. She worked hard to hide the animosity she felt for her father from her mother. But she wasn't always successful. Those times she always came out the loser because overt hostility didn't bother her father at all, and it ripped Hope apart when she knew that she'd upset her mom. Stress wasn't good for any recovery.

Hope sat next to her mom and looked at the lap pool. Out of the corner of her eye, she saw her father take a chair. Then Bing, and finally Mack McCann.

Her father leaned forward, his arms on the table. "Bing brought Mack here today because I asked for assistance. Mack provides PPS."

Her father had the most irritating habit of assigning acronyms to things and then acting surprised when other people didn't know them. She didn't rise to the bait. She thought about the water temperature of the pool.

She heard her mother sigh. "Personal protective services, Hope. He's a bodyguard."

Oh, good grief. Her father was going to add a bodyguard to his entourage. That would mean there wouldn't be a seat in the limo for either his hairdresser or his accountant.

She bet the hairdresser got tossed. Or maybe he'd just have the church buy a bigger limo.

"There have been some threats," her father said.

"Threats," she repeated, making sure her tone said *boring*.

Uncle Bing looked at her father. There was no reaction from Mack McCann.

"Threats on *your* life," her father said.

Hope looked at her mother. She could not be falling

for this. But the look on her mother's face said that she'd been reeled in.

"We've hired Mack to protect you," her mother said. "He's your shadow for the next ten days while we're traveling."

Hope pushed her chair back. Took a deep breath, held it. Then she turned to the stranger. "Mr. McCann, I hope you didn't come too far for this appointment because that's time you're never going to get back. I don't need or want a bodyguard." It was the understatement of the year. A bodyguard would ruin everything. Make it impossible to do the things that needed to be done.

She bent down and kissed her mother's cheek. Then she straightened. "I'm going shopping."

THE ONLY SOUND on the veranda after Hope made her departure was the tinkle of water from the frog's mouth at one end of the pool.

"Archie?" Bing asked.

"She doesn't have a choice," Reverend Minnow said, folding his arms across his broad chest.

"She doesn't seem too concerned," Mack said. He'd been prepared for her to be upset, maybe cry a little, or be a little angry that someone would dare to threaten her. He hadn't expected to be dismissed.

"She needs to understand the full impact of the situation," Patricia Minnow said. "I'll talk to her." The woman reached for the papers that Reverend Minnow held folded in his hands.

Mack reached over the frail, yet lovely woman. "I'll do it," he said. When he'd first read the threats, he'd been incensed that Hope was being targeted because someone had a bone to pick with Archibald Minnow. It was damn cowardly to go after someone's child, even if that child was an adult. He'd been grateful that he'd accepted the assignment.

But he wasn't going to guard an uncooperative subject. She had to go along with the plan or all bets were off. He wanted to talk to Hope alone. There'd been some strange dynamic at the table. He hadn't had time yet to figure it out and nobody was tipping their hand.

"May I?" he asked, inclining his head toward the house.

"Of course," said Patricia. "But you better be fast. Hope moves quickly when she wants to."

Mack pushed back his chair. So far, he wasn't overly impressed with Hope's speed or initiative. When he and Bing had arrived at the reverend's house and learned that Hope was still in bed, that she was always in bed until early afternoon, he'd been disgusted. The party girl needed to get her very nice butt home and get to bed at a reasonable time so she could stop wasting her life away. He knew he was probably too much the other extreme, but he was generally up by four, had read a couple newspapers by five, worked out and eaten breakfast before the sun was up.

He entered the air-conditioned house just in time to see Hope, with keys in hand, exit through a door that he assumed led to the garage. He cut through the immense living room, then the study and out the front door just as the garage door went up.

She backed out fast, slowing just a little to close the garage door behind her. Mack didn't miss his opportunity. He opened the passenger door and swung into the still-moving car.

Chapter Three

"Hey!" she yelled.

"A minute of your time," he said. "That's all I'm asking for."

She jammed on the brakes, almost causing him to pitch forward. He could tell that she wanted to tell him to go to hell, but good manners or something had her shoving the car into Park. "You've got sixty seconds."

Now that they were sitting close and there were no competing fragrances from the chemical-rich pool, he could smell just her. The scent was something light, elegant, and it made him think of the rare orchids that his father grew.

Her bare arms were tanned and fit and he suspected that at some point they did more than just lift a martini glass. She probably had a personal trainer on call.

One polished fingernail tapped impatiently on the steering wheel. He glanced at her toes. Yep, they matched. He not only knew his bridal-gown designers now, but he was also pretty up to speed on polish colors, too. There'd been a lengthy discussion over lunch about those. Hope favored something a little hotter, a little sexier, than the pink champagne that his sister and her bridesmaids were wearing.

"You're wasting time," she said.

"I talk fast," he said, and gave her his best friendly smile. It had unarmed bad guys all over the world, but didn't seem to faze her. Her jaw remained stiff. He wished he could see her eyes but she'd put on her sunglasses.

"I guess I really just want to know why you're so damned determined to be careless with your personal safety?"

She pressed her lips together.

He opened the folded papers. "I think you should see these." He handed her the least insulting one. She started to reach for it and stopped.

"You can touch it. These are copies. The police have the originals and the envelopes that they came in. They were hand-addressed and delivered by mail to your father's office. This one came about a week ago." Reverend Minnow had shared that he'd asked Chief Anderson, the local cop in charge, to keep the letters confidential unless there was a specific reason for the information to be shared. Evidently the chief was a devout follower. Reverend Minnow had given Mack the chief's private number and he'd entered it into his phone.

She took the paper. Read it. Her expression didn't change.

That pissed him off. He leaned close and read aloud. "'Dear Reverend Minnow. I lost my son because of you. You need to know the same pain.'"

"This one came just two days ago." He spread the paper out. "'Dear Reverend Minnow. An eye for an eye. My son. Your daughter.'"

She finally looked at him. "I'm not sure what you want me to say?"

"Maybe something like, 'wow, I'm kind of worried.'"

"But I'm not." She took a deep breath. "Do you know that my father has a new book coming out soon?"

Mack nodded.

"My mother's cancer is in remission. Good news, of course. Not great timing for my father. You see, she'd been recently diagnosed when his last book hit the shelves. Gave him the boost he needed for it to hit the *New York Times* list."

Okay. A few things were starting to make sense. First things first. "I'm sorry that your mom was ill." His own mother had died of cancer when he was just a teenager. "And I'm glad that she's getting better."

"Thank you," she said, her voice very soft.

"You really think that your father would engineer something like this just to get some attention?"

"Definitely. Don't underestimate my father. Others have and they've paid the price."

"Bing believes these threats are real."

"Uncle Bing is a wonderful man. But his friendship with my father, which I do not understand, is apparently clouding his judgment."

"What if you're wrong?" Mack asked. "Do you have so little regard for your life that you're willing to take the chance?"

She moved the gearshift to Reverse. "Mr. McCann, you've used up more than your sixty seconds. Get out."

He would have thought she was absolutely as cool as a cucumber, but she had a profound tell. Her pretty hot-pink toes on her left foot were moving. Her foot wasn't tapping. No. Just the toes, expending her nervous energy. If she'd had on shoes or if they'd been seated at a table, he'd never have been the wiser. He opened the door. "Don't be a fool, Hope."

He watched her drive away. Let her get to the end of the block before he moved. Then he ran for his car, which was parked around the corner. Before she got to I-280

East, he'd picked up the car and settled in, staying a discreet three car lengths behind.

He called Bing from the car. "I'm following Hope."

"I'll let her parents know," Bing said and hung up.

She drove competently, staying up with the nonrush-hour traffic. They crossed through the Holland Tunnel and weaved their way through lower Manhattan, then up to midtown. Then she pulled into a parking garage one block off of Fifth Avenue that charged a ridiculous thirty-five dollars per hour. He idled in a no-parking zone, giving her time to get out of her car and down the sidewalk. Then he pulled into the same lot and quickly parked.

This portion of Fifth Avenue was one designer store after another. The shoppers were an eclectic bunch. Parents with children, likely on vacation to the Big Apple, and much more likely, he figured, to be window-shopping rather than buying at the overpriced stores. There were business types—men and women—with briefcases or expensive leather bags on their shoulders and cell phones in their hands. Maybe they shopped but he thought not. Probably en route from one meeting to the next and using the expensive street as a convenient thoroughfare.

And then there were the real shoppers, the people like Hope Minnow, who had the means and the inclination to pay for a designer name and some personalized service. He caught up with her in a small store that was somehow managing to pay their rent selling purses, scarves and shoes.

He stayed outside because the interior was too narrow to provide him any cover. He stood off to the side of the big windows, pulled his cell phone off his belt and pretended to make a call.

He knew there was some chance that he could lose her if she decided to run out the back door but it was a calculated risk. He was confident that she didn't realize she was being followed.

Wedding dresses, nail polish, now the accessories. He could feel his masculinity eroding. He needed some scratching and spitting.

It was a good thing he owed Brody Donovan a call. The two of them were going to throw Ethan a hell of a bachelor party, but first Brody needed to get back into the country. He'd been working on the front lines for a long time, patching up soldiers who had the misfortune to lose limbs to roadside IEDs. The last time Mack had spoken to Brody, just after Chandler had surfaced in Ethan's capable hands, the man was looking forward to getting back to the States. He intended to join the trauma team at one of Southern California's most prestigious hospitals.

The three of them were going to have some fun in Vegas first. Mack had seen the movies. He could do better.

But now, his only real responsibility in life was following a woman intent upon spending her daddy's money.

When she walked out of the store fifteen minutes later, she was carrying just one bag that, by the shape, appeared to be shoes. It made him think of her pretty pink toes again. Shame to cover those up.

She went to three more stores and the pattern pretty much repeated itself. She went in, spent about twenty minutes and came out carrying another bag. Their shapes were not as definitive as the shoe bag, but given the types of stores, he suspected she'd purchased jewelry, dark chocolate and clothing. She was just about to enter a huge toy store when she suddenly detoured from her path and headed toward a bus stop at the corner. There was a group of people but she sought out a woman who was standing with a stroller in front of her and two other young children, one on each side. The woman wore a fast-food worker's uniform. Mack suspected she was either just getting off or just going to work.

He couldn't figure out what Hope had in common with the woman. But it didn't take him long because suddenly Hope was handing the woman all her packages. The woman appeared hesitant to accept them, but Hope must have said something to convince her because she finally accepted the bundle.

He wished he could hear the conversation but he couldn't afford to get any closer. In fact, when Hope turned quickly, retracing her steps, he had to jump behind a group that was waiting for the crosswalk light to come on.

What the hell? She'd spent two hours shopping only to give away the merchandise? He was confident the woman with the children hadn't been expecting to meet Hope.

He followed her as she headed in the direction of her car. They were still two blocks away when she pulled her cell phone out of her purse. She glanced at the phone and answered. Then she walked and talked, an animated conversationalist, shaking her head, even waving an arm. The call continued all the way back to the parking lot and for another ten minutes after Hope was in her car. When she finally put her phone down, she slumped over the steering wheel for a few seconds.

Even from a distance, he could tell that she seemed defeated, and he had the most insane urge to storm the car and demand to know what was wrong. He wanted to fix it. Why, he wasn't sure. She'd snubbed him, kicked him out of her car and made him waste two hours of his life on Fifth Avenue.

But before he could make the decision to show himself, she straightened up, started her car and pulled out of the lot. He got in his own car and followed her back onto the highway, dropping off when she turned the corner to return to her home.

He called Bing again. "She's back, safe and sound. The only thing that was in danger was her wallet."

"I was just about to call you. I'm out to an early dinner with Patsy and Archie before we catch our plane. Patsy called Hope while she was shopping and they had a long conversation. She's agreed to have you provide security."

That explained the phone call.

"Why the change of heart?"

"I could only hear Patsy's side of the conversation. At first, it didn't appear as if Hope was going to give in. But Patsy kept insisting, almost begging her. I guess she finally agreed."

"When is she expecting me?"

"Tonight. But don't expect her to cook you dinner."

He'd be lucky if she didn't throw her dinner at him.

Chapter Four

Hope had just finished her salmon and asparagus when Mack McCann walked up from the backyard. She'd eaten outside because the weather forecasters had been wrong. The rain had held off.

Mack carried an expensive leather bag with a strap over one shoulder and held something else in his hands. When he got closer, she could see it was lightbulbs.

That seemed like an odd thing to pack. He had changed into worn jeans, T-shirt and sandals. He had the job. Obviously no need to dress to impress.

But oddly, he still did impress. It was the confidence he moved with, the assurance that every step he took was exactly the right one.

She envied that. She'd been waffling for months, not able to make a decision about her next steps.

"We have a front door," she said when he got close enough to hear. "Most people use it." She stared at the gun that he holstered at his hip. Of course he was armed. She should have expected it but she'd never been all that fond of guns, especially after her father had demanded that she go with him on a deer-hunting expedition when she was about thirteen.

She shifted her eyes, determined to focus on something else besides the black gun. She frowned at the package of lightbulbs. "You didn't have to bring your own," she said. "We provide them for our guests."

He shrugged. "When your father took Bing and me for a tour this morning, I noticed there were some lights out on the other side of the pool house. Light is one of the simplest and best deterrents to unwelcome activity."

She should probably appreciate his attention to detail. But it was hard to appreciate somebody who was interrupting what would have been ten days of peace. Almost two whole weeks of not pretending to be something that she wasn't. At least while she was in her own home.

"I still think it's ridiculous that you're here," she said.

He nodded and pulled out a chair. He angled it and she realized he did that so he could see both the house and the backyard. He evidently was still buying in to the fact that the threats were real.

"If you think it's so ridiculous, why did you agree to the protection?"

"Because my mother asked me to," she said, blurting out the truth. "She said it was the one thing that I could do to ensure that she enjoyed her trip." She tapped her index nail against the side of her dirty plate. "My mother has wanted to go to Europe for many years. A year ago, when she was so sick that she couldn't even lift her head off her pillow, she had accepted that she was never going to get there. And it broke my heart. Such a simple thing to ask for, but time had run out."

"But she's getting to go after all," he said, "and you're not going to do anything to dull the shine of the experience."

"I love her too much," she said. "And when my parents check in with you, as I'm sure they will, I'd appreciate it if you'd remember that I don't want my mother to have any reason to worry about me. I'll play my part, Mr. McCann. I hope you will, too."

"Mack," he said. "We're going to be living together for the next ten days."

Living together. He made it sound so intimate. And a part of her that had been cold for a very long time heated up, making her almost ache with need.

They would not be alone in the house. "Mavis is my mother's assistant and does some basic cooking and cleaning. About four months ago, she let the lease on her apartment go and moved in here. Right now she's out to dinner with friends, but you should expect her back around nine. It would be good if you didn't shoot her."

She pushed back from the table, making the legs of the wrought-iron chair scrape against the brick patio. "I'm going to my room. Before she left, Mavis told me that the guest room on the second floor is ready for you. Top of the stairs, take a right, third door on the left. There's an attached bath. I like to sleep late. I'd appreciate it if you're quiet in the morning."

HE KNEW WHERE the guest room was. After agreeing to the assignment, he'd reviewed the house's blueprints and examined pictures of the exterior and the grounds, which were extensive. In this exclusive rural area of New Jersey, all the lots were at least ten acres. The trees were mature, providing lots of privacy.

From a security perspective, that could be a good and a bad thing. Good because it wasn't likely that anybody would simply stumble upon the house. That made it easy to separate the good guys from the bad guys. If you weren't an expected guest, you automatically went into the bad-guy column.

Most of the Minnows' neighbors raised horses. They

had barns and fenced-in pastures and horses that sold for thousands of dollars. When Reverend Minnow had walked them around the grounds, Mack had asked about the barn.

"Been empty since we moved in," Reverend Minnow had said. "We're not the horsey type. Hope had a cat for a few years when she was growing up but when it died, I didn't want any more animals around."

Mack would have preferred the barn to be bustling with animals. They, at least, would let him know if someone strange was around. Now the barn was just a large empty structure that provided lots of hiding spaces. That, along with the relative remoteness of the Minnow property, presented some security challenges.

Plus, he had to contend with lots of ground-floor windows and multiple points of access. Hell, even the second floor had direct access—right to Hope's room. There was a lovely little balcony off her bedroom. Only good thing was there wasn't any easy way up to the balcony and the door was hooked up to the security system. However, he'd looked at the specs of the system and he wasn't impressed. It was ridiculously basic and a tenth grader could probably bypass it. And if the alarm were triggered, the responders were from a well-to-do suburban police force that rarely saw any real crime. They wouldn't be much help.

This morning, when he'd been touring the property, he'd debated requesting that Hope take a more secure room in the house. But had ultimately decided it wasn't necessary. If anybody tried to access the balcony, he'd hear the movement and motion outside and have time to respond.

After five minutes, he followed Hope into the house and walked upstairs. He was okay with stashing his stuff in the guest room, but he sure as hell didn't plan to sleep there. He'd sleep downstairs on a couch or in a chair, somewhere where he could easily respond if the home were breached.

It took him just minutes to unpack. He left the room, but instead of going downstairs, he started opening doors. It was one thing to study a blueprint, an entirely different thing to walk through and get a feel for the layout of the rooms.

The big staircase split the upstairs, with two bedrooms and two baths on each side. He and Mavis were sharing a side. When he opened her door, he saw that the bedrooms were laid out much the same, although it was clear that Mavis had a special fondness for giraffes. They were scattered all over the dresser and chest, in all materials and sizes. There was an especially beautiful one in glass and a real ugly one made out of burlap. In the corner, there was a metal one that was tall enough that it looked him in the eye.

He crossed the hallway and checked out the bedroom next to Hope's. It was another guest room and quite frankly, based on the dust that was on the dresser, it hadn't been used recently. He avoided Hope's room, knowing that she wouldn't appreciate him knocking on the door.

Next he went downstairs. Archibald and Patricia Minnow's room was just off the kitchen. The bedroom was spacious, with a king-size bed. There was a separate sitting space, with a desk and several comfortable chairs. Then a huge bath and two walk-in closets, both jammed with clothes.

He glanced into the kitchen, which was painted a nice pale green and had lots of stainless steel. Hope had rinsed her dirty dinner dishes and neatly stacked them in the sink. Somebody had made a loaf of what smelled like banana bread and left it cooling on a rack near the stove.

Other rooms on the first floor were a family room with a wall of books and a big-screen television, a formal living room with overstuffed leather furniture and expensive artwork and, finally, the study. Nice windows, more books on built-in shelves and a desk that he recognized. In the center of the desk was a big Bible. Every week Archibald Minnow recorded his weekly television show from this room. He started and ended the program with his hand on the Bible. Mack had watched a few episodes in preparation of the assignment.

The camera liked Reverend Archibald Minnow. No doubt about it. The man came across as passionate about his faith and committed to his flock. In the segments Mack had watched, Reverend Minnow had spoken lovingly about his wife. He had not mentioned his daughter.

Mack searched the basement next. The house was almost eighty years old and the basement showed it. The walls were big blocks of white stone and the space had not been remodeled or fixed up, like in so many of the newer homes. The floor was cement. There was a treadmill and a weight bench in the largest space. The rest was storage and at the far end, the furnace and water heater.

Confident that he understood the house, he went back upstairs and settled in on the couch. Mavis would return shortly. He'd met the woman earlier in the day, when he and Bing had first arrived. She'd shown them into the living room, where they'd waited until Reverend Minnow had come to get them. Bing had met the woman before and the two of them chatted easily. Mack's impression of Mavis was that she was competent and fiercely loyal to the Minnow family, especially Patricia.

Mack heard a car approach shortly before nine. He

went to the window and pulled back the curtain. Mavis parked her Toyota next to his BMW and came in through the front door. When the alarm went off, the woman entered the code on the keypad to shut it off. Then she reset it.

"Mr. McCann," she said, turning to greet him. "I'm glad to see you. I was hoping Hope wouldn't have a change of heart and run you off."

Mack smiled. "I'm not that easy to shake."

Mavis shrugged. "And Hope Minnow is tougher than she looks." The woman put her foot on the bottom step. "I'm tired so I think I'll turn in right away. What time would you like breakfast, Mr. McCann?"

"It's Mack, please. And don't cook for me. I can take care of myself."

"You sound just like Hope. Looks as if these next ten days are going to be a vacation for me, too. Good night."

Mack watched the older woman walk up the stairs and listened for her room door to open and shut. Then he re-checked the security system to make sure it was on. Finally, he shut off the television and followed her upstairs.

He took a quick shower and pulled his jeans back on. They were comfortable enough to sleep in and he didn't want to get caught with his pants down or off. Then, cognizant that Mavis and Hope were asleep, he very quietly left his room, walked downstairs and stretched out on the couch in the family room.

And he didn't wake up until he heard the very soft beep of the security system being turned off. Then the distinct sound of the front door opening and softly closing.

In seconds, he was up and at the window, gun in hand. He saw a woman walking down the long lane, headed for the road. If he'd been even a second slower, he'd have lost her in the heavy tree line.

What the hell? It had to be Hope. Right height, right weight. Same sexy walk. But her hair was short and dark.

He slipped on his jacket, patted his pocket to make sure that his small flashlight was still there and followed, gun in hand. She was walking fast, her head down, likely watching to make sure she didn't trip.

An ankle injury would put a damper on her escape plans.

Was she running away? That was crazy. He knew she wasn't happy, but running away was for temperamental teens. And she had it made at her dad's house. No real responsibilities. Plenty of funding.

Out for a night on the town? In a disguise? Maybe. But she was dressed in a dark sweatshirt and baggy khaki pants. Not right for the club scene, even in Jersey. And why walk? She had a perfectly good car.

She stopped when she reached the road. She had her arms wrapped around her middle. Her head was no longer down. She was looking to the left, as if she were waiting for someone.

He considered approaching. He should, really.

But he knew that if he did, she'd simply lie about what had driven her to leave her warm bed at midnight.

And he'd be no closer to figuring out what made this woman tick.

So he stayed quiet, hidden by the trees. And in less than five minutes, an old car came along, slowing well before they could have seen Hope. When the car stopped, Hope stepped from the trees and opened the passenger-side door.

The car's interior light came on, showing the driver.

A woman. Dressed in dark blue or black scrubs. Probably ten years older than Hope.

Hope slid in and shut the door. The car drove away, leaving Mack McCann, who rarely got surprised by anything, standing at the side of the road, with his mouth hanging open.

Chapter Five

Hope leaned back against the headrest of the old car and sighed. It had been an emotionally draining day, and while she normally slept for a few hours before Sasha picked her up, she'd been unable to drift off tonight. Because of *him*.

Mack McCann. A necessary precaution, her mother had cajoled. Trusted friend, claimed Uncle Bing.

Brilliant strategy, she suspected, from her father's perspective.

Didn't really much matter what anybody else thought. She pretty much had him pegged as a thorn in her side.

She'd heard him come upstairs after Mavis had gotten home. Had heard the pipes of the old house groan when he'd showered. Could admit that she'd spent a few warm moments imagining how his naked body might look and had told herself it was normal to fantasize a bit, given that she hadn't had sex in almost two years.

And he was seriously handsome with his dark hair and hazel eyes. And physically fit. She knew he'd graduated from the naval academy with honors, spoke several languages fluently and was an expert marksman. Her mother had listed off those attributes this afternoon.

She hadn't been thinking one bit about those things when she'd spent several valuable minutes of her life wondering if he'd packed pajamas in his leather bag. Finally, she'd punched her pillow for the tenth time, closed her eyes tight and thought about the surprise and the delight on the stranger's face earlier that day when the woman realized that Hope intended for her to take all the packages that Hope had managed to accumulate while grazing on Fifth Avenue.

It had been an excellent way to end the day.

"Tired?" Sasha asked, her tone kind.

"No," Hope lied. If anyone had a right to be tired, it was Sasha. She always picked Hope up after she'd finished her three-to-eleven shift at the nursing home. "How was work?"

"Charlie Fenton ran away again tonight. Without his clothes on."

That wasn't a pretty picture. Hope recalled that Mr. Fenton was almost ninety. "Where did you find him this time?"

"Where we always find him. Buying donuts down the street. He was bringing them back for Delores. They're dating."

"That's sweet. How old is Delores?"

"A spry eighty-three. They're talking about getting married."

"You've got to be kidding," Hope said, laughing.

"You would think. Can you imagine?" Sasha gave her a quick sideways look. "Sorry," she added.

Sasha was one of the few who knew the real reason that Hope's brief marriage had crumbled. She'd been there to pick up the pieces. That was how the two women had met. "No problem," Hope said easily. She'd never be able to laugh about her own situation, but she wasn't so jaded that she couldn't feel good about these two old people sneaking around, as much as one could sneak when using a walker, acting like teenagers again.

"Think we'll be busy tonight?" Sasha asked, attempting to change the conversation.

It was a rhetorical question. No one could ever predict what kind of night it would be. The hotline had been quiet for a few nights so maybe it would heat up. They'd had a brand-new client and her two children two nights ago. She'd had two black eyes, a chipped tooth and a broken finger. Her young children had hung on to her the entire night, their little hands tightly clenching her cheap cotton T-shirt. Fortunately, they hadn't had a mark on them, but they'd evidently watched what their father had done to their mom.

Finally, Hope had gotten the four-year-old girl and five-year-old boy to follow her into the old kitchen. She'd convinced them to help her make some cupcakes so that Sasha and Jackie could work with the mom and get her started on rebuilding her life, one that didn't include regularly getting the hell beat out of her.

Sasha pulled her car into the parking lot of the nondescript one-story building. From the outside, it looked quiet enough. Always did. There were no neon signs blinking in these windows. Just a small sign on the door, one you had to be close to in order to read.

Gloria's Path. Named for the founder, Gloria Portland, who'd scraped together grants and private donations to open the ten-bed shelter eight years earlier. Now Gloria worked mostly days, leaving the night work to trusted volunteers and just a few paid staff.

Hope opened her door and got out. As she did, something fluttered to the ground. She bent and picked it up. She leaned into the car, using the interior light to see what it was.

It was a strip of vertical photos of Sasha and a man. "What's this?" she asked, holding the strip up so that Sasha, who was already out of the car, could see.

The woman waved a hand. "Oh, nothing. I went to my cousin's wedding last week and they had a photo booth there with a bunch of props."

When she didn't mention the man, Hope didn't pry. She knew that Sasha had been married and divorced twice. Maybe she was dipping her toes in the dating water again.

Hope gently tossed the strip back onto the passenger seat. "The purple glasses were a nice touch."

"It was that or a felt Santa hat."

The two women walked down the dark sidewalk and Sasha used her key to unlock the back door. The interior was softly lit, in deference to the late hour. But Hope knew that there would be activity. There always was. Previously abused women didn't sleep well. They were worried about their futures, their children's futures. And sometimes it was in the middle of the night that they most needed a supportive shoulder to lean upon.

Hope headed for the small kitchen to grab a cup of coffee. There was a woman sitting at the table. She had a half-empty cup sitting in front of her and she was playing with her smartphone.

Serena was a repeat client, first arriving almost six months ago, shortly after Hope had started her volunteer work. Serena had spent a few days at Gloria's Path, only to return home after her husband had pleaded with her and pledged that he'd do better. When she'd shown up almost two weeks ago, her face bruised and cut, she'd said that she was finally ready to leave her husband, because *better* still regularly included a sharp uppercut to the jaw.

She had no children and no other family in the immediate area. By the sounds of it, all she had was a very angry spouse who couldn't accept that his wife of three years had finally had enough.

"I was hoping you'd have a minute to talk," Serena said, suggesting that she'd been waiting for Hope's arrival. "I think I finally have a plan."

Hope smiled. Her night had begun.

MACK SAT IN his quiet car, debating what to do next. The second after he'd watched Hope get into the car, he'd been racing back to the house to get his own vehicle.

Fortunately, his keys had been in his jacket pocket and he'd been on the road fast. He'd caught up with the old Ford three minutes later, two miles outside the city limits of Weatherbie, the affluent commuter community of less than ten thousand in Western Essex County.

Because traffic was almost nonexistent, he'd had to drop back twice to ensure that they didn't realize they were being followed. He'd assumed they were going to roll through town and had almost lost them when they'd turned off the main street. He'd circled back and wasted time looking for them.

He'd found the car three blocks off the main drag, parked next to a square, one-story, frame building with a brick front on the corner of Marsh and Wooten. There was one other car in the small lot. There were narrow sidewalks and a couple of streetlights that provided inadequate illumination of what appeared to be a quiet area. He'd driven around the block once to get the lay of the land, then parked a block away, pulling into an empty spot on the street. He had a good visual of the front door.

During the daytime, there was likely some foot traffic due to the apartment buildings on both sides and a hair salon and an oil change shop across the street. However, in the middle of the night, there was nobody around.

At least not visible. Mack always expected somebody to be hiding in the shadows. It was what had kept him alive to the ripe old age of thirty-eight.

It was the second time in less than twelve hours that he'd chased after Hope. It was starting to be a rather tiresome activity. At least it hadn't been all the way back to New York City. She'd stayed local this time.

But why?

And what the hell was she doing inside the building?

Buying drugs? Possible. But she didn't look like a user. She had beautiful skin, shiny hair, pretty white teeth.

Prostitution? That made his skin crawl. And he felt a surge of jealousy in his gut that he didn't even attempt to analyze.

Gambling? Maybe. She had a lot of money and she didn't seem terribly upset about parting with it.

Dog fighting? He thumped the heel of his hand against his forehead. He was getting ridiculous.

He was just about to get out of his car, knock on the damn door and demand an explanation when an old El Camino with dual exhaust roared down the street. It slowed in front of the building just long enough for the passenger to toss something out of the window. Mack saw the flash.

Holy hell. It was a Molotov cocktail and thrown hard enough that when it hit the front window, it broke through. He could see flames dance upward.

The building was on fire and Hope was inside.

Mack dialed 911 as he raced toward the building. When the operator answered, he reported the fire and indicated the cross streets. Then he described the car

that had fled the scene before he hung up on the operator, who was instructing him to stay on the line.

The front door was locked. He had to kick it twice
before it gave and he was able to push his way through.
The small lobby area was already filling with smoke.
He could see flames climbing the curtains, spreading
onto the small couch, licking their way across the carpet. Heard a woman screaming.

He didn't think it was Hope. That didn't make him
feel any better.

He tried the interior door. Locked. His other option
was going over the waist-high counter that separated the
lobby from a small reception area. He braced his hands
on the counter and easily vaulted the barrier. On the desk
was a fire extinguisher, on its side, as if it had been tossed
there. The pin had been pulled. Mack picked it up and
pressed the handle, but nothing happened.

It was either empty or defective. Didn't matter. It
wasn't helping.

There was another door. This one not locked. It opened
into a long, dimly lit hallway with doors off to both sides.
Women and children, all in their pajamas, were stumbling out of those doors, shell-shocked.

Whoever had been screaming had stopped. The
woman who had picked up Hope stood at the end of the
hallway, her back against a partially open exit door, urg-
ing everyone to hurry.

There was no sign of Hope. Where the hell was she?

Then he saw her. She came out of a room, one arm
around a woman who had to be nine months pregnant,
the other holding a sleeping toddler. Her face was pale
against her chin-length auburn wig, but she was calm.

She looked down the hallway as if she were counting

heads and she saw him. Her face registered surprise and something else. Maybe relief?

"Check the rooms," she yelled, not missing a beat.

The hallway was filling with smoke. He used the flashlight on his key chain. It was small but powerful and he could see enough. The rooms were empty. By the time he got to the back door, he realized that Hope had changed places with the other woman. She was bracing the door open and she no longer held the child. He could hear the sounds of approaching emergency vehicles.

Her eyes met his. "I did a quick head count," she said. "I think everyone is out."

"Rooms are empty," he confirmed.

"Thank God." She glanced nervously over her shoulder. The other woman had moved the group to the end of the small parking lot, where they would be out of the firefighters' way.

"I have to get out of here," she said, insistent. "I can't be here when fire and police arrive. Will you help me?"

He had a thousand questions. "What…?"

The look in her pretty eyes stopped him. Fear. Real fear. He didn't know what the hell was up but he wanted her out of there. He wanted her safe.

He grabbed her hand, pulled her around the corner of the building and they raced for his car down the street.

They got inside and she immediately huddled down, as if trying to stay out of sight. He pulled out just as the fire truck rounded the curve.

He drove for three minutes before he couldn't stand it any longer. "What the hell is going on, Hope?"

She straightened up. "Did they see us?" she asked.

He shook his head. "I don't think so. But people inside the building saw you."

"Sasha knows that I got out. I told her I was leaving. She understands. She won't say anything about me being there."

"What about everyone else?"

"I guess I have to hope that the police talk to Sasha. She'll do her best to keep me out of it."

They had reached the main highway. He looked in his rearview mirror. Nobody was following them. "What the hell is that place and what were you doing there? And why are you wearing a wig and dressed like that?"

She didn't answer.

He slowed the car down and flipped on his turn signal, as if he might be turning around.

"Oh, fine," she said, her tone exasperated. "It's a women's shelter. For victims of domestic abuse. I volunteer there. They know me as Paula."

Because he'd had the benefit of seeing the past few minutes, he wasn't as surprised as he might have been. He'd been able to process the scene. But still, her words were pretty damn shocking.

It would have been helpful if Archibald Minnow had mentioned this when he'd given Bing and him the tour of the Minnow estate. "Nobody said anything to me about this," he said.

"Nobody knows," she said. "Well, that's not exactly true. Mavis knows. But she'd never say anything." She paused for a minute. "I assume you somehow managed to follow me."

"Yes." He figured she'd blast him for that. But she simply shook her head in disgust.

"I can't even manage to sneak out of a house."

"Don't beat yourself up. I'm a little more observant than your average houseguest. Who's the woman that picked you up?"

"Sasha. She has a paid position with Gloria's Path. That's the name of the shelter," she added.

"She must know the truth about who you are," he stated.

"She does."

He waited for some additional explanation, but it didn't appear that any was forthcoming. Okay. He'd circle back to that later. "The two of you were doing a good job getting people out of there."

"We got lucky. Sasha was in the reception area when the firebomb or whatever it was came through the window. She tried to use the fire extinguisher but it didn't work. She yelled and I got the person I was with out the door and went back in for more."

That made him feel sick. "You shouldn't have gone back in," he said. "Once you're out of a burning building, you stay out."

She shook her head. "There's no way I would do that," she said simply.

It wasn't said in a boastful way. Just a statement of fact. And he realized that there was much more to Hope Minnow than he had anticipated.

"It was a Molotov cocktail and some guy riding shotgun in an old yellow El Camino threw it through the window. I told the police that when I made the 911 call. That vehicle ring a bell?"

She shook her head. "No. But I imagine the police will want to know if it rings a bell with any of the clients. It's likely someone trying to make trouble for one of them. We work really hard to keep the location of the shelter a secret. It's by referral only and there's no signage on the street. But it is possible that some estranged spouse or significant other got lucky and figured it out."

He turned to look at her. "Maybe somebody was trying to make trouble for you? You're the one receiving the threats."

She shook her head. "I know you don't believe me, but those threats are bogus. Besides, nobody knows that I volunteer there. It's a secret that I've been very careful to keep."

"Something isn't a secret if more than one person knows. You just said that Mavis and Sasha both know."

She shrugged. "I trust Mavis and, well, the same for Sasha. She had a chance to sell me out before when it would have been really bad for me. She didn't take the opportunity then. She won't take it now."

He was starting to get a very bad feeling. "How did you meet Sasha?"

She was quiet for a long time. Finally, she spoke very softly. "She's worked at Gloria's Path for several years. Lucky for me, she was the counselor on duty the night I showed up beaten and broken."

Chapter Six

It was the first time she'd said the words out loud to anyone besides her father. Mack showed no reaction. That made it easier somehow. If he'd looked shocked or surprised in any way that someone like her had been battered, she'd have wanted to kick him.

"Your ex?" he asked, his voice tight.

She nodded. "William Baylor the third. Never met the first and the second seemed like a nice guy. I guess maybe the apple fell pretty far from that tree."

"How badly were you hurt?"

"Broken nose. Fractured jaw. Bruised larynx. He tried to choke me," she added. "Two cracked ribs. Assorted other bumps and bruises."

"I hope to hell you pressed charges," he said, his voice sounding hard.

This is where it got difficult for her. "No, I didn't."

He seemed to consider his next question. "Why not?" he asked finally.

They were pulling into her long driveway. She waited to answer until he'd parked the car and turned it off. "I didn't press charges because I didn't tell anyone except my father. My mother was very ill at the time. We thought she was dying. My father asked me to keep it from her and I ultimately agreed."

There was just enough moonlight coming in through the sunroof that she could tell that he was puzzled about something. She knew what the next question would be.

"Your ex still works in your dad's ministry? What's with that?"

Indeed. What was with that? "That was my father's decision," she said. "You'd have to talk to him about that."

She opened her car door and shut it quietly, even though she desperately wanted to slam it. She didn't want to wake Mavis, regardless of how it made her feel to talk about her father's betrayal. No wonder she never felt compelled to tell anybody about what had happened. When would the hurt stop? Her father had a choice. He could have chosen Hope. Instead, he'd chosen Wills.

And she was never going to forget that.

She unlocked the front door and went inside. She heard Mack follow her in. Heard him set the alarm.

She was going to bed. Going to try to forget the last hour.

"Hope?"

Damn. It had already been a heck of a night. She kept walking. She had her foot on the fourth step when he tried again.

"Please?"

She hadn't expected that. "Yes," she said, without turning around.

"I'm sorry that happened to you. Baylor deserved to have his ass kicked by somebody bigger and stronger."

It was the quiet conviction that was almost her undoing. To fight her own dangerous impulses, she took a deep breath, then another. "It doesn't matter anymore." Then she lifted her foot and kept going until she reached the top of the stairs and walked down the hallway to her room.

DOESN'T MATTER. The hell it didn't. The idea of a man hitting a woman was unconscionable and the fact that Reverend Archibald Minnow kept the abuser within the ministry was absurd.

It was no wonder that Hope detested her father. What was the man thinking? Mack wanted to call him up and demand an answer. Then he wanted to raise some hell with the ex, cause him some serious pain.

Whatever he'd expected when he'd watched Hope get in that car, it certainly hadn't been that she was volunteering at a battered women's shelter. He hadn't expected that she'd run back into a burning building to save someone else. And he certainly hadn't expected that she'd run from the limelight.

Run? Hide was more like it.

And now she was upstairs, doing more of the same. And he was letting her because quite frankly, he wasn't sure what to say to her. *I'm sorry* seemed painfully inadequate. It had been the best he could do.

She'd been quick to again dismiss the possibility that the attack on the shelter had anything to do with her. He wasn't as easily convinced. But there wasn't a lot he could do about it at one in the morning.

Mack sank down on the couch, leaned his head back and closed his eyes. He wondered how badly the building had been damaged. The fire department had responded quickly. No doubt the lobby area was gone, but they likely had kept the fire from spreading far into the main living area. There would be smoke damage but there were companies that could effectively remove that.

Even in the best of circumstances, the clients would need to be relocated to other shelters until repairs could be done. Would Hope want to volunteer at the new location? She needed to understand that there wasn't going to be any more sneaking around. Everything had worked out okay tonight. They might not be so lucky the next time.

He slowed his breathing. Years of living on the edge had taught him the importance of being able to quickly wind down, relax and catch a few hours of sleep. As he drifted off, he wondered which Hope Minnow he was going to encounter in the morning.

When he awoke, exactly three hours later at half past four, the house was quiet. He checked the security system, even though he was confident that it was still intact. Hope had stayed in her room and Mavis was not yet up.

He drank a glass of water. Then he pulled on his running shoes and headed for the treadmill in the basement. He'd always been a runner and preferred running outdoors when he could. In college, he'd been on the cross-country team at the naval academy and had spent countless hours running the track that was across the Severn River. It had wound through a golf course filled with military personnel and politicians who had swings with wicked right hooks.

It was likely where he'd learn the valuable skill of ducking and darting.

Twenty-eight minutes and five miles later, he was feeling much better. He pulled his T-shirt off and used it to wipe the sweat off his face. He wrapped it around his neck, intending to head for the shower.

As he walked up the stairs, he heard the faint sound of a chair scraping across the tile floor. Mavis? Possibly. He silently walked up the rest of the steps and cautiously looked around the corner.

Hope was at the table, sitting cross-legged, with her bare legs tucked under her butt, wearing pajamas that had—yep, those were dolphins on them. She had left her awful wig behind and her long blond hair was loosely pulled back into a low ponytail. Her face was makeup-free. She was reading the newspaper.

She was really very beautiful.

And what the hell was she doing up at five in the morning?

"Hi," he said.

She jumped about a foot and pages flew. And when she landed, she had her hand on her heart. She stared at him and her cheeks got pink.

"Don't ever do that again," she said, bending to gather up the newspaper on the floor.

He caught a glimpse of tanned skin as her pajama top pulled away from her shorts. It made him think that Hope likely spent some time outside by the pool. Her skin was silky smooth and when she straightened up, he had to look away fast.

He walked over to the coffeepot that now had fresh coffee. He made himself busy opening cupboards, looking for exactly the right cup. Damn. He'd been hot when he'd finished his run but he was feeling even warmer now.

Get a grip, he told himself. He was here in the role of bodyguard. "Sorry I scared you," he said. "I didn't expect you to be up." He looked over his shoulder.

"I couldn't sleep." She was fiddling with the handle of her coffee cup.

"Have you talked to your friend Sasha?"

"I did," she said, not looking up. "I sent her a text last night and she called about two hours after we got home."

That meant she'd had almost no sleep. If there were ever a day that she deserved to sleep past noon, today was it.

"What did she have to say?" he asked, turning back to pour that wonderful first cup. He didn't put the pot down. Instead, he carried it over to the table. He filled

Hope's half-empty cup. He returned the pot to the burner, grabbed his cup and took a chair at the other end of the table from Hope.

She evidently wasn't interested in sharing space because she pushed her chair back and walked over to the sink. She stood at the window, looking out, her back to him. "They were able to work out an arrangement with one of the hotels in town. All the clients stayed there last night. They have space for them for the next few days. However, there's a big soccer tournament this weekend and the hotel is booked then. Unfortunately, that means the clients will have to move again."

"Back to Wooten Street?"

Hope shook her head. "Sasha didn't know. Today they will have contractors come in to assess the damage and see how long it will take to repair the lobby and get the smoke out of the rest of the building."

"The police have any idea who did this?" He wished she would turn around. It was disconcerting to talk to her back even though he appreciated the view of her very nicely rounded rear end. No wonder the dolphins looked happy.

"Sasha didn't think so. The investigating officer did ask the clients if they had any knowledge of a yellow El Camino and all of them said no. They could, however, be lying. Battered women sometimes protect the wrong people."

It wasn't only battered women who did that. Over the years, he'd investigated countless situations where, had the truth been told initially, it would have been bad, but definitely not as bad as the cover-up that generally began when one sailor lied to protect another.

"They don't do it to cause a problem," she added, finally turning to face him. She evidently had taken his silence as condemnation.

He held up a hand. "No judgment here. I've learned along the way that the truth is always somewhere in the middle."

She smiled but there was no joy there. "As a child, you are taught to always tell the truth. Then you become an adult and you realize that everyone lies. It's quite a coming-of-age moment." She turned again and dumped her coffee in the sink.

"Not everyone lies," he said, again talking to her back. "And certainly not all the time."

She shrugged. "Maybe not. Perhaps the small corner of the world where I live is just different." She shoved a hand through her hair. "I'm going back to bed."

"You don't have to hide in your room," he said.

She straightened her lovely spine. "I'm not hiding."

"Last night you said that the only person you told was your father. But you also said that Mavis knows. That doesn't match."

She turned to face him. "Mavis knows that I work at the shelter. She doesn't know why. She was cleaning up my room one day and discovered Paula's clothes and wig. She asked about it and I had to tell her something. She thinks that I'm keeping it a secret because I believe my father would use it to his advantage—that he would somehow look even better to the followers if it got out that I was volunteering my time at a women's shelter. She knows that I'm not interested in helping my father build his empire."

"Don't you think she's curious about why you picked Gloria's Path?"

Hope shook her head. "She's never really asked."

Speaking of Mavis, Mack heard the woman coming

down the stairs. She was talking to someone. When she rounded the corner of the kitchen, he could see that she had her cell phone up to her ear. Her hair wasn't combed and her shirt had been misbuttoned so one side was hanging lower than the other.

He took his shirt that was wrapped around his neck, shook it out and pulled it back on.

"I want to come, I do. But I just don't know. I'll have to get back to you. Stay strong, sis. Tell Walt that I'm praying for him." Mavis pushed the end button on her phone.

"What's wrong?" Hope asked, moving close to the older woman.

"My sister's husband in Mobile, Alabama, had a heart attack. He's not doing so well. Their only child died of cancer years ago so Greta's trying to deal with this on her own."

"You have to go be with her," Hope said immediately. "I'll get you a plane ticket for this morning."

Mavis shook her head. Then she walked over to the refrigerator and pulled off the top calendar page. It was one of those where every day had its own page. She crumpled up the paper, opened a cupboard under the sink and tossed the ball into the trash. "I told your mother that I'd be here while she was gone, that I'd watch out for you."

Hope looked exasperated. "*He's* supposed to watch out for me," she said, pointing to Mack.

"Nice of you to acknowledge that," he said. He turned to Mavis. "Look, I've got this under control. You do what you need to do. We'll be fine."

The older woman looked from Hope to Mack and back again. Then she walked back to her calendar and flipped pages. She stopped at one several days in and pointed at a handwritten note. "I'm supposed to volunteer at the library fund-raiser. It's a car wash. They need every volunteer they can get."

"No problem," Hope said. "That's more than a week away. If you're not back by then, I'll take your place. I know how to wash a car."

"You're sure?"

"Sure that I know how to wash a car or sure that I'll volunteer?" Hope asked, her voice teasing.

Mavis just shook her head. "I was going to buy groceries this morning."

"I'm pretty sure that between the two of us, we can handle that," Hope answered.

"I don't have anything baked," Mavis said.

"I make a mean chocolate cake," Mack replied.

Hope raised her eyebrows.

"You wait. You'll be begging for another piece."

Mavis looked between the two of them. "Be kind to each other," she said. She turned to Hope. "You be careful. Don't underestimate the threats."

Hope nodded. "I won't. Now get going. And you may want to take another pass at those buttons," she said, gently wrapping her arm around the woman's shoulder. "I'll help you pack."

The kitchen was strangely quiet after the two women left. Mack sat and drank his coffee. It appeared that he and Hope were going to be playing house for a few days. He'd seen how Hope moderated her actions around Mavis. Last night, she'd been very quiet coming into the house, likely because she hadn't wanted to wake her up. Without Mavis around, all bets were off. The amount of mischief Hope could get into was probably limited only by her imagination.

Great. He better get some new locks for the doors.

Chapter Seven

Hope went downstairs to see off Mavis and then she retreated back to her bedroom for a nap. She didn't see Mack when she was on the first floor, but realized he was outside when, through the open window, she overheard him telling Mavis goodbye.

She didn't care what he was doing. As long as he wasn't bothering her.

She had to admit, he'd been helpful last night. She'd looked up and through the smoke, he'd appeared, like some superhero. And he'd checked every room, saving her from having to go back down the hallway to do it.

Then, she'd heard those police and fire sirens and known that she needed a quick escape. If the newspapers were interested in when she had a drink at some charity event in the city, they'd be all over a story like this.

The whole ugly truth would come out.

Byron Ferguson would drool with delight. The photojournalist had taken an interest in the Minnow family several years ago. Ferguson had been a general nuisance, snapping pictures at events that Hope or her parents attended. He'd partnered up with a writer at the newspaper and they'd done a whole series that had chronicled Reverend Archibald Minnow's rise from small-town preacher to world-wide religious icon. The piece had been good enough to win several awards, although not good enough for a Pulitzer. Still, Hope had anticipated it would rocket Ferguson out of Weatherbie and into the Big Apple.

But Byron Ferguson had stayed in Weatherbie. He'd gotten a new title and she assumed he'd gotten more work. However, he still had time to always be there, every time the Minnows were creating any news.

From her perspective, it was a bit of a love/hate relationship. He'd been helpful several times when she'd decided to give the press a photo opportunity of Hope Minnow, party-girl extraordinaire. She was sure he'd snapped the picture that had run with the *People* article. She wondered how much he'd been paid for that.

If she'd have wanted to tell anyone about getting beaten by her husband, Byron would have been happy to document the damage. It could have been front-page news.

And there had been times—many times, especially in the first few months after the incident—that she'd been tempted to tell the whole story, to expose her ex for the bastard that he was. But she'd given her father her word.

And her father's request wasn't unreasonable. Her mother had reveled in the match that Hope had made with her marriage to William Baylor the third. His family was old money, with a huge apartment near Central Park, an estate in the Hamptons and another one in Vail.

It would have bothered her mother terribly to know that she'd been so wrong about William, that she'd encouraged her daughter to marry a man with a violent temper.

Her mother had been too sick to hear that kind of news. Her father had been right about that.

And as time went by, she became less and less inclined to want to talk about it. Last night had proven that. She'd barely been able to get the words out of her mouth. *My husband beat me.*

It would hurt her mother if she learned the news now. It would cause problems between her parents. There was no way that her mom had rebuilt her strength enough for that kind of strife.

It might cause trouble for her father's ministry and she was okay with that, but once again, that would be hard on her mom. It all came back to that.

She'd keep her secret. Although Mack was right. Once more than one person knew, it was no longer really a secret. She trusted Sasha. Now Mack had the real story. Could she trust him?

She hoped so. He'd surprised her this morning when he'd walked upstairs after working out, looking all hot and sweaty. She'd seen his naked chest and all those muscles and her own body had heated up, all the way to the top of her head.

She'd fought back by standing at the sink, with her back to him. She'd been relieved when Mavis had walked in and he'd put his shirt back on. But truly, it had been a shame to cover up such male beauty. He'd evidently been hitting the treadmill this morning, but she suspected he did more than that to maintain that kind of physical condition.

She lay back on her bed and tried to forget that it was just her and Mack in the big house. The place was plenty big enough for the two of them. There was no need for them to be even in the same room at the same time. They would coexist. Not cohabitate. She closed her eyes, satisfied that she had a plan.

When she awoke several hours later, her stomach was telling her it was lunchtime. She took a quick shower and dried her hair. She pulled on black leggings and a simple black silky T-shirt. Then she carefully assembled her "work" clothes: baggy gray denim pants, a loose lightweight, long-sleeved shirt, tennis shoes and, of course, her wig. She hated the wig. It was hot and itchy but she knew it was absolutely necessary. Thanks to Byron Ferguson, she'd been photographed enough in the last couple of years that her blond hair was likely recognizable to many people in Weatherbie.

Before the fire had started, she and Serena had been in the kitchen, working out the details for Serena's move. The young woman had contacted her mother, who lived out of state. Divorced herself, the mom had limited funds to help Serena get a new start. Still, she'd managed to scrape together several hundred dollars for her daughter. Serena was hoping that money, along with what she'd gotten when she'd pawned the jewelry her husband had given her, would be enough to rent a small apartment in Weatherbie.

Hope wasn't so sure. While the rent there didn't begin to compare with the rent that someone would pay in New York City, it still wasn't cheap.

As Hope gathered up her work clothes, by habit she reached for her leather satchel that she always used to carry them. She stopped, hand in midair, realizing that she didn't need to hide the items. In the past, she would leave the house as Hope Minnow, stop at the convenience store two miles down the road, use the ladies' restroom to change and emerge as Paula.

It was rather liberating to realize that, for the first time ever, she'd be able to walk out of her room and not have to hide Paula, whom she rather liked. At least she liked her a whole lot better than Hope, who was drifting these days, caught in a place where she'd let her old life go, but she hadn't yet fully embraced a new path.

Hope acted upon her aggression toward her father by spending his money and getting photographed in situations that he might find uncomfortable or at odds with his public persona.

Her master's degree wasn't in psychology, but that didn't mean that she didn't understand what she was doing. She acted out in a rather classically passive-aggressive way toward her father. Because she was angry at him. *Very, very angry,* to coin a phrase from Richard Gere in *Pretty Woman*. She loved that scene. He and Julia Roberts were in the bathtub and after he admitted that he was very angry with his father, she wrapped her legs around him, citing some amazing fact that her legs were forty-four inches long so that she could offer eighty-eight inches of therapy.

She couldn't help but wonder how long Mack's legs might be.

Good grief. She needed *real* therapy.

She pulled her pants and shirt on over her leggings and T-shirt. She put the shoes on. She pulled Paula's cell phone out of the leather bag where she always kept it. Then she walked down the big staircase, carrying her wig and the phone. She could smell bacon. When she got to the kitchen, she stopped in the doorway. Mack stood behind the counter, a cutting board in front of him. He was slicing tomatoes. There was already a stack of lettuce leaves on a plate.

"Hello, Paula," he said. "Sleep well?"

The fact that he'd so clearly grasped that she wasn't just pretending to be someone different, but that she really was someone different when she pulled on Paula's clothes, struck her hard.

"Pretty well," she said.

"New outfit?" he asked.

"Even Paula can't wear khaki pants every day," she said, smiling.

"New phone?" he asked, looking at the simple flip phone.

"Hope has a smartphone," she said. "I buy a prepaid phone at the drugstore and that's what Paula uses."

"You're pretty good at this double life," he said.

"Good enough," she agreed. She'd been doing it for eight months and nobody had caught on yet. "I noticed that my other clothes reek of smoke. I'm going to put them in the wash." She hesitated. "I could throw your jeans from last night in, too, if you'd like."

"No need. Already did a load this morning when you were sleeping. Hope you like BLTs," he said, as if it were the most natural thing in the world for him to make her a sandwich. "I cut up some fruit, too," he said, pointing to a bowl on the counter.

She was truly flabbergasted. Her bodyguard also did laundry and cooked. "How much is my father paying you?"

The minute she said it, she was sorry. It sounded so bitchy. "I certainly didn't expect this," she added, trying to soften the harshness of her earlier words.

"We have to eat. I shine at breakfast, can muddle my way through lunch and if you like steak, I'm good for dinner, too. But Mavis was right. We need to make a grocery run. Maybe we could do that this afternoon?"

Her stomach growled. Loudly. She pulled a plate out of the cupboard and started building her sandwich. Ten minutes later, halfway through lunch, she put down her fork. "This is really good. Thank you."

"You're welcome," he said. He stared pointedly at the wig that she'd placed at the end of the counter. "What are your plans for the day, Paula?"

She took a drink of water. Then a second one.

He waited patiently, as if he had all day.

"There's a woman who needs to find an apartment. She's been at the shelter close to the maximum time that she can stay there. I told her that I'd help her look this afternoon."

He nodded. "In Weatherbie?"

"Yes. While she might prefer leaving, she has a good job in town as an occupational-therapy assistant and she doesn't want to leave it."

"What's her story?"

"Dated her high-school sweetheart for several years. They were going to get married. But before that could happen, he got blown up by a roadside bomb in Afghanistan. Six months later, a friend introduced her to Wayne. They dated for about six months before they got married. He hit her for the first time on their second anniversary. He was upset that they hadn't yet managed to get pregnant. Evidently, he's big on children."

"So, she left him?"

"Not right away. She actually first sought help from Gloria's Path about six months ago. However, he promised to be good and she so desperately wanted to believe him."

"She still loved him after that?" Mack asked, his tone disbelieving.

"Maybe. And maybe it was just hard for her to admit publicly that she made a big mistake by choosing him. Anyway, it took a couple more trips to the emergency room before she finally decided that she'd had enough. That's when she came to Gloria's Path a second time."

"She tell the police?"

"Yes. This time. And he was arrested. Spent a night in jail before he bonded out. He's not very happy with her."

"What's Wayne's last name?"

"Smother. Wayne Smother."

He raised an eyebrow. "Smother? Really? He doesn't walk around with a pillow, does he?"

She smiled. "I know. It's a ridiculous name. But really, who am I to talk? Minnow?"

"Bet that was fun in middle school."

She nodded. "Minnow became Catfish, Guppy, Goldfish because of my hair, and then there was the perennial favorite, when they messed with both my first and last names, and I became Hopeless Fish Bait."

"Hopeless Fish Bait," he repeated. "I like it. Sounds like a rock band from the nineties."

"Lovely." With a smile, she pushed her plate away and stood up. "I'll only be gone for a few hours. I can stop at the store on my way home."

"Where you go, I go," he said, taking a big bite of his sandwich. He chewed.

"That's impossible," she said. "Listen, it's the middle of the day. Broad daylight. Nothing is going to happen to me."

"You're right. Nothing is going to happen to you." He used his napkin to wipe off his mouth.

"How am I going to explain you?" she asked, her voice rising. "Paula doesn't have a bodyguard."

He shrugged, looking unconcerned. "Pick another *B*."

"What?"

"Brother, boyfriend, babysitter, butler, banker—"

"Stop. You're being ridiculous."

"No, ridiculous is being careless with your personal safety. Your father, mother, Bing and Mavis all think that the threats are legit. That's good enough for me. I'm your shadow. Now that you've been fed, are you willing to listen to the rules?"

"Rules?" She raised an eyebrow.

"Yeah, rules. Rule number one—don't go anywhere without telling me where you're going. Rule number two—when I tell you to do something, do it right away, no questions asked. For example, if I say get down, then hit the dirt. Don't debate me."

"I recall Uncle Bing mentioning that you'd been in the navy. You must have been in charge." She made sure he understood that it wasn't a compliment.

He put his chin in the air. "Think I'm bossy, huh? I come by it naturally. I have a younger sister."

She hadn't thought about him having family. He wasn't wearing a ring so she didn't think he was married. Plus, what wife would let her husband play bodyguard to another woman?

"How old is your sister?"

"Almost thirty. Eight years younger than me. She's getting married this summer. I guess she's old enough."

For sure. "I was thirty when I got married. Divorced at thirty-two. I hope she has better luck."

"She's marrying a great guy. One of the best."

"Good for her." She figured she might as well ask. "How about you? Are you married, Mack?"

"Nope. I haven't been in one spot long enough in the last sixteen years to get married."

"But now you're done with the military?"

"Yeah. I'm going to put down some roots in Colorado. That's where my sister and my dad live."

"Are your parents divorced?"

"My mom died when I was in high school. Cancer."

The most awful *C* word in the world. "I'm sorry," she said, swallowing hard. "I was older when my mother got sick and it was still so very hard. I can't imagine what it was like for you in high school. And for your sister. She was just a little girl when she lost her mother. And how sad for your dad."

He looked away and for once, she caught just a hint of vulnerability on his handsome face. "It was hard on the whole family. My mom was pretty special. My dad didn't remarry for twenty years and then when he did, his new wife turned out to be a traitor. Six months ago, after she tried to kill my sister, she was arrested for attempted murder and treason. She's going to be in prison for a long time."

Wow. And she'd thought her life had some drama. She pushed her hair back behind her ears. The silence in the room was deafening. "Have you guys thought about becoming a reality-television show?"

It was a little irreverent but it broke the tension immediately. He winked at her. "Want to make a guest-star appearance?"

"Maybe sometime," she said. "Paula doesn't have a bodyguard or a butler or a banker. But she could have a brother. And that appears to be a role you could convincingly play. Let's go. Serena will be waiting for me."

Chapter Eight

They were halfway to town before Hope spoke again. "Serena's not too keen on men right now."

He glanced sideways at her. She had left off her wig for the ride to town, thank goodness. It rested in her lap like a fox fur. "I imagine not," he said. He waited a minute. "So, are you my younger or older sister?"

She gave him a dirty look. "Younger. Much. We have very little in common."

"What's your favorite color?"

"Why?"

"I think I'd know that about you. That would have been the used-up color in your crayon box."

"Yellow." She paused. "You?"

"Men don't have favorite colors. And if I'm much older, then my crayons would have disappeared long before you came along."

She considered that. "Favorite food?"

"Chicken enchiladas. Spicy."

"I thought you said that the only dinner you could make was a mean steak?"

"I don't have to be able to make it myself to love it. Best enchilada maker was aboard the *USS Higgins*. I was on ship for several months and I never got tired of enchilada night."

"I thought you were an intelligence officer. Did you actually spend time on board a ship?"

"Absolutely. At different times, in different places. Sometimes my stays were as short as a couple hours, sometimes as long as a couple months. Sometimes the ship was in port and sometimes, at sea."

"I assume an intelligence officer gathers intelligence. Right?"

"Gathers. Analyzes. Tries to figure out what's real and what's been leaked to keep you chasing your tail. After 9/11, there was data overload. Somebody had to figure out what was important and connect the dots between pieces of information gathered from all over the world."

"And that somebody was you?"

"I was always good at puzzles."

They were at the edge of town. Hope pulled on her wig and even though he'd expected it, he was still startled by her change in appearance. It was no wonder she'd been successful at keeping from being recognized. Unless somebody looked past the ugly clothes and dull hair, they would never realize it was Hope Minnow, all dressed down.

But she wouldn't have had to have been recognized. Two people knew her secret. Her friend Sasha and Mavis. If they had each told two people who had each told two people, the math became exponentially dangerous.

They entered the unimpressive lobby of the chain motel and passed by the reservation desk. Hope punched the elevator button. She'd gotten the room number from Sasha. On the third floor, they got out and knocked on 310. "Remember," Hope stressed, "it's Paula."

"This is not my first time at the dance," he said, somewhat irritated that she'd underestimated his ability to quickly go undercover. Hell, for six months in Afghanistan he'd been someone very different than Mack McCann, and the information he'd managed to gain had been very valuable.

A woman, mid-twenties, with some crazy railroad-track tattoo on her neck, opened the door. She smiled at *Paula* and then her gaze shifted to him. Her eyes turned wary.

He smiled and tried to look harmless.

"Serena, this is my brother, Mack. He's visiting from out of town. I told him he could come along today."

Mack considered extending his arm for a handshake but decided to let her make the first move. All he got was a nod.

"Ready?" Hope asked.

"I got a text from Wayne," Serena said.

"And?" Hope prompted.

"He said that he'll go for counseling."

"Do you believe him?" Hope replied, her tone neutral.

"I believe that he believes he will. But when it comes right down to it, he won't go. Just like before."

"Did you answer the text?"

"I told him I was getting an apartment. Not where, of course."

Mack doubted there were all that many apartments in the pricy suburb. Lots of estates like the Minnows' and probably some nice condos, too. The rental market was probably not so great. Renters were expected to move along to the cheaper suburbs.

"All right," Hope said.

He got the impression that she wasn't thrilled that Serena had communicated with her estranged husband. But perhaps she'd expected it.

"We'd better get going," Hope said.

They were barely in the car before Serena leaned forward from the backseat, as if she were a little kid excited about going on a journey. "Thank you, Paula," she said. "I know I should be able to do this by myself but I just feel so much better having you here."

"I'm happy I can help," Hope said.

She was, he thought. He keyed in the address that Serena read off to him into his GPS. The apartment was less than three miles from the hotel.

"I didn't know you had a brother," Serena said. "You never mentioned that."

"Mack and I don't see that much of each other," Hope said easily.

"What do you do for a living, Mack?" Serena asked.

"Just got out of the navy," he said. It was always best to stick as close to the truth as possible, even when one was lying.

"Wayne was in the navy, too," Serena said. "Before we were married. He didn't talk about it much. I don't think he liked it."

"Military service isn't for everyone," Mack said. True. But maybe Wayne, who apparently had an anger management problem, hadn't been able to abide by the rules that were necessary to keep the military running smoothly.

The apartment building was a three-story brick-and-frame combination, circa 1970, with nice square windows and a roof that looked recently patched. There were sliding glass doors that led to small balconies on both the second and third floors. The parking lot next to the building was empty with the exception of two cars. Likely most everybody was working during the middle of the day. The trees around the building were mature and the grass needed to be mowed. It was close enough to the train station that renters could easily catch a train into the city for work or play.

All in all, it looked as if it might suit a young woman looking for a fresh start.

"I hope I can afford this," Serena said.

"Let's see the inside before you start worrying about money," Hope said.

The three of them got out of the car and walked inside. The landlord, a man of almost sixty with a slight limp, met them in the lobby, and led them up the staircase. When he unlocked the door of the second-floor apartment, Serena was the first inside. It took her just a few minutes to look in both bedrooms and the bathroom, and then return to the space that served as both kitchen and living room. She stood still for just seconds before she pulled open the vertical blinds that evidently came with the apartment and opened the sliding glass door. The balcony was probably only three-by-two, barely large enough for a couple of lawn chairs. She stepped outside and looked over the railing.

A princess surveying her new kingdom.

A survivor grateful for another day.

She came back inside, carefully locking the door behind her. She seemed less agitated than before, as if she'd come to a decision.

"What do you think?" the landlord asked.

It was okay, Mack thought. Lots of white walls and beige carpet. But it was better than living on the street or in a women's shelter. Much better than living with somebody who used you as a punching bag. Evidently Serena was thinking the same thing because she was nodding her head.

"I think it could work," she said. "How much?"

"First and last month's rent plus a security deposit of 800 dollars. Total of 2,400 dollars."

The woman's face fell. "I didn't think about the security deposit. I should have. I just don't have that much."

Mack was about to step up and offer to cover the deposit but Hope beat him to it. "May we have a minute?" she said to the landlord.

"Sure." He walked out into the hallway, leaving the door open a crack.

"Do you like it?" Hope asked.

"I do. And the train is so close, I wouldn't need to buy a car to get to work. But I don't have that much cash. I could probably cover the first and last month's rent if I didn't eat much for a couple weeks, but the security deposit makes it way too much."

"We have some funds available through the shelter. How about we cover the security deposit plus we'll advance you a couple hundred to cover food and other expenses until you get your first paycheck?"

Serena's eyes filled with tears. "Really? Gloria's Path would do that?"

Gloria's Path wasn't writing any checks. Mack was confident of that. Hope Minnow was going to fund this woman's escape on her own dime. He figured it wasn't the first time.

"Absolutely," Hope said. She opened the door and motioned the landlord back inside. He produced a lease, Hope and Serena read it and then Serena signed on the dotted line.

"I'll need the money before I turn over any keys," the landlord said.

"She'll be back tomorrow," Hope said. "At noon."

Serena practically skipped back to the car and Mack realized that a heavy weight had been lifted from the woman's shoulders.

He drove back to the hotel and they dropped off Serena. Once it was just the two of them in the car, he turned to Hope. "You do that often? Give money to the clients?"

"Who said I was giving her money?" Hope asked innocently.

"I did."

She shrugged. "It's no big deal. She needs it and I have it. The important thing is making sure that no woman ever goes back to her abusive spouse simply because she doesn't have the financial resources to live on her own." She pulled off her red wig and shook out her long blond hair.

Mack desperately wanted to run his fingers through it. Instead, he kept his hands tightly clenched around the steering wheel.

Then she took off her shirt and her baggy pants.

She had black leggings and a black T-shirt underneath. He hadn't realized that when she'd started ripping off her clothes.

"We need to buy groceries," he said. See, he could act normal even when his heart was skipping every other beat.

"Turn left at the next corner," she said. "There's a store two blocks down on the right. I can run in."

"Where you go, I go," he reminded her, proud that his voice didn't crack. She had no idea how gorgeous she was.

She rolled her eyes. Even that was cute.

"People in Weatherbie know that I don't have a brother," she said.

"There are *B*'s left," he said, reminding her of their earlier conversation. "If none of them suit you, work your way to the *C*'s."

"I have one. How about Crazy?"

"Works for me. I'll be your Crazy Cousin Charlie."

She held up a hand. "Stop. I have to live here long after you've forgotten my name. Let's just go inside, buy some groceries like normal people and if anybody asks, I'll tell them that you're a friend visiting from out of town. Just don't strike up a conversation with anybody."

Chapter Nine

"Do you shop here regularly?" he asked as they walked from the car into the store.

She shook her head. "No. But Weatherbie is a small town. I'm bound to know somebody here."

It didn't take him long to realize that regardless of whether Hope knew anybody, she was *known*.

There was one woman checking out groceries with a man bagging. Both looked up, glanced at him and then settled their gazes on Hope. Then they looked at each other.

Hope ignored them and pulled a cart from the rack. She proceeded to load it up with fresh fruits and vegetables, some chicken, fish, whole-wheat pasta and freshly made marinara sauce from the in-store kitchen. He threw in two nice-looking steaks and some baked potatoes. When he realized she was going to pass up the chip aisle, he grabbed several bags and a jar of salsa. She frowned at them. He ignored her and picked up a gallon of ice cream.

"I would not have expected you to eat junk," she said.

"I eat all the basic food groups," he said, throwing in a bag of red licorice. "It's just that I've spent some time in places where you can't get ice cream or candy or many of the things that make life worth living. When

I can get my hands on something I like, I don't pass up the opportunity."

She hit the cleaning-products aisle and started grabbing things right and left. There was practically no room left in the cart when she finished.

"Your house doesn't look dirty," he said.

"It's for Serena. Cleaning products are expensive. She's not going to have a lot of extra money for things like this."

Would she ever stop surprising him?

They rounded the end of the last aisle and she stopped so suddenly that he almost rammed into her.

"Damn," she groaned. "I have the worst luck."

He looked over her shoulder. A man was walking toward them. Mack recognized him from the pictures that he'd studied.

William Baylor. Hope's abusive ex-husband.

Mack stepped in front of Hope. *Give me a reason, Baylor. Give me a reason.*

"Don't make a scene," Hope hissed and grabbed his arm.

"Hello, Hope," Baylor said, his tone conveying his own surprise. "I didn't know you shopped here."

Hope glanced at the front of the store. The two clerks were staring back. "In the area," she said quickly, likely trying to follow her own advice not to attract too much attention. "Excuse us. We're in a hurry."

Did Baylor know who he really was? Archibald Minnow had sworn that there were only seven people who knew about the threats—himself, his wife, Hope, Mavis, Bing, Chief Anderson and Mack.

Had he conveniently forgotten to mention that he'd told William Baylor? Mack didn't think so given the way Baylor was looking him over.

"I don't think we've met," Baylor said. "I'm William Baylor, Hope's ex-husband." He extended his arm to shake.

Before Mack could speak, Hope stepped forward. "This is Mack McCann, my boyfriend."

Boyfriend. She'd gone with a *B* word after all.

And, hell's bells, was that her arm wrapping itself around his waist? He kept his face neutral.

Baylor's face, however, was getting red. "I didn't realize you were dating anyone," he said, as if he had a right to know.

Mack wrapped his own arm around Hope's shoulders and pulled her close. "I think we're a little past dating," he said. He brushed a kiss across her forehead and to her credit, she didn't pull back.

"Honey, I'm starving," he said. "Let's go home and get these steaks on the grill."

With one arm still around Hope, he used his other to push the cart around Baylor. He could see that both cashiers were still looking at them. He knew a little about small towns, having spent some time in them over the years. Word was going to spread that Hope Minnow had herself a boyfriend.

They checked out and he pushed the grocery cart to the car. Hope helped him load the groceries without saying anything. She got in and sort of collapsed down onto the seat.

"I'm sorry," she said, after a long moment of silence.

"What for?" he asked.

She looked at him as if he was losing his mind. "For using you. I just didn't expect to see him. I wasn't prepared. He's such a smug bastard."

"Just forget him," Mack said. He started the car and pulled out of the lot.

"He likes to pretend that our marriage didn't work because I was too young, too flighty. If I'd worked harder at it, we would have made it. That's the story he tells himself. And anybody else who will listen."

He kept quiet. She was on a roll.

"I had this crazy need to one-up him. To prove that I was moving on. You…you were convenient."

That hurt a little. "Don't beat yourself up." He drove a little farther. "You know, I got the general impression that William Baylor the third isn't necessarily over you."

"Well, I'm done with him," she said, her tone adamant.

"And you're sure he doesn't know anything about you volunteering at Gloria's Path?"

She shook her head. "If he knew, then my father would know. And I'd have heard about that, trust me."

Trust me. Strangely enough, he did. A day ago, he'd have bet his last nickel that he could trust Hope Minnow about as far as he could throw her. But the Hope Minnow that the world knew was the very tip of the iceberg. Under the water was a whole other person. Somebody interesting. Somebody he liked. Respected.

"How do you like your steak?" he asked.

She grabbed the change of topic as if it were a lifeline. "Medium rare. And I don't bother with baked potatoes unless there is sour cream."

"Understood. I'll cook tonight. You can have tomorrow."

"Fair enough," she said.

He pulled into the long lane and drove the quarter mile up to the house. When Hope reached for her door handle, he said, "I'll go first. I'll come back for the groceries once I check the house."

She reached for her purse, pulled out an emery board and starting filing her nails. He got the message. He could act as if the threat were real. She, in turn, was going to make her point that he was nuttier than a squirrel because it was all some bogus publicity stunt dreamed up by her father.

He got out of the car, locking the doors behind him. He walked up the steps, unlocked the front door and was happy to hear the security-system alarm. He keyed in the code and looked around. The rug near the door was slightly off-center, just as he'd left it. The center desk drawer was open an inch. He'd done that right before they'd left. He turned the handle of the basement door. Locked. Just the way it should be.

He ran upstairs, gave it a quick run-through, and when he was happy it was secure, he went downstairs and back outside.

And realized the car was empty.

Using the house to protect this back, he pulled his gun, raised his arm to shoulder height and rotated in a semicircle. There was no sign of her.

He glanced at the brick driveway. It offered no clues.

He left the relative safety of the porch and ran to the passenger-side door. He glanced inside. No sign of struggle. Her purse was still on the floor. The emery board had been tossed on the gearshift console that separated the two front seats.

With the car at his back, he looked around. He'd been gone less than a minute. Even if someone had been waiting for them, they could not have taken her far.

He stood perfectly still, listening. No car, either approaching or leaving. No barking dogs. Nothing unusual at all.

Except that there was a flock of sparrows near the door of what would have been the horse barn if the Minnows had been the horsey type, swooping and diving, as if they'd recently been disturbed.

He ran toward the building and pulled open the door. It was dark inside and musty-smelling. He waited for his eyes to adjust, then eased around the corner.

And there was Hope.

Chapter Ten

Hope was sitting on the cement floor, holding a white cat that was as big as a midsize dog.

Well, maybe not really, but his perception was a bit off because he was damn happy to see her and damn angry that she hadn't stayed in the car.

"What the hell are you doing?" he said.

Her head jerked up and she must have tightened her arms because the cat, sensing a change, shifted its big body and squirmed away. He ran and slipped under the lower rung of a wooden gate that led deeper into the big barn.

"Fred!" Hope called.

Fred evidently didn't intend to stick around for introductions. Hope got up from the dirty cement floor and dusted off her butt.

And damn him, he couldn't take his eyes off the motion.

"I told you to stay in the car," he said.

"I'm sorry," she said. "I saw Fred come around the corner of the barn and squeeze through the door. I haven't seen him for weeks."

He remembered the reverend's comments about Hope having a cat at one time. "I thought there were no animals," he said.

"Fred belongs to the Websters. They have the place next door. He spends a lot of time here. Probably because I feed him," she admitted. "Now be quiet."

She pointed to a place behind a wooden gate that might have at one time penned in horses or cattle. Now, there was one orange tabby cat and three very small kittens. Not newborns, but probably just a week or two old. Two of them were scrambling over one another, playing, and the third was getting a snack from Mom.

"Fred brought his family here," she whispered, soundly deeply satisfied. "I don't think they were born here, but somehow Mama and Papa managed to move their babies here. I'm going to need to buy some cat food tomorrow. Let's leave them alone now. I don't want them to get scared." She backed away from the stall and then quietly left the barn.

He wanted to stay mad at her for leaving the car but couldn't find it in him. "Please don't do that again," he said, when they were outside. "Don't run off."

"I didn't exactly run off," she said.

"Look, I know you don't believe the threats are real, but if they are, it's important that you and I are on the same page. At all times."

"I understand," she said. "I do. You have a job to do and I'm making it more difficult. I'm sorry about that."

Now he really couldn't be mad at her. "Let's get the groceries inside."

It took them two trips. Then, they worked together to get things put away. He took everything that went in the refrigerator while she stocked the cupboards. When they were finished, she turned to him.

"Mavis would be proud of us." She yawned, covering her mouth with her fist. "I think I'll lie down for a while before dinner. I didn't get much sleep last night."

"No problem. I'm going to go sit outside on the patio."

"Veranda," she corrected with a smile. "That's what my mother always calls it."

"The veranda," he repeated, nodding his head. "Okay if I start the steaks around seven?"

"Perfect." She left the kitchen.

He waited until he heard her bedroom door open, then close, before grabbing two potatoes. He scrubbed them up, poked a few holes in them with a fork and stuck them into the oven at 350. Then he grabbed a bottle of water from the fridge and opened the door to go outside.

He owed both his dad and his sister a call. And then he needed to reach out to Brody Donovan, too. They had a bachelor party to plan.

He called his sister first. After their stepmother was arrested, there had been some speculation that Linder Automation would collapse. But the one good thing that Margaret Linder McCann had done was build a fairly strong management team. The corporation would survive intact and people's jobs were saved.

Although not Chandler's. By her choice. She'd found a new job. Same type of work as a computer analyst but better hours, better pay and, best of all, as she was fond of saying, nobody there was selling secrets to the enemy.

The phone rang several times before going to voice mail. He looked at his watch. While it was almost six on the east coast, it was only four in Denver. She was probably hard at work, had her phone on vibrate and didn't even realize she was getting a call. He waited for the beep.

"Hey, Cat Eyes. How's it going? Just checking in. I'll be at this job for another nine days but back in plenty of time to finish the cabin for this shindig you and Ethan seem determined to go through with. Call when you can."

He dialed Ethan next. The man had been one of his

best friends for years, and in six weeks he was going to become his brother-in-law. Ethan, who had landed a job flying medical helicopters, answered on the second ring.

"Hi, Mack," he said.

"Hey, Ethan. You got cold feet yet?"

"Not yet."

It was a stupid question and they both knew it. Ethan wasn't going to get cold feet *ever* about marrying Chandler. It would have been embarrassing how smitten the fool was if it weren't over his sister, who deserved every good thing she got.

"How's the protection detail?" Ethan asked.

Mack started to give him some flip answer but realized that it might be good to have another perspective, especially from someone as solid as Ethan Moore. "Surprising," he admitted.

Ethan paused. "You're never surprised. You're the consummate anticipator, you overprepare for everything."

"It's not a character flaw," Mack protested.

"I know that. What's so surprising?"

"Hope Minnow. I expected... I don't know, I guess I expected a light beer, uncomplicated and not very interesting. She's more of a delicious amber, flavors carefully melded, unique."

"You're comparing her to a microbrew?"

"Only in the broadest sense," Mack said. He couldn't tell Ethan how he really felt. That he'd known Hope Minnow for less than forty-eight hours and he was afraid that he liked her better than any woman that he'd known in his previous thirty-eight years.

Ethan didn't respond. That made Mack nervous.

"Well?" he prompted his friend.

"Well, you don't usually *drink* on the job," Ethan said, his tone carefully neutral.

"I didn't say I was drinking," Mack protested weakly. Hell, he wanted a drink of Hope Minnow. Maybe a whole night of indulging.

Something told him that she would be a very nice cocktail and worth a hell of a hangover.

"Have you heard from Brody?" Mack asked, needing to change the subject.

"Yeah. He's coming back to the States next week. He's going to be a guest at the White House. Guess our boy somehow saved a bunch of lives when there were bombs exploding around him."

"Nerves of steel. He always had them. I got a text from him, asking me to call. He's next on my list. I just wanted to make sure you were taking care of my sister."

"No worries. It's easy work."

Mack smiled. "Talk to you soon." He ended the call and left his phone on the table. He walked back inside to check the potatoes and decided to wait to put the steaks on until Hope was awake. They wouldn't take long. He pulled a bag of lettuce out of the refrigerator. It was one of those where the Caesar dressing and the shredded cheese were in the same package. He opened it, dumped the contents into a bowl and spread the salad dressing around. Then he pulled out the loaf of French bread that Hope had tossed in the cart. He cut half the loaf into slices, buttered the pieces and wrapped them in foil. He'd throw the bread on the grill while the steaks were cooking.

He went back outside and picked up his phone. He pushed the button for Brody Donovan.

"Donovan," his friend answered.

"Dr. Donovan, I presume," Mack said. "*The* Dr. Donovan who has been invited to the White House to be honored."

"I know. Pretty good for a kid who almost failed high-school English."

Brody had almost failed because he'd been in love with the teacher. Fresh out of college, Miss Taper had been a mere four years older than the students she was teaching. She'd walked into the room, smiled at the class and Brody had fallen head over heels in lust. Now, some students might excel when put in the position of trying to impress the teacher. Not Brody. He'd been so enamored that he'd failed to turn in over 50 percent of his homework assignments that semester.

That had not been the last time Brody had been in love. It happened again his first year of medical school.

He and Elle dated for years and he'd evidently figured out how to worship a woman and study for finals because he'd graduated at the top of his class. They were to marry the summer before he started his residency.

But there hadn't been any wedding. Brody had almost been left at the altar. Elle had left town nine days before the wedding, and four months later, his mother returned the wedding gifts that had arrived early.

As far as Mack knew, that was the last serious relationship Brody had. And he never talked about what happened. Gave his friends some line about changing priorities and lack of common ground.

At the time, neither Ethan nor Mack had pushed for the truth. They respected that their friend was guarding his secrets. But they worried. And when he enlisted in the air force following completion of his residency, they wondered what he was running from. And each of them in their own way had tried to ask, but Brody shut them both down. Nicely. But definitely.

Some secrets were evidently not meant to be shared.

"So, you saved a few lives. Big deal," Mack teased.

"All in a day's work," Brody said. "But here's the thing. Tomorrow I leave Afghanistan, headed for Germany. I've got to finish out a few things and then I'll be back in the States for the White House event. They invited my parents, which was nice. Unfortunately, they're out of the country. Dad is researching a book set in Russia. So I have two tickets. I thought of you and Ethan, but Ethan is tied up making your sister happy. Are you in?"

Dinner at the White House. Again. The first time had been almost four years ago and it hadn't been some fancy dinner. No. In a little country where they hated Americans, he'd discovered key intelligence, so sensitive that it warranted a meeting with those at the very top of the food chain.

He'd had pizza and beer in the Oval Office.

The joint looked bigger on television.

"I'm doing protective-services work in New Jersey," Mack said. "Hope Minnow."

There was a pause. "Nice work if you can get it," Brody said, his tone appropriately reverent. "We get *People* magazine here, too."

"She's different than you might think," Mack said immediately.

"I would hope not. She seemed pretty near perfect in that picture. Hell, bring her along. She'll take the attention off me and we'll all be happy."

Most people would jump through hoops for an invitation to dinner at the White House. Mack had no idea how Hope would respond. New York Party Girl would be in her element. Paula would think it was *ridiculous,* to use one of Hope's favorite words.

He hated to disappoint Brody but his first responsibility was to Hope. If she insisted on staying in New Jersey, it wasn't going to be possible to provide that protection from a chair in the west wing dining room. "I'll ask her and let you know."

"Good. We'll talk later." Brody hung up.

Mack put his phone down. He wasn't sure how long he sat before the French doors opened. Hope walked out, looking beautiful in a casual pink dress that tied at the neck. Her feet were bare.

"Hey," he said. He stood up and pulled out a chair for her.

She took it. "Thanks for letting me sleep. I feel a hundred percent better."

"No problem. The potatoes are probably done. I'll start the steaks."

"I'm starving," she admitted.

He pushed his chair back. "Would you like some wine?"

She looked startled and he realized that as comfortable as it all seemed, he may have overstepped. He was, after all, hired help.

"Sorry," he said. "Didn't mean to—"

"I'd love some. I didn't realize I was so awkward at this," she said, with a nervous laugh. "This just proves how ridiculous Sasha was last night. I don't have the skill set to graciously accept a drink. In my own home, no less."

He was a little lost. "What did Sasha do that was ridiculous?"

"It's not what she did, it's what she said. She made some offhand remark about me getting married again."

Married again? "Who's the lucky guy?" he asked, working hard to keep his tone light.

She gave him a blank stare. "Huh?"

"The guy you're going to marry. Who is it?"

She threw her head back and laughed. "There's no guy. Trust me, I'm never getting married again."

His stomach suddenly stopped hurting. "You're young," he said. "You'll change your mind."

She shrugged. "I don't think so. Between what I've experienced myself and what I've seen at Gloria's Path, marriage doesn't look all that appealing."

He could certainly understand her perspective. He took two steps toward the house. "I'm hoping you enjoy the steak enough that you'll feel compelled to do the dishes," he said.

"Consider it done," she said. She turned her chair a little so that she could look over the pool. While it was early evening, the temperature was still in the low eighties. She tilted her head back, allowing her face to catch the very last sunshine of the day.

"Are you intending to go back to the hotel tonight?" he asked.

"Not tonight. I usually volunteer three or four nights a week."

"It's probably a good night to stay home. I checked the weather on my phone and we're supposed to get a heck of a storm."

She didn't answer until he came back with the steaks. "I hope you're right. I have loved storms ever since I was a child," she said. "I distinctly remember my ninth birthday party. I had a sleepover and all night there raged a huge summer storm. My little friends cowered under the covers, screaming every time the lightning cracked. That's when we lived in our old house, which was much smaller. I managed to hang outside my upstairs window, my pajamas getting drenched with rain, watching the tree branches whip around. My friends thought I was crazy."

He figured she'd been a real cute kid. "I'll bet that made your parents happy," he said.

"I don't think they knew."

The steaks sizzled when he put them on the hot grill. "Well, promise me there will no hanging out of the windows tonight."

She smiled and shook her head. "Can't ever promise that."

He sat a bottle of red wine on the table. "This wine takes me back a couple years. I was in northeastern Spain, maybe thirty miles from the coast, the last time I had it. The vineyard that produces it was just down the road. In that area, the ground is more rock than soil and the grapevines were these scraggly-looking things. When I first saw them, I doubted they even produced grapes. But they did. I was there long enough that I saw the harvest."

"You've been a lot of places, I guess," she said, watching him open the wine.

"Yeah. Traveling on Uncle Sam's dime. It was fun, but it got old after a while."

"Is that why you retired?"

"I didn't really retire. I couldn't because I didn't have twenty years in. Lots of people thought I was crazy. Why leave now, they asked, when all I had to do was stay four more years, give a full twenty to Uncle Sam and I could retire with full benefits."

"Why didn't you?"

"I guess I was too impatient. My friend Ethan managed to do that. He enlisted right out of high school and got his twenty in. I, however, chose a different route. I went to the naval academy for four years, but those don't count toward a person's military service."

"But you probably don't regret going to the naval academy?"

"Not one bit. Of course, when I was there I missed my friends, Ethan and Brody. But we kept in touch. Still do."

"So, what's next for you once this assignment is over?" she asked.

"I'm starting a job at Matrice Biomedics as their director of security."

"In Colorado?"

"Yeah. Northwest of Denver. I leased a place in the foothills of the Rockies."

"Sounds nice," she said, taking a sip of the wine he poured. "Oh, this is good."

"Who buys the wine in this house?"

"My mother."

He poured some in his own glass and then lifted it in a toast. "To your mother's good taste."

She laughed. "My mother would appreciate that. She underestimates her own talents. According to her, she's just a girl from Texas who believed until the ripe old age of twenty-two that big hair was the answer to most of the world's problems."

"I've been to a lot of places in the world. Trust me on this, I've met many people who believe stranger things." He flipped the steaks. "Miss Texas, right?"

She took another sip of wine. "I know she didn't tell you, and my father, who married her because she was Miss Texas, now doesn't like to mention it. He wouldn't want to cop to the frailty of worshipping personal beauty."

"How do you know that's why he married her?"

"She told me. When people are very sick, when they think they're dying, they like to reflect upon their lives. And the only thing I could do was listen. She wasn't angry about it. Just the opposite. It amused her that theirs was a marriage based on so little substance that had survived the test of time."

"Forty years, right?"

"Yes, that's right." She looked thoughtful. "You know, my father's fame has been rather recent. Things were different in the old days. Perhaps that helped." She stared off into space for several minutes before switching her gaze back. She didn't make eye contact. Instead, she glanced at the grill. "And maybe it's because he, too, makes a mean steak."

"I imagine marriages have stayed together for less," he said, letting her off the hook. Her eyes took on a sad look whenever she talked about her father.

And he didn't really want Hope Minnow to ever be sad.

Chapter Eleven

They ate in silence, both lost in their own thoughts. "This is delicious," she said, finally looking up from her steak. She reached for the sour cream and put her third teaspoon—yes, third—on her potato. She picked up her glass of wine and realized that it was empty.

Mack reached for the bottle and poured. She held up her hand at half. She wasn't a big drinker. "Thank you," she said. "You've set the bar pretty high."

"You haven't even had my chocolate cake yet."

"You made cake?"

He shook his head. "Had to save something back," he said.

She laughed. And then realized that it had been forever since she'd had a nice dinner with a man and laughed. It felt good. She took a few more bites and pushed her plate away. "I'm stuffed. Absolutely feet-up stuffed."

"Feet-up stuffed?" he repeated.

"Something we used to say in college after we'd pig out. You know, so stuffed you can only sit in the recliner you borrowed from your parents' basement with your feet up and your jeans unbuttoned."

"That's an image I didn't need," he said, pushing his own plate away.

The storm was closer, she could feel it. Darkness had

set in. There would be no pretty reds or lavenders in the sunset tonight. The cloud cover was heavy and the overall impression was a palette of swirling grays.

He picked up his wineglass. He'd drunk less than she had. He was still on his first glass. Probably didn't want to be impaired in any way.

Good cook. Nice guy. Dedicated. Understood the importance of sour cream.

"Tell me about college," he said.

"I went to New York University and fell in love with living in the city. Toward the end of my freshman year, I got a job waitressing at a little restaurant in SoHo and I met the most wonderful people. I was a good student, not a great one, and ultimately got a bachelor's in art history and a master's in visual arts administration."

"Bing mentioned that you worked for the Metropolitan Museum of Art."

"I did. I wanted to stay in Manhattan and working at the Met was really a dream job. I got an apartment with another girl, who had worked at the same restaurant. Meridith had gone to culinary school and she was crazy about food. The rent was so expensive but between the two of us, we managed to cover it. Of course, there wasn't a lot left over for anything else."

"Well educated, struggling professions," Mack said.

"Exactly. Meridith's parents probably could have helped. He some big lawyer and she was a doctor. But Meridith was determined to make it on her own. That was before my father's rise to fame and my parents had already paid for my education. I certainly wasn't going to ask them to pay for anything else. And it really didn't matter that we didn't have a lot of money. We were having fun."

"Lots to do in the city," Mack said.

"We stayed in a lot. Whatever extra money we had, we spent on food. Meridith was a great cook and it's because of her that I now know how to do more than boil water. She taught me how to make a basic red sauce, then a white sauce. How to roast pork and how to sear scallops. How to make peach cobbler. The list goes on and on."

Mack lifted his glass. "Here's to Meridith."

Hope smiled. It felt good to talk about her friend. "Meridith worked at a restaurant so her weekends were booked. But she had Thursday nights off. Almost every week, on Thursday, we would have some kind of dinner party. Friends from college, friends from work. Sometimes the parties were intimate, sometimes they were raucous affairs with too much tequila that caused the neighbors to pound on the door. That's when we started inviting people from the building."

"Good plan."

"Yes." She took another sip of wine. "It was at one of those parties that I met Wills."

"You don't have to talk about him if it makes you uncomfortable," Mack said quickly.

"It's weird. I never talk about him. With anyone." She looked at her dirty plate. "This is the sour cream talking."

"Oh, yes. In the navy, we frequently used dairy when we were trying to get information from the enemy."

She laughed. "Anyway, Wills came to a party with a friend. When he introduced himself, I realized that I had met him years before, actually several times. My mother, his mother and Mavis, too, had all been sorority sisters at Texas A&M. I knew he was living in the city because my mother kept telling me to *call up that nice boy, William Baylor.* I just never got around to doing it, so it was weird that he just showed up at my apartment one night."

"So you started dating?" Mack asked, his tone giving nothing away.

"We did. And we had fun together. We'd been dating for four months when I took him home to meet my parents at Christmas. My father and Wills hit it off, better than I could have imagined. To make a long story short, within a year, Wills had left his banking position and was working with my father in the ministry that was picking up steam. He commuted from the city for a while, but after a year or so, he moved out to Weatherbie."

"But you stayed in the city?"

"I did. I continued to live with Meridith. My job was going really well. I had been promoted a couple times. A couple years went by and my mother kept suggesting that it was *time*."

Mack didn't say anything.

"So, when Wills asked me to marry him on my twenty-ninth birthday, I said yes. We were married fourteen months later and I moved into the house in Weatherbie and commuted into the city to my job.

"The first time he hit me, I'd gotten back late from the city."

"The first time?" Mack said. "It was more than once?" His voice was hard.

"Yes. I'm not very proud of that. Makes me seem like a bit of a doormat, doesn't it?"

He reached out for her hand and it seemed the most natural thing in the world to let him hold it. "*You* were not the problem," he said.

"I know. Anyway, I'd gone to visit Meridith and her new husband. They had carried on the tradition of Thursday night parties. Wills knew I was going. I'd invited him to go with, but he was too busy with the church. My father's occasional appearance on television had turned into a weekly show and the money was flowing in."

His thumb was stroking her palm. It was enough to give her the courage to finish.

"I had a wonderful time, but when I got home I could tell that Wills was in a terrible mood, one of the worst I'd ever seen. He said that a big donor had decided that he wasn't going to fulfill his pledge. This was a donor that Wills had personally courted."

She paused, still able to remember that night like it was yesterday. "I wanted to give him something else to think about so I started showing him the pictures that I'd taken on my cell phone of Meridith's new apartment. She and her husband had done a good job decorating it. I had forgotten that Meridith had used my phone to take a couple pictures of me dancing with her brother-in-law. He'd been showing me his steps. He was taking dance lessons to surprise his wife."

"Baylor didn't like the pictures?" Mack asked.

"I tried to explain that it was Meridith's brother-in-law, who was happily married with two children. He refused to listen and we argued. Still, I was unprepared when he backhanded me across the face."

Mack's grip tightened but his face showed no emotion.

"It happened so fast and after it was over, he was so apologetic. And like a fool, I let it go. He said he loved me, he was practically sobbing. He begged me to forgive him. And I did. At least I told him I did. I'm not sure if you ever really forgive someone for doing that. It stays in the back of your mind, nagging at you, coming back at you when you least expect it."

"And you didn't tell anybody?" Mack asked.

"No. Not my mother, my father, or even Meridith. I was embarrassed and, as crazy as it now seems, even thought that somehow I'd played a role. I shouldn't have gone to the city. I shouldn't have danced with Meridith's brother-in-law. Anyway, we never talked about it again."

She sat silently for a couple minutes, staring at their linked hands. Mack's hand was bigger and his skin was darker. The bruise on his index finger was healing.

"It was just a few months later that my mom got sick. For a while, I tried to balance everything. I worked during the day and when I got back to Weatherbie, I went to my mom's house. I was there every weekend. It took a toll on me, plus my mom was continuing to fail. Four months into the cancer diagnosis, I quit my job so that I could tend to Mom full-time."

She looked up. "Wills said he supported that decision. But we'd gotten used to living on two incomes. I could have asked my parents for money because by that time their own financial situation had greatly improved, but I didn't want to do that. Wills and I started to argue about money but he never hit me."

"Until he did again," Mack said softly.

"Yes. Wills was now regularly appearing on my father's television show. He had asked me to pick up some dry cleaning, but I had taken my mother to a chemotherapy appointment and we got caught in traffic coming out of the city. The dry cleaner was closed by the time I pulled into the lot. I didn't give it much thought, knowing that he had another dozen shirts in his closet. My mom was so sick by then that it was hard to worry about anything else. That night I spent most of the night at my mom's and had gotten home around two in the morning. A couple hours later, I was in bed, trying to catch a little sleep, when Wills discovered that his favorite blue shirt wasn't there."

She pulled her hand back. He let it go. She couldn't

touch Mack, not now. "He'd dragged me out of bed by my hair and just went crazy. I fought back but he was bigger and he…he got the best of me."

"Hope," Mack said, his voice sounding hoarse. "You don't—"

"After he left me lying on the bedroom floor, I managed to pull myself up and I called my dad. I knew I needed a doctor. He came to the house and I told him what had happened. He took me to the emergency room, not in Weatherbie, but in Hazelton, two suburbs away. I was in so much pain and in shock, I wasn't really tracking what he was doing. He said it would be better to get treatment there. He didn't come in with me, just dropped me off at the door. It didn't dawn on me until the next day that it was *better* because we were someplace where people weren't as likely to connect that Hope Baylor was Reverend Archibald Minnow's daughter."

"I'm sorry," Mack said.

"Well, you pretty much know the rest. At his request, I told the nurses that I'd fallen down the basement stairs and I ignored the knowing looks in their eyes. One of them gave me information on Gloria's Path. After I got out of the hospital, my father arranged for me to go to a hotel to recover."

"That's when you went to Gloria's Path?"

"Yes. I didn't cancel my hotel room, though. I let my father pay for it. That's when my rather obsessive habit of spending my father's money began."

"Didn't your mother wonder where you were?"

"My father told her that I was out of town, doing a one-time consulting assignment for my old employer."

"What about Baylor?"

"He tried to call me, sometimes I'd get twenty-five calls a day from him. But I wouldn't see him. I started divorce proceedings immediately and communicated with him only through my attorney. I never went back to the house. I simply bought new clothes and moved into my old bedroom. I told my mother and Mavis that Wills and I had grown apart. My mom was certainly sad, but given that she was in a fight for her life, she had other things to worry about. Most everyone thought it was a very amicable split because Wills continued to work in the ministry, as my father's assistant."

"I was pretty damned civilized about the whole thing. It's really a good skill to be able to remain outwardly calm even when you're inwardly furious."

"I don't know what your father was thinking," Mack said. "If I'd seen that, I'd have killed Baylor."

Chapter Twelve

Mack said it with such solid conviction that she believed him. He would not let someone hurt his family. Her father had evidently felt differently. But what did it matter? Old water, old bridge.

She pushed back her chair and gathered both their plates. He started to push his chair back.

"I've got these," she said quickly. "A deal is a deal." She needed to get away from Mack and get a little perspective. Blame it on the sour cream or the wine or the fact that she'd simply just needed to finally tell someone. Whatever the reason, she'd shared a lot and was emotionally spent. "I said I'd do the dishes," she added, knowing that she sounded a little harsh.

"Okay," he said, settling back into his chair.

Hope half expected Mack to follow her inside. But he remained at the table, staring off into the distance. She turned on the water, let it get hot, then rinsed the plates and silverware. Then she loaded everything into the stainless-steel dishwasher, carefully placing the heavy stoneware in the racks.

She was tired. That explained it. The brief nap she'd had this afternoon had helped, but she was still several hours shy of the six hours of sleep a day that it took to keep her body going.

She folded the dish towel, hung it over the bar on the stove and looked through the French doors that led to the veranda. Mack was still sitting at the table. His cell phone to his ear. He'd turned his chair so that he was able to see her working in the kitchen.

Maybe he was talking to her father. She suspected that they'd prearranged times to talk. Was her father getting an all-is-well-in-Weatherbie report? Somehow, she doubted that Mack was offering the details. *Had a nice steak dinner with your daughter. We drank some wine. Had a few laughs. She told me what an ass you are.*

Too much information, for sure.

Was he waiting for her to join him again? Deliberately, she turned away. It had been a nice dinner, but there was no need to give him any reason to think that she wanted to extend the evening. She had things to do, her own calls to make.

She shut off the lights in the kitchen and walked upstairs to her room. She sat on the edge of her bed and reached for her cell on the nightstand table. She'd tried Mavis earlier to see how things were going at her sister's house, but hadn't been able to reach the woman. She hadn't left a message. She scrolled through her numbers and hit Call.

It rang four times before going to voice mail again. Instead of hanging up, she waited for the beep. "Hi, Mavis," Hope said. "Just checking in to make sure you got there okay. Hope your sister's husband is doing better. Call if you need anything."

She knew that Mavis was probably working like crazy to take care of things. Probably baking and cleaning and finding time in the middle of all that to visit her brother-in-law and pamper her sister a bit. The woman was a dynamo. She defined the words *active senior*. It was such a shame that she'd lost her husband and was alone during what was supposed to be her golden years. And she didn't seem inclined to go down that path again.

Hope distinctly remembered walking in on her mother and Mavis during one of their afternoon teas. They'd been talking about the neighbor woman across the road who was in her late sixties and recently remarried. Her mom had gently suggested to Mavis that perhaps it was time to start dating again.

Mavis, who had been standing at the sink, steeping the bags of tea, had gotten the oddest expression on her face. Then she'd seen Hope and her expression cleared.

Hope could understand the feeling. She hadn't been kidding when she'd told Mack that she was done with marriage.

She put her cell down, confident that Mavis would return the call when she was able to. She got up, walked across the room and opened the door that led to her balcony. Of all the space in the house, she loved this the most. It was just big enough for two lounge chairs and a few plants that she'd potted herself. Because it faced the west, she got the benefit of the most amazing sunsets.

The storm was getting closer. The air felt hot and wild and she could smell the approaching rain. Tonight, she'd stay out as long as she possibly could, hopefully for the duration of the storm. She didn't mind getting wet.

She closed her eyes, wanting to use her other senses to experience the storm. She deliberately slowed her breathing, drawing air deep into her lungs. Holding it for just a second. Letting go.

It was dark when she woke up to a sharp crack of lightning and then a subsequent explosion. The lights in her bedroom went out. Same for the tall yard light.

As she was thinking that the lightning had likely hit a

nearby transformer, knocking out their power and likely their neighbors', too, incessant pounding started at her bedroom door.

"Hope?" Mack yelled. There was a short break in the pounding. "Open the door or I'm shooting the lock off."

"Hang on," she yelled. She hurried across her pitch-black bedroom. She felt for the doorknob, unlocked it and swung the door open.

Mack shined a flashlight in her eyes.

She put up her hand.

"Sorry," he said, lowering the light and pointing it at the floor. "Are you okay?"

"I'm fine." There was just enough illumination reflecting upward to see that he looked rumpled and sexy. His T-shirt was pulled out of his jeans, as if the storm may have woken him up from a deep sleep.

Tempting.

"Thanks for checking," she added, before she tried to shut the door.

He stuck his foot out, stopping the door's momentum. "I want you to come downstairs."

"Why?"

"Without power, the security system won't work. You should have a battery backup but you don't. I want you downstairs where I can see you."

"What time is it?" she said, attempting to get her bearings.

"Eleven," he said.

She could hear thunder rumbling and then another crack of lightning. The storm was very close and she didn't intend to miss it.

"I'm fine," she said. She tried to close the door again but it was like trying to push against a brick wall. "Good grief," she said. She turned around, saw the flicker of light and knew that he was tracking her movements with his flashlight. She walked back to her balcony.

She took a seat on one of the lounge chairs. Within seconds, he was lowering himself down on the other one. "I guess it's slightly safer than hanging out the window," he muttered.

The first splatter of rain hit her bare lower legs. She waited for him to add that she was going to get soaked. But he didn't say anything.

The wind was whipping through the trees and when the rain came, it hit at a slant, a driving shower. It was a cacophony of sensation: the rumble of the thunder, the crack of the lightning, the whistle of wind, coupled with the shock of the cold rain on her warm skin.

She felt more alive than she had in years. More carefree. Maybe even reckless.

The hard rain lasted for maybe ten minutes and stopped almost as quickly as it had started. By this time, she was soaked and knew he had to be, as well. But still, he'd said nothing.

Suddenly, she heard him shift on his chair, get up and walk into her bedroom. He returned with some soft towels from her bathroom and the blanket from the end of her bed. "You're going to get cold," he said, handing it all to her.

She reached up. Their hands connected.

And a flash, every bit as intense as the lightning they'd witnessed, shot up her arm. Instinctively, she pushed her fingers between his, wrapping them over the edge of his hand.

Then she pulled her arm back, pulling his hand and arm, his body, toward her. She heard his breath catch but he didn't resist.

She rested their linked hands on her heart, which was

thumping in her chest. To keep his balance, he'd put one knee on the lounge chair. She could feel it next to her bare leg. She sensed, more than saw, that his face was less than a foot from hers. She could feel the tension in his hand and knew that maybe she'd managed to shake cool, calm Mack McCann just a little.

"Hope?" he asked.

"Shush," she said gently. Then she leaned forward and, with her free hand, cupped his chin. His face was wet, slick with rain. With the pad of her thumb, she felt for his lips. It was so dark, so erotic to be touching him, learning him.

"Kiss me," she whispered.

When he hesitated, she used her hand to pull his face closer. And when his lips brushed against hers, nerve endings that had been dormant for a long time starting singing. She could feel her body heat up and moisture begin to gather between her legs.

His lips hovered and she felt his warm, sweet breath on her face. He was about to pull back, she could feel it.

Hope Minnow, who had been living in limbo for the last two years, took control. She moved his hand, which she still had clenched tight in hers, to her breast. She arched her back, pressing her aching body into his warm grasp.

"Sweet mother of God," he said, running his thumb across the wet material that was molded to her skin. Her nipple, already hard, responded to his touch.

Then he kissed her. Hard. And her body came alive.

And still, he was holding back. She could feel it. "I need you to know something," she said, her mouth close to his ear. "I haven't had sex in two years. And if you turn me down, it's going to be devastating to my self-esteem. Worse even than Hopeless Fish Bait."

He was still for several seconds. Then he felt for her hand, took it in his and moved it down his body. He arched his hips toward her and pressed her hand against him. He was so hard. It was erotic and bold and sensation swamped her needy body. "You do this to me," he said, his voice low, sexy. "You. How's that working for your self-esteem, Hopeless?"

"Pretty good," she said, and she nipped at his lower lip.

He took charge, pulling at the tie of her sundress, peeling the wet material down her body until she was bare to the waist. The warm night air washed over her.

They didn't need light. He used his hands and his mouth to learn her body. Soft licks to the inner skin of her elbows. A brush of lips across her collarbone, a nip on her earlobe. Long succulent feasts on her nipples. Deep kisses with his tongue in her mouth.

And when her body was literally writhing with want, he gathered her up and carried her inside to the bed, leaving the door to the balcony open. He laid her down and she could hear him removing his clothes. Then he pulled her dress off all the way, her panties.

And then his mouth did all kinds of delicious things to her lower half until finally he stopped. She heard the rip of a condom and then finally, finally, he was inside of her.

He moved gently, letting her adjust, letting her get used to him. And when he was finally seated deep, he put his hands under her rear, pulled her apart even more and started to move.

When she came, it was shockingly intense, so much so that she thought she might have actually blacked out for a moment. He let her ride out the moment.

"Okay?" he asked, his voice husky with need.

"Oh, yes," she said. "That was better than sour cream."

She could feel his smile against her shoulder. Then he

began to move again and she could feel him inside of her, even bigger, more powerful. She felt full and stretched and when she arched and took him even deeper, she could feel the shudder roll down the powerful muscles of his back.

She kissed his shoulder and realized that the rain had dried but now his body was slick with sweat.

"I'm going to come," he groaned.

He moved inside of her, even faster now, his strokes long. She felt her own need build again and she clenched him tight. As she exploded around him, he stiffened, his body no longer able to resist.

MACK DRIFTED BACK to consciousness with the realization that he'd just had the most amazing sex of his life. With Hope Minnow. His head would have likely spun if he had the strength to lift it.

He had a thousand questions. Should he apologize? Plead temporary insanity? Admit that his knees were still weak? Wait fifteen minutes and go for round two?

The biggest question of all: Why had Hope waited two years to have sex, only to have sex with him?

A better man would have said no. He'd intended to until she'd pushed her lovely breast into his hand and literally begged him.

She hadn't been drunk or impaired in any way. He had absolutely nothing to feel guilty about.

With the exception that he was supposed to be guarding her.

They were going to have to talk about it, but maybe not right now. He pulled away from Hope and went to the bathroom to clean up the best he could without the use of water. They would have to wait for the electricity to come back on before the well would work.

It didn't take him but a second to realize that he had a problem. *They* potentially had a problem. He stood in the dark and felt his heart rate accelerate.

The condom broke.

Chapter Thirteen

What the hell was he going to tell her? Could he hide something like this? Absolutely not.

On his way back to bed, he closed the balcony door and locked it. No sense giving her an opportunity to make a leap for it. Then he climbed back into bed.

Hope had turned on her side. He moved close, spooning her, his arm around her waist as he pulled her close.

"Hope?" he asked.

"Yes," she said, sounding sleepy.

Not for long. He was about to drop a bomb. "I think we may have an issue."

She turned in his arms and faced him. "What?" she whispered, as if she thought someone had managed to sneak in the house.

No, *that* would be easy to deal with. There was no good way to say it. "The condom broke."

"What?" she said again, only this time it had a totally different ring.

"Are you on any type of birth control?" he asked.

"No. Of course not. I haven't been having sex," she said indignantly. She sat up in bed.

He scrambled to sit up, as well. He wanted to reach out and hold her, but didn't know if his touch would be welcome.

He heard a humorless chuckle. "Well, I guess there's an upside. Everything I've done up to this point to irritate my dad will be child's play if I'm suddenly an unwed mother."

His child would have a father. A father and a mother that were married. "It wouldn't have to be that way," he said tentatively. When she didn't answer, he decided to go for broke. "If there's a child, there's a reason to get married."

"Oh, good grief. I'm not getting married again, Mack. I told you that."

If she were pregnant, all bets were off. "We may be worrying about nothing," he said.

He could feel the air leave her body. "You're probably right. I wasn't on birth control when I was married and I never got pregnant. It's probably fine."

She lay back down, but not close enough that he could hold her. She was crowding her edge of the bed. The message was loud and clear. Cuddling time was over. He lay back as well, careful not to cross over the invisible middle line in the bed.

A child. Tonight he may have fathered a child.

That changed everything.

THE LIGHTS CAME back on at 3:07 a.m. Hope had rolled over to her stomach, with one arm flung out. She was still blissfully naked and he took a moment to study her.

Her skin was tan against the white sheets and so soft. He could see the ridge of her spine and then the gentle curve of her butt. Her long hair spilled over her shoulders, almost covering her face.

Gorgeous.

So damn sexy. And like a crazy fool, he imagined her

body, ripe with child. Her breasts heavy, her belly growing with new life.

His child.

He eased himself out of bed, careful not to wake her. He pulled on his jeans but didn't bother zipping them. He walked downstairs and shut off the lights that had been on before the blackout. He reset the security system.

He went back upstairs and saw that Hope was awake, sitting up in bed. The sheet was pulled up to her neck and her face was very pale.

"Morning," he said, working hard for casual. His insides were churning.

"Good morning. I didn't dream our conversation, did I?"

"No."

"Oh, good Lord." She put a hand over her eyes. "I cannot believe that the first time I have sex in years, the condom breaks. Who has that kind of luck? You know who? Hopeless Fish Bait, that's who."

"I guess," he said, trying to keep it light. But then he realized that there was something that he really needed to say, he really needed her to understand. "Listen, Hope. I want you to know that if you are pregnant, you don't have to do this alone. I'll be there."

She stared at him. "We can never do this again."

"Let's not be rash," he said.

She shook her head. "Listen, I realize that this is my fault. I asked you to have sex with me. I'm a big girl, Mack. I take responsibility for my own actions. I've potentially put both of us in a very difficult situation."

"Don't beat yourself up. Nobody put a gun to my head. If anybody needs to feel bad about what happened, it's me. I'm supposed to be ensuring that you stay safe. But the reality is, that while there's probably plenty of blame to go around, we are both single adults. Single adults can have sex. We shouldn't feel badly about it. In fact, I think we should be kind of happy. This was really great sex."

She smiled. Finally.

It was going to be okay. He took a step toward the bed when the phone on his belt vibrated. Who the hell was calling him at three-thirty in the morning? He looked at the number. Brody. He read the text.

Are you and the lovely Hope M. coming to the dinner? I have to notify the WH. They need time to run security checks on her. You evidently still pass.

He supposed now was as good a time as any to ask. "May I?" he said, motioning to the edge of the bed. He waited until she nodded.

He sat. "My good friend Dr. Brody Donovan has been patching up soldiers on the front lines for more than ten years. He's recently left the air force but he's going to be honored at the White House next week at a dinner. I was wondering…well, I was wondering if you'd like to attend. With me."

"Dinner at the White House?" she repeated.

"Yes. Dinner. A few speeches. Obligatory clapping. Good desserts as I recall."

She let go of her sheet and it slipped several inches, but not far enough that he had a really good glimpse of her beautiful breasts. "You recall?" she repeated. "You've been to the White House before."

He waved a hand. "It was years ago. Something informal. But I do remember the cheesecake."

"I'm busy," she said.

"I didn't even tell you which night," he said, attempting to keep his tone even.

"It doesn't matter. I'll be busy."

He tapped his index finger on the white sheets. "Why?" he asked finally.

She sighed. "Is it important? Listen, you're here for another week or so. I don't really think that my lack of attendance at this event is going to impact the future course of your life."

"I just thought you might enjoy it. And I thought," he said, his throat feeling tight, "that maybe *this* made a difference."

She shook her head. "You said it yourself. Single adults have sex. This wasn't special, Mack."

"Wasn't special," he repeated. Then wanted to kick himself for rising to the bait.

"No," she said. "Listen, I would like to get some more sleep. Can you make sure you shut the door tight when you leave?" She turned over in bed, giving him her back.

He knew he could easily force her to give him her undivided attention. But that wasn't something Mack would ever do.

Regardless of how much her rejection hurt.

He left the room without another word, closing the door quietly behind him.

HOPE WAITED A full minute after hearing the door shut before she flipped over in bed. In the darkness, she stared upward. *Dinner at the White House.* Her father would be ecstatic. It would be the kind of publicity that he regularly tried to buy.

What the hell was Mack thinking?

Never mind that. What had she been thinking? She'd slept with a man who lived in a world where he regularly received invitations to the White House. People who lived in that kind of world were ripe for public scrutiny. More of what she'd been living since her father's rise to fame.

She couldn't do it. Not anymore.

But she hadn't needed to be so damn petty about it. Hadn't needed to dismiss the best sex she'd ever had. Hadn't needed to make Mack feel badly when she, quite frankly, ladies and gentlemen of the jury, had been the aggressor.

She started to swing her legs over the side of the bed and stopped. What the hell was she going to do if she were pregnant with Mack's child?

It wasn't as if she didn't want a child. It wasn't something she generally talked about, but at thirty-four she could feel her biological clock starting to wind down. Just last week she read an article about a television star who was having her first baby at thirty-six. It said that everyone over the age of thirty-five was now considered high-risk.

Time was running out. But still, she'd never considered getting pregnant. Children needed two parents. She'd simply been spouting off when she'd let Mack think that she was cool with raising a child on her own.

She lay back down and stared upward. It reminded her of when she'd been a little girl. Her father would walk her to her room, read her a story and, right before he left, she would lie in her bed and stare at the ceiling. He would stand at the door and listen to her prayers.

She folded her hands. "Dear God…" she began.

Chapter Fourteen

Mack took his aggression out on his arm and leg muscles, using the treadmill and the weight machine as his weapons of choice. He worked his body until fatigue would have made additional exercise dangerous.

Then he dragged his body off for a cold shower.

It appeared he was going to be taking a lot of them. *We can never do this again.*

It would have been easy to pack his things and go lick his wounds in private. But there was no way. The stakes had always been high. Now they were even higher. Hope could be pregnant with his child.

What the hell would her parents say? And Bing? Would he regret asking Mack to come in the first place?

None of that could be helped. They would sort through all of it.

Chandler would be thrilled to be an aunt. His dad would be happy for him. Brody and Ethan would have cigars ready.

Assuming he could convince Hope to marry him. Because he wasn't interested in being a long-distance dad, somebody his child associated with the airport.

After his shower, he got dressed and cooked some breakfast. There was no sign of Hope and he figured she was avoiding him. If she intended to go into town to help Serena move into her new apartment, she was going to have to get over that fast. The rules hadn't changed. Where she went, he went.

He'd just have to be a little more careful *how far* he followed.

At twelve-thirty, Hope walked into the kitchen. Mack looked up from the newspaper that he wasn't really reading. She carried Paula's clothes and wig in her hands. She again wore her black leggings, but this time she had on a long gray-and-black silky T-shirt. Her hair was piled on top of her head.

"Morning," he said.

"Good morning," she answered. She pulled a glass from the cupboard and filled it with water from the faucet. She drained the glass in two long drinks.

He knew he was in for a bad time of it when even the working of her soft, sexy throat made him hard.

"Would you like some lunch?" he asked. He needed to do something besides stare at her.

"Just some toast," she said. "I'll get it."

He didn't respond. Just looked at his hands. He listened while she pulled the bread out of its wrapper and pushed the toaster lever down. Heard the pop. Then, the turn of the lid to the peanut butter.

She surprised him when she pulled out the chair next to him. "I'm sorry," she said.

He waited.

"I didn't mean to hurt you."

"I'm a big boy, Hope. I'll survive it," he said, his tone harsher than he intended. He took a breath, channeling the control that was usually easy for him. It felt out of reach.

"I know you will. But I could have been much kinder."

He took a chance. "It's not kindness that I'm looking

for from you. I just want you to have an open mind about the possibilities."

"This got complicated quickly," she said. "I want you to know that last night was wonderful and…"

He waited.

"And it was also a mistake. Those terms are not necessarily mutually exclusive."

He could feel his damn throat struggle to work. "Sometimes things aren't as complicated as we make them."

She smiled but it didn't reach her pretty eyes. "Listen, we need to get going. I assume that you're coming with me to move Serena into her new apartment. I have a request."

"Okay," he said. As long as it didn't involve anything that would compromise her safety, he was willing to listen.

"I don't want to have any more discussion about a possible pregnancy. We'll know soon enough. I'd like to just pretend that it's not even a possibility. And, of course, neither one of us should talk to anybody else about it."

He didn't need to talk about it, but it was in the forefront of his mind. He couldn't help that. "That's fine. Consider it done." He looked at her toast. "You going to eat that?"

She pushed it toward the middle of the table. "I'm not really hungry." She pulled her cell phone out of her purse. She looked at the screen and frowned.

"What's wrong?" he asked.

"I left a message for Mavis and she hasn't called me back yet. I'm worried about her."

"Mavis seems as if she can take care of herself pretty well."

She put her phone away. "You're right. I'm sure she'll call soon."

They left the house and drove into town. They didn't talk until they reached the hotel. Mack drove around it twice before he parked in a spot a block away from the front door.

Serena was waiting for them in the lobby. The two women exchanged hugs.

"I didn't realize you'd still be here," Serena said to him. "Must be wonderful to have such a nice long visit with your sister."

"Wonderful," Mack echoed, not making eye contact with Hope. He picked up Serena's suitcase. Serena carried a box. It was the kind that had cutouts in the sides, making it easier to carry. It also gave him a look into the box. It was filled with books, a crystal vase and a couple of picture frames turned inward so he couldn't see the photos.

He'd always traveled light. The military taught a person how to do that. But he'd always had the security of knowing that his stuff was back home in storage. If he ultimately could only have one box, what would he take? Pictures of his family? A given. Proof that his grades at the academy had earned him a spot on the superintendent's list most semesters? Not likely. His old Jimmy Buffett CDs, almost antiques by now? For sure.

He used his key fob to pop open the trunk. They stowed her things inside and then got into the car. Hope gave him directions.

"Wayne sent me a text, wanting to know if I'd rented an apartment," Serena said. "I told him I did."

"Did you tell him where?" Hope asked.

"No. He didn't ask, either. He said he'd registered for some internet dating site. I asked him which one but he wouldn't say."

It was like high school, Mack thought. Boy acts bad.

Girl gets mad and kicks Boy to curb. Boy doesn't want to idle at curb and schemes to get Girl back. Boy acts disinterested and says he's moving on, hoping Girl comes crawling back.

Except the stakes were a lot higher than not having a date for the homecoming dance. When Wayne acted up, he started using Serena as a punching bag. If Serena went back, it was anyone's guess how bad her injuries might be the next time.

He could tell Hope was tracking along the same lines. "Does it matter what site?" she asked gently.

In his rearview mirror, Mack could see Serena shrug. "I guess not," she said.

Mack drove to the apartment. He maneuvered through the lot, passing several empty parking spaces. Nothing seemed unusual. It was about half-full. Nobody was loitering near the doors. He knew he hadn't been followed from the hotel.

Safe enough. He parked in an empty spot, twenty feet away from the nearest car.

"My brother likes to find the perfect parking spot," Hope said, evidently trying to explain his behavior.

He didn't think Serena cared. She was staring out the window, looking at her new eight-unit apartment building, likely remembering the house that she'd run from. Comparing. Maybe coming up short.

He waited for her to say that she couldn't do it. Instead, she opened her purse and he could see her clench a stack of twenties.

Hope opened her purse, too. She pulled out ten one-hundred-dollar bills. He knew she hadn't gone to the bank. She must keep a stash somewhere in her room, for occasions just like this. She handed the money to Serena.

The woman's hand shook when she reached for the

money. "I don't know when I'll be able to repay it," she said softly.

"It doesn't matter," said Hope. "I know you will."

They got out. Like before, the landlord was waiting for them inside. The transaction went pretty fast. Serena turned over the money, the landlord gave her the key and a potted geranium for her small balcony. Then he left.

Standing in her kitchen, Serena turned in circles. "Home sweet home," she said, her voice sounding small in the empty space. Forlorn. "I guess I'll have to figure something out for furniture."

"Gloria's Path works with a secondhand store. I'll arrange for them to drop off a couch, a bed and a dresser, as well as some dishes, pots and pans, bedding and towels. That will get you started."

"Thank you." Serena's eyes had tears in them. "I wish I would have thought about a coffeepot. I love coffee," she added, her tone wistful.

"You know what," Hope said, "Mack and I need to pick up a few things. We'll grab a coffeepot and some coffee from Tate Drugs and drop them off here on our way back."

He could see that Serena was close to her breaking point and perhaps Hope sensed it, too, because they made a fast exit. Once they were back in the car, they sat in silence.

"It's weird," he said finally. "She's so immature at times and yet, so mature at other times."

"Yes. She's only 26. I guess that's normal."

"Where's Tate Drugs?" he asked.

She gave him directions as he drove. She took off her wig and she shimmied out of her shirt and pants. It made him remember how he'd undressed her the night before, how terribly erotic it had been to untie her dress, to feel the wet, heavy material fall to her waist, knowing that her breasts were fully exposed to the night air, and to him.

"How come Paula never goes shopping?" he asked, reaching for the mundane.

"I don't know. Hope shops. Paula helps battered women." She took off the ugly tennis shoes and put on sandals.

He gave her a sidelong look. "You know that Hope and Paula are the same woman?"

She looked down her pretty nose at him. "Thank you, Dr. Phil."

He drove into the parking lot of the mom-and-pop drugstore, the kind that only existed anymore in small towns that hadn't caught the attention of Target and Walmart. It was part of a strip mall with four other re-tailers.

They got out of the car and walked across the parking lot that was in need of some repair. The woman at the front counter looked up when they opened the door. He caught the flare of recognition in her eyes.

"Hi, Hope," she said.

"Hey, Jane," Hope responded politely, not stopping.

"Friend?" he asked quietly once they were past.

"Acquaintance. We went to high school together. Four years of gym proved that she was a better soccer player than me but couldn't play tennis to save her life."

"How's her golf?"

"Don't ask."

It was a good day for golf but not a good day for shopping. The store was warm, almost stuffy. The high for the day was expected to be eighty-five and it had to be close to that already.

They found the aisle for coffeepots. There were only

three brands to choose from. Hope dutifully read the descriptions on each box before finally picking the basic, least expensive model.

"You're ruining your image," he whispered.

"I know. But Paula is really buying this. And Paula is a good bargain shopper."

"I don't know how you keep all this straight in your head."

It took them several minutes to find the coffee. It was at the end of an aisle, along with a few boxes of cereal, some macaroni and cheese that went in the microwave and small round tins of mixed nuts.

Mack looked at the price of the coffee and saw that it was twice what they would pay for it at a grocery store. He didn't suggest doing any comparison shopping. He sure as hell didn't want to take the chance of running into Hope's ex-husband again.

Yesterday, he'd managed to hold back. Now, after holding her body, knowing first-hand how delicately she was made, it made him crazy to think that she'd been beaten by the man. He desperately wanted to smash his fist in Baylor's mouth.

Hope picked up some toothpaste and a few other items. They rounded an aisle and ran smack-dab into the home-pregnancy testing kits. Remembering his promise, he didn't say a word. He saw Hope look at them for several long seconds. Then she turned to him. "First of all, I'm not pregnant," she whispered. "Secondly, I sure as hell can't buy one of these here. The whole town will know in minutes." Then she hurried out of the aisle.

They were almost out of the store when she remembered that she needed cat food. The store only carried small bags of dry food. "Better than nothing," Hope said.

"Fred's probably doing his best to catch mice. This will be the backup plan."

Jane checked them out. "How have you been?" she asked.

"Great. You?" Hope replied.

"Good. Just working, you know." She rang the cat food through. "Must have a cat."

"I do," Hope said, sounding happy. When Jane gave her the total, she pulled out the correct change. Jane bagged their items, giving him several looks in the process.

He didn't say anything. He wasn't sure what *B* word Hope would use today to describe him. Brief encounter. Bad mistake. He didn't like any of those.

Baby daddy.

He was losing it.

"Thanks, Jane," Hope said, picking up her sack. "See you around." She pushed open the glass door.

Mack glanced over the parking lot. He didn't see anything unusual.

They were thirty feet from the store when Hope bent down suddenly, to shake a rock out of her sandal. At that exact moment, a bullet hit the store window behind them, shattering the glass.

Chapter Fifteen

"Get down!" he yelled. He leaped toward Hope, twisting his body so that when his momentum carried both of them to the pavement, he took the hardest hit. He felt the hot pavement grind into his back and knew he was going to have a knot on the back of his head.

Once on the ground, he quickly got to his feet. Bent at the waist, he pulled Hope up and hauled her in between a blue Toyota Camry and a pale gray Mazda.

A woman two rows over started screaming and someone hit the hazard button on their car keys, starting a loud beeping.

He looked at Hope. Her face was white and her eyes were big. "Are you okay?" he asked. Without thought, he looked at her absolutely flat stomach. She had her hand splayed across her abdomen.

"I'm okay," she said. "I am," she reassured him.

He pulled his gun from its holster. "Stay down," he instructed. He raised up, looked in the direction from where the shot had come. A gray van and a blue SUV were the only vehicles moving in the parking lot. They were going in opposite directions.

He wanted to get closer, to force a confrontation with the gunman, but he didn't move. It was possible that the shot had been a distraction, something to separate him from her. If he pursued the shooter, a second assailant might make his move on Hope. Mack wouldn't take that chance.

He saw a man who might be a manager run out of the store, a cell phone to his ear. Mack pulled his own cell phone off his belt. He scanned his numbers, found the one he was looking for. He had Police Chief Anderson on the line within seconds.

Mack swiftly identified who he was, why he was calling and their location. He also described the two vehicles that had been in the lot. He got an assurance that the chief would be there quickly.

By the time he finished the call, the first cop car arrived, sirens blaring, lights going. An ambulance followed them.

Even then, he kept Hope down, protected by the cars. It would take the chief a few minutes to get there and he didn't intend to talk to anybody else.

However, he wasn't counting on the woman who'd been screaming suddenly pointing at them and yelling, "They were shooting at them."

That got everybody's attention. He put his gun away.

He helped Hope stand up. That's when he got his first good look at her and realized that the right knee on her leggings was shredded. And he could see blood.

"Damn it, you're hurt," he said. He could see a male and a female officer approaching. He made sure his shirt was covering his gun. He didn't want them to start panicking if they saw that he was carrying.

"It's a scratch," she responded, waving her hand.

"Sir, ma'am, we'd like to ask you some questions," the male officer said.

Mack shook his head. "Not until somebody looks at her knee," he said.

The two cops looked at each other. Likely they weren't used to somebody telling them no. Finally, the woman nodded. "Okay." She waved a paramedic over. It was a girl of about eighteen and Mack almost demanded that they send someone more experienced, more knowledgeable.

But he kept his mouth shut because the young woman seemed very competent. She checked Hope's pulse, her blood pressure and her pupils. Evidently satisfied that there was no immediate need for concern, she carefully cut away the material, cleaned out the cuts and placed a bandage on Hope's knee.

Mack stood two feet away, watching everything.

"You're going to want to put some ice on that," the paramedic said. "I usually have some cold bags but somebody must have forgotten to restock them. When you get home, twenty minutes on, twenty minutes off. Sooner the better."

"I will. Thank you so much," Hope said, being her naturally kind self.

Mack wasn't feeling kind. He wanted blood. But he forced himself to remain calm, to not generate any more attention than they already had.

After the paramedic finished, the male and female officers approached a second time. When asked, both he and Hope provided their names and showed their driver's licenses as identification. He could tell the minute the officers connected that the victim was the daughter of Weatherbie's most known celebrity.

The male officer became more differential, perceptibly more polite. The female officer just the opposite. He could see the disdain in her eyes that she wasn't trying very hard to hide.

He knew that Hope picked up on it right away. She

remained polite but the natural warmth that he'd come to expect was missing. She was distant and he could see how others would perceive that she thought she was better than everybody else.

They were saved from having to answer any more questions because at that moment a Crown Victoria rolled into the parking lot and an older man got out. The two officers exchanged glances. Mack could read the look. *What's the chief doing here?*

The man greeted his officers, nodded in Mack and Hope's direction and said, "I'll take over here."

Mack could tell the female officer wanted to argue but she kept her mouth shut. Both of them walked away.

"I'm Chief Anderson," the man said.

Mack stuck out his arm. "Mack McCann. Thank you for coming."

The chief shook his hand, then Hope's. He glanced down at her knee. "Ms. Minnow, are you injured?"

"Bruised knee. A couple cuts. Nothing serious," Hope said.

"Do you want to sit in my car?" he asked.

Hope started to shake her head. "Yes," said Mack. It would make their conversation more private and it would provide protection for Hope in the event that somebody was crazy enough to try to take a second shot. "She needs some ice for her knee," Mack added.

"It's fine," Hope said.

The chief held up a finger. Then he walked over to where his officers were gathered around their vehicle. One of them opened the trunk and fiddled around with something inside. Then the chief was walking back with a cold bag.

He cracked it in the middle and handed it to Hope.

"Thank you," she murmured.

She was embarrassed. Mack didn't care.

The chief led them over to his car. The vehicle had warmed in the few minutes that it had been sitting in the sun. He started the engine to get the air conditioner going. He and Mack took the front seat, Hope a spot in the back.

"What the hell happened here?" Chief Anderson asked.

"I'm not sure," Mack said. "We were inside for maybe ten minutes. We came outside and got about thirty feet from the door before the shot was fired. Based on the sound and the damage to the window, I'd say it was a rifle. I believe it came from either the gray van or blue SUV that I previously described."

"You're right about the weapon," the chief said. "I heard from one of my officers on the way over. The bullet hit a display rack. We've recovered it. Not sure about where it came from. Other witnesses have also described the two vehicles but nobody got a license-plate number on either one. I've got an officer checking to see if there were cameras in the lot."

"What about street cameras?"

"Not here. This is usually a quiet community, Mr. Mc-Cann. Hard to get the city council to agree to spend that kind of money. Do you think this has anything to do with the notes that Reverend Minnow received?"

Mack knew it was possible that he and Hope had merely been in the wrong place at the wrong time. But he didn't think it was likely. The shot had been aimed at Hope. He was confident of that. By some stroke of luck, she'd bent down to get the rock out of her sandal.

That had saved her life. Maybe their baby's life.

"I don't know. I know that Hope and I were not followed to the store. I guess it's possible that somebody saw her inside."

The older man rubbed a hand across his jaw. "Mr. Mc-Cann, I don't normally invite victims to participate in the investigation, but Reverend Minnow shared some of your background with me. I think, in this case, it might be helpful. Do you want to come with me when I talk to the store manager?"

"Definitely. Hope comes, too," he added. He wasn't letting her out of his sight. He got out, opened the back door and held out a hand.

She took it.

Her touch was warm and it reminded him of how close he'd come to standing over her cold, dead body. He wanted to pull her tight, to hold her close, but he knew now wasn't the time. "Bring your ice," he said. "We'll get you a chair inside."

He positioned her between him and the chief as they walked into the store. There was glass on the floor and the display that the bullet had hit was pretty much trashed. Other than that, the store looked fine. They'd be back in business once they could get the window repaired and the glass swept up.

It didn't take them long to figure out some of what had happened once they spoke to the manager. "I'm dreadfully sorry," he said, mostly looking at Hope. "Jane, my cashier, did something that she should not have. She Tweets," the man added.

"What did she Tweet?" Mack asked, already having a pretty good idea.

"Your picture. We have a security system that takes still shots of everybody who walks in the door. She downloaded the picture, Tweeted it, and within minutes, it evidently got picked up by one of those online news agencies and retweeted." Now the man turned his glance to Mack.

"The text that went along with the picture was 'Hope Minnow and a sexy stranger.'"

"Double *S*," Hope murmured.

Chief Anderson and the store manager looked at her oddly. Mack smiled at her. He wasn't a stranger. Hope might want to delegate him to that role but he wasn't having any of that. Sexy? As long as she thought so.

"You'll follow up?" Mack asked the chief.

"Yes. I've got somebody on my staff that's really good at this kind of thing."

Mack was really good at it, but he couldn't take the time away from Hope to sift through all that data. "Okay. You can reach me on my cell."

He and Hope walked out of the store. There was no sign of Jane. Maybe she was off somewhere disabling her social-media accounts. There was, however, a photographer who snapped a picture.

Mack started to reach for the camera, intending to shove it down the man's throat.

"Hey, Hope," the man said, stepping back fast. "Making news again?"

"Byron," Hope said, a resigned note in her voice. "Long time," she added.

"Slow news day. This will help."

"Great. Mack, this is Byron Ferguson. He's a reporter with the local paper. Byron, this is Mack McCann. He's a family friend."

On to the *F*'s. Mack realized what she was doing. She was laying out the facts, trying to make it a nonstory.

"Family friend?" Ferguson repeated. "Not what I hear. I heard he's a bodyguard. That your family has received threatening letters and that you're the target."

Mack was going to wring somebody's neck. "We don't

have any comment," he said coolly. He cupped his hand underneath Hope's elbow.

The man moved with them. "Somebody took a shot at you today, Hope. Do you have any comment on that?"

Hope shrugged. "I think you're reaching for a story and you're a better journalist than that. Somebody shot at the window of the store and I just happened to be in the way."

"I wonder if that's what the police will say," Byron challenged.

They might, if the guy talked to Chief Anderson. The man would understand the family's hopes to downplay the situation.

"Let's go," Mack said. Even once they were past the reporter, Mack could hear the soft click of the man's digital camera.

He had no doubt that he and Hope were going to be front-page news tomorrow.

Chapter Sixteen

"That was more than a lucky guess. He knew about the letters. About you," Hope said under her breath as they walked to the car.

"Appears that way," Mack replied, disgusted. "You and I didn't tell him, your parents and Bing are all out of the country, and Mavis is out of town. That's everybody except for Chief Anderson."

"Maybe the chief gave something away when he walked over and talked to his officers. He probably felt as if he had to give some kind of explanation about why he'd suddenly showed up at the scene."

"You could be right. And then one of his officers let something slip to the reporter. Either on purpose or accidentally."

"I guess in the big scheme of things, it doesn't really matter whether people know about the letters or think I have a bodyguard or not."

"It would be better if people didn't know," Mack said.

"Well, we can't do much about it now."

"I'm going to have a conversation with Chief Anderson about it," Mack said, setting his jaw.

Hope almost felt sorry for the man. "Oh, my gosh, look at that," she said, thankful for something else to talk about.

They had reached Mack's car and the coffeepot, still in its sack, was sitting on the trunk of the car. Someone had been thoughtful enough to put it there. She opened the lid of the box. "It's fine. Nothing broke. We need to take it to Serena."

Mack looked like he wanted to argue. But he didn't. "I guess we can," he said. "She's going to wonder what took us so long."

"Maybe not. I think she has a program on her smartphone that tracks the police-scanner activity. She was using it the other night when I walked into the break area. She probably heard that there was an incident in the parking lot at Tate Drugs. I better call her, she'll be worried."

"I'm going to want to talk to Wayne," Mack said.

"Why?"

"Because he's got a reason to have a grudge against you. You're helping his wife to leave him."

"Not me. Paula." She started to pull her disguise back on. The pants, the shirt, the shoes. Finally, the wig.

"Maybe he knows you're one and the same."

"I don't see how." She knew it was a useless argument. If Mack had decided it was important to talk to Wayne, then he was going to talk to him.

"I'm also going to want to talk to your ex."

"Wills is not trying to kill me."

"Does he have a gun?"

"Several. He went hunting with his father."

"Is he a good shot?"

"I have no idea. He acted like he was. But then again, he acted as if he was good at everything. I know that wasn't true."

He gave her a look and she could feel the warmth spread from her chest to the tip of her head. Was he thinking that she was referring to Wills's prowess in the bedroom? Had she been? She'd commented on Serena's immaturity earlier. How mature was it to compare lovers?

There'd been no comparison. When Mack had left her bed this morning to go into the bathroom, her body had still been humming with the sweet afterglow of two really wonderful orgasms. He'd been a considerate lover, yet demanding. Gentle, but just rough enough to quickly bring her to a feverish pitch. Slow at the right times, yet very fast when it mattered. He'd evoked responses from her body that quite frankly had scared her.

Then he'd returned to the bed for the oops-the-condom-broke conversation, and she'd decided she was never having sex again.

Even as she'd been saying it, she'd known it was a damn shame.

"We're here," she said, stating the obvious as he pulled into Serena's lot. "I'll just run this in." She needed some air, even if it was hot, humid air.

He shook his head. "Call her. Tell her that I'll stick it inside by the front door." He got out, flipping the locks, even though he'd parked within fifteen feet of the door.

If he'd been hard to shake before, he was going to stick like glue now. She had to admit, she might not be all that eager to get rid of him. Hearing that window break had been horrific. Knowing that the bullet would have hit her had been terrifying.

When the paramedic had been checking her vital signs, she'd almost admitted that she felt sick, that she was awfully afraid that she was going to throw up. But those several minutes when she'd been receiving first aid had given her a chance to regroup, to catch her breath.

There was no proof that the bullet had been aimed at

her. And she'd tried to hang on to that thought the entire time they'd been talking to the police and the store manager. She'd done a pretty good job of it. It had gotten her through the ordeal.

Now she really just wanted to go home and cry.

Mack returned to the car and opened the door. He slid into the seat and looked at her.

"What's wrong?"

Ten minutes. That's all she had to last. "Nothing." She turned her face to the window.

"What happened? Did someone call?" He grabbed her phone, looked at it, searching for calls.

"No one called," she protested.

"Then what's wrong?" he demanded. He reached out and felt her forehead. "You're cold. I'm taking you to the hospital. You're in shock."

She pulled away from him. "I've been sitting here in front of the air-conditioner vent. I am not in shock."

He did not look convinced. She was sixty seconds from a visit to the emergency room.

"Listen, you idiot. If you want the truth, I was sitting here thinking about the fact that I almost died today. I don't want to die. I'm too young to die." Her voice cracked but she kept going. "And if I am pregnant, I didn't want my baby to die. I want to hold her in my arms. I want to teach her how to color and play with her in the park. I want to walk her to her first day of kindergarten and help her with her fifth-grade science project. I want it all, and today…today it almost ended. And I would have had none of it."

Then the dam broke and the tears that she'd believed could be held off another ten minutes came in a rush.

And she did not resist when he pulled her close and

held her. She cried hard, her face pressed to his chest, his hand stroking her hair. She cried until she could not cry anymore, until her body was spent with emotion. Only then did she lift her head.

And then he gently took the pad of his thumb and brushed away the tears that lingered on her cheeks and he kissed her forehead.

"I'm sorry," she said. Even when her ex-husband had beaten her and through their subsequent divorce, she hadn't cried that hard.

"You don't have anything to be sorry for. It's been a tough day. Let's go home," he said.

Home. Her home for now. But not necessarily for long. Weeks ago she'd started looking online for jobs, had actually applied for one. It wasn't exactly what she'd done before—she accepted that she'd already had her dream job, now she just needed work.

The company had called her the day before Mack had arrived to set up an interview. If it panned out, she was going to have some decisions to make. If not, well, maybe she could get an apartment down the hall from Serena. Two formerly battered women, trying to get their lives back on track. She'd have to tell Serena the truth about her identity—no way was she wearing Paula's ugly clothes forever.

Except it would be much easier to hide a pregnancy in them.

Good Lord, what was she going to do if she were pregnant? She'd need a very good job because it wouldn't be just her that she needed to provide for.

She'd need a job that offered flexibility and maternity leave and one that had good health-insurance benefits. Things could get more complicated quickly.

What was it that Mack had said earlier, something

along the lines of "sometimes we make things more complicated than they need to be"?

Yeah, well, he wasn't the one who was going to have a traveling companion for nine months.

And for the first time since they'd had the awkward *oops* conversation, she didn't break out in a cold sweat at the thought of being pregnant.

She would handle it. She could handle it. These last several years had proven to her that she could handle a whole lot.

Like getting shot at.

The thought of that had her shaking her head. The things you worry about in life were rarely the things that happened. It was a good lesson in worrying less.

"What are you thinking about?" Mack asked gently.

"I'm hungry," she lied. "I didn't eat breakfast or lunch and my stomach is letting me know. It's my turn to cook tonight."

He put the car in Drive and pulled out of the lot. "What's on the menu?" he asked.

"Chicken enchiladas. I know you've got a high standard of comparison, but I'm willing to see how mine stack up."

"Confidence. I like it." He drove for another few minutes.

I like it. Who would have thought three simple words would make her insides heat up? Her crying jag had left her vulnerable. That was the only explanation.

Was she willing to admit that she liked the idea of cooking him dinner? Of chatting with him while they sipped margaritas and snacked on chips and salsa? Of making sopaipillas for dessert and taking the warm fried dough, dripping with honey, up to bed with them?

Of licking honey off his wonderful body.

Having him lick if off her.

She turned the vent toward her face, which was very warm.

No, she was definitely not willing to admit that.

There wasn't going to be any licking, not of plates or bodies. Maybe some gnashing of teeth due to sexual frustration but that was it. They'd made a mistake last night and slept together. And time would tell if there were lasting consequences from that lapse. They didn't need to compound it and make it worse by doing it again.

She owned the lion's share of the blame for last night. She'd admitted that to Mack. She could be stronger. She would be stronger.

This was temporary duty for him. For her, a brief interlude before the rest of her life started.

He pulled into her driveway. "Let me go in first," he reminded her when he'd stopped the car.

She opened her door. "I want to check on Fred and his new family," she said. She grabbed the bag of cat food from the sack.

He rolled his eyes. "Okay. We'll go there first."

They walked into the barn, with Mack leading the way. There was nobody inside but Mama Kitty and her babies. Hope didn't try to touch any of them. She simply ripped open the sack and dumped some food on the cement about three feet away.

"Fred's AWOL," Mack said, stating the obvious.

"He'll be back," Hope said confidently. "He'll be a good daddy."

Mack's eyes heated up and she regretted the offhand remark. Was he thinking that he'd make a good daddy, too?

She didn't doubt that. And while she'd been very serious when she'd told him that she never intended to marry again, she would never keep a child away from the father. They would figure out a way to work through the logistics of having parents in different states. People did it all the time.

They walked out of the barn and toward the house. "I don't think your father is going to be crazy about more cats," he said.

She shrugged. "I'm going to be moving out soon. Maybe I can take one with me. I'll try to find a home for the other two."

"Moving? Where?"

"Not sure yet," she said. She waited while Mack unlocked the front door. "But it's time. I've never lived anywhere but the east coast. I imagine I'll stay in this region."

He stared at her, likely remembering his promise that he wouldn't bring up the subject of pregnancy, but also probably wanting to know whether a pregnancy would make a difference to her decision. But he stayed true to his promise and didn't force the topic. Instead, he simply opened the door and turned off the security system. "Stay here," he said. "If you hear anything unusual, get the hell out."

Before she might have been tempted to roll her eyes, much like he'd done when she'd demanded to see the kittens, but now she simply nodded and waited like a good girl.

He took the steps quickly. She didn't hear his footsteps on the old floorboards or hear any doors squeak as they were opened. Yet, she knew he was doing a thorough search.

Mack McCann had a nice touch at things.

Boy, did he.

He came down the steps. "Listen, I've been thinking.

Maybe it would be a good idea if you simply got out of town for a while. I have someplace you could go."

Now he had her curious. "Where?"

"You said that you've never lived anywhere besides the east coast. I'm giving you an opportunity to explore another state. I'd like you to go to Colorado with me. There's a place in the mountains, a cabin. Actually, two cabins. One was recently damaged in a fire and we're re-building that. The other cabin, which belongs to a friend, is available. We could go today."

"I can't go to Colorado," she said. What was he thinking?

"Why? You'll be safe in Colorado," Mack challenged.

"I have an interview in New York in three days, on May ninth. I have to stay here."

"An interview? Nobody told me anything about an interview."

"I'm sorry. I hadn't told anybody. I got the call just a few days ago. I applied for a position at a nonprofit in Brooklyn that supports after-school art programs in low-income areas."

He considered her. "It's not the Met," he said finally.

"No, it's not," she said lightly.

And while she might miss doing the work that she'd done there and having the responsibility, what bothered her most was that if she moved back to the city, she'd probably have to give up her volunteer work at Gloria's Path. It had been her salvation for the past year and, quite frankly, had kept her in Weatherbie these last couple of months, even when she'd been confident that her mother was well on the road to recovery.

She wasn't going to Colorado, she wasn't going back to the Met. The only place she was headed to was the kitchen. "I'm going to start the enchiladas," she said.

Chapter Seventeen

While Hope was busy making enchiladas, Mack called Chief Anderson. The man was friendly enough until Mack told him that he suspected that one of his officers had leaked information to the reporter.

"That's impossible," Chief Anderson said. "I understand you're a friend of the Minnow family, but I certainly don't appreciate those kinds of accusations."

"The reporter had information that had to have come from a knowledgeable source."

"And I'm telling you that he didn't get it from me or from one of my officers."

Mack didn't know whether he believed him or not, but there was little to be gained by continuing to harp on it. If they had leaked the information, they'd be more careful in the future. If not, well, then, Chief Anderson had a right to be pissed at Mack's accusations.

"I need to run some errands," Mack said. "I don't want to leave Hope unprotected."

"I'll come myself. And if it makes you feel any better, Mr. McCann, I won't tell anybody what I'm doing."

Mack hung up and went to find Hope. She was chopping onions on a cutting board.

"I talked to Chief Anderson. He says the leak didn't

come from him or his officers, that your reporter friend got it from someone else."

"First of all, Byron Ferguson is not my friend. I don't think he's necessarily my enemy, either, but that's neither here nor there." She tapped her knife on the butcher-block cutting board. "You know, there is another possible explanation."

"What?"

"Maybe my father gave Byron the information before he left town."

"What? Why?" Mack asked, shaking his head.

"Publicity. It's not a four-letter word and generally not considered a sin. Even if it was, I don't believe that would dissuade my father from pursuing it."

"I don't know," Mack said. "I just don't see him doing that."

Hope shrugged and started noisily chopping her onions again.

Mack put his hand up to still the noise. "I need to leave for a little while. Run some errands. Chief Anderson will be here while I'm gone. I want you to tell him about Gloria's Path."

She held the knife suspended in the air. "That doesn't seem like a great idea. The police don't appear to be able to handle sensitive information well. Plus, I'm not sure if you picked up on it or not, but the female officer today showed some overt animosity toward me. Not everyone on the force may have my best interest at heart."

He nodded. "You may be right. But the chief and his officers are what we have to work with right now. At least if the chief knows and something comes up during the course of the investigation that is connected to Gloria's Path, he won't dismiss it. I want you to tell him about Paula."

She stared at him. "I'll tell him about Paula and Gloria's Path," she said finally, "but I'm not going to tell him what led me there."

"It would be helpful if the police knew the truth about your ex. They would want to talk to him."

"It's enough that they know I have an ex-husband. That should automatically put him on the list. I don't need to air all my dirty laundry."

"You know, it's a crime to deliberately thwart a police investigation by keeping evidence a secret."

"I don't care."

Mack ran his hands through his hair.

"I don't know what you're upset about," Hope said. "Heck, people are Tweeting that you're a sexy stranger. I, on the other hand, have people disliking me before they even know me." She gave the onion a deliberate slice.

"It happens all the time. We judge people by the color of their skin, their ethnicity, their socioeconomic status, their marital status, everything."

"It's wrong."

"It is. We can't control that. About all we can control is giving Chief Anderson information that may be helpful to him. Trust me on this. I'm going to make sure that he understands that he needs to investigate anybody who might have a bone to pick with your father."

"It's so ironic," she said. "Someone is mad at my father and they want to take it out on me. Hell, *I'm* mad at my father. What do I need to do? Take an ad out in the newspaper and let this crazy know that they're not alone?"

"Maybe it's really you they're mad at."

"Me?"

"We can't discount that someone is deliberately trying to lead us down a dead-end path. I need you to tell

Chief Anderson the names of any person who might be upset with you or want to cause you trouble."

She rubbed between her eyes. "In fifth grade, I stole a two-dollar ring from the drugstore and I let my friend take the blame. She got grounded for a week. Does that count?"

"Put it on the list," he said, making sure she understood that he wasn't budging on this.

She shook her head. "Errands to run? You don't have any dry cleaning to pick up or banking to do. You're going to go see Wills. Aren't you?" She laid her knife down.

"You're damn right I am. And if I have any reason to believe that he has anything to do with this, I'm not going to be responsible for keeping anybody's secret."

WILLIAM BAYLOR THE THIRD answered the door wearing old running shorts, a T-shirt that used to be white and a sweatband around his head.

His mouth fell open when he saw Mack. "Oh. I thought you were the delivery guy. I ordered Chinese."

"No fortune cookies anywhere on me," Mack said. "I need a minute." He stepped forward, forcing *Wills* to take a step back.

The house was nice, but it didn't feel like Hope. It was too formal, with stiff-looking furniture and lots of dark wood. It was a large, two-story Colonial, way too big for a single guy.

"Look, I'm kind of busy," Baylor said.

"You don't look busy. You know what you look like? A wife beater. That's right. Some ass who decides to beat up somebody half his size just because he can."

Baylor's ruddy complexion turned a dull gray to match his shirt. "I don't know what the hell Hope told you, but if you think you're going to malign my good name, you've got another thing coming. I'll ruin you."

"I want to know what the hell you were doing between two and three o'clock today."

Baylor frowned at him. "I don't have to tell you anything. Just because you're screwing—"

Mack shoved him up against the wall, pinning him there, with his feet dangling in the air. "Shut up," he said. "Between two and three."

"I was at work. At the church. In a meeting with the administrative staff. There are eight people who can verify it."

Mack let him hang for another few seconds before he lowered him down. And then just for principle, Mack shoved him hard enough that Baylor's head snapped back and hit the wall.

"Get out of my house," Baylor said, his voice cracking at the end.

"If I have any reason to believe that you're causing one bit of trouble for Hope, you'll answer to me," Mack said.

He left without letting Baylor get the last word in. He intended to give Chief Anderson the vanilla version of this exchange and ask him to make sure that Baylor's alibi held water.

Maybe he was visible to those eight people at the meeting because he'd somehow discovered that Hope was going to be in that parking lot at that time and knew he'd need a strong alibi. Maybe Baylor had hired somebody else to do his dirty work.

It was a stretch, he had to admit, but if his visit had served no other purpose than to put Baylor on notice that he was being watched, it was worth it. And it had felt damn good to push Baylor around.

Mack keyed Wayne Smother's address into his GPS.

When he got there, there was no car parked in front of the small, frame-sided ranch and there was no garage. He rang the doorbell, then knocked. No answer. He walked around behind the house, through the small overgrown yard, and knocked on the back door. He heard a noise behind him and whirled.

"He's not home," said a woman wearing a big gardening hat, a long-sleeved shirt and jeans. "At about ten this morning, I saw him put a suitcase in his trunk. I told him last week I was going to report him to the city if he didn't mow his grass. I called them right after he left."

"Any idea where he might be going?" Mack asked.

"I have no idea. I think he has family in Texas. Not sure where. I'm trying to sell my house and it's not helping that this eyesore is in my backyard."

He didn't think it would help if he told her he really didn't care. He wanted to know where Wayne had been this afternoon. He pulled a business card out of his pocket. "Will you call me if you see him come back?"

"I guess. Can you make him cut the grass?"

"You call me and I'll cut the damn grass if I have to."

WHEN HE GOT back to the house, Hope was finishing the chicken enchiladas and Chief Anderson was enjoying a cup of coffee and some cookies. They both looked relaxed.

That made the knot in his stomach loosen just a little.

"Hi," he said. "Everything okay?"

"Very good," Chief Anderson said, then wiped his mouth with a paper napkin. "I appreciate you encouraging Hope to tell me about her volunteer work at Gloria's Path. Good organization, by the way. And helpful to know about Hope's connection to clients and their families. She's confident that nobody knows her as Hope Minnow, but still, it's good to have the information."

"I went to see Hope's ex-husband, William Baylor the third," Mack said, helping himself to a cookie from the plate on the counter.

The chief shook his head. "I know earlier today I invited you in to hear some witness reports. That wasn't an open invitation for you to start investigating the case."

"I wasn't waiting for an invitation. He says he was in a meeting with staff members this afternoon. I'd like that alibi to be verified."

"It will be. But do yourself a favor. Reverend Minnow said you were hired to provide extra protection for Hope. Why don't you concentrate on that and let us concentrate on getting the bastard who is doing this."

He wasn't going to make any promises he couldn't keep. "I'll try to keep out of your way, Chief, as long as I'm confident that you and your officers are doing everything they can to figure out who is behind these threats and the shooting today."

"We will. Don't worry about us." And with that, he got up and walked out the front door.

Mack sat down on one of the counter stools. "It's hard to have a lot of faith in a man with cookie crumbs on his face."

Hope smiled. "A cook takes that as a compliment. My cookies were so good that he was inhaling them."

"The cookies are good," he admitted. "How are the enchiladas coming?"

"So far, they appear to be right on track. Dinner will be ready in about an hour."

"Need some help?"

She looked surprised. "I guess. Do you know how to make guacamole?"

"Avocados, tomatoes, onions, salt. Lime or no lime?"

"Lime," she said, frowning at him.

"Jalapeños?"

"Un poquito," she said, pinching her fingers together.

"Sí, senorita. I'll merely wave the pepper over the dish."

MACK'S GUACAMOLE WAS GOOD, the enchiladas were some of her best work yet and the margaritas, well, they were stellar. Maybe, just maybe, because she'd come close to never having the chance to enjoy another margarita. Perspective made tequila sweeter.

She and Mack had dinner on the veranda. He'd lit several lanterns and found a television channel that played Mexican music. He'd put a speaker on the porch and she was now tapping her toes to "La Bamba" by Ritchie Valens, who had been dead long before she was born.

Mack pushed his chair away from the table. "That was so good," he said. "Seriously, your enchiladas have now taken first place. I'll be back once a week for eternity."

She picked up her glass and saluted him. Then she carefully set the glass down. "Have you spoken to my father about what happened this afternoon?"

"Not yet. Our agreement was that I would email him at night. I've done that the last couple of nights already."

"I'd appreciate it if you wouldn't tell him what happened today. I don't want them to worry."

"Them?" Mack queried. "Not just your mother?"

"Them. Her. Look, I'm still not convinced this is all real."

"You didn't hear the glass break behind you today when the bullet shattered it?"

She waved a hand. "That's not what I meant. Of course today was real. But the bullet may have not been aimed at me. It could have been a random shooting. Maybe the shooter wasn't even trying to hit anything. He or she was just out screwing around."

"This is not a game," Mack said.

"I know that. But if you tell my father what happened today, and he tells my mother, and she insists upon coming home, I'm never going to forgive myself. Please."

He nodded. "For now," he said grudgingly. "I'll keep it to myself for now, but I'm not making any promises into the future."

"Fair enough," she said. "By the way, I finally heard from Mavis today. She called while Chief Anderson was here. Her brother-in-law is holding his own. He had bypass surgery and is going home tomorrow. She'll be gone for a few days yet."

"Did you tell her what happened?"

"Absolutely not. She has enough to worry about. She lives to take care of others."

He picked up her plate, then his. "My turn for KP. Are you going to stay outside?"

"For a little while," she said.

"Okay. Please don't leave the veranda without telling me. No chasing after Fred if he happens to make an appearance," he added, trying to keep it light.

"Agreed," she said. She sat back in her chair and watched the lights dance over the pool water. She appreciated that Mack hadn't brought up her crying jag again. Nor had he belabored the points that she'd spewed out in her sudden need to make him understand why she was crying.

She'd basically admitted that she wanted a baby. She put her hand on her flat stomach. She'd ask him not to mention it again, but it didn't keep her from thinking about it. As delicious as the margaritas had been, she'd sipped just a little of hers, conscious of the fact that alcohol wouldn't be good for a baby.

Would her child be a blonde like her or a brunette like Mack? As a teenager, she'd yearned to have anything but blond hair and blue eyes. It was so boring. She'd wanted to be exotic, to have smoky dark eyes and hair so black that it almost looked blue.

Mack had dark hair and dark eyes.

Would her child be short or tall? She was just an average height for a woman but Mack was pretty tall.

The possibilities were endless.

But it was probably a whole lot of speculation about nothing. She wasn't pregnant. She was going to have her period next week and she'd be making jokes about escaping another bullet.

After about ten minutes, Mack came back out to the veranda. By then she'd moved to a lounge chair, closer to the pool.

He had a dish towel over one shoulder. "All done," he said. He pulled out a chair and sat.

It was a beautiful, warm spring night and the big trees and the soft lighting around the pool made it seem as if they were in a cocoon, separate from the real world, where windows got shot out and secrets got shared.

She closed her eyes. She could feel him beside her.

Watching over her.

And she felt safe.

"HEY, SLEEPYHEAD," he said, his voice very close, very soft. She opened her eyes. "You fell asleep," he said. "I didn't want to scare you, but I also didn't want you spending the night out here." He was leaning over her, his arms on the side of her lounge chair.

She stretched her arms over her head, and realized it

was a mistake when his eyes followed the movement of her breasts. His look was hot and hungry and it caused the need that she'd managed to hold at bay all day to surge forward.

It was crazy. They were both adults. Both single. The sex had been wonderful.

She reached up to touch his jaw. She felt the roughness of new beard. She ran the pad of her thumb over his bottom lip.

He held himself perfectly still.

She ran her tongue across her own top lip. His eyes followed the movement.

"Sometimes I'm hasty," she said.

"I'm listening."

"And I say things I regret," she said softly.

"Uh-huh," he said. He turned his face and kissed the palm of her hand.

The heat shot straight down her center. "Mack," she whispered.

He moved his mouth, traveling up the length of her arm. He licked the inside of her elbow, kissed her biceps, nuzzled her shoulder. Then his mouth found the delicate skin of her earlobe. "What did you say that you regret?" he whispered.

She was on fire. She turned her head, found his lips and they kissed. It was wet and sensual and she knew that she was not nearly as strong as she needed to be.

"That I wasn't going to sleep with you again," she admitted. "I take it all back."

She could feel the energy in his body. "Are you sure?" he asked.

"Yes," she said. Nothing had ever felt this right.

He gathered her up in his arms and carried her inside.

After kicking the door shut behind him and flipping the lock shut, he strode up the stairs.

He gently deposited her on the bed. The lights were off but the illumination from the yard light seeped through her sheer curtains. She could see the need on his face, could feel the heat radiating off his strong body.

"Make love to me," she said. "All night long."

Chapter Eighteen

Mack slept until nine o'clock, something rather unheard of for him. To be fair, he thought, as he grabbed workout clothes and tugged them on, he hadn't done all that much sleeping.

Which is why he was being very quiet. Hope was still asleep, lying on her side. Her naked body was wrapped in a sheet and her hair fell over her shoulder, as if sometime during the night she'd gathered it up and pulled it to the side.

He rubbed his fingers together, still able to feel the silkiness as he'd run his fingers through her hair when she'd bent over him and taken him in his mouth.

They'd used birth control every time and it had not failed. While they'd had no discussion about it, the knowledge that they might have been closing the gate once the horse was already out of the barn lingered in the back of his mind.

He'd been having sex for a good many years and never worried about an unplanned pregnancy. He'd been very careful. And it wasn't as if he'd been careless the other night.

Equipment malfunction. In the navy, that had the potential to take lives. Here, it had the potential to give life. It was a humbling thought.

He left the bedroom, walked downstairs, checked the alarm and did a quick look around the house. He glanced out the windows, surveying both the front and backyards. It was a beautiful morning.

And if Hope hadn't bent down to shake a rock out of her sandal, she might not be here to see it. The thought of that had him hitting the treadmill hard, pushing his body to the limit.

When he was finished, he walked upstairs. And just like she had been that first morning, Hope was sitting at the table, drinking a cup of coffee. She was not reading the paper this time. It was still folded up inside its plastic sack.

When he entered the room, she gave him a long, measured look that had his body temperature rising even higher.

"Good morning," she said. "If you're getting coffee, I'll take a refill."

He walked over to the counter, grabbed the pot and an empty cup and brought both back to the table. He refilled her cup first, then poured one for himself.

"Going to look at the paper?" he asked.

"I'm sort of afraid to," she admitted.

"How bad can it be?"

"Pretty bad. Byron Ferguson has a flair for the dramatic."

"Why is he so interested in you?"

"It's not just me. It's the whole family. And I'm not sure. I thought he'd tire of us. We really aren't that interesting."

Mack opened the paper. The headline wasn't good.

Hope Minnow Nearly Gunned Down

There was a picture of Hope and him, as they walked out of the store. It had to be one of those that he'd taken right as they saw him. The quality was good. Hope looked as beautiful as ever and Mack looked as if he wanted to bite somebody's head off.

Which proved the camera never lied.

He scanned the article. Some of it was fact: time and location of shooting, type of shell, amount of store damage. Then it got more sensitive. Family had recently hired a bodyguard after receiving threatening letters; everyone in the family was at risk; Reverend and Mrs. Minnow had chosen to leave town.

"This is not journalism," Mack said.

Hope shrugged. "It's what people like to read. It's scintillating. Probably sells a few papers."

Ferguson did not identify Mack by name in the piece. Which was odd, Mack thought, given that Hope had introduced him. Probably thought it made the piece more interesting to imply that he was some sort of mysterious bodyguard.

"He found out that your parents are out of town."

She shrugged. "That would have been easy. There are several people on my father's staff at the church. Any one of them could have innocently let it slip that he was out of the country."

She skimmed the article again. She looked up at him, shaking her head. "I know it's very immature of me, but I guess my biggest regret about this article is that Wills probably feels better about you, now that he knows you were hired to be with me."

Mack reached his hand toward her and cupped her chin. He gently tilted her face up. "Let's be really clear on this, Hope. I was not hired to *be with you*. What we have together is something very different. It doesn't have anything to do with what I was hired to do."

She stared at him. And for just a second, he thought she might be ready to have the what-if-I'm-pregnant conversation. But then she suddenly shoved her chair back and got up. "I have to change the date," she said, pointing to the calendar on the refrigerator. "Mavis always takes care of that. She keeps the rest of us on track."

Okay, they weren't going to talk. Now, that was. He was only going to let her put it off for so long.

Hope ripped off the page, wadded it up and threw it in the wastebasket, just as he'd seen Mavis do that the first morning. Muscle memory. As upset as the woman had been about her sister's news, she'd walked over and ripped off the top sheet, exposing the correct date. Probably because that's what she did every morning of her life.

He walked over to take a closer look and flipped through a couple pages. On Friday, May 9th, someone had written a note under the date. *Pick up symphony tickets.* "Somebody going to the symphony?" he asked.

Hope read it, too. "The junior college in Weatherbie has a nice little orchestra and my mother, who still plays the violin, is a big supporter. It's sort of a small-time operation. They don't have any administrative staff so they usually only offer advance tickets on one day. Otherwise, people get them at the window on the night of the show. My mother hates doing that."

Hope looked at the note closer. "That's Mavis's handwriting. She was probably planning on picking them up for Mom. That's the day of my interview but I can still take care of it."

"I'll bet you bought this calendar," he said.

She nodded. "Yes. How did you know that?"

He took his thumb and flipped through the pages.

"Every page has a picture of an animal in the corner along with some fascinating fact about them." He got close to the small print under the picture. "'Seals molt once a year. It can take up to six weeks.'" He smiled at her. "Fascinating."

She wrinkled her nose, dismissing his comment. "If it was up to me, I'd have a whole barn full of animals. Well, obviously not seals, but you get the idea. Horses, cows, chickens, dogs, cats. Bring it on. It's number three on my bucket list."

"What are numbers one and two?" he asked.

"Learn sign language and take a zip line across the jungle."

He laughed. "Sort of two extremes."

She shrugged. "Whatever. How about you? What's on your bucket list?"

"I don't have a bucket list."

She frowned at him. "Everyone should have a bucket list."

He snapped his fingers. "Okay. I've got one. To never be more than fifty yards away from a refrigerator with ice-cold beer."

She let out a huff of air and turned her chair so that her back was facing him. "I'm done with you," she said.

"Oh, no, you're not," he said. Then he scooped her off the chair, carried her upstairs and into the shower. "I just thought of something else," he said, right before he turned the water on.

FOR THE NEXT two days, things were about as perfect as they could be. They took turns cooking and Mack was a good student when she taught him how to make a pesto sauce using fresh basil. In turn, he helped her add biscuits and gravy to her repertoire. They watched movies on television, argued about whether the Colorado Rockies were a better baseball team than the New York Mets and they made love.

She tried not to think about the fact that in just days Mack would be leaving. He would go back to Colorado and she would do something, yet to be determined.

Neither of them talked about the possibility of pregnancy and they were very careful about using birth control. They did not talk about guns or reporters or threatening letters.

Mack may have read the paper. She did not.

On the morning of Friday, May 9th, she awoke to a beautiful day. The sky was bright blue and even though it was early, the temperature was already climbing toward the expected high of eighty.

"Breakfast," Mack said, walking into the room carrying a tray. "French toast and bacon. Coffee, too, of course."

She scooted up in bed. "It smells wonderful," she said.

He crawled in bed next to her, wearing just his underwear. They both grabbed a plate off the tray and started to eat. He'd warmed the syrup and put it in a small pitcher. She picked it up halfway through her meal to add a little more. It made her remember her honey fantasy.

"Why the smile?" he asked.

"Well, do you know what sopaipillas are?"

"Sure. Deep-fried dough with cinnamon and honey. Why?"

"I had this fantasy that we made sopaipillas, ate them in bed, and we dribbled honey over the other and licked it off."

His eyes lit up. "Really. You have lots of fantasies like that?"

"Maybe I have a few others. This particular one was very nice. Very sweet, as I recall."

He took her plate away from her.

"Hey," she said. "I wasn't done."

"Yes, you are." He pulled off his shorts and picked up the small pitcher. "Sometimes you just have to make do with what you got."

THEY WERE LATE getting out of bed and had to hurry to get ready. Hope's interview was at 1:30 p.m., so they wanted to leave the house by noon to ensure that they arrived in Brooklyn on time.

Traffic flowed pretty well and they were able to find a parking spot near the corner of Fifth Avenue and Ninth Street. "We'll need to walk from here," Mack said.

They found the building, took the elevator to the third floor and found the office. "You can't come in with me," she said. "It will look as if I was afraid to come to the job interview on my own, that I had to drag my boyfriend with me."

"Boyfriend," he repeated, smiling.

"I'm saying that's what their receptionist will think. And they'll mention it to the hiring manager and my name will be crossed off the list and they'll write some crazy notation in the margin like 'does not appear to be able to act independently,'" she said, making air quotes.

He studied her. "Fine. I'll walk you to the door and hang around in the hallway. You didn't tell anybody about this interview, did you?"

"No."

"Then there's no reason to think that there is any danger. I know we weren't followed. I made sure of that."

"There's a coffee shop just down the street," she said. "You could kill some time there."

"Don't worry about me. Are you nervous? You seem nervous."

She ran a hand through her hair. "Of course I'm nervous. I've only interviewed for a couple jobs in my entire life. I don't even know if I want this job, but still, I want them to want me. Does that make sense?"

"Sure. You want to be the one to say no. Not the other way around."

"Exactly. Okay, I'm going in." She opened the door.

"Hey," he whispered. "You're going to knock their socks off."

The door closed, separating her from Mack. She was smiling when the receptionist looked up.

"Good afternoon. I'm Hope Minnow." *And I'm here to knock your socks off,* she added silently.

"The director will be right with you," the young woman said, her hands still on her keyboard. "Please have a seat."

The waiting area looked a little bit like the one in Gloria's Path. Well, how Gloria's Path had looked before the fire. Which reminded her that she needed to check in with Sasha. She normally volunteered on Friday nights. It was usually a busy night. Probably had something to do with the fact that people had finished out their work week and decided to have a few drinks. Two drinks turned into four, sometimes six, and tempers became harder to control.

The clients were going to have to move out of the hotel tonight because of the soccer tournament. She needed to know where to show up for work.

Hope sat on the couch and picked up a magazine off the table. She put it back down. She didn't really want to read gossip about anybody else when her own situation was getting so much attention.

She was going to have to figure out a way to get Byron Ferguson off her back. He'd been helpful in the past, when the publicity had been uncomfortable for her father, but suddenly, that no longer seemed so important.

Was it possible that she was done being mad?

Certainly not done with being hurt. But anger was a pretty useless emotion. She'd known this for some time, of course, but within the past couple of days everything had gotten much clearer.

Getting shot at and falling in love had a way of doing that.

Oh, dear Lord, falling in love? She picked up the magazine and fanned her face, which was suddenly hot.

Was it possible? Had she really fallen in love with Mack McCann? No. It was just sex. And some good conversation. Nice dinners. Laughter.

Oh, no.

"Hope, the director will see you now."

MACK SAT FOR a while, then prowled the halls, never letting the office door out of his sight. Hope had been so nervous. It was the first time he'd seen her like that. It was sort of cute.

Hell, Hope would be cute wearing prison stripes, picking up garbage off the side of the road.

He knew she'd do well in the interview. And if she got the job, what would that mean? She'd move back to the city, maybe even live in Brooklyn and be close to her work. He walked over to the window that was at the end of the hallway and looked out. It was a clear day. He could see quite a ways. Brooklyn didn't have the flash that Manhattan had. The buildings were older and there were more big trees. There were no skyscrapers.

Could he live here? He'd certainly lived in less attractive places over the past years. But his heart had been set on Colorado. He'd accepted the job with Matrice Biomedics so that he could stay there.

None of that mattered, he realized. What mattered was being where Hope was. And maybe, where their child was.

He'd live on the moon if that's what it took. But first he was going to have to convince Hope that this wasn't a temporary affair, that he was in it for the long haul. He was going to have to convince her to try marriage again.

He turned when he heard the office door open. Hope walked out, looking beautiful as usual, although more formal in her black dress and heels. She'd pulled her long hair up and pinned it in the back. He'd seen his sister do similar things with her hair. He remembered his father telling him that a woman's ability to style her hair was God's way of showing that women were the superior species. He wondered what Reverend Minnow would say to that.

"How did it go?" he asked.

"Okay, I think. They said they'd let me know. I'm just glad it's over with."

"Do you want to spend some time in the city? We could drive over to Manhattan."

She shook her head. "I need to get back to pick up the symphony tickets for Mavis. I'll bet you ten bucks that she's going to call and ask about them."

"If she remembers what she wrote on the calendar," Mack said, opening the door for Hope.

"Everything she writes on the calendar, she enters into her smartphone, too. She started doing that because she was out running errands once and came home, only to realize that she'd forgotten to do something that she'd written on the calendar. She had to go back out and she didn't like that. Like I said, superefficient."

The drive back to New Jersey didn't go as smoothly as the drive in. There was an accident on the highway and traffic was backed up for miles.

They were sitting still when Mack's cell phone rang. He looked at the number. "Chief Anderson," he said to Hope.

"Put it on speaker," she requested.

"McCann," he answered.

"It's Chief Anderson. I've got some news for you."

Chapter Nineteen

"I've got you on speaker," Mack said. "Hope is here."

"I figured as much. Anyway, this afternoon we arrested Wayne Smother on charges of attempted murder. We got a signed confession from him. He's the one who shot at you the other day. He's the one who sent the letters."

Mack looked at Hope. Her mouth was open.

Somehow Smother had connected Paula to Hope. Hope had been confident that only two people knew the truth—Sasha and Mavis. He could tell by the sudden distress in Hope's eyes that she'd just come to that same conclusion.

"How did he know that Hope and Paula were one in the same?" Mack asked.

"His wife, Serena, told him. She evidently recognized Hope the first time she met Paula but she didn't say anything. She was pretty impressed by the fact that her volunteer counselor was Hope Minnow and she told Wayne."

It fit. Serena and Wayne had a relationship where they were often trying to one-up the other.

"Smother was also responsible for the fire at Gloria's Path so there will be some additional, very serious charges against him and his friend, who evidently owns an old yellow El Camino. Serena suspected that Wayne was responsible for the fire but didn't tell anyone. In her own way, she didn't want to get her husband in trouble. In the end, however, she did the right thing. She read Byron Ferguson's story in the paper and called us, saying why she thought her husband might be responsible. We got a search warrant for his house and we found a notebook where he'd scribbled down the address of your father's office."

"Where did you find him?"

"He was staying with his friend who owned the El Camino. Serena led us in that direction. I think he was sort of glad we'd figured it out. It was almost as if he'd gotten himself into something that he couldn't get out of."

Hope leaned forward in her seat. "But the threats referenced the loss of a child. I don't think Wayne and Serena Smother had any children."

"You're right. He did that to throw suspicion in other directions. He didn't realize that your parents weren't aware of Paula. He figured once there were threats against you, they would demand that you stop volunteering at Gloria's Path. He thought you were talking Serena into leaving him. When you didn't stop volunteering, he decided he had to take it a step further. His wife getting her own apartment was the final straw."

"How did he know we were at that store?" Mack asked. He knew that he had not been followed from the apartment.

"Serena sent him a text, bragging about how nice her apartment was, how close it was to the train and how helpful everyone from Gloria's Path had been. So helpful in fact, that they were getting her a coffeepot at the store. He didn't know for sure where the apartment was, but he had a pretty good idea of the general area. He took a guess at which store and he got lucky. He said that he'd almost given up when he saw the two of you walking out of the store. He took it as some kind of sign."

"Has he posted bail?" Mack asked.

"Nope. And I don't think he'll be able to. He's going to sit in jail until his trial. Of course, that counts as time served."

"Will you let us know if he does make bail?" Hope asked.

The chief indicated he would. Mack didn't care. He'd put things in place to monitor Wayne Smother until the man was safe behind prison bars. The man would never, ever have a chance to get close to Hope again.

"The press is aware of the arrest," the chief said. "Ferguson has already interviewed Serena Smother. I'm afraid the truth about your volunteer work in disguise is no longer a secret. He called and asked me about it and I basically shut it down with a no-comment response. Unfortunately, he can be a bit of an ankle biter when he smells a story. I thought you should be prepared."

Mack looked at Hope. Her eyes were troubled and he suspected that she was wondering if the full secret would somehow unravel. Would Byron Ferguson give up until he knew what had brought Hope to Gloria's Path?

"Thank you," Hope said. "I appreciate knowing that. Can't wait for tomorrow's paper," she added drily.

The chief laughed. "That's how I feel every morning. Just try to remember, every news story blows over eventually."

"Of course," Hope said, not sounding confident. "Thank you, Chief. I do appreciate your assistance with everything."

"Well," the man said, suddenly sounding unsure, "I have admired your father for a long time. He's got to be very proud of you."

Hope smiled at Mack. "Yes. Yes, I'm sure he is."

"Thanks, Chief," Mack said quickly. "Let us know if anything else comes up."

"I will. I'm just glad it's over," the man said, and hung up.

They drove in silence for several minutes. Finally, she turned to him. "It really is over, isn't it?"

"Looks that way," he said.

She leaned her head back against the headrest. "I'm so sorry," she said.

That wasn't exactly the reaction he'd expected. "What for?"

"For not taking the threats seriously. You did. You were right. My family was right. I was just so busy being mad at my dad that I couldn't see anything else. I couldn't see the possibilities."

"You have a right to be mad. Keeping Baylor at the ministry was a big mistake. Your dad had to know that."

She smiled. "You know, earlier I told you that it didn't matter. And I was lying then. It did matter. But suddenly it really doesn't." She looked down at her hands. Then at him. "I owe you for that. I do."

"You don't owe me anything."

She smiled at him. "Let's agree to disagree."

"I think I should tell your parents what has happened. They deserve to know."

She nodded. "You're right. I'm sure they will be very relieved to know that the threat is over."

"But I'm not leaving, even if they tell me I can."

FERGUSON HAD LEFT three messages on the house phone's voice mail. He was working on a story for tomorrow's paper and he wanted to give her a chance to comment.

She listened to the first one and deleted the other two without listening.

"He's probably going to talk to other people who work at Gloria's Path," Mack said. "The truth about how you came to be a volunteer there may come out."

"It could," Hope admitted. "I don't think it will, however. Sasha is the only one who knows, but I don't think she'll tell him."

"Why?"

"Well, for one thing, she hates the local paper," Hope said, grateful to talk about something else. "Her ex-husband from her second marriage sells advertising for them. She hates the local car dealer, as well," she added, with a smile. "First ex-husband works there."

"Two exes. Bad luck or bad choices?"

"I don't know. Sasha was helpful to me at a time when I desperately needed help. And I think she's got a good attitude about things. She works at a nursing home, and while it can be a sad place, she finds fun in it. She's always talking about this one elderly man, Charlie Fenton, who manages to leave, without any of his clothes, because he's intent upon buying donuts for his girlfriend, who also lives there. Sasha is a good storyteller."

"Sounds as if you think she's a good friend, too. Are you going in tonight?"

"I usually do volunteer on Fridays, but I think I'll let Sasha know not to expect me for a couple nights. By then, some of the interest will die down. Ferguson may have found another hot story by then."

"In Weatherbie?" Mack asked.

"It's almost time for the seniors to be done with their classes for the year. Maybe we'll get lucky and they'll pull some good pranks that will get some attention. Goats loose on the track. Underwear up the flagpole."

"Got to love small-town America," Mack said, shaking his head. "So let me get this straight. You don't have any obligations tonight or into the foreseeable future?"

"Well, on Tuesday—the thirteenth—I have to cover Mavis's volunteer shift for the library fund-raiser. She said that she'll be back that day, but not until the evening."

"Okay," he said, "we can fit that in."

"Fit it in?"

Mack picked up his phone and started dialing.

"Who are you calling?" she asked.

"The pizza guy. We're sure as hell not cooking tonight, or tomorrow night, or any night until Mavis comes home."

"Oh, really?" she asked, her tone challenging. "I thought we were having fun cooking."

"It was fun. But comparatively speaking, there are other things I enjoy more."

"I wonder what that is?" she teased.

"Keep thinking," he said. "Let's see. Pizza tonight, then Thai, and maybe even gyros from the little Greek place on the corner."

She smiled at him. "You know I do love to support the local economy."

ON TUESDAY, AT ten minutes before seven, she slipped out of Mack's arms. Of course, when he immediately sat up in bed, she realized he was already awake.

"Time to wash cars?" he asked, voice husky.

"Yes. I'm going to take a quick shower, grab something to eat and get over there."

He swung his legs over the bed and she found it difficult to take her eyes off of him. He was naked and so amazingly gorgeous. "We'll shower together," he said.

"Oh, no," she answered, already moving toward the bathroom door. "I'll be an hour late."

"But happy when we get there," he countered.

"We? You don't have to go. The threat is over, it will be perfectly safe."

"I want to go," he said. "I already checked today's paper. After running articles for two days, you'll be happy to know that Ferguson finally took a day off today. But still, people will likely be talking about what's happened. I don't want you to have to face that alone."

"At least Byron didn't dig too deep into the reasons I chose Gloria's Path."

"No, he didn't. I think he's a lazy journalist."

"I'm grateful for that. I'll have to be careful if he's there today."

"Don't worry. I'll handle him," Mack said.

She leaned in and kissed him on the cheek. "I'm a big girl, Mack."

"I know that. And capable as hell. It's just that Ferguson rubs me the wrong way."

She tossed her hair over one shoulder. "If he gets too nosy, I'll just hit him with the hose."

THE ORGANIZERS OF the car wash practically fell all over themselves when both he and Hope showed up. "I heard Mavis was out of town," the woman who was registering volunteers said, "so I thought we'd be one short."

"Mavis made sure it was covered," Hope said and accepted the stack of towels the woman handed her.

"That was a terrible thing that man tried to do," the woman said in a loud whisper.

"Yes, yes it was," Hope said, moving down the line to pick up sponges.

They joined the twenty or so other volunteers and then

divided to make three lines with someone spraying, a few people washing and several more drying.

The event was held in the parking lot of the library that was going to get all new windows if they could raise enough money. At one point, when Mack looked up from drying a car, and the line of cars stretched to the end of the block, he figured the building might get a new roof out of the day, too.

By noon, the temperature had hit eighty-eight. There wasn't a cloud in the sky. People were friendly and happy to donate twenty bucks for a free car wash.

"I need more towels," a woman in their group said.

"I'll get them," Hope said. She put down her hose and started walking toward the pallets at the far end of the parking lot, where extra supplies were stored. Ferguson had not shown up, but still Mack kept one eye on her as she crossed the lot and squatted down to pick up towels.

He saw her stand up.

But then she dropped her towels, put a hand to her forehead, and sank to the ground.

Chapter Twenty

The former cross-country star sprinted across the lot. And when he pushed his way past the four or five people who had already gathered around Hope, her face was pale and she was blinking fast.

"What happened?" she asked.

"I think you fainted," a woman said.

"Call 911," Mack said. He reached for Hope's wrist to check her pulse.

"No," Hope said. She smiled at the woman, offering reassurance. "I'm fine. Really. I think I just had too much sun."

"You fell on the pavement," Mack said. "You might have hit your head."

She shook her head. "I didn't. Really, Mack, I'm okay."

Well, bully for her, Mack thought, because he was a wreck. When she'd gone down, his first thought was that she'd been shot at again, and this time had been hit. His heart had stopped in his damn chest.

"Can I get you something to drink?" This from the woman who had given the fainting diagnosis.

"Thank you. Maybe some lemonade," Hope said.

"She'll drink it over there," Mack said to the woman. Then he scooped up Hope into his arms and carried her over to sit under the shade tree.

"Oh, good grief," Hope said. "Put me down."

He ignored her until they got to the grassy area where big oak trees provided lots of shade. Then he gently put her down. He sat next to her.

"What happened?" he asked.

"I'm not sure," she admitted. "I picked up the towels, stood up and suddenly, everything went gray to black. Fast. I've never fainted before. I don't like it."

"Me, either. You scared me," he admitted. "Are you sure you won't go to a doctor?"

She shook her head. "No. I don't think that's necessary. I just got too warm, maybe a little dehy—"

She stopped because the woman was carrying over two lemonades. She handed them each one. "Enjoy," she said and walked off.

Hope took a big drink.

"We'll take off once you finish that," he said.

"We can't leave. We have to finish the car wash."

"Oh, no. You're not finishing anything. You're done. The most pressing thing you need to do is finish your lemonade."

"But—"

"But nothing. I'll compromise. If you'll sit in the shade and drink your lemonade, I'll keep washing and drying cars. If you insist on helping, all bets are off."

She rolled her eyes. "Fine. Can I sit at the table and accept the money?"

"As long as the table is in the shade. And then we're going back to your house. And you're going to rest."

"I have a request," Hope said.

"I'm listening."

"I want you to go to the dinner tonight for Brody at the White House. I do. Your name is still on the guest list. You have plenty of time to take the train if you leave soon."

"I don't want to leave you. I could make a few calls, probably get you on the list."

She shook her head. "The media circus is somewhat controlled here. But at the White House, the story could get legs again and that's not fair to you."

"I can handle the media," Mack said.

She smiled. "You've proven that you can handle most anything. But you shouldn't have to. Just go. Please. Brody is one of your best friends. You're never going to have another chance to honor him in this way."

He'd been feeling badly that he was going to have to bail on Brody. But hadn't wanted to pressure Hope to go.

"Are you sure?" he asked.

"Yes. I'll be fine. Mavis will be back tonight and we'll hang out."

"I'll only be gone for a few hours. And I don't think I'll do the train. A plane will be faster. Then dinner for a couple hours and I'll be back before you know it."

"I know. Don't worry. The danger is over."

He knew that, but still, he'd come too close to losing Hope. "Your parents will be back tonight," he said.

"I know. I'm going to talk to my father. I need to understand his side of the story."

MACK HAD CONSIDERED taking a commercial flight to D.C., but decided that a small plane out of a private airstrip suited his needs better. It would reduce the amount of time he needed to be away from Hope even more.

Still, he'd been at the airport for less than twenty minutes and he was already missing her. He knew he should stop worrying. But he couldn't. He wanted to wrap her up in cotton and carry her around on soft pillows. Of course, she wanted none of that. She wanted to wash cars all day in the hot sun.

She and Mavis would be fine now that Wayne Smother was locked up. And Patsy and Archibald Minnow would be home late tonight.

He would no longer be needed.

Too bad.

He loved Hope and didn't intend to walk away. He understood why she was so nervous about getting married again. He could be patient, but he wasn't giving up.

He couldn't wait to tell Brody all about her. And when he felt the plane start to taxi down the runway, he knew that he'd be able to do just that in less than an hour. He was meeting his friend at the hotel. Then they would travel together to the White House for dinner.

He closed his eyes, hoping to catch a catnap. That thought had him smiling. Catnap. As in cat. He'd arranged to purchase Fred from the Websters. He knew he was playing dirty, but he didn't care. He was playing to win.

Forty-five minutes later, the wheels touched down and he was off the plane. He carried the tux that he had Chandler ship to him days ago, just in case. She was happy to do it, she'd said, because it gave her official permission to snoop in her brother's closet.

He hailed a cab and drummed his fingers on the door when they hit D.C. traffic and moved at a snail's pace. Finally, he was at the hotel. It was big and splashy with lots of marble in the lobby. He didn't care about that. He cared a whole lot when he spied Brody Donovan unfold his lean body from one of the couches.

Brody looked good. Tanned. Fit. There were some lines around his eyes that hadn't been there two years ago when Mack had last seen him. Of course, Brody had spent most of those two years on the front lines, working miracles for soldiers. That would tend to put a little wear and tear on the body.

Mack gave his friend a big hug. "Good to see you," he said.

"Glad you could make it," Brody replied. "Is your assignment in New Jersey all done?"

"Almost. Hope's parents return to the States late tonight."

"You managed to keep her out of jail. Good for you."

Mack pulled back. He knew Brody was kidding, but he couldn't let it go. "I'm going to marry her."

Brody squinted his eyes at him, assessing. "Damn. I think you're serious."

"As a heart attack. She's amazing, Brody. Beautiful and smart and fun. She's kind and thoughtful and giving. Oh, and she makes the best enchiladas."

"Well, then, get a license and get it done."

"I haven't gotten her to say yes yet."

Brody grabbed him by the elbow and started to drag him to the bar.

"What are you doing?" Mack said. "We have to get dressed and get going."

"Oh, no. I just learned that some woman has my best friend in knots. You can't drop a bombshell like that and think the conversation is over. Come on. I'm buying."

HOPE WAITED FOR twenty minutes after Mack left the house before she got in the car and drove to the drugstore. Fortunately, Jane wasn't working. Hope didn't recognize the clerk on duty.

She didn't care.

She bought two home pregnancy-test kits. For days

she'd been thinking about it. But this morning, the fainting episode had pushed her over the edge.

She'd told Mack the truth. She never fainted.

But she hadn't told him that she'd woken up feeling a little nauseous this morning. He wouldn't have left her side. And she needed to do this by herself.

When she got home, she went upstairs, read the directions and went into the bathroom. Then she repeated the test a second time.

Both results were the same.

Pregnant. With a capital *P*.

Hope Minnow was going to have a baby.

She felt like dancing around the room. But she didn't because she heard the security alarm go off and knew that Mavis had returned. She picked up all the trash, put it in a bag and then shoved it under her bed. She didn't want anybody seeing this.

Not until she'd had a chance to tell Mack. He deserved to know first. He'd be back by midnight at the latest. Eight hours. No big deal.

She took the steps to the first floor, laughing silently when she realized that her hand was hovering over the handrail. She'd been taking these steps for years and never considered using the handrail.

But now a fall might not impact just her. It was amazing how pregnancy changed one's perspective.

"Hey, Mavis," she said, entering the kitchen.

"Hi, Hope. I missed you," she said, giving her a hug. "I didn't see Mack's car."

"He's at an event honoring an old friend. In Washington, D.C. He'll be back late tonight. Probably about the same time as my parents. He figured it was safe to go now that Smother is in jail."

"Makes sense," Mavis said.

"How's your brother-in-law? And your sister?"

"Better."

"Glad to hear it. And glad that you're home. I'm going to go downstairs and walk on the treadmill for a while."

"Okay," Mavis said. "I bought stuff for Chinese for dinner."

"Perfect. I'll see you in a half hour."

WHEN HOPE CAME UPSTAIRS, she was surprised to see that the kitchen was empty. She looked through the French doors to see if Mavis was on the veranda. No sign of her.

"Mavis?" she yelled. A sense of foreboding traveled through her body. Mavis was always really good about telling her if she was leaving the house.

She reached for the house phone, intending to try Mavis's cell number. That's when she saw the note on the calendar.

Ran to the store—needed cornstarch. Will be back in a little while.

She realized that Mavis had put the note where she thought it was likely that Hope would see it. The woman wouldn't be gone long. Maybe she'd just sit outside and enjoy the late-afternoon sun while she waited for her.

She was just about to open the back door when she heard a cell phone ringing. It took her a minute to realize that it was Paula's phone that was still in her purse. She pulled it out, recognized the number as Gloria's Path and answered it. "This is Hope," she said, relishing the fact that she didn't have to hide her identify any longer.

"Hey, it's Sasha."

"What's going on? I heard you were out of town for a couple days."

"Had to visit my mom unexpectedly. She broke a hip."

"Oh, I'm sorry. Is she okay?"

"Yeah, except she's getting discharged from the hospital today. I really need to be there. However, we got a call on the hotline. There's a new client and I was going to pick her up. She's at the Smart Gas station, just east of town. A neighbor gave her a ride there."

"Is she okay?"

"Fine, now. She got out of the hospital two days ago after her husband knocked her around. She went home, but woke up this morning and decided that she wasn't going to take it anymore. Her name is Dana. Mid-forties. Short brown hair. I didn't want to tell her that there wasn't anyone available to meet with her. Jackie is willing to come in early but can't get there for a couple hours. Could you pick up Dana and get her settled at Gloria's Path? Jackie will relieve you as soon as possible."

She'd told Mack that she intended to stay home. "There's no one else?"

"No. I checked. I wouldn't ask if…"

It was true. Sasha had always demonstrated her willingness to take an extra shift or complete a dirty job. She never asked one of the volunteers to do what she wouldn't do. "Just for a couple of hours?" Hope asked.

"Definitely."

She would be home before Mack got done with his rubber chicken or whatever it was that they served at White House dinners.

"Okay. I'll do it. Good luck with your mom." Hope hung up the phone and picked up a pen. On the calendar, below Mavis's writing, she scribbled, *Need to help a client. Eat without me and I'll grab something when I get home.*

She grabbed her purse, grateful that she didn't have

to put on the ridiculous disguise anymore. She got into her car and secured her seat belt. Five minutes into her drive, her cell phone rang. She looked at the number. The school in Brooklyn. "This is Hope," she answered.

Ten minutes later, she pulled into the parking lot of Smart Gas. It was a locally owned gas station and did a big business with the trucks that lumbered through New Jersey on their way to New York City, as well as the commuters who burned through tanks of gas a week.

She did not see a lone woman standing outside. She parked in front of the convenience-store portion of the gas station and went inside. There were only three aisles. No women customers. Hope approached the cashier. "Hi. I was supposed to meet a woman here. Mid-forties. Short brown hair."

"I just gave her the key to the ladies room," the man said, pointing outside. He turned to help the next customer.

Smart Gas had been built thirty years ago, when gas stations had exterior entrances to their restrooms. It had remained in the Smart family for all these years and they'd evidently found no need to change that.

Hope went outside, walked down the length of the store, turned the corner and didn't see the man who stepped out of the shadows until it was too late.

He put a hand over her mouth and jerked her head backward. "Cooperate or you're dead," he said.

Chapter Twenty-One

The bar served a pretty good microbrew and Mack was happy enough to participate in a toast to his good fortune. He felt lucky as hell. He'd accepted this assignment never realizing that he was going to meet a wonderful woman, somebody that he would want to spend the rest of his life with.

"Have you told Chandler yet?" Brody asked.

Mack shook his head. "No way. I want to see her face. But I also don't want to impose upon her big day. I'll tell her afterward."

"Maybe she'd want a double wedding?" Brody suggested.

"If I throw a wrench into things and end up delaying Ethan and Chandler's wedding, I don't think I'll be around to enjoy my own. Ethan will get me for sure."

"It's so cool that Ethan and Chandler ended up together," Brody said, setting down his empty glass. "It's pretty amazing when you think about the chances."

"It is. Although, I don't know why I'm surprised," Mack said. "When I think back, he was always looking out for her. Always wanted to let her tag along."

Brody nodded. "He's come full circle. And I barely have a chance to get used to that news before my other best friend takes the plunge."

"You're next," Mack said, standing up. It was time for them to get to the White House.

"I don't think so," Brody said, dismissing the idea immediately. "What's next for me is a nice little vacation. I'm going to South America. Going to lie on a beach somewhere and enjoy ice-cold rum drinks."

"That sounds pretty good."

Brody slapped him on the back. "It sounds excellent. And there aren't going to be any bombs going off or bullets whizzing by. That sounds even better." He started walking. "Come on. I hate to make the president wait on me."

The two men dressed in Brody's room, with Brody in military dress and Mack in his tux. "You clean up pretty good," Mack said.

"Likewise. Although I expected it from you. An outcome of your James Bond genetic material."

"If you say things like that tonight, they're going to take back the award."

"Let 'em try."

Mack pulled out his phone. "I'm going to send a quick text to Hope." He typed in his message and hit Send.

The two men left the room and took the elevator downstairs. They exited the lobby, intending to walk the four blocks to the White House. Mack checked his phone three times on the way. Nothing.

"No response?" Brody asked, obviously picking up on his preoccupation.

"No."

"Maybe she's in the shower?"

"Maybe." He didn't think so. Hope had already showered once that day. He knew that because he'd showered with her. Who could have known that raspberry shower gel could be put to so much good use? They'd been in there so damn long that the hot water had run out.

There was no reason to think there should be any problems. But none of that logic did anything to settle the unrest that had lodged itself in his chest.

They walked the remaining two blocks. There was a small group of attendees waiting to get cleared by security. They took their place in line. As they shuffled forward, Mack once again pulled out his phone. He pressed Hope's number and listened to it ring. It went to voice mail. "Call me," he said quickly. It was their turn for security.

They showed identification and were allowed to pass through a set of electronic gates to complete the screening. Once past that, they were greeted by a woman at the door, wearing a long black dress. She escorted them to their seats in the State Dining Room.

People were milling around, taking seats, and there were servers floating through with trays of wineglasses. There was music playing in the background. It seemed everyone wanted a chance to meet Brody, to congratulate him on his service. He, in turn, introduced Mack.

It should have given Mack plenty to think about.

But all he could think about was Hope. And that his phone wasn't ringing.

He tried her again. Voice mail again.

He called the house. No answer there, either.

The president was approaching, shaking hands as he came. Mack searched through his numbers, found the one he needed and pushed Send. It was answered on the third ring. He explained what he needed, gave her the number of Hope's cell phone and hung up.

"Who was that?" Brody asked.

"Pam Brogan. Best data analyst I ever worked with. I'm tracking the location of Hope's cell phone."

Within two minutes, his phone was buzzing. He answered and felt the quick burn of panic spread across his chest. He clicked the end button just as the president stepped in front of them.

"Good to see you again, Mack," the man said.

"Thank you, sir."

The leader of the free world shifted his attention to Brody. "Dr. Donovan," he said. "It's a pleasure." The president went on to thank Brody for his service and said he admired both his skill and courage.

Once the president had moved on, Mack leaned into Brody and whispered in his ear. "I hate to do this. You are my best friend and I want to be here to see you honored. But I can't stay. Pam tracked the location of Hope's cell phone to the middle of a field. Something is very wrong."

"Let's go," Brody said.

"You can't go. You're one of the people getting honored."

Brody waved a hand. "There are three other honorees here. I shook the president's hand. That's good enough for me. You're my friend. If there's trouble, then I want to be there to help you. But you have to do one thing for me."

"Name it," Mack said, already moving toward the door.

"Let me be the best man."

HOPE HAD NO idea where the men had taken her because as soon as she'd been pushed into the van, they'd tied a blindfold around her eyes and shoved her down on the floor. She'd hit her head hard.

She felt her attacker grab the strap of her crossover purse and yank it over her head and down her arm. Then the van had taken off fast. She'd spread her hands and tried to keep from bouncing around too much. She felt sick to her stomach and so terribly frightened that it was hard to keep from crying out.

But she kept still. And tried to listen to what the men were saying to one another. But it was useless. They were speaking in a language that she didn't understand.

She heard what sounded like a zipper and then the rush of wind as a window was lowered. One of the men said something, the other laughed and the window was shut.

Had something been tossed out the window? Her purse? Something else?

She did not think her capture had been random. The man had been waiting for her to come around the corner. He'd clapped his hand over her mouth and within seconds, she'd been inside the van. The van had been ready for her.

There must have been a woman. She'd asked about a woman, mid-forties with short brown hair, just the way Sasha had described her. The clerk had told her that there was a woman in the restroom.

Sasha was mid-forties with short brown hair.

Hope hadn't been scheduled to work. She'd only worked because Sasha had called her.

She felt sick. Had her friend betrayed her?

What did these men want? Ransom? Her parents would pay, she was sure of that.

Oh, God. Mack. He would be crazy with worry.

Their baby. Oh, please let their baby survive.

MACK AND BRODY caught a taxi outside the White House. From there, Mack called the pilot who had flown him in, and told him to get the plane ready, that he and Brody would be there in fifteen minutes to take off.

It was the longest fifteen minutes of Mack's life. He tried Hope's home number twice more. He didn't bother leaving messages.

The next call he made was to Chief Anderson. When the man answered, he sounded sleepy.

"Yes," he said.

"This is Mack McCann. I couldn't reach Hope and I had her cell phone tracked. It's in some kind of field next to Highway 52. She's in trouble. I need you to get somebody to her home and see if anyone is there."

"But, but…" the man sputtered. Then he sighed. "I'll go myself. I live pretty close to the Minnows." He hung up.

The cab stopped and Mack threw some money at the driver. He and Brody hit the pavement at a hard run. They boarded the plane, the pilot finished his take-off routine, and they were in the air in less than three minutes.

"It's going to be okay," Brody said.

Mack nodded. "It has to be." It had never mattered more.

HOPE TRIED TO keep track of the distance they were traveling by counting in her head. One, one thousand, two, one thousand, three, one thousand, all the way up to sixty, one thousand. She got through five full rounds and was halfway through a sixth before the van came to a pretty sudden stop. She heard doors opening.

She wasn't sure of the speed, but she thought it was likely within the speed limit, to not attract attention. That meant they were roughly five or six miles from the gas station where she'd been abducted.

It didn't tell her much but it did tell her something. She tried to listen for background noise. Was that a train in the distance? There were a couple of rail tracks, both freight and passenger, that ran through Weatherbie. Most were on the north end.

"Let's go." A hand gripped her upper arm and yanked her up. With her eyes still blindfolded, she missed a step and fell onto the ground.

Grass. Long grass.

The hand yanked her up again. They walked for just a minute and she heard a door open. Then she felt a temperature change as they entered a hot, stuffy building. A strong hand on her shoulder pushed her down onto a chair.

Finally, somebody ripped off her blindfold and she was looking at her abductors.

And she didn't have a clue who they were. Two men. Both with olive-colored skin and dark hair. Probably in their late thirties or early forties. One wore jeans and a white T-shirt. The other had on khaki pants and a long-sleeved dress shirt.

Most importantly, both had guns in their hands. It was hard to focus on anything but that. She forced herself to look back at the men's faces.

There was something about the man wearing the khaki pants.

The roundness of his face. The broad forehead.

And suddenly she remembered. The strip of photos in Sasha's car. The date for her cousin's wedding. It was definitely him.

More proof that Sasha was involved.

She swallowed, terribly afraid that she was going to throw up. Why would her friend do this?

She shifted her gaze, not wanting the man to see any flare of recognition in her eyes. The building was a metal structure with a cement floor. There was an old tractor and a hayrack stored at one end. Where they'd placed

her, they had a cheap patio table with four chairs. There
was a small refrigerator, the kind she'd had in college,
near the table, with an extension cord running across the
room to a wall outlet.

"Who are you?" Hope asked.

Neither man answered. The one in jeans opened the
refrigerator and pulled out a beer. He tossed it to the
other man and then pulled out a second one for himself.

"What do you want?" she asked.

"Shut up," Jeans-man said, this time in English.

When she heard his voice, she realized that was who
had spoken to her in the van. Khaki-guy must have
been driving. That meant that the keys were likely in
his pocket.

The minute she got the chance, she was going for the
keys and getting the heck out of here. But when Jeans-
man suddenly put down his beer and grabbed a rope that
was hanging on the wall, she knew her chances for escape
had gotten much slimmer.

Chapter Twenty-Two

Mack and Brody touched down at the small private airstrip outside Weatherbie at exactly 8:00 p.m. Two minutes later, as they were driving toward the Minnow home, Mack got the call he'd been waiting for.

"I'm here at the Minnow house," Chief Anderson said. "Mavis got home about twenty minutes ago. There was no sign of Hope. Her car is gone. So is her purse. No sign of struggle. Mavis said the alarm was set when she let herself in."

"No note? No explanation?"

"No. I asked her and I checked myself. I didn't see anything."

There was no need for him to go to the house. He plugged the address that Pam Brogan had given him into his GPS. Then he repeated it to Chief Anderson, and added, "I'm headed there now. Meet me."

There was very little traffic and it took eight minutes to get there. It was on the outskirts of Weatherbie, where the pretty community started to turn more rural. There was a McDonald's on one corner, a gas station on another, a church with a big parking lot on the third corner and the fourth was still an empty field with a For Sale sign posted on it.

"That's got to be it," Brody said.

"Yeah." Mack parked and the men got out. They stood at the edge of the foot-high grass. It was going to be like looking for a needle in a haystack. Except not really. He dialed Hope's cell phone. Then he listened. Nothing. They separated, each man frantically redialing her number, hoping to hear a ring from somewhere. They were losing the daylight.

It took ten minutes before Brody called out. "I've got it."

Mack ran to his friend, crashing through the tall grass. There it was, sort of lying on top of the long grass. Like it would have been if someone had tossed it from the road.

None of the grass in the area was beaten down or showed any damage, except the paths that Brody and Mack had taken. He was sure that neither Hope nor her captor had actually been in the field.

Out of the corner of his eye, he saw flashing blue lights and knew that Chief Anderson had arrived. There were two squad cars with him.

The chief and the two other officers walked into the field. Mack nodded at the men. "This is my friend, Brody Donovan." Then he pointed to Hope's phone. "I'm sure it's Hope's, but I haven't touched it yet. I don't have any gloves."

One of the officers snapped on a pair and reached for the phone. "We need to check her calls," Mack said.

The chief nodded and the officer pressed a button. He showed Mack the screen. She hadn't made any calls that day. The only incoming calls were the ones he'd made in D.C. and the thirty or forty calls that he and Brody had made in the last few minutes.

"Check the texts," he said next.

There was his text from D.C. Nothing else. Damn it. He turned to the chief. "Hope was near here. I don't know why, but she was. We need to question everyone in the area. I think the lowest possibility is the church. There are no cars in the parking lot and quite frankly, if she drove somewhere, I don't think it was to visit an empty church. But she could have run to get gas or to pick up some food, although I've yet to see her eat any fast food."

Chief Anderson pointed to one of the officers. "Check the church." He pointed to the other. "You go with Brody and check McDonald's. Mack and I'll take Smart Gas. Switch your radios to channel two for secure communication."

"Wait," Mack said. He pulled his cell phone out of his shirt pocket, opened up his pictures and found one of Hope. "Here's Hope's picture," he said, holding it out so the men could have a good look. Then he looked at his friend. "I'll forward it to your phone so that you can show people."

"Got it," Brody said. Then he looked at Mack. "We're going to find her."

Mack didn't answer. He had a horrible feeling that time was not their friend.

WHEN HE AND Chief Anderson went into the gas station, there was one clerk and three people waiting to get checked out. The chief pulled his badge, said "excuse me" a couple times and they were suddenly at the front of the line. In the meantime, Mack had checked each aisle.

"Good luck," said the male clerk to the customer who had just bought a lottery ticket.

They needed all the luck right now. He and Chief Anderson stepped close to the counter.

The chief flashed his badge again. "My name is Chief Anderson from the Weatherbie Police Department. We're looking for this woman." He motioned for Mack to hold out his phone.

The man looked at it. "Pretty. She do something wrong?"

"She's…missing," the chief said.

Mack hated hearing that word. *Missing.* "Have you seen her?"

"I just came on about a half hour ago. Hank would have been working the register before that, but he's gone for the day."

Damn. "Do you have a security camera?" Mack asked.

The man frowned at him. "Of course."

"We need to see it," Mack said. "Everything from this evening."

"You'll have to talk to my manager, Tammy, for that."

Mack leaned his face in close. "Get Tammy out here. Now."

JEANS-MAN HAD PULLED her hands behind her back, led her over to a wooden stake that she suspected had been installed just for her and tied her to it. Then he and Khaki-guy had left the building.

Her shoulders burned, her head hurt from where she'd hit it on the van floor, but the pain in her heart was the worst.

Sasha had been a trusted confidante when Hope had first come to Gloria's Path. She'd helped Hope have the courage to leave Wills and, ultimately, the resolve to come back and volunteer. They were friends.

At least she'd thought they were.

She'd thought that there could never be a betrayal that would be as horrible or as painful as when her father had chosen Wills over her. But this somehow felt worse.

Her father had been motivated by his greed for fame and money. While she detested that, she understood it.

What had Sasha's motivation been?

It didn't matter, Hope realized. All that mattered is that she had to stay alive. Whatever it took, whatever she ultimately had to endure.

She owed that to herself, to Mack and most of all, to the child that she carried in her womb. Mack would come back, he'd see the note on the calendar on the refrigerator and he'd start to put the pieces together. He would find her. If anyone could. And she was going to be alive when he did.

TAMMY BURDEN WAS barely five feet tall, but she carried herself like a woman who tolerated very little bull. Chief Anderson introduced himself and Mack before quickly and quietly explaining the situation.

Tammy stared at them. "Hope Minnow was my tennis partner in high school. Oh, good Lord. You're the sexy stranger that Jane was Tweeting about."

Mack nodded.

Tammy shook her head. "Jane never did have any common sense. Come on. Let's go take a look."

The quality of the security camera video was not great, but certainly better than some he'd worked with. Plus, it wasn't like he was trying to pick someone out of a lineup. He was looking for the woman he loved. And he found her easily enough.

"There she is," he said. He checked the time on the tape—6:14 p.m. Almost two hours ago now. "She's talking to your clerk." He tried to read her lips. "Meet a woman." He got that much. The clerk was pointing toward something. What the hell was he pointing at?

Tammy was already picking up the phone. She dialed,

then spoke. "Hank, it's Tammy. Sorry to bother you but I have a quick question. About a half hour before your shift ended, a pretty blond woman came in. She spoke to you, maybe asked you something about meeting a woman and you pointed outside. Do you remember that?"

Mack wanted to jerk the phone out of her hand, to demand to talk to Hank, but Tammy had been pretty helpful so far. He didn't want to push his luck. He looked at Chief Anderson and got the impression that he was thinking the same thing.

"Okay, thanks," Tammy said and hung up her phone. "Hank definitely remembers Hope. Said she had come in, looked around, then asked whether there was a brown-haired woman in her mid-forties in the store. He told her that he'd just given the restroom key to someone who fit that description. He said that he assumed that she went to find her. He was mad because nobody ever came back in with the key. When his shift was over, he went out to check and the key was on the bathroom floor. He hung it back up." She pointed to a key with a foot-long metal rod for a handle. It was hanging on the wall behind the clerk's head.

"Don't touch that key again. Don't give it to anybody. Don't let anybody use that restroom," Chief Anderson instructed. He spoke into the radio that was on his lapel. "Report to Smart Gas. Repeat, report to Smart Gas."

He looked at Mack. "I'll get my two officers back here to process the scene."

"Is there a security camera by the restrooms?" Mack asked.

"I'm sorry, but not on that side of the building."

"On your pumps?" he persisted.

"Of course. You think she got gas?"

He doubted that. There were two possibilities. One, the

brown-haired woman was in as much trouble as Hope. Two, the brown-haired woman had been a ruse and someone accosted Hope on her way to the ladies room. They'd driven off with her. Maybe they would get lucky and at least get some sort of vehicle description. "I want to see everything from six o'clock to about six-twenty."

Tammy quickly typed in some commands on her desktop and soon she was showing a view of the pump area. There were three pumps, with cars pulling up on both sides. They watched. Nothing seemed unusual. Until Mack saw the blue work van. It passed by the far end of the pumps, but the driver, middle-aged, wearing a ball cap low on his forehead, didn't pull in to fill up his tank.

They lost him from the screen. "Where did he go?" Mack asked. "Where the hell did he go?"

"Maybe he pulled in to turn around," Tammy said. "That happens a lot out here. People looking for stuff in Weatherbie and suddenly realizing that they're getting out of the city limits."

There was no way to know because the camera did not provide a view of the entryway off the street. "Go back to the other camera," Mack said. "See if he came inside to buy something."

They looked. No men in baseball caps entered. In fact, no men at all entered.

Mack made eye contact with the chief. The older man nodded. Then he spoke into his radio, asking for all officers to be aware of a blue van with a dent on the right rear fender panel. Once he finished, he made eye contact. "Okay. That will get communicated statewide."

Tammy looked at the two men. "I'm sorry," she said. "I wish we had more for you, but nothing bad ever happens in Weatherbie."

Mack knew that bad stuff happened everywhere. And

sometimes it was random. But that wasn't the case here. Hope had come looking for someone. But who? And who had sent her on the wild-goose chase? If he could figure that out, he would find her.

"I think we've done what we can do," Chief Anderson said. "I suggest you go back to the Minnows' place and hopefully, we'll get a demand call. I'm going to contact the FBI and ask for some assistance."

Mack looked at his watch. The Minnows were due to land at JFK International Airport in New York in less than two hours. It was going to be impossible to keep a lid on the fact that the missing woman was Hope Minnow. He could not let them hear this news from anyone but him.

Hope had been his responsibility and he'd failed her.

The only thing worse than that was the possibility that he'd lost her forever.

Chapter Twenty-Three

Hope wasn't sure how long the men left her alone in the shed, but she thought it was several hours. She was tired of standing, her throat was raw from screaming, her shoulders and back ached terribly from the awkward position of having her hands tied behind her back and she desperately needed to use the bathroom.

But it was the feeling of isolation, of being so very alone, that was the worst. What if no one ever came back? What if they had left her here to die? How long would it take? Days? A week before her body started to shut down from lack of water, lack of nutrients? It was a horrible thought. And it played with her mind.

When the door finally opened, she was almost grateful to see the faces of her kidnappers. They looked at her, little emotion on their faces. Khaki-guy with the buffed fingernails had changed his shirt. It was still long-sleeved but now blue instead of a gray-and-white stripe. His hair looked cleaner, too.

Had he showered and changed clothes? The fact that he could do something so mundane after kidnapping someone made her stomach roll. Had he gone to Sasha's house?

She made eye contact with him. "I need to use the restroom. Badly."

He seemed to hesitate. Then he walked over and untied her. She rolled her shoulders forward, praying that she wouldn't pass out when the tendons and ligaments protested. He grabbed her upper arm tightly.

"Don't do anything stupid," he said. He led her to the door that he and Jeans-man had been using. He opened it and Hope could see that it was a small office area. There was a television on the wall showing a soccer game. Remnants of the fast-food dinner the two men had consumed were still on the desk. Her stomach rumbled loudly.

He ignored it and pointed toward the bathroom. "If you're not out in a minute, I'm coming in."

The bathroom was small with just a toilet and a sink. If the man had showered, he'd done it somewhere else. Maybe when he'd picked up the food. She hadn't heard the van start or return but she believed that at least one of them had left.

Would they do that again? It would be easier to fight one than two. She would use every bit of her strength, her teeth, whatever it took.

Hope used the toilet and tried to find something that she could use as a weapon. But there was nothing. No hairspray, no razors, no nothing. Just a bar of soap and some paper towels.

She flushed, washed her hands and opened the door. Khaki-guy was watching the television.

"What do you want?" she asked. "It's not too late to fix this."

He just looked at her. "Let's go," he said.

"May I have something to drink?" she asked, trying to sound submissive, nonthreatening.

He didn't answer. Just led her back into the big room. On their way past the refrigerator, he grabbed her a bottle of water. He watched as she opened it and took a big drink.

She heard his phone buzz and he reached into his khaki pants and pulled it out. He looked at the screen, then looked at Jeans-man. "It's starting," he said. "Won't be long now."

Jeans-man nodded several times, as if he were nervous.

What was starting?

He pulled the half-drunk bottle of water away from her. "That's enough."

Then he led her back to the pole and tied her up again.

MACK USED HIS connections to get through airport security so that he could be waiting at the gate when the plane landed. Now he waited, pacing back and forth.

He'd called Mavis from the car. The woman had been calm, certainly calmer than he felt. He'd told her to expect the police and the FBI to arrive shortly. "I'll be here," she'd told him.

He saw Bing first. Then Patsy Minnow, with Archie Minnow bringing up the rear. They all looked tired.

"Mack?" Bing said, slightly apprehensive. Nobody met travelers at the gate anymore.

Mack's throat almost closed with emotion, and he shook his head. "I'm sorry," he said. Then he turned to Patsy and Archie. "Hope went missing tonight, approximately six hours ago. The local police and the FBI have been alerted. So far, we have not received a ransom demand."

Patsy let out a soft squeal, like a wounded puppy might make. Archie's face lost all color. Bing's dark eyes drilled him.

"But that awful man was caught," Patsy said. He could hear her bewilderment.

"It's someone else," Mack said. He wanted to swear

to them that he'd figure it out, bring Hope home, but he had nothing, absolutely nothing, to go on. "Mavis is at the house. I know she's anxious to be with both of you."

But before they were out of the airport, Mack's phone rang. He yanked it out of his pocket. *Brody*. "What do we know?" he answered.

"We got a call," Brody said. "They made a ransom demand. Five million dollars. By noon tomorrow."

"Proof of life? Did you get it?" Mack demanded.

"We did. Hope's alive. They told her to say something and she said, 'Tell Mack that I loved the north donuts.'"

Loved the north donuts. What the hell? "You're sure that's what she said?"

"I heard it myself. We had it on speakerphone."

North as in a company name? Donuts? He'd never bought her donuts from North Donuts or any other donut shop. They'd never even talked about donuts.

Except they had. She'd been talking about a story that she'd heard about an old guy in a nursing home who escaped, naked, to buy his elderly girlfriend a donut.

She was being held at a nursing home? A nursing home called North.

No. That didn't make sense. Near a nursing home? On the north side of town? Maybe.

Held by someone who was old?

Held by someone who worked at a nursing home? Held by the person who told the story?

Sasha.

He stepped away from the rest of the group. "Brody, I need you to do something, but don't say anything to anyone else." He didn't know whom he could trust. "I think the woman that Hope worked with at Gloria's Path, one of the paid staff, is involved. Her first name is Sasha.

Don't know the last name or her address, but I'm betting we can get it from somebody at that shelter."

"I'm on it," Brody said.

They exited the airport. It was a quiet ride back to the Minnows' house. Everyone seemed lost in their own thoughts.

The only thing Reverend Minnow said was that he intended to pay. He would go to his bank in the morning.

Mack was grateful that the man wasn't balking at the request. He could have come up with a sizable portion himself, but it would have taken him a few days to raise the rest. Time they might not have.

They might not have it anyway, he knew. Kidnapping cases rarely ended well, even when the ransom demands were met. Kidnappers got nervous and killed the victim, sometimes before they got the money, sometimes immediately after.

But for now, Hope was alive. At least she had been fifteen minutes earlier.

They turned down the long driveway and parked behind several police cars. When they entered the house, at least six agents and several more officers in uniforms looked up. Mavis had made coffee and there was a big plate of cookies on the counter.

It could have been a damn party except that everybody looked very serious.

"Local press was here," Chief Anderson said, pulling him aside. "No one, of course, said anything about a ransom demand, but I still think it's going to get big play, especially after what happened last week to Hope."

Publicity. It was what Hope hated the most. She'd been so convinced that the threats against her were a publicity stunt. Was it possible that she was right? Was her father so hungry for press coverage that he'd do something like this?

Mack approached Reverend Minnow, who appeared to have aged ten years since he'd gotten off the plane. But Mack wasn't about to let that stop him. "May I speak with you privately?" he asked.

Archie Minnow nodded. "Of course." He led him to the library and closed the French doors.

Mack didn't waste any time. "I know that you and your daughter have a strained relationship. I also know that William Baylor beat the hell out of her and that for some crazy reason, you continue to employ him."

Archie pursed his lips, but didn't say anything.

"Hope initially dismissed the threats against her because she believed that it might be a publicity stunt to push your book sales. But the threats were real and Wayne Smother was real. We thought it was over. But now this. I'm going to ask just once. Are you involved in this in any way?" He expected the man to bristle but he didn't.

Archie merely shook his head. "I made a mistake with William. He was like a son to me, long before he married Hope. I liked him. Hell, I loved him. And I knew that I would not have achieved the success I had without his help. He's really very brilliant. Seemed to know exactly the right steps for me to take. And when the two of them started having trouble, I got scared. I thought I'd fail if William wasn't part of my team, and I'd worked my whole damn life to get where I was."

Mack really wanted to slam a fist in the man's mouth. But he kept silent.

"I was surprised when Hope told me what had happened. And I saw her injuries. They were bad. I talked to William about it. His story was different. I wasn't there,

I told myself. How could I know? What I did know for sure was that if the story got out, it would be bad for the ministry. Everyone knew that William was my right-hand man, my hand-picked successor, in fact."

"Hope believes you chose William over her."

"I know that. She's wrong, you know," he said, his voice thick with emotion. "I did something worse. And I have regretted it for a very long time. I can't expect her to forgive me. You see, I chose myself over her. And that's not what a parent is supposed to do. Parents put the needs of their children first. I didn't do that. I'm not proud of what I did. And ultimately, I'll be judged by my god and I can only pray for His forgiveness. I've already told her mother the truth. I did it after you called us in Paris. We almost lost Hope. I knew I finally needed to be honest with Patsy."

"And what did she say?"

"She was upset, of course. But I think she understands. Patsy has always understood how important the ministry was to me. It's important to her, too." The man cleared his throat, then looked toward the doors, as if checking to make sure they were still shut. "You need to know something. The two threats that we received, those letters, Patsy leaked the information to Byron Ferguson. And told him that Hope had a bodyguard. That's where he got his information."

Of all the things that Mack had expected to hear, this wasn't one of them. "Why?"

"In the past, I've gotten strange letters from parishioners and followers. Some are very zealous about their faith. While these were different, Patsy told me that she didn't really believe that Hope was in danger, especially with you around. She thought the publicity would be good for book sales. She did it for me."

Mack thought his head might burst. "I want you to know something. I love your daughter. Very much. And she loves me." He drew in a deep breath. "I'm going to marry her."

Archie Minnow stared at him. Finally, he spoke. "Although you may not believe it, I really am a very spiritual man. I am praying for Hope. I'm praying for all of us."

"I'm going to find her," Mack said. "If it's the last thing I do."

MACK RETURNED TO the kitchen. With the ransom demand in, everyone was mainly in wait-and-see mode. Agents were talking quietly in small groups. Someone had brought in pizza and the aroma filled the small kitchen.

Mavis was at the far counter. She was wearing the same shirt as the morning when she'd come in with it buttoned wrong. The morning she'd been reluctant to leave Hope and Mack alone. The morning she'd gone through the calendar with them.

He looked at the wall.

The calendar was already showing tomorrow's date.

That wasn't right. Mavis tore off the previous day's sheet every morning. He'd seen her. Sure, it was possible that someone else had changed the date. But how likely was that?

Not very. The calendar was Mavis's domain.

If Mavis had done it early by chance, then she'd likely thrown it away in the garbage. Old habits were hard to break.

Casually, he pulled a paper napkin out of the dispenser and spit out the piece of gum he was chewing into it. He folded it up, walked over to the sink and opened the cupboard door that was below the sink. He tossed in the napkin.

To an empty garbage can. Absolutely empty.

He distinctly remembered emptying coffee grounds into that garbage can just that morning. Somebody had taken the garbage out. In the middle of a crisis?

He shut the door and poured himself a glass of water. Drank it, standing at the sink. Nobody was paying any attention to him. Mavis had moved into the living room and sat next to Hope's mother, talking quietly to her.

He walked outside to the veranda. It was a warm night and he stood, watching the pool. Anyone watching him would think that he was gathering his thoughts.

After a minute, he moved to the corner of the house, toward the garbage cans that lined the side of the garage. He lifted the lid and pulled out the plastic bag on top. He opened the bag and used the flashlight on his key ring to look at the contents.

Amidst coffee grounds, leftover spaghetti, and newspapers, he found what he was looking for. He unfolded the ball of paper and smoothed it out.

Ran to the store—needed cornstarch. Will be back in a little while. That was in Mavis's handwriting.

Need to help a client. Eat without me and I'll grab something when I get home. Hope's reply.

Mavis had deliberately withheld this information. Why would she do that?

The only possible explanation was that Mavis was in this up to her eyeballs.

Chapter Twenty-Four

He pulled out his phone to call Brody. "Where are you?"

"Just left Gloria's Path. The woman is Sasha Roher, and I have her address."

"From who?"

"From nobody. There was nobody in the lobby area. It's still damaged from the fire. They haven't started re-building. But they also haven't cleared out any of their paperwork. It was still in the steel filing cabinet. I managed to get it open and there were tax forms for all the employees. There was only one Sasha. I'm on my way to her house now."

"Swing by and pick me up," Mack said. "I'll be waiting for you at the end of the lane." He didn't intend to announce to anybody that he was leaving.

Brody pulled up in Mack's car a couple minutes later. He got out so that Mack could drive. When Mack told him about the calendar page in the garbage, his friend hissed through his teeth.

Exactly.

He put Sasha Roher's address into his GPS and took off fast. They were at their destination in less than ten minutes. It was a small-frame house, maybe a two-bedroom. There was a narrow driveway that led to the garage, which backed up to the alley. The garage door was down. There was a light on in the back of the house.

"Take the back door," Mack said. "I'm going in through the front."

He walked up the three front steps, opened the screen door and turned the knob of the front door. Locked. He could hear music playing, something loud with a lot of drums. Finally, something was going his way.

He lifted his leg and kicked the door handle. Two quick kicks and the wood frame splintered. He pushed through the door. The house smelled like cinnamon. He glanced into the kitchen. Clean, nothing out of place. Same with the small living room. Nothing to make him think that any violence had occurred here. That made him feel only slightly better.

He passed the bathroom as he walked down the hall. He stuck his head around the corner of the room where the light was on. Sasha had her back to him. She was dancing to the beat of the music while she packed a suitcase on her unmade bed. There was also an open purse on the bed. In it, a small handgun.

He put his gun against her temple and wrapped an arm around her neck.

She tried to jump but couldn't budge him. "Going somewhere?" he asked, his mouth close to her ear.

"How did you get in?" she asked, her voice trembling.

Good. He wanted her scared. "I'm going to give you three seconds to tell me where Hope Minnow is. If you don't, I'm going to shoot you. One. Two." He took a breath. Opened his mouth.

"How would I know?" she asked, trying to act tough.

He took a chance. "Because you picked a partner who doesn't stand up to questioning very well. Mavis may look tough but she's a cupcake. She rolled over on you like a dog wanting his belly scratched."

He could feel the air leave the woman's body. "Damn it," she said.

"The only way for you to help yourself now is to tell me where Hope is."

"I don't know where she is."

The woman was lying. He pulled out his cell phone and dialed Brody. When he answered, he spoke fast. "Officer Donovan," he said. "I need you to contact Officer Ethan Moore. Tell him that Ms. Roher resisted arrest and I was forced to shoot her in self-defense."

He held the phone away from his ear so that Sasha could hear Brody's response.

"Roger that," Brody said. "I'll call the coroner, too."

He shoved Sasha away from him, spinning her so that she faced him. There was less than three feet that separated them.

"Goodbye, Sasha," he said. He pointed his gun at her heart.

"Wait," she cried. "They have her in an old machine shed. Off County Road C where it crosses Route 126."

That was north of town. "Who?" Mack demanded.

"My boyfriend and his brother. But this was all Mavis's idea. She's the one who thought up this crazy scheme. She told my boyfriend that it would work."

"How does she know your boyfriend?"

"He's her younger brother."

Mack dialed Brody. "Get in here. Use the front door."

When Brody walked into the bedroom, Mack smiled at him. "Roger that?"

Brody shrugged. "I don't get the chance to watch many police dramas."

Mack nodded at the open purse. "Get that gun and make sure it's loaded."

Brody knew his way around guns. As kids, they'd hunted in the mountains and Brody always had a good shot. Steady hands that served him well as a surgeon.

"It's loaded. Six bullets."

"Take a test shot. Make sure it shoots."

Brody put a round into the headboard. "Fires a hair to the right. I can correct for that."

"I'm counting on that. Keep your gun on her. Don't hesitate to shoot if she tries anything. I'm going to call Chief Anderson and they'll be here to back you up within a couple minutes."

"Where are you going?" Brody asked.

"I'm going to go find the woman I love. When the cops get here, you can tell them that they'll find me at the corner of County C Road and Route 126."

"You don't want to wait?" Brody asked.

"Hell, no," Mack said and left the house.

He wasn't going to take a chance that the cavalry would descend upon the machine shed and Hope would get caught in the crossfire. He was going in quiet.

He drove fast and arrived seven minutes later. He parked his car a half mile away and ran the rest of the distance. He wasn't even breathing hard when he got there.

When he saw the blue van outside of the building, his heart started beating a little fast. He walked around the building. Two doors. One was a regular house door. The other at the rear of the building was a garage door big enough to pull machinery in and out.

There were three windows on each side, but way too high to be useful to him. He was going to have to go through the front door. He needed to figure out a way to make them open the door without making them suspicious that they were under attack.

He looked around and considered his options. He studied the van. It might work. There was a patch of grass between the front of the van and the building, maybe three feet wide. Just a little downward slope. Maybe enough.

He opened the door of the van, hoping that the idiots had left the keys inside. They hadn't.

Okay. Plan B. He got out, got flat on his back and moved underneath the van. Using his flashlight, he carefully located the cable running alongside the transmission that had a switch and lever connected to it. He disconnected the cable and pushed on the lever until it clicked twice. The van moved forward just a little, telling him he had managed to get it in Neutral.

He crawled out. Then he braced his back against the rear of the van and pushed like hell until the thing started rolling forward. Then he ran.

He rounded the corner of the machine shed just as the van hit the building. It wasn't going fast enough to go through, but it dented the side of the building and made a hell of a noise.

That's what he'd been counting on.

The door opened and a man stuck his head out, looking around. He had a flashlight. "What the hell?" he said, when he saw the van. He shined the light around a little more and was evidently satisfied when he didn't see any other vehicles. He walked out, leaving the door open behind him.

Mack let him get close to the van before he walked up behind him and knocked him in the head with his gun. The man crumpled to the ground. Mack opened the van door, dragged the man inside and used a rope he found in the back to tie the man's hands behind his back. Then he backed out of the van, flipping the door locks to lock the man in.

He walked through the door of the machine shed, into a small office area. There was a television going in the corner and a half-empty beer on the old metal desk.

He opened the door that connected the office to the back part of the machine shed. The door creaked and he moved fast, knowing that he'd lost the element of surprise.

But he didn't move fast enough. He saw Hope, then the second man just as they saw him.

The man, who had been untying Hope's hands, grabbed her and pulled her in front of him, taking his shot away.

His heart plummeted. He'd come so far, he could not lose her now.

Then he saw Hope knot her hands together, raise them over her shoulder and knock the man hard enough in his larynx that he stumbled back.

It was all Mack needed.

By the time the man recovered, Mack had his gun pointed at the man's chest.

And he heard the sounds of approaching sirens.

THIRTY MINUTES LATER, Mack was sitting on the grass, with his back against the machine shed, Hope in his arms. The cool night air felt good.

"I knew you would come," she said.

"You were so smart," he said, kissing her forehead. She was alive. "I wouldn't have got it without the donut clue."

When he'd called Chief Anderson after leaving Sasha's house, he'd given the man a quick rundown of what was going on. The man had agreed to contain Mavis and send backup for Brody. He'd told Mack, in no uncertain terms, to do nothing else, to leave it to the police.

So the man had been a little irritated after he'd gotten the address from Brody to find that Mack had one suspect tied up in the van and the other held at gunpoint. But he'd rallied quickly and spent a little of the last half hour filling them in.

When the chief had confronted Mavis, she initially denied any role in Hope's disappearance. Then, when Reverend Minnow asked her to please tell them the truth, she'd broken down. Had admitted that she'd overheard Patsy on the telephone, leaking information to Byron Ferguson about the threats. Had thought that if something bad actually happened to Hope, that it would all come out and that Archie would be so angry with his wife that he would turn to her for solace.

"She admitted," the chief had said, "in front of a whole room of people that she was in love with Reverend Minnow, that she'd been in love with him since she and Patsy were sorority sisters and Archie had chosen Patsy over her."

Mavis had sought help from her brother, who recently started dating Sasha Roher, and they devised a plan to kidnap Hope. It was supposed to happen after the Minnows were home and Mack was gone. When Mavis had learned that Mack was out of town for the evening, she'd put the plan in play.

"I thought Sasha was my friend," Hope said, sounding sad. "And Mavis? She's been living in our home all this time."

"She was jealous of your mother. Had been for years. I guess that kind of emotion can wear a person down after a while and make them do crazy things."

"I recognized the man when I saw him. I knew it was

the man in the pictures with Sasha. And I kept thinking there was something else very familiar about him. I guess I was seeing the resemblance to Mavis."

"He enlisted the help of his brother-in-law. It was a regular family affair. Maybe they can all get cells close together." He stroked her hair. "By the way, you gave that guy a pretty good shot in there, with your hands clasped together like that."

She smiled. "I wonder if I should call Wills and thank him."

"Huh?"

"I felt very vulnerable after what had happened with Wills. It led me to six months of self-defense training. That was one of the moves our instructor showed us. Guess it goes to show that a little good comes out of everything."

"I don't think you're going to have to worry much about running into your ex. Something tells me he's not going to be working at the ministry much longer."

"You know something I don't know?" she asked.

He shrugged. "I think you need to talk to your parents."

"I do. I want to see them. I…have a lot to tell them," Hope said.

"I'll be right there with you," he said.

"There's something I should tell you first," Hope said, turning in his arms to face him.

"Okay."

"I got offered the job in Brooklyn."

He smiled. "That's good news, right?" He could live in Brooklyn. He could live anywhere that Hope was.

"I turned it down."

"Why?"

"There's something else I have to tell you."

He waited.

"I'm pregnant."

He could feel the blood in his veins pumping. "How do you know?"

"I took a pregnancy test. Two of them, in fact. I am definitely pregnant."

Now his heart was swelling in his chest. Pregnant. He was going to be a father.

"And I have something else I need to tell you," she said.

"My head is starting to whirl, darlin'," he said.

"Yes."

"Yes, what?"

"Yes, I will marry you. I love you. I trust you. I know that I'm not making a mistake. I want to live in Colorado with you. I want to see those cabins that you've talked about. I want our child to see them."

Mack leaned close and kissed her. Softly. Then he stood up and held out his hand for her. "And I want to tell our child about the day I fell in love with Hope Minnow, aka Hopeless Fish Bait. A woman so beautiful, so kind and so amazingly brave, who has made me the happiest man ever."

* * * * *

THE MEN OF CROW HOLLOW *comes to an exciting conclusion next month.*
Look for Beverly Long's TRAPPED!

MILLS & BOON®

Want to get more from Mills & Boon?

Here's what's available to you if you join the
exclusive **Mills & Boon eBook Club** today:

✦ *Convenience – choose your books each month*
✦ *Exclusive – receive your books a month before*
  anywhere else
✦ *Flexibility – change your subscription at any time*
✦ *Variety – gain access to eBook-only series*
✦ *Value – subscriptions from just £1.99 a month*

So visit **www.millsandboon.co.uk/esubs** today
to be a part of this exclusive eBook Club!

MILLS & BOON®

The Little Shop of Hopes & Dreams

* cover in development

Much loved author Fiona Harper brings you the
story of Nicole, a born organiser and true romantic,
whose life is spent making the dream proposals of
others come true. All is well until she is enlisted
to plan the proposal of gorgeous photographer
Alex Black—the same Alex Black with whom
Nicole shared a New Year's kiss that she is
unable to forget…

Get your copy today at
www.millsandboon.co.uk/dreams

MILLS & BOON®

Why shop at millsandboon.co.uk?

Each year, thousands of romance readers find their perfect read at millsandboon.co.uk. That's because we're passionate about bringing you the very best romantic fiction. Here are some of the advantages of shopping at www.millsandboon.co.uk:

* **Get new books first**—you'll be able to buy your favourite books one month before they hit the shops

* **Get exclusive discounts**—you'll also be able to buy our specially created monthly collections, with up to 50% off the RRP

* **Find your favourite authors**—latest news, interviews and new releases for all your favourite authors and series on our website, plus ideas for what to try next

* **Join in**—once you've bought your favourite books, don't forget to register with us to rate, review and join in the discussions

Visit **www.millsandboon.co.uk**
for all this and more today!